A DISCARDED SON

THE FITZGERALDS OF DUBLIN BOOK THREE

LORNA PEEL

Copyright © 2019 Lorna Peel
All rights reserved.

No part of this publication may be reproduced or transmitted in any form or by any means, electronic or mechanical, including photography, recording, or any information storage and retrieval system without the prior written consent from the publisher and author, except in the instance of quotes for reviews. No part of this book may be uploaded without the permission of the publisher and author, nor be otherwise circulated in any form of binding or cover other than that in which it is originally published.

This is a work of fiction and any resemblance to persons, living or dead, or places, actual events or locales is purely coincidental. The characters and names are products of the author's imagination and used fictitiously.

The publisher and author acknowledge the trademark status and trademark ownership of all trademarks, service marks and word marks mentioned in this book.

Cover photo credit: Wilhelm Roentgen (1845-1923), German physicist, received the first Nobel Prize for Physics, in 1901, for his discovery of X-rays in 1895: Everett Historical/Shutterstock.com and Portrait of a man in a top hat and morning suit holding a cane: Everett Historical/Shutterstock.com

Cover photo credit: Florence Court, County Fermanagh, Northern Ireland: phb.cz/Depositphotos.com

Cover by Rebecca K. Sterling, Sterling Design Studio
Formatting by Polgarus Studio

Chapter One

Dublin, Ireland. Saturday, December 10th, 1881

Will exchanged a smile with Isobel as she came slowly down the stairs from the nursery holding his nephew, John, by the hand. His wife's matron-of-honour dress was a high-necked emerald green satin creation with a gold-coloured trim and ribbons of the same green were woven into her thick brown hair. By contrast, the three-year-old boy didn't look at all happy, glaring at his navy blue sailor suit with disgust.

"You look wonderful," he said all the same and kissed them both.

"I hate my dress," John declared and Will glanced at the knee-length box-pleated skirt. "Why can't I wear a frock coat and trousers like you?"

"It's only for Grandmamma Martha's wedding," he assured the boy for what seemed like the umpteenth time. "And she did choose it especially for you. Afterwards, you'll be back in your short trousers, I promise."

"But it's a dress. Everyone will laugh at me."

"Well, to be precise, it's a skirt." Crouching down, Will tilted John's chin up and met the boy's dark eyes, a legacy from his Indian mother. "If anyone says something nasty to you, tell them Roman soldiers wore what could be described as skirts and no-one dared to laugh at them. Isn't that right, Isobel?"

"Yes, it is."

"Are Ben and Belle fed and asleep?" he asked, mentioning the twins in the hope they would take the boy's mind off his 'dress'. "Good," he replied as John nodded. "Shall, we go? We can't keep Grandmamma Martha waiting on her special day." Picking the boy up, they went downstairs to the hall where Zaineb, one of their house-parlourmaids, smiled at John before opening the front door for them. "Thank you, Zaineb," he said as they left the house. "See you later."

It was a chilly morning but, thankfully, there were no signs of rain and they walked around the private railed-off Fitzwilliam Square garden to number 55 – home to Isobel's mother and brother. Two carriages were waiting outside and Alfie Stevens gave them a grin from the front door as they approached.

"The Fitzgeralds – good morning. Isobel, I think our darling mother is going to be late. May has been sent to the servants' hall for something or other twice since you left."

"Everything was fine fifteen minutes ago," Isobel muttered, shaking her head. "I'll go and hurry Mother up."

She went inside and Alfie shrugged his shoulders as he came down the steps to the pavement.

"It's hired," he explained, gesturing to his frock coat. "And I think I'm the first man to have worn it. You both look very smart."

"Thank you." Will peered at his own new frock coat and silver-grey cravat. "But John doesn't like his outfit, it was all

Isobel and I could do to persuade him to wear the 'dress'," he told Alfie in a low voice.

"It's only for today," Alfie reminded the boy. "After the wedding, I'll be back in my far more comfortable morning coat and you'll be back in your short trousers. Yes?"

"Yes," John replied firmly and Alfie gave him another grin.

Fifteen minutes passed with Will and Alfie glancing impatiently at each other and their pocket watches until Isobel and her mother came down the stairs to the hall. Mrs Henderson's wedding dress was identical to Isobel's, only that it was gold-coloured satin with an emerald green trim and ribbons of the same gold were woven into her greying brown hair. She paused to lift a bouquet of gold and emerald satin roses from the hall table before continuing on out of the house with Isobel following her. Alfie assisted his mother into the first carriage, gave Will a quick wave then climbed in after her.

Relieved they weren't going to be excessively late, Will helped Isobel and John into the second carriage. He got in and lifted the boy onto his lap so John could see out of the window and the short procession left Fitzwilliam Square.

Isobel and young John took their places behind her mother and Alfie at the door to St Peter's Church on Aungier Street. Will hurried inside and, less than a minute later, the wedding march began. Almost halfway up the right-hand aisle, an elderly man with a snow-white beard and hair and wearing small round spectacles caught her attention. His black woollen overcoat was far too big for him and a long white scarf was wound around his neck. He was seated twisted around in his pew while everyone else was standing to view the bridal party so Isobel couldn't help but stare until the penny dropped and his eyes also widened in recognition as she passed him. Nearing the chancel steps, John tried to pull his hand away from hers and she looked down at the boy, realising she had been squeezing it tightly.

"I'm sorry," she whispered, rubbing his fingers with her thumb.

Taking the bouquet from her mother, she and John sat beside Will in the front pew as the ceremony began. Will lifted John onto his lap so the boy had a clear view of his Grandmamma Martha and soon-to-be Grandpapa James before clasping her hand.

"What is it?" he whispered anxiously during the first hymn. "You're both freezing and on edge."

"I've just seen Mr Greene – Mother's father," she replied and his jaw dropped.

"Here in the church?" He threw an incredulous glance behind them. "Are you sure?"

"Yes. Mother has only one photograph of her parents and her father has aged, of course, but it's definitely him. He is sitting behind us in this central block of pews about halfway down the church and is wearing a white scarf. I don't know why he's here – he and my grandmother broke off all contact with Mother when she ran away from home to marry Father against their wishes."

"What do you want to do?" he asked and she gave a helpless little shrug.

"I don't know, because Mother and James are going to greet everyone at the door and I'm dreading a scene."

He nodded as the hymn ended and they sat down. She

did her best to enjoy the service but it was all she could do not to push past Will and John, run down the aisle and drag her grandfather out of the church. Alfie gave their mother away and joined them in their pew and, as the wedding concluded, she reached over and touched his arm.

"John would like to walk out of the church with you," she said and both Alfie and the boy smiled. "And Will and I shall walk out together, too."

Standing behind the new Mr and Mrs Ellison with Alfie and John bringing up the rear, they proceeded down the left-hand aisle. Spotting her grandfather through a sea of faces, Isobel noted how his eyes were fixed only on his daughter and that, thankfully, she had not seen him yet.

They greeted the happy couple at the church door, Isobel kissing them on both cheeks so she could quickly whisper in James' ear;

"Lewis Greene – Mother's father – is in the church. He is wearing a black overcoat and a white scarf wound around his neck."

Her step-father's brown eyes bulged in alarm but he nodded and she and Will moved on towards the gates to Aungier Street.

"Isobel?" Hearing Alfie's fierce whisper, they both turned. "What on earth is the matter?" he demanded, leading John towards them. "You and Will were whispering through every hymn and now you've told James something that's made him go as white as a sheet and—" He broke off and gasped as he recognised the elderly man emerging from the church clutching a top hat and a walking cane.

Mrs Ellison's eyes widened in first disbelief and then shock before she forced a smile and greeted her father warmly and no different than anyone else. James shook his father-in-law's hand then Mr Greene walked on and, to Isobel's consternation, made a beeline for the four of them.

"You must be Isobel," he said, leaning on his cane and looking her up and down. "You know exactly who I am."

"I do. What do you want?"

One of her grandfather's eyebrows rose at her bluntness but he didn't respond and turned to Alfie.

"And you must be Alfred?"

"Yes, I am, but everyone calls me Alfie."

"And who is this?" Her grandfather nodded to John, who was still clutching Alfie's hand. The boy's dark eyes were darting from Alfie to her and to Will, clearly sensing the animosity and suspicion amongst the three of them towards the stranger. "Your son?"

"No, my nephew, John Fitzgerald," Will replied, holding out a hand. "I am Isobel's husband, Dr Will Fitzgerald."

"I see," Mr Greene replied but made no attempt to shake Will's hand.

"You haven't answered my question," Isobel persisted as Will picked John up. "What do you want?"

"I would prefer not to discuss the matter here in front of all and sundry."

All and sundry? It was just as well the other members of the congregation were paying them little attention.

"Well," she replied stiffly. "I am afraid it is here or not at all."

Her grandfather's eyebrow rose again. "I am dying, Isobel," he said with equal bluntness and she heard Alfie gasp again. "And I wish to make my peace with your mother and get to know my new son-in-law and you and your brother before I die."

This time, Isobel looked him up and down. Mr Greene was leaning heavily on his walking cane, beginning to wheeze and she hoped he had a cab waiting for him.

"Mother and James leave for a week's honeymoon in London late this afternoon. It is bad enough you turn up at their wedding without warning but you will not break such news to Mother until she returns to Dublin. Is that understood?" she insisted and her grandfather exhaled a phlegmy laugh.

"I learned of your mother's wedding purely by chance, I can assure you. But I understand."

"Where are you staying? The Shelbourne Hotel?"

"Your grandmother and I have rented a house on Fitzwilliam Square," he replied and Isobel's heart sank. "Number 7."

"I live on Fuzwillan Square with Will and Isobel," John announced. "So does Grandmamma Martha. And Grandpapa James will live there, too."

Her grandfather glanced at the boy in surprise before looking up at Will plainly of the opinion that children should be seen and not heard. "This boy lives with you, Dr Fitzgerald?"

"John is my late brother's son," Will explained. "He lives with Isobel and I and Ben and Belle."

"Ben and Belle?" his grandfather-in-law inquired with a frown.

"Our twin son and daughter," Isobel informed him. "Your great-grandchildren."

"I have great-grandchildren." Mr Greene produced another phlegm-filled laugh. "Your mother was a twin."

"So I was told. Please do not upset her further on her

wedding day – please go – and we shall call on you tomorrow."

"Until tomorrow, then." Putting on his top hat, her grandfather walked away and was soon lost in the crowd which had spilled out onto the pavement.

"Isobel?" A hand grabbed her arm from behind and she turned to face her mother. "Where is he? Where is my father?"

"I'm afraid he had to leave."

"Had to leave?" her mother echoed incredulously and James turned briefly to the street. "Whatever was he doing here?"

"He and Grandmother live in Dublin now."

"Where?" James asked.

"He did not say," she lied.

"Oh, Isobel, I can hardly believe it." Her mother fought back tears. "I thought I would never see my father again."

"Never say never," Isobel told her with a smile. "Congratulations again, Mother. And you, too, James."

"Thank you, Isobel," he replied and gestured to the gates. "I think we should make our way to our carriages."

"I agree," Will added. "It is far too cold to stand about here."

As soon as they returned to number 55, Mrs Ellison insisted on speaking to her in private and, reluctantly, Isobel followed her mother into the morning room. Closing the door, she looked at the hearth. A fire had been set that morning but not lit and the room felt unusually cool.

"You may now tell me the truth," Mrs Ellison began. "Where are my father and mother living?"

Isobel grimaced. Was she so bad a liar these days? "I don't—"

"The truth, Isobel," her mother interrupted crisply.

"They have rented a house here on the square – number 7," she said and Mrs Ellison went straight to the window and looked out at the street. "And you will call on them when you return from London."

"No. I want them both here – now."

"Mother, no," she begged. "You have been looking forward to this day for such a long time don't allow them to ruin it."

"They are my parents," Mrs Ellison replied, her voice rising.

"The same parents who cut you off when you married Father and who are now suddenly here in Dublin for your marriage to a gentleman they approve of."

That made her mother flinch and Isobel hoped she hadn't gone too far.

"I want them both here – now," Mrs Ellison repeated quietly, walking to the rope and ringing for a servant.

"Very well." Isobel reached for the doorknob.

"And I want you, Alfie, James and Will here when they arrive."

Letting her hand drop to her side, Isobel walked to the window turning momentarily to the door as the butler came in then watched a ginger cat squeeze between the railings surrounding the Fitzwilliam Square gardens before disappearing from view.

"You rang, Mrs Ellison."

"Gorman, please, send someone to number 7 and ask that Mr and Mrs Greene join Mr and Mrs Ellison for luncheon and to meet their families. Oh, and this means there will be two extra for luncheon."

"Yes, Mrs Ellison."

"And ask my husband, son and son-in-law to join myself and my daughter here."

"Yes, Mrs Ellison."

The butler left the room and Isobel pulled a face, only turning around again when the door opened and James, Alfie and Will came in.

"I have sent for my parents," Mrs Ellison announced and Isobel met Will's brown eyes for a moment. "And, no, Isobel does not approve of my decision but I want them both here on my wedding day."

There was no response, Mrs Ellison gave a little shrug and the five of them waited in a tense silence until voices were heard in the hall and the butler came into the room.

"Mr Greene," Gorman announced, the elderly gentleman walked in and Isobel peered behind him. Where was his wife? Why wasn't she here? And why hadn't she accompanied her husband to St Peter's Church?

"Martha." Mr Greene went to his daughter reaching out his hands. "Oh, let me look at you." Clasping her hands, he stood back with a smile. "Oh, how I have missed you."

Isobel clenched her fists and banged them against her thighs in frustration as her mother burst into tears. How could she be so forgiving?

"And I have missed you." Her mother smiled through her tears. "Oh, Father…" Holding him to her, the two cried unashamedly.

Isobel glanced at Will who returned a helpless expression while Alfie began to shuffle uncomfortably and James examined his hands.

When the two finally stopped sobbing, Mrs Ellison

wiped her tears away with her fingers and looked over her father's shoulder.

"I must introduce you to my family, Father. This is James Ellison – my husband."

James joined them and greeted his new and unexpected father-in-law with admirable calm politeness.

"Alfie?" his mother called and he shuffled forward. "My son, Alfie, is a medical student at Trinity College."

"A budding doctor, eh?" his grandfather commented.

"I have wanted to be nothing else," he replied.

"And this is my daughter, Isobel, and her husband, Will," her mother continued and she braced herself as Will took her hand, led her to them and her grandfather inclined his head politely.

"Your concern for your mother is commendable, Isobel."

"I do not wish to see my mother upset – especially on today of all days."

"But I am not upset," her mother protested with an almost hysterical laugh which made her cringe. "I am absolutely delighted to have my father here today."

"Where is Grandmother?" she asked on behalf of them all and he gave her a little smile, no doubt having expected her question.

"Resting," he answered simply and she didn't believe him for a second.

Quickly realising she wasn't going to reply, her mother gestured to Will.

"This is my son-in-law, Dr Will Fitzgerald."

"Are you a Dublin man?" Mr Greene inquired.

"Yes, I am," Will replied. "I was born and brought up on Merrion Square."

"Isobel and Will have twins – a boy and a girl – Ben and Belle – who are five months old," Mrs Ellison went on. "And they are raising Will's nephew, John, who is almost four."

"I am a great-grandfather." Mr Greene smiled and shook his head. "Good gracious me. I may be as old as the century, but this news makes me feel utterly antiquated."

"I think we should go upstairs and introduce Mr Greene to our guests," James suggested and his wife nodded.

"And luncheon will be served soon."

They went up the stairs to the pleasantly warm drawing room where Mrs Ellison introduced her father – wheezing after the climb – to the guests. Will's mother, in particular, was astonished, Sarah having assumed her friend's parents were both long dead.

"You don't seem at all happy to finally meet your grandfather, Isobel," Will's father commented and she sighed, taking his arm and leading him to a relatively quiet corner.

"My grandparents cut Mother off when she ran away from home to marry my father just days after her twenty-first birthday and yet here they both are in Dublin – twenty-five years later."

"Your grandfather has the pallor and laboured breathing of a very ill man," he said as they observed Mr Greene now leaning heavily on her mother's arm and she nodded.

"Grandfather is dying and my mother does not know – and will not know – until she and James return from London."

"Of course. They live in Co Mayo, don't they?"

"They did, but not anymore, apparently. They are renting number 7."

"Here on Fitzwilliam Square?" John Fitzgerald's eyebrows shot up.

"Yes. I think their move to Dublin and my grandfather's 'sudden' appearance at the church were very carefully planned, despite his words to the contrary," she said as Will came to them.

"James seems rather stunned, what do you think of all this?" his father asked.

"Poor James is walking on eggshells," Will replied. "He did not expect to acquire parents-in-law. I agree with Isobel that Mr Greene's 'sudden' appearance has taken careful planning, so I am rather… wary."

"Well, do not agree to be your grandfather-in-law's doctor whatever you do."

Will shot his father a sharp look. "I'm sure Mr Greene already has a doctor."

"My namesake didn't look too happy to be wearing a skirt." John swiftly changed the subject.

"He wasn't happy," Will confirmed. "He hated his 'dress'. But when I left him at number 30 with Zaineb, he went running up the stairs ahead of her for his short trousers immediately."

A quarter of an hour later, they all sat down to the wedding luncheon – a place setting for Mrs Greene having been added and then quickly taken away. Isobel glanced at Will's estranged parents, placed opposite each other at the huge dining table. Living separately – although under the same roof at number 67 Merrion Square – John and Sarah had behaved impeccably at Ben, Belle and young John's joint christenings and could put on a show of togetherness when required.

Isobel was seated between John and one of James' brothers and, although she spoke politely with both men, she couldn't rid herself of the shock and anger of her grandfather's unexpected arrival. She had rarely thought of either her paternal or maternal grandparents over the years. Her father's parents had both died long before Alfie and she were born and she had never expected to meet her mother's father and mother.

Mr and Mrs Ellison were to leave by cab at five o'clock. It would take them to the North Wall Quay passenger terminus and the boat to Holyhead in Wales. From there, they would travel to London by train. Isobel went upstairs with her mother and helped her to put on an exquisite three-quarter length 'going away' coat and hat made from the same gold and emerald green satin as the wedding dress.

"Promise me one thing," Mrs Ellison said as Isobel opened the bedroom door. "Promise me you won't row with your grandfather while James and I are in London. I know you are not at all happy at his rather sudden appearance."

"I cannot promise you that, Mother," she replied truthfully.

"In that case, I would like you to keep away from him – and your grandmother."

Isobel's jaw dropped. "Keep away?"

"Yes, Isobel, keep away. Yes, they hurt me deeply – cutting me off when I married your father – and I appreciate your wish to protect me from any further distress. But until I have the opportunity to sit down with them and determine whether their move to Dublin is temporary or permanent and what either could mean for us all, I would like you to keep away from them – please?"

Isobel gave a little shrug. "I can only promise you that I shall not call on them. But if they call on me…" She tailed off intentionally and her mother sighed but nodded.

"Yes, it is natural that they would wish to see their great-grandchildren."

Is it, Isobel wondered. Today was the first occasion Mr Greene had set eyes on his grandchildren, never mind his great-grandchildren, even though he has no doubt known of us all and where we live for quite some time.

"And now it is time for you to go," she said, hugging and kissing her mother. "Have a lovely time in London."

"I'll try."

They went downstairs and she kissed James goodbye. He smiled before giving her a firm nod, silently telling her he would ensure his new wife enjoyed her honeymoon.

The wedding guests stood on the steps of number 55 waving the cab off and as it left the square Mr Greene turned to her.

"I shall take my leave now, too."

"Goodbye," Isobel said simply and her grandfather's eyebrows rose, no doubt having expected something a little more acerbic. Turning away, she went back into the hall with Will following her. "My grandfather is returning to number 7," she informed Gorman who lifted Mr Greene's overcoat down from the stand. "And I hope the other guests leave soon as well," she added to Will. "Because I don't know for how long I can remain polite and make inane small talk."

It took two hours for the last guests to leave and as soon as Will closed the drawing room door, Isobel exploded – throwing her hands up into the air.

"Twenty-five years—"

"Isobel." Will clasped her hands and kissed them. "Let's try and remain calm – we need to remain calm. Alfie, tell me what you know about your grandparents while I pour us a drink."

"Well," Alfie began, rubbing his forehead as Will went to the drinks tray. "They live – or lived – at Greene Hall in Co Mayo – not far from Westport. Their estate borders the Marquess of Sligo's estate."

"Their estate?" Will echoed, reaching for one of the decanters. "How much land do they have?"

"A lot," Isobel replied, trying to recall what she had been told over the years. "About ten thousand acres. Some of it is peat bog and mountain and only fit for sheep, but there is also some good land. The house is large, too, according to what Mother used to say. But I've never seen a painting or a photograph of it, so I don't know how accurate her description is. Mother took one photograph of her parents with her when she ran away to marry Father, that is all."

"And they cut your mother off completely?" Will asked her while pouring the drinks. "There was no secret correspondence?"

"Not as far as I know. Do you know any different, Alfie?" she asked and he made a helpless gesture with his hands. "What about when Father died?"

"When Father died, Mother and I both decided to move to Dublin more or less straight away. If there were any letters, I knew nothing of them."

Will passed her a glass of brandy and Alfie one of whiskey before holding up his own whiskey glass.

"Well, apart from your grandfather appearing, the day was very pleasant. Long life and happiness to the Ellisons."

They touched glasses and drank.

"Today would have been an emotional one for your mother even if your grandfather hadn't turned up at the church," he continued. "So, let's see what her state of mind is when she returns from London."

"Hopefully, James will be able to talk some sense into her," she added as the door opened and Gorman came in.

"Mr Greene has called and is asking to speak to Mr Stevens and Mrs Fitzgerald."

"What does he want now?" Isobel muttered, rolling her eyes.

"Mr Greene needs to sit down, Dr Fitzgerald," the butler added. "He is puffing and panting rather alarmingly."

Will quickly put his glass on the mantelpiece, her glass and Alfie's joined it and they went downstairs to the hall. Her grandfather was standing at the front door, leaning heavily on his walking cane and wheezing. Taking Mr Greene's arm, Will guided him into the morning room and sat him down on the sofa while Alfie and Gorman lit the gas lamps.

"Breathe as slowly and deeply as you can," Will instructed as she closed the door.

Mr Greene exhaled a phlegm-filled laugh. "That is easier said than done."

"Would you like whiskey, sherry or brandy?" Isobel asked and he glanced up at her in surprise.

"Brandy. Thank you."

She nodded and went to the decanters. Returning with a large glass of brandy, she passed it to him but his hand shook and Will had to grab the glass before it fell onto the rug. With Will holding the glass, the elderly man took a sip and sat back, pulling a handkerchief from his overcoat pocket and mopping his forehead.

"I don't like sherry," he announced. "I can tolerate a single malt whiskey, but I much prefer brandy."

She almost smiled, as she had exactly the same taste in alcohol. Who knows what else she had in common with him.

"Why come to Dublin?" she asked and the butler discreetly left the room. "Why turn up unannounced at Mother's wedding? Why did Grandmother not attend the wedding with you? Why did she not attend the wedding luncheon? Why is she not here with you now?"

"Because, Isobel," he said, taking the glass from Will. "I am about to tell you something your grandmother wishes to keep secret."

"Well?" she prompted irritably as he enjoyed another sip of brandy and handed the glass back to Will.

"It was wholly my idea to attend your mother's wedding," he told her. "Your grandmother wished to stay away but I wanted to see my daughter marry so I insisted I attend, even though it went against my doctor's strict advice. I have chronic lung disease," he added, with a glance towards both Will and Alfie. "I am dying, and there are many things I have done over the course of my life I want to try and put right before it is too late. I wish to get to know my darling daughter again. I wish to get to know my grandchildren and my great-grandchildren. But I also have a son and it is my dearest wish that I see him once more before I die."

Mr Greene took the glass from Will and downed the contents in two gulps before placing it on a side table.

"Your son is dead," Isobel said, and Will heard her voice shake. "Mother said—"

"Your mother was told what everyone was told," Mr Greene informed her in a weary tone. "That Miles had died of whooping cough when he was a year old. It was a lie. Theirs was a difficult birth. We had not known your grandmother was carrying twins. Your mother was born first but her brother took an age to be born. When he was born, all seemed fine in the beginning, but he did not feed well, he did not laugh or make any sounds and he did not crawl or attempt to walk. By the time he was a year old, we had him examined and the result only confirmed what we had suspected – that Miles was a simpleton – an idiot."

"What did you do with Miles?" Will asked as gently as he could.

"My wife blamed herself – she could hardly bear to look at Miles – so I thought it best to get the boy away from Greene Hall – away from Co Mayo altogether – so I arranged that he be taken to an asylum in Dublin – one which would give him the care we could not."

"Which asylum?"

"St Patrick's Hospital."

"And you visited Miles?" Will asked, even though he knew the answer.

"I have not seen my son since the day I watched him being driven away in a carriage down the drive."

Tears began to spill down his cheeks and Alfie grabbed the glass from the side table, went to the decanters and sloshed more brandy into it.

"Drink this," he said, passing the glass to him and Mr Greene nodded his thanks.

"My wife and I hoped we would have more sons but, sadly, it was not to be."

"How on earth did you hide the fact your son was not dead?" Isobel demanded.

"We have loyal servants," he replied before taking a sip of brandy and putting the glass down on the side table. "And a rather large funeral was held for him."

Isobel closed her eyes for a moment but – to Will's relief – said nothing. She simply turned her back on them and walked to the window with her hands on her hips.

"Does your wife wish to see Miles again?" he asked and Mr Greene shook his head.

"He is dead to her – as is your mother-in-law. Tilda did not wish to come to Dublin but I insisted and here we are."

"Did you engage an inquiry agent?" Isobel asked, turning away from the window. "You knew we all lived here on Fitzwilliam Square."

"There was no need for an inquiry agent. I always read the announcements and notices in *The Irish Times* and Knox, my butler, is a Dublin man. He made a few discreet inquiries to determine when and where the wedding would take place and where you all resided. Isobel, I simply wish to see my son again. Then, I want to go home to Greene Hall to die. I do not have long left. My wife and I will not trouble you for longer than one month." He struggled to his feet and Will passed him his walking cane. "Isobel, Alfred, thank you for seeing me. Dr Fitzgerald, may I speak privately with you in the hall?"

"Of course." Will followed him as he made his way out of the room and closed the door.

"Have you dealt with a simpleton before, Dr Fitzgerald?" Mr Greene asked.

"I have dealt with a psychiatric case before, yes."

"And?"

"I cannot discuss the case with you, Mr Greene."

The older man nodded. "I understand. I would be grateful if you would make inquiries with the asylum as to when would be the best time to visit my son – morning, afternoon, evening – it does not matter when."

"I will. Shall I escort you back to number 7?" he offered.

"No, there is no need. I will take my time, thank you."

"Very well." Will handed Mr Greene's top hat to him before opening the front door.

"I shall expect to hear from you in due course, Dr Fitzgerald," Mr Greene said, putting the hat on and Will waited until the elderly man safely reached the pavement before closing the door and returning to the morning room.

Both Isobel and Alfie were standing exactly where they had been when he left the room and he squeezed Alfie's shoulder as he passed him before kissing Isobel's cheek.

"Just when I thought your brother placing his baby son in a children's home was as bad as things could get," she said bitterly.

"Have you ever been to St Patrick's Hospital?" Alfie asked him.

"Yes, once, with Fred and Jerry. It's also known as Swift's Hospital and as institutions go, it is very respectable. Even though tomorrow is Sunday, I think the three of us should go there in the afternoon. We might not be allowed to visit Miles, but I would like to speak with someone there and gain an understanding of his condition."

"What do you think happened to Miles?" Alfie added curiously.

"I can only surmise that he was deprived of oxygen during the prolonged birth," he replied and saw Isobel's eyes widen in horror. "Belle was not oxygen-deprived," he assured her firmly. "She is a perfectly normal baby girl, I promise you." She nodded and he continued; "We will take this matter one step at a time – we will visit Swift's Hospital tomorrow afternoon – agreed?"

"Agreed," they both replied and he nodded.

"Good. Let's get a good night's sleep, it's been quite a day."

Outside on the pavement, Isobel put her hands on her hips and swore in the most unladylike way she could think of to try and rid herself of her anger.

"Fuck. Fuck them for coming to Dublin. This was supposed to be a fucking happy day for Mother and James – for all of us. And how could they do that? How could they send their child away to a fucking asylum?"

"If something had happened to Belle during her birth, you would never have forgiven yourself either," Will told her softly.

"No, I wouldn't, but I would never have sent her away and pretended she was dead to everyone and go through the charade of a large funeral."

"No. That was..." He tailed off and shook his head. "Come with me, I want to kiss you and try and forget about the Greenes until tomorrow."

Taking her hand, they crossed the street to the railings surrounding the gardens. In the darkness between two gas lamps, he pulled at her lips with his and his hands slid up her body to her breasts. They were heavy and tender and she groaned as he caressed them.

"I'm sorry. I need to express more milk before you can play with them."

"It's not every husband who gives his wife a breast pump for her birthday, is it?" he murmured and she felt his lips on her neck. "I do love your very full breasts, though, and I'll miss them when the twins are weaned."

"You'd better make the most of them then because the twins are being weaned in a few week's time."

"I shall – we'll go to bed straight after dinner," he said and kissed her lips again. "Let's go home."

Sitting in the padded chair in their bedroom on the second floor, Isobel expressed the milk and brought it upstairs to the nursery. She and Bridget, one of their two nursery maids, fed Belle and Ben and Will joined them in the children's bedroom to help young John to bed.

"I don't ever want to wear a dress again," John told them as they tucked him in.

"You won't," Will replied. "It will be short trousers only from now on."

"Will you make Ben wear a dress ever?"

"Not now we know from you that he won't like it."

"Good," John replied firmly, snuggling down into the bed. "Night-night."

"Night-night." They kissed him and the twins and went out to the nursery, trying not to laugh.

"The 'dress'?" Florrie, their other nursery maid, guessed correctly.

"The 'dress'." Isobel laughed. "Other than that, I think he enjoyed the wedding."

"Florrie," Will added. "We shall be taking Master John

and the twins to St Stephen's Green tomorrow morning rather than the afternoon."

"Yes, Dr Fitzgerald."

After the huge wedding luncheon, they could only manage a light dinner and, instead of escorting her from the breakfast room into the morning room, Will led her up the stairs to their bedroom. He pushed the door shut with his foot and kissed her hand before letting it go. He lit the oil lamp on his bedside table before opening the drawer and lifting out a red box of condoms.

"I need to order more," he said, more to himself than to her while she went to the hearth and placed a few small coals on the newly-lit fire.

They slowly undressed each other, hung their clothes up in their wardrobes and she extracted the pins and ribbons and let down her hair.

"When we got married, I didn't anticipate us having to make time for this," he told her, sweeping her hair to one side and kissing her neck before extinguishing the gas lamps. "But – events and emergencies aside – Saturday afternoons and evenings are ours – I insist on that."

For now, while the children are young, she added silently as he stood behind her and held her breasts in his hands smoothing his thumbs over her nipples.

"Dr Fitzgerald?" They both froze, hearing Zaineb's voice and a hesitant tap at the door. "Dr Fitzgerald?"

"Damn it," he whispered and let her breasts drop. Shrugging on his dressing gown, he opened the door a couple of inches.

"I'm sorry to disturb you, Dr Fitzgerald," Zaineb began. "But there's a maid here from number 7. She says Mr Greene has been found collapsed across the street from the house and could you please come and attend to him at once."

"I'll come," he said and closed the door.

They pulled on their clothes removed so lovingly only moments before. There wasn't time to pin up her hair so she tied it back with one of the green satin ribbons, threw a black fringed shawl around her shoulders and followed Will downstairs. He picked up his medical bag from the hall table and they left the house.

Hurrying to the east side of the square as heavy drizzle began to fall, she saw a small group of people bending over a figure lying on the pavement which surrounded the railings and the gardens.

"I am Dr Fitzgerald, stand back, please," Will instructed and they did as he asked. She crouched down on one side of Mr Greene while Will knelt on the other and felt her grandfather's neck for a pulse. "He's alive," he told her before running his fingers across the elderly man's scalp. "But only just. And he's very cold but, thankfully, there is no head injury. Are all of you servants in number 7?" he asked the group and one smartly-dressed man in his fifties stepped forward with Mr Greene's top hat and walking cane in his hands.

"Yes, we are, Dr Fitzgerald," he replied. "I am Knox, Mr and Mrs Greene's butler."

"Please ask for some water to be heated and round up as many hot water bottles as you can find."

"Yes, Dr Fitzgerald." The butler turned to a maid who accepted the top hat and cane from him and ran across the street and down the areaway steps.

"Please help me carry Mr Greene upstairs to a bedroom."

Isobel picked up Will's medical bag as he took Mr Greene's shoulders and Knox gripped Mr Greene's ankles. She tailed them as her grandfather was borne across the street, up the steps and into the gas-lit hall but she halted at the front door.

"Where is Mrs Greene?" she asked a red-haired maid about to go down the areaway steps.

"I am here," a severe voice announced from behind her and Isobel turned around.

At five feet eight inches, Isobel was considered tall for a woman. Standing in the morning room doorway, her grandmother was equally tall but as thin as Isobel was curvaceous. Plaited wavy grey hair was wound into a bun at the nape of her neck and she wore a purple satin dress. Mrs Greene looked her and then Will up and down, taking in her hastily tied-back hair and his lack of hat, collar and cravat. An eyebrow rose and Isobel fought to control a flush of embarrassment.

"Tell me what is needed and you shall have it," her grandmother added crisply.

"Thank you, we shall," Isobel replied before closing the front door and following the others up the stairs.

Her grandfather was brought to a large bedroom on the second floor at the front of the house and laid on the double bed. Will unbuttoned Mr Greene's overcoat and raised him into a sitting position so the butler could peel it off. Discreetly turning her back, Isobel accepted her grandfather's clothes from Knox as they were removed layer by layer. The overcoat was wet and the other clothes were damp and couldn't be hung up in the huge mahogany wardrobe so she draped them over the back of a balloon-back bedroom chair so they could be taken away to be dried and aired.

When she turned back, Mr Greene was lying on the bed dressed in a white nightshirt and Will was returning a thermometer to his medical bag. Lifting out his stethoscope, he raised her grandfather into a sitting position again and Knox held Mr Greene's shoulders while Will listened to his phlegmatic breathing and put the stethoscope away fighting back a grimace. Her grandfather was painfully thin and as Will lifted him up, Isobel pulled the bedcovers back. Mr Greene was placed in the bed and she covered him up to his chin.

"I asked for hot water bottles, where are they?" Will asked.

"I'll go and see, Dr Fitzgerald." The butler strode to the door and left the room.

"Does he have hypothermia?" she asked.

"No, but it could develop," Will replied as the door opened again and her grandmother came in. "He must have been lying on the pavement since he left number 55 two hours ago."

"My husband was determined to return there and speak with you and I assumed he was still with you," Mrs Greene informed them. "Did not one of you offer to escort him back here?"

"I did," Will said. "But he declined."

"Will he live?" she asked, walking to the bed and gently smoothing long and bony fingers over her husband's sparse white hair.

"Mr Greene is very cold but his temperature must be raised slowly," Will said as a footman and two maids hurried into the room each carrying two hot water bottles and Isobel lowered the bedcovers. "Place all of them in the bed – not too close to Mr Greene – good. Thank you."

"Can nothing else be done for him?" her grandmother asked as the servants left the bedroom and Isobel pulled the bedcovers up again.

"Sit with him, Mrs Greene, have the hot water bottles refilled every two hours, and raise his temperature."

"Well." Mrs Greene went to the bedroom chair and sat down, clasping her hands tightly together on her lap. "The boy has finally proved to be the death of my husband. My husband insisted on coming to Dublin. He insisted on reacquainting himself with Martha. And he insisted on telling you about the boy."

'The boy' was now a man in his mid-forties but Isobel bit her tongue.

"You did not want Grandfather to meet Mother again?" Isobel asked and her grandmother fixed a cold stare on her.

"Your mother could have married into Lord Sligo's family but she chose to run away from home and marry the curate of Ballyglas Parish. I knew the marriage would be disastrous and so it proved. She sent many letters bemoaning her situation and begging my husband and I to take her and her children in but, as you make your bed, so you must lie in it."

"She told you Father was violent and you did nothing?" Isobel demanded.

"I burned the letters," her grandmother replied matter-of-factly. "Your mother had made her choice and so she must live with that choice."

"I did grasp your initial meaning," Isobel replied tightly.

"I am so glad the items she stole from Greene Hall to pay for your excessively expensive education at Cheltenham Ladies College and for your brother's at Harrow didn't altogether go to waste."

Isobel's jaw dropped. "She stole from Greene Hall?"

"You thought that despite our pleas to your mother not to marry a man unworthy of her, your grandfather paid her marriage portion?" Mrs Greene smiled humourlessly. "No. He did not. Yours and your brother's education were paid for by stolen property. Unfortunately, you chose to waste every penny by whoring yourself to a farm boy."

"I did not whore myself to James," she retorted, clenching her fists but unable to stop herself shaking with rage. "He seduced me."

"You exude an overt sensuality, Isobel, which men are unable to resist," her grandmother told her crisply, making a point of looking her up and down again. "I doubt very much if he needed too much of an excuse to get you on your back."

"That is enough," Will snapped and Mrs Greene gave him an icy smile.

"Took a fancy to Isobel in her parlourmaid's uniform, did you, Dr Fitzgerald? Most men would not wish to touch soiled goods."

"You have said quite enough. Isobel – we're leaving."

Mrs Greene inclined her head. "Thank you for tending to my husband, Dr Fitzgerald, you and your wife may now return to your bed."

Isobel flung open the bedroom door and stomped down the stairs to the hall with Will following her.

"Isobel, wait a moment," he called as she reached for the

front door handle. "Which doctor has been attending to Mr Greene since his arrival in Dublin?" he asked a red-haired maid who was coming up the steps from the servants' hall carrying an ewer and a bar of soap in a basin and a towel over her arm.

"A Dr Smythe, Dr Fitzgerald," the young woman replied and Will swore under his breath.

"I see. Well, if there is any deterioration in Mr Greene's condition overnight, please send for me, not Dr Smythe."

"Yes, Dr Fitzgerald. I was bringing these upstairs so you could wash your hands."

"That's very kind, thank you. I'll do it here."

The maid placed them on the hall table and Will washed and dried his hands, thanked her again and she saw them out.

Isobel took Will's hand, they ran back around the gardens in now heavy rain to number 30 and in the hall, she clasped his face in her hands and kissed him.

"My grandmother is a bitter and cruel old woman who thinks exuding an overt sensuality is something to be ashamed of," she said. "I can't help being the way I am, I'm not ashamed of it, and I'm not ashamed to admit that I want you."

They kissed their way upstairs and into their bedroom. Closing the door with her behind, she undid Will's trouser buttons and pushed his trousers and drawers down while he lifted up her skirts and pulled down her drawers. She stepped out of them then reached for him. She adored touching him and holding him in her hand, making him groan.

"Let me just—" He reached into the red box, slid a condom on, then cleared some space on the dressing table. Lifting her up, he sat her on it and pushed into her. Smoothing her hands down his back to his buttocks, she held him inside her and he rested his forehead against hers, exhaling a long breath. "I'm not ashamed to admit that I adore being inside you."

"For my grandmother to know about James Shawcross and I, someone must have been engaged to make inquiries in Ballybeg. What if Grandmother knows about Sally Maher's brothel, too?" she asked in a small voice, hating to have to even think of it, and he raised his head.

"I think if she had known, she would have thrown it at you, too, or had you removed from the house. When you came to Dublin, you changed your name."

"Yes, I did – to Rose Green – Greene without an 'e' – but Green or Greene – they both sound the same."

"Even so, your grandmother only seems to know of you being in Dublin from your time at the Harveys' onwards when your real identity was uncovered after you had been caught using the Maisie Byrne name. It was wise of you to change your name again and I'm confident your grandmother doesn't know about your time in the brothel."

She gasped as he began moving inside her, pulling out and sliding in until his hips found a rhythm. Her breathing became short ragged gasps as he brushed against her sweet spot every time slowly building a fire within her. Scraping her nails across his buttocks, he grinned and kissed her lips. He pulled at her bottom lip before pushing his tongue into her mouth and she met it with her own, swirling around it and then sucking it strongly. Writhing, she let out a deep moan and he quickened his pace, relentlessly pounding into her and she felt as though she couldn't catch her breath as she neared her release.

"Oh, God, Will, there, I—" she cried out as he snapped his hips up forcefully, tipping her over the edge screaming his name.

He held himself inside her as he rode out his own climax, grunting before letting her go and leaning on both hands on the dressing table, catching his breath.

"Come to bed," she said. "You can kiss and play with my breasts before we go to sleep."

For the second time that evening, they got undressed and she hung her matron-of-honour dress up in her wardrobe. They got into bed, lay down and she stroked Will's hair as he licked and kissed her breasts. Would her grandfather die during the night? She hoped not. Despite everything, she wanted him to see his son before it was too late.

"You're miles away."

Hearing Will's voice, she opened her eyes and sighed. "I'm sorry."

"Isobel, your grandfather's lungs are in an appalling state. I can only hope he survives the night."

"I know," she replied simply.

"And don't take to heart what your grandmother said to you. She was upset and she is jealous of you. You are the mother of healthy twins."

"That is thanks to you."

"Just try and forget what she said."

She nodded and he twisted around and turned down the oil lamp.

Chapter Two

In the morning, while Isobel went upstairs to the nursery to feed the twins and help John with his favourite breakfast of a soft boiled egg and toast 'soldiers', Will walked to Fitzwilliam Square East. Taking off his hat, he rang number 7's front doorbell and the red-haired maid opened the door.

"Did Mr Greene survive the night?" he asked her.

"Yes, he did, Dr Fitzgerald," she replied, much to his relief.

"And has Dr Smythe been sent for?"

"Mrs Greene sent for Dr Smythe immediately after you and Mrs Fitzgerald left and he has been with Mr Greene all night and—"

"Who is at the door?"

Hearing Mrs Greene's sharp voice, the maid jumped and tensed and Will held a finger to his lips, silently telling the young woman not to say he was there.

"A gentleman looking for the previous residents, Mrs Greene," the maid replied and Will admired her quick thinking.

"Well, they are long gone. Send the gentleman on his way."

"Yes, Mrs Greene," she said, Will heard a door close and

the maid relaxed. "I don't think Dr Smythe knows what he's doing," she told him bravely, confirming Will's fears.

"I'm afraid I can't interfere with Dr Smythe's treatment – I was only called last evening because it was an emergency – and I asked you that I be called instead of Dr Smythe because I was angry – I shouldn't have said it and I'm sorry."

"I understand, Dr Fitzgerald, and I understand that you can't interfere but is there anything – anything at all – that can be done for Mr Greene?" she asked.

"You can help Mr Greene a little by ensuring he does not smoke," he said and she nodded. "If there are cigarettes, cigars or pipe tobacco in his bedroom, please remove them. If he asks where they are, tell him I instructed you to remove them last night when I was called here. And do not allow the air in the room to become stale. Open the window for a few minutes every two hours to let in some fresh air. What Mr Greene really needs is to inhale oxygen from an oxygen cylinder. Dr Smythe hasn't mentioned one by any chance?"

"No, Dr Fitzgerald," she replied and his heart sank.

"Well, keep the room ventilated but keep Mr Greene warm at the same time."

"Yes, Dr Fitzgerald."

"Good. Thank you..?"

"Ida, Dr Fitzgerald."

"Thank you, Ida." Turning away, he rolled his eyes and put on his hat before returning to number 30.

"Well?" Isobel asked from the morning room doorway as he placed his medical bag on the hall table then hung his hat and overcoat on the stand.

"Mr Greene is still alive but Dr Smythe is with him now and I can't interfere," he replied, hearing the front doorbell jangle down in the servants' hall. "I managed to have a word with Ida, the red-haired maid, and she admitted Dr Smythe doesn't know what he's doing," he added, opening the door. "Good morning, Father. Come in."

"Thank you." His father took off his hat and stepped into the hall. "I have to admit the reason for my call is nosiness, plain and simple," he said as Will closed the door. "Your grandparents, Isobel, what is their real reason for being in Dublin?"

Will exchanged a glance with her, wondering if they should keep it to themselves, but she waved a hand in assent, lifted the skirt of her sapphire blue dress and went back into the morning room.

"After you," he said, taking his father's hat and overcoat, hanging them on the stand beside his own and they followed Isobel.

They sat down and Will told his father all. It was some considerable time since he had seen his father look quite so astonished.

"And Miles Greene is still in Swift's Hospital?" he asked.

"Yes, he is," Will replied. "But, at present, it's his father I am more concerned about. Dr Smythe's blundering could kill him."

"You cannot interfere, Will."

"I know but, Father, when I said to you it would take the unnecessary death of one of Dr Smythe's patients for him to stop practising medicine, I hadn't expected that the patient could very well be Isobel's grandfather."

"Chronic lung disease?"

Will nodded. "He urgently needs to inhale pure oxygen but I doubt if that has even crossed Dr Smythe's mind."

"What if I were to call to number 7 now – feign complete ignorance of Mr Greene's illness – hope Dr Smythe is still there – and try and have a word with him?"

"You can't push your way in there, Father, it will be viewed as interfering on my behalf."

"Will, it's worth a try," Isobel said and he sighed.

"Very well, but we might not be here when you return, we're taking John and the twins to St Stephen's Green this morning."

"Your visit to feed the ducks is usually on Sunday afternoons."

"This afternoon, Alfie, Will and I are going to try and visit Miles," Isobel explained.

"I see. Well, call to number 67 on your way home."

Twenty minutes later, the five of them made their way to St Stephen's Green. The perambulator was cumbersome and difficult for Will to manoeuvre but, for the present, it was the easiest way of transporting Ben and Belle any distance. Wrapped up warm and sitting at each end, the five-month-old twins were noticing more and more with each outing. John was also starting to point things out to them, taking his role of cousin very seriously.

With a brown paper bag containing bread crusts from Mrs Dillon, their cook-housekeeper, John soon had what seemed like every duck in Dublin crowding around him at the lake squawking for a piece.

"I don't know if my father is actually capable of feigning complete ignorance," Will said as Isobel pointed out a huge drake to John. "But we'll see. John, throw a piece of crust to him and see if he feeds it to any of his wives."

John threw a piece at the drake but the duck wasn't in a

generous mood, snatched it off the grass and swam away with it.

"Charming," Isobel muttered. "How most ungentlemanly. Throw some crusts for the female ducks so they all get some."

Soon, the bag of crusts was empty and a disappointed John watched the ducks realise that was all for now and swim away.

"Do we have to go home yet?" he asked, passing the bag to Isobel and she put it in her handbag.

"Not just yet," Will replied. "We'll make a circuit of the park and then go home."

"Thank you," John cried and ran ahead of them along the path.

"Don't go too far," Isobel called after him.

"I won't."

"Will?" His father was approaching them. "Thank goodness."

"I thought we were to call to number 67?"

"This couldn't wait," his father said, raising his hat to Isobel. "When I called to number 7, Mrs Greene had just dismissed Dr Smythe after finding him asleep at her husband's bedside."

"I see," Will replied cautiously.

"And Mr Greene wants you to attend to him."

"I see," Will replied again and his father gave him a puzzled stare. "You told me not to become his doctor."

"That was before I knew about Miles. Mr Greene is lucid now but it may not always be the case and I think it would be best to keep what the Greenes did with Miles 'within the family', so to speak, for as long as possible. Or would you rather suggest Dr David Powell? I presume he is trustworthy?"

"Yes, he is but, no, not David. Between the two practices, he has enough patients to deal with and I don't want any possibility of his relationship with Alfie becoming common knowledge. Isobel – yes or no?" he asked but she wasn't there. Turning around, he saw her hurrying along the path in the direction John had just run. "Isobel?"

"I don't know where young John is," she shouted back at him.

"Please stay here with the twins in case he comes back," Will instructed his father and caught up with Isobel. "John's probably trying to find all the ducks again. I'll keep going this way – you make your way to the bridge and see if you can spot him from there."

They separated and he raced as fast as he could along the path around the lake to the opposite bank hoping John hadn't taken it into his head to – oh, Christ – yes, he had. The boy was sitting down and sliding off the path and into the water in pursuit of the huge drake. As Will reached the bank, John disappeared under the water for a heart-stopping moment before surfacing and gasping as he discovered his feet didn't touch the bottom. He flailed about, his dark eyes bulging in terror and Will dropped to his knees. Grabbing the collar of John's overcoat then one of the boy's wrists, Will hauled him out of the water and sat him down on the path.

"You're all right – you're safe now," he said, fighting an urge to cry with relief while John coughed and spluttered. "Breathe slowly and deeply in and out – that's it – good. What were you trying to do?" he asked as matter-of-factly as he could, sitting on the path beside the boy and putting an arm around his shoulders.

"Follow him," John replied, pointing to the drake who was now back on the far side of the lake with all his wives.

"Is the water cold?"

"Yes."

"Is it deep?"

"Yes."

"Can you swim?"

"No."

"That is why the lake is for ducks only," Will explained gently.

"I won't do it again," John assured him in a small voice.

"Good," Will said as the boy burst into tears and he kissed John's cheeks then looked around for Isobel and spotted her on the bridge, her distinctive coat of black velvet leaves on a white velvet background with matching hat marking her out from the other visitors to the park. "Isobel's coming. She's going to be angry with you."

"I know," John said, quickly wiping the tears away with his fingers.

"What were you thinking?" Isobel demanded as she ran towards them. Kneeling down, she hugged John to her and kissed the top of his head. "You could have drowned."

"I'm sorry, Isobel," John whispered and began to shiver.

"It's too cold for him to walk home as he is," Will told her, getting to his feet then helping John up and taking his hand. "We need to take his clothes off, dry him and put a blanket from the perambulator around him."

Will met his father's eyes as they returned to him and the twins, silently telling him not to scold the boy that the fright had been punishment enough.

"Tried to swim like a duck, eh, John?" his father inquired instead.

"I can't swim, Grandfather," the boy replied quietly as Will crouched down and unbuttoned his overcoat.

"That will have to be remedied. Isobel, take some of these blankets – there are at least six in here."

"Bridget didn't want the twins to catch a chill," she said and lifted three out of the perambulator. "Will, dry John with this one and then wrap the others around him."

Will undressed John, passed her the wet clothes and as he dried the boy's hair and body, she wrung them out before bundling them and John's boots into the damp blanket. She placed the bundle in the perambulator between the curious twins while Will draped a blanket around John's shoulders and tucked another around the boy's waist. John was shivering violently and Will picked him up and rubbed his arms, legs and feet to warm them.

"Yes or no to me attending to Mr Greene?" he asked Isobel.

"Who is Mr Greene?" John tugged at the lapel of Will's overcoat.

"A gentleman who has recently moved into the square," she explained and hesitated before answering Will.

"Give John to me," his father instructed. "I'll rub his arms and legs and warm him," he added and Will passed the boy to him with a grateful smile before walking a few yards along the path with Isobel.

"You swore never again to attend to someone you knew socially or were related to," she said.

"This will have to be different," he replied. "I will not tolerate any more of last evening's behaviour from your grandmother. And when your mother returns from London and is told of her father's condition, she will have to be dealt with equally firmly. Neither she, nor her mother will interfere with, or take issue with my treatment."

"Of course."

"So, are we agreed?" he asked and she nodded.

"Yes."

"Very well. I obtained an oxygen cylinder for the practice. I'll go to the practice house now and fetch it. Ask Father to help you bring the children home, instruct Florrie and Bridget to give John a bath, and please apologise to Mrs Dillon as I may be late for luncheon, but the sooner I start your grandfather's treatment the better."

Will hurried away and Isobel went back to his father, the twins and an inquisitive young John.

"You have agreed?" Will's father asked.

"We have. Can you help me bring the children home, please?"

"It will be a pleasure."

"Where's Will going?" young John demanded, peering past her.

"He has to go and attend to a patient. He'll be home later."

"And I shall carry you and escort Isobel and your cousins home instead," his grandfather said and the boy grinned at him.

Isobel struggled with the perambulator as they made their way to Fitzwilliam Square, getting the contraption off and onto pavements especially. Either the twins' weight had doubled or the wheels had a mind of their own.

"Damn and blast the fecking thing," she finally exploded and both Johns shot her surprised glances. "I'm sorry. Will has much more of a knack of controlling this thing than I do."

"Perhaps, if you turned it around and pulled it onto the pavement, rather than trying to push it?" her father-in-law suggested.

She nodded, turned the perambulator to face the way they had just come, and heaved it onto the pavement. Suddenly Belle let out a squeal of laughter at her efforts, followed by Ben and they all stared at the twins in astonishment.

"Well, they have just told me what they think of my perambulator driving," she muttered and they set off again.

"Do they laugh a lot?" their grandfather asked.

"A little. That was the first time the two of them laughed together. Will shall be sorry to have missed it."

"I missed both Edward and Will's first words. But I did see them both take their first steps. These two," he indicated the twins, "will be walking before their first birthday."

"I had better warn Will, Florrie and Bridget, then."

The perambulator was carried into the hall of number 30, Zaineb ran up the stairs to the nursery for Florrie and Bridget and the two nursery maids came downstairs, their eyes widening when they saw young John's damp hair and him wearing two blankets.

"He went into the lake after the huge drake and needs a bath and these two have just laughed at my lack of perambulator driving skills," she explained, passing Ben to Bridget and Belle to Florrie. "So, if he repeats what I should not have said, tell me, and I'll have a word with him."

"I'm hungry," the boy announced as his grandfather set him down on his feet and Isobel bent and kissed his cheek. "Up you go ahead of them and open the door to the nursery.

Florrie and Bridget will give you a bath and luncheon will be served afterwards."

John nodded and she and Will's father watched as he began to climb the stairs with the two maids tailing him.

"I was on the bridge and I saw him disappear under the water. It was only for a moment but it seemed like an age…" She shook her head, undoing her coat buttons as she went into the morning room. "Thank you for assisting."

"Not at all. Are you not going to number 7 as well?" he asked, following her.

"I'd rather not row with my grandmother while Will is making my grandfather comfortable," she said as he closed the door. "She did not wish to come to Dublin and acquaint herself with any of us and she does not want to meet her son again. She knows of my past and wasted no time in throwing it in my face."

"How? Did she engage an inquiry agent?"

"Grandfather told me there was no need for one but Grandmother knew of my seduction so someone must have been engaged to make inquiries in Ballybeg," she replied, extracting the pin from her hat and taking it off. "Perhaps, Grandmother engaged someone without Grandfather's knowledge, I don't know. That I am a fallen woman is no secret but your living arrangements are very much a secret. Are your servants discreet?"

"Our servants are discreet and loyal."

"Good," she said, pushing the pin back into the hat. "I shall call to number 67 – possibly tomorrow – and bring Sarah up to date."

"Are you still going to Swift's Hospital this afternoon?"

Isobel glanced at the clock on the mantelpiece. It was just after one o'clock.

"That all depends on what time Will comes home and when we eat. Have you ever been to Swift's Hospital?" she asked.

"Yes, I have. I had a patient committed about fifteen years ago. As asylums go, it is very respectable."

"That's what Will said. You really should go home for your own meal."

John nodded. "I will."

She saw him out herself and as she closed the front door, hung her hat on the stand and shrugged off her coat, she heard footsteps behind her. Zaineb was coming up the steps from the servants' hall.

"Mrs Dillon was wondering whether to serve luncheon, Mrs Fitzgerald."

"Please, tell Mrs Dillon she can, but just for myself," she said, hanging up her coat. "My husband is with a patient."

"Yes, Mrs Fitzgerald."

As Zaineb turned away, the front door opened and Will came in, a little surprised to find them both in the hall.

"Luncheon is about to be served," she told him. "Come to the breakfast room and tell me all."

Will hurried as fast as he could from St Stephen's Green to the practice house on Merrion Street Upper. He collected the oxygen cylinder, tube and face mask then took a cab back to Fitzwilliam Square and retrieved his medical bag from the hall table at number 30. Knox admitted him to number 7 and he followed the butler upstairs, hearing Mr Greene's mucousy coughing.

Mrs Greene was seated at her husband's bedside wearing a chocolate brown dress and she nodded a greeting to him as she placed a glass of water on the bedside table.

"May I be of any assistance to you, Dr Fitzgerald?" she offered.

"Thank you, but no."

"Very well," she said, getting up and kissing her husband's cheek. "Come to the morning room before you leave."

Mrs Greene and the butler left the room and Will went to the bed. Mr Greene was lying back against three pillows and gave Will's hand a squeeze.

"Thank you for coming, Dr Fitzgerald, and for attending to me last night. I thought I was able to return here myself but the distance was simply too much for me."

"You were found just in time," Will told him. "I'm afraid I must advise you not to go out unaccompanied again."

"Very well," he replied in a resigned tone. "My wife dismissed Dr Smythe. He was recommended to us but it is clear that at his age, practising medicine is now beyond him."

Not wishing to discuss the failings of a fellow doctor with Mr Greene, Will held up the oxygen cylinder instead. "I have brought you pure oxygen to inhale. It will make your breathing a little easier."

"Do whatever it is you have to do."

Will busied himself in giving Mr Greene a full examination before connecting the oxygen cylinder to the tube and face mask and setting the pressure.

"Place the face mask over your nose and mouth and breathe in," he instructed. "That's it. Now, lift it a little to exhale – good – and when you want to sleep, place it at a slightly crooked angle leaving a small gap so you can exhale without having to lift the mask."

"Like this?" Mr Greene asked, turning the mask a little

so there was a gap of about a quarter of an inch at the sides.

"Yes, like that – good. Isobel and I took the children to St Stephen's Green this morning. John loves the ducks but gave us quite a scare by sliding on his bottom into the lake to go after a drake. I managed to haul him out," he added quickly as the elderly man gave him an anxious glance. "He is cold but quite all right and is being carried home wrapped in two blankets."

"Boys will be boys," Mr Greene said, lowering the face mask.

"Yes." Will replaced the face mask over Mr Greene's nose and mouth. "Now, rest, and remember – use the face mask to breathe in – but lift it a little to exhale – and angle it when you want to sleep. I will call to you again this evening."

An ewer of water, soap and a towel had been left on the washstand in a corner and he washed and dried his hands before leaving the bedroom. Knox was waiting on the landing, escorted Will downstairs and showed him into the gloomy morning room. A huge sofa and two armchairs all upholstered in burgundy velvet which almost matched the wallpaper were solid and serviceable, rather than fashionable, and ideal for a rental property. The Greenes evidently did not intend to stay long in Dublin as, apart from a small clock on the mantelpiece, the room was devoid of any ornaments or personal items.

"Well, Dr Fitzgerald?" Mrs Greene glanced apprehensively at him before getting up from the sofa.

"Your husband is inhaling pure oxygen," he told her. "It is not a cure but it will ease his breathing for a time."

"A time," Mrs Greene repeated, sitting down again and motioning for Will to do likewise. "I understand."

"Mrs Greene," he continued, sitting in the armchair nearest to her. "The immediate priority is keeping your husband as comfortable as possible. At present, he is not in a fit state to travel even a short distance, so a visit to your son is currently out of the question. This will both frustrate and upset him but we must try and ensure it is kept to a minimum. I must also state that I will not tolerate a repeat of your disgraceful behaviour towards my wife last evening."

He was gratified to see her shuffle uncomfortably. "It will not happen again, Dr Fitzgerald," she replied quietly.

"Good. Can you please tell me the name and address of the doctor who attends to your husband at Greene Hall?"

"His name is Dr Richard Bourke and his address is The Mall, Westport, Co Mayo."

"Thank you. Generally, I do not intervene if someone is the patient of another doctor but, in this case, I must. I shall write to Dr Bourke, inform him of your husband's condition and tell him that I shall attend to your husband for as long as he remains in Dublin."

"Dr Bourke will understand."

"And in the next few days, I would like to introduce your husband to Ben and Belle, and also to John. Would you like to meet them as well?"

Mrs Greene looked momentarily startled. "I…" she began but tailed off.

"Consider it."

"I shall."

"I understand this must be very difficult for you but—"

"I did not wish to come to Dublin," she interrupted. "But my husband insisted on it. As soon as he is able, we shall be returning to Greene Hall."

Never to see any of you again, Will finished silently and got to his feet.

"Well, as I said, the immediate priority is keeping your husband comfortable. I will call again this evening. Good afternoon to you."

Alfie called to number 30 just before two o'clock and was brought up to date as they walked to Baggot Street Lower to hail a cab.

"Mother is going to be very upset, Isobel," he said as one stopped for him and he opened the door.

"Yes," she replied and climbed inside. "But it is James I feel the sorriest for."

They got out of the cab at the gateway facing St Patrick's Hospital. Will paid the cabman then introduced himself to the porter, explained their reason for visiting and they were admitted to the grounds.

The porter escorted them to the seven-bay, two-storey over basement hospital which had further buildings to its rear she could only partially see as they approached. The area in front of the hospital, separated from Bow Lane by a substantial wall, was planted with trees and had a lawn surrounded by a gravel path. Outwardly, it all appeared very serene.

They went inside, up a beautiful cantilevered staircase and she and Alfie waited in the entrance hall while Will and the porter went in search of the matron. The sounds of a man sobbing echoed towards them and Isobel exchanged a nervous glance with Alfie.

"…No, Dr Fitzgerald, Miles is not on one of the wards." They turned as Will, the porter and a middle-aged woman dressed in a black dress and a white nurse's cap walked towards them. "I am Matron Rice," she said, shaking first Isobel's and then Alfie's hands. "You are very welcome to St Patrick's Hospital. Miles is what is known as a chamber-boarder. He has his own apartment and a servant."

"An apartment and a servant?" Isobel exclaimed and the matron nodded.

"Oh, yes, Mrs Fitzgerald. Miles is very comfortable here."

"How…" Isobel tailed off, racking her brains. "Is he?" she concluded the question feebly.

"Miles is a very gentle soul. Although, he is not as sharp-witted as you or I, he is certainly not considered an 'idiot' or a 'lunatic'."

"Then, should he really be here?" she asked.

"To be quite honest with you, Mrs Fitzgerald, Miles is here simply because his parents did not want a 'dim-witted' son."

"We did not know of his existence here until yesterday," Isobel said quietly.

"So your husband told me. It is nothing to be ashamed of, many families tuck their husbands, wives, sons and daughters away in establishments such as this. Please, come with me," she said and they thanked the porter as he took his leave.

They followed Matron Rice along a gallery with windows situated high enough to be out of the reach of patients until the matron halted outside a door to their left.

"It would be best if you went in one at a time. Perhaps, you first, Mrs Fitzgerald. Miles, it's Matron," she said, opening the door. "I have a visitor for you."

Isobel went inside, her heart thumping as Matron Rice closed the door, and couldn't help but gaze around the parlour in a mixture of pleasant surprise and relief. The large window was sited at a standard height which could only mean the occupant was not deemed to be either at risk of trying to escape or taking their own life. The walls were papered with a pattern of green leaves on a cream background and on the floor was a rug, also with a leaf design.

To the right of the door was a small dining table and two chairs and to its left was a tall mahogany bookcase overflowing with volumes of all sizes. Two armchairs upholstered in green velvet stood on either side of the fireplace, above which hung a huge mirror. Sitting at a walnut writing desk at the window and reading a book was her uncle. He twisted around in the chair and looked her up and down, taking in her coat and hat's leaf pattern and she smiled. Like his father, he had a beard but wore no spectacles.

"Good afternoon, Miles," she said softly.

"Are you a new nurse?" he asked, getting to his feet and doing up the buttons of a black morning coat.

"No, my name is Isobel. What are you reading?" she inquired, edging forward.

"*Jane Eyre.*"

"Are you enjoying it?"

"Yes, I am. Do take a seat," he said, gesturing to one of the armchairs.

"Thank you." She sat down, trying not to make it obvious she was staring at him as he retook his seat at the desk. Dark-haired like her mother, he also had her mother's high forehead and brown eyes and reminded Isobel of Mr Parnell, leader of the Home Rulers and president of the Land League.

"If you are not a nurse then, who, may I ask, are you?"

"Has anyone spoken to you about your family?"

"I have no living family," he replied, turning his attention back to the book.

"That is not true," she said and he lifted his head. "Miles, you are my mother's brother – you are my uncle."

He stared at her and she smiled again as he digested her words. "I am your uncle," he stated and she nodded. "Why have you not visited me before?"

"Because until yesterday I did not know you were here. Out there," she gestured to the gallery, "are my brother and my husband. Would you like to meet them?"

"Are you going to bring me home with you?" he asked and she stared at him in consternation.

"Matron Rice says you are very comfortable here," she said instead of answering. "You have a lovely parlour and a lovely view," she added, stretching her neck and catching a glimpse of the lawn and gravel path.

"I am lucky. Some of the other patients have cells. I am really your uncle?"

"Yes, you are," she said. "My name is Isobel Fitzgerald and I have one brother called Alfie. My husband is called Will. Would you like to meet them?"

"Yes, I would, thank you."

"I'll go and fetch them." She got up, went to the door and opened it. "Come in and meet Miles."

They followed her into the parlour and she caught Alfie glancing around the room in surprise, having expected, like her, for it to be far more austere.

"Miles," she said and he got up from the chair. "This is my brother, Alfie Stevens. And this is my husband, Will Fitzgerald."

"I am delighted to meet you." Miles greeted them formally. "Do you live in Dublin?"

"We all live on Fitzwilliam Square," Alfie replied. "And I am studying medicine at Trinity College."

"I am a doctor," Will told him. "But I'm off duty today."

"Are you going to bring me home with you?" Miles asked again and Alfie threw her a startled glance.

"No, we are not," Will replied gently and Miles' face fell.

"But we shall come here and visit you regularly," she added. "I would very much like to take a walk with you around the lawn."

"Why will you not bring me home with you?" Miles persisted.

"When did you last leave this hospital?" Will pointed to the gates.

"I..." Miles tailed off and his shoulders slumped. "Never."

"We will come here and visit you," she repeated, hesitantly reaching out and squeezing his hand. "Now we have met you, we will not forget you."

"Promise?"

"I promise."

"Good. That's settled, then."

"Is there a book you would like me to bring you when I come to visit?"

"Well." Miles' face creased as he pondered her question. "I have almost finished *Jane Eyre* and I would like to continue with the Brontës – perhaps *Wuthering Heights*?"

"*Wuthering Heights* it is," she said.

"When will you visit again?"

"In the next few days, I promise."

"Thank you."

Isobel returned to the gallery and rejoined Matron Rice with Will and Alfie following, hoping she wouldn't cry. Alfie closed the door to the apartment and they went downstairs.

"You will visit again?" the matron inquired.

"Yes, we will," she replied.

"Good, because we have had promises before."

"I don't make promises I will not keep," she said. "Miles has asked for a book – *Wuthering Heights* – is it suitable for him?"

"Yes, it is."

"And mince pies?"

Matron Rice smiled. "He will enjoy them very much."

They walked in silence to James' Street where Will hailed a cab. They climbed in and sat down but she couldn't stop the tears coming.

"There is barely anything wrong with him," she sobbed.

"Matron Rice explained that he appears to have the reasoning of a fifteen-year-old boy," Will said, putting an arm around her. "When we return during the week, I will speak with Dr Harrison the medical superintendent."

"When he asked me if we were going to take him home with us, I didn't know what to say." She fumbled in her sleeve for a handkerchief and blew her nose. "We can't take him home with us."

"But I could take him home with me," Alfie said and grimaced. "What I mean is – if it would benefit Miles not to live in a hospital, then, number 55 would be ideal."

"I shall mention it to Dr Harrison," Will told him. "But there is the small matter of your mother and James, who are expecting to return from honeymoon to a quiet married life. As well as that, your grandmother doesn't want anything to do with Miles, so we must not tell her husband we have seen him in case it causes friction between them. There are many things to take into account but first and foremost is what Dr Harrison has to say. We do nothing until I have spoken to him."

That evening, after feeding the twins and helping young John – who was none the worse for his scare in St Stephen's Green – to bed, Isobel and Will called to number 7. Knox brought them upstairs, showed them into Mr Greene's bedroom and her grandfather kissed her hand then gave Will a smile as he put his medical bag down on the bedside table.

"This oxygen is wonderful."

"I'm glad." Will took out his stethoscope and listened to Mr Greene's chest. "Good," he said. "The oxygen is definitely helping."

"May I get up?" Mr Greene asked eagerly.

"I'd like you to have complete bed rest for now," Will replied and Mr Greene's face fell. "But when I do allow you to get up, you must continue to inhale the oxygen and I want you to use a bath chair so you don't over-exert yourself."

"How? I am up here on the second floor?"

"Your bed must be carried downstairs to the morning room," Will explained. "You must climb as few stairs as possible – preferably none."

"Can my bed be placed near the window?"

"As long as the servants' bell is within your reach, yes."

"Thank you. I cannot tell you how dull being up here is."

"I can bring you some books or newspapers?" Isobel offered and he nodded.

"A selection of newspapers would help to pass the time. Is Mr Parnell still in Kilmainham Gaol?" he asked Will.

"Yes, he is," she replied and her grandfather turned back to her in a little surprise. It was clear he did not approve of women reading newspapers. "I take it from your tone you do not approve of him?"

"I certainly do not approve of Mr Parnell," he replied shortly. "I happened to be in Westport back in 1879 when a land meeting was taking place. I could hardly believe my ears – Charles Stewart Parnell – a landlord himself – was attacking the entire principal of landlordism – wanting to dismantle it and allow tenants to purchase their land. Where would I be if my tenants purchased their land? Out on the side of the road, that is where. Thanks to my land agent and his excellent management of the Greene Hall estate, there has been little or no trouble from the Land League and their followers," he added before she could ask. "So I do not need Mr Parnell inciting violence – he deserved to be imprisoned – Mr Parnell is a disgrace to his class – the longer he is kept locked up the better for all—" He broke off in a fit of coughing and grabbed the face mask.

"Mr Parnell was imprisoned because the government were convinced he was attempting to thwart Mr Gladstone's land-reform bill," she clarified. "Would you like a Mayo newspaper, too?" she continued before he could carry on with his one-sided argument and he inhaled and exhaled a few times before replying.

"I arranged for the *Connaught Telegraph* to be posted here but thank you for asking."

"I will see what other newspapers and periodicals I can find for you," she said and he patted her hand in reply.

"We now must speak with your wife," Will said. "Rest, and I will call on you in the morning."

They went downstairs and were shown into the morning room. Mrs Greene tensed on seeing her but Will cleared his throat and Mrs Greene looked at him.

"Your husband is a little improved but I have told him he still needs bed rest."

As Will related what he had said to Mr Greene regarding the moving of his bed downstairs, Isobel went to the fireplace and warmed her hands. Apart from a small plain mahogany clock, the mantelpiece was bare, as was the entire room. The burgundy wallpaper, the black curtains and the mahogany sofa and two armchairs upholstered in burgundy velvet which didn't quite match the wallpaper only served to add to the air of gloom.

"The house came furnished," Mrs Greene informed her. "But that was all."

"I am bringing Grandfather some newspapers and periodicals," she said. "Do you read them? Or would you prefer some novels?"

"Well, I…" Her grandmother tailed off, not knowing how to respond to her kind offer.

"Mother reads a great number of periodicals," Isobel went on regardless. "I shall bring some to you."

Without responding, Mrs Greene turned back to Will. "When you deem my husband well enough, inform me, and I shall instruct the servants to move his bed."

"I will, and Knox and I shall carry Mr Greene downstairs – he is not to walk."

"Thank you for what you have done for my husband so far. The oxygen greatly eases his breathing but I know his condition will not improve and that it is simply a case of keeping him comfortable."

"Yes, it is," Will replied. "But to have him here with you, rather than alone two floors up, will be good for him."

"I agree."

"I will call again in the morning. Good evening to you."

As they left the house and went down the steps to the pavement, Will put on his hat and took out his watch.

"What time is it?" she asked.

"Just after half past seven – good – it's not too late to call to number 67."

They walked to Merrion Square and Maura, one of Will's parents' house-parlourmaids, admitted them to the house and they parted in the hall. Will went upstairs to speak to his father while Isobel was shown into the morning room, where she related the events of the past two days to an increasingly incredulous Sarah.

"So your grandparents' coming to Dublin was orchestrated by your grandfather, not your grandmother?"

"Yes," Isobel replied. "And I know I should be looking forward to Mother and James returning from London but, truthfully, I'm dreading it," she admitted. "My grandmother ignored all of Mother's letters over the years – letters which told Grandmother that Father was violent and asking if she could return to live at Greene Hall with Alfie and I. When Mother realises this – and all the things which have been kept from her – it will be terrible. Grandmother does not wish to be reunited with Mother – she did not wish to meet any of us. I really should be looking forward to Christmas, but I'm not," she concluded miserably.

"Take one step at a time," Sarah advised gently.

"That's what Will said. When we visit Miles again, Will is going to speak to the medical superintendent."

"And James is a level-headed man. He will comfort your mother."

"But would you want to have to cope with all of this when you are just returned from your honeymoon?" Isobel asked and Sarah grimaced, giving Isobel her answer. "I thought that once Mother and James were married, all would be well – how stupid—"

She stopped abruptly as the door opened and both Will and his father came in. Beside her on the green velvet sofa, Sarah tensed but said nothing.

"Father knows Dr Harrison in Swift's Hospital and will be coming with us on Wednesday afternoon," Will said. "Can you come to number 30 and visit the children in the morning instead, Mother?"

"Yes, I can."

"Thank you, Sarah," Isobel replied. "And while the two of you are here, I would like to invite you to number 30 for Christmas Day. The twins will sleep through it all but Will and I would like to make the day especially enjoyable for young John."

"Of course," Will's father replied. "I would be delighted to come. Sarah?"

"Thank you for the invitation, Isobel," his wife replied without looking at her husband. "I shall gladly come for the day."

Will had one urgent house call to make on Wednesday afternoon but met Isobel and his father at number 67 at half past three and they took a cab to St Patrick's Hospital. Isobel went straight to Miles' apartment with a copy of *Wuthering Heights* and a tin of mince pies, while Will and his father went to the medical superintendent's office.

"Miles Greene has the mental capacity of a fifteen-year-old boy," Dr Harrison told them. "He is not violent or aggressive – never has been – even when he sometimes struggles to express himself – and if it were not for the fact that his parents did not want a 'slow' or 'simpleton' child, he could have lived with them perfectly well and not be tucked away here."

"So, Miles is capable of living in an ordinary home?" Will asked and Dr Harrison nodded.

"Miles likes everything tidy, orderly and just so. I believe he could live a happy life in a quiet home with some supervision. Can you give him a home, Dr Fitzgerald?"

"No, I'm afraid not," Will replied. "My wife and I have three young children but Miles could be accommodated in my wife's mother's home. Except—" He sighed. "My mother-in-law is currently away on honeymoon and she has always believed her brother to have died at a year old. The news will have to be broken to her and to her new husband when they return and the possibility of giving Miles a home discussed."

"And Miles' parents?" Dr Harrison added.

"Mr Greene is too ill to visit him and Mrs Greene continues to want nothing to do with her son," Will explained.

"I see that it is a delicate matter all round."

"Yes, it is."

"Well, discuss the matter and let me know the outcome.

If Miles can be given a home, the hospital shall need written consent from Mr Greene for Miles to be released from our care into the care of his sister and brother-in-law."

Will and his father left the office and as they approached Miles' apartment, Will could hear laughing and on opening the door saw Isobel performing an elaborate curtsy to her uncle.

"I have just taught Miles how to waltz," she said. "Miles, come and meet Will's father. Miles, this is John Fitzgerald. John, this is Miles Greene."

"I'm very pleased to meet you, sir." Miles shook Will's father's hand. "Isobel tells me you are a doctor, too."

"I am retired from practising medicine," he clarified. "I now edit the *Journal of Irish Medicine*."

"Dr Harrison reads that periodical, I have seen a copy on his desk."

"Good. So, you have mastered the waltz?" he asked and Miles smiled.

"I wouldn't say that, sir, but I now know all the steps. Thank you for visiting me."

"You are very welcome, Miles."

"When will you visit me again?" Miles turned back to Isobel.

"In the next few days, I promise," she said, reaching up and kissing his cheek before leaving the apartment. "Well?" she asked as the porter showed them out of the hospital grounds. "Is Miles capable of living away from here?"

"Yes, he is," Will replied. "But remember, Isobel, one thing at a time – it needs to be broken gently to your mother how ill her father is and then that Miles is alive – and she will need time in order to digest the news."

"Yes, and I am dreading telling her – and James."

"You won't be alone," he said, lifting her hand and kissing it. "Alfie and I will be with you. And we must not interfere – the final decision must be hers and James'."

Mr and Mrs Ellison were due back in Dublin on late Saturday afternoon. Isobel and Will had just returned to number 30 from their weekly coffee outing to a café on Grafton Street followed by a visit to the National Gallery when Alfie was shown into the morning room.

"They're back," he said. "And Mother wants to see both of you. Now."

Isobel exchanged a glance with Will. This was it.

They accompanied Alfie to number 55 and in the morning room, she hugged and kissed her mother and step-father.

"We had such a lovely time," Mrs Ellison proclaimed. "London is a wonderful city to visit – even in December. Now, tell me, are my parents still here, Isobel?"

"Yes, they are."

"Good," her mother replied, lifting her 'going away' hat from a side table and extracting the pin. "I must call on them—"

"Martha, we are home barely ten minutes and you have not even taken off your coat." James gently took the hat and pin from his wife and placed them on a side table near the door. "You can call on your parents tomorrow."

"Shall we have some tea?" Isobel suggested, silently thanking him for his calm intervention.

"I have drunk gallons of tea over the past week," her mother said, ringing for a servant before sitting on the enormous sofa upholstered in gold-coloured velvet. "Shall we have coffee instead?"

"Yes, please," she replied, despite not wanting any more, and she and Alfie sat down on either side of their mother on the sofa while Will and James sat in the armchairs.

When the coffee was carried in Isobel poured, added milk and passed the cup and saucer to her mother with a hand which shook. Coffee slopped into the saucer and she swore under her breath.

"What is wrong, Isobel?" her mother asked, her eyes suddenly widening in horror. "Is my father dead?" she demanded and Alfie quickly took the cup and saucer from her. "Is he dead, Isobel?"

"No, he is not dead," Will told her. "But he is very ill. He has chronic lung disease and he collapsed last Saturday evening. To cut a long story short, I am now his doctor. Your father is inhaling pure oxygen which eases his breathing and his bed is now downstairs in the morning room as I have forbidden him to climb any stairs."

"Chronic?" Mrs Ellison whispered. "That means he will not recover, doesn't it?"

"All is being done to keep him as comfortable as possible," Will replied. "But, no, he will not recover."

"How long does he have left?"

"That is impossible to say but what I can tell you is that this Christmas will be his last."

"And Mrs Greene?" James asked as his wife exhaled a long and shaky breath.

"Mrs Greene appears to be in good health."

"But there is something else, isn't there?" James continued and Isobel nodded.

"Yes, there is. Mother, do you remember anything of your brother, Miles?" she asked and her mother shot her a puzzled glance.

"No, nothing. He died aged a year old. Why?"

Clasping her mother's hands, Isobel held them tightly. "Miles did not die aged a year old. He is alive. He is here in Dublin."

Her mother gave her a blank stare and then peered at James but all he could do was shrug helplessly so she looked back at Isobel.

"But – but – he died – there is a grave…"

"Miles is alive," Isobel said. "You were born first but Miles' birth was a difficult one and he took a long time to be born. He seemed fine initially but he did not feed well, he did not laugh or make any sounds and he did not attempt to walk. When Miles was a year old, he was examined and it was determined that he was not like other children."

"Not like other children?" Mrs Ellison was bewildered. "I don't understand."

"Miles does not have the mental capacity of an adult," Will told her softly. "And he never will. So your father arranged that he be taken from Greene Hall to a hospital in Dublin and cared for there."

"Which hospital?"

"St Patrick's Hospital. It is also known as Swift's Hospital. Miles has his own apartment – separate from the other patients – and a servant."

"But why did Father and Mother lie to me?" her mother demanded, her voice little more than a squeak. "Why have me believe he had died?"

"Martha, your parents must not have wanted to be known as the father and mother of an 'idiot'," James explained gently.

"But that's the thing," Will said and they all turned to him. "Miles is not a 'simpleton' nor an 'idiot'. Nor is he violent or aggressive. According to Dr Harrison, the medical superintendent, Miles has the mental reasoning of a fifteen-year-old boy."

"You have spoken to his doctor – you have seen Miles?" Mrs Ellison asked and Will nodded.

"We have visited Miles twice and on our second visit on Wednesday afternoon my father and I spoke with Dr Harrison while Isobel brought Miles a copy of *Wuthering Heights* and some of Mrs Dillon's mince pies."

This was too much for Mrs Ellison and she burst into tears. Her husband quickly knelt beside the sofa, putting his arms around her and she sobbed on his shoulder.

"It is a lot to take in," James said, as much for himself as for his wife.

"We were dreading telling you this, Mother," Alfie spoke up. "We knew how upset you would be."

"You have seen Miles, too?" his mother inquired.

"Yes, but just the once. I could not go on Wednesday as I had lectures."

"Drink some coffee, Martha," James advised her and she took the cup and saucer from Alfie. "Is there anything else?" he asked rather warily as his wife took a sip.

"Yes, but not now," Isobel replied and the cup went down onto the saucer and they were handed straight back to Alfie.

"Yes, now," her mother insisted and Isobel's heart sank. "Tell me."

"You wrote many times to your parents – to tell them Father was violent – to ask if they would take you, Alfie and I in and give us a home at Greene Hall. When you received no reply to any of the letters, you probably thought the postmaster in Ballybeg had intercepted your letters and passed them on to Father. But the postmaster hadn't passed them on to Father. Your letters did reach Greene Hall. And—" She sighed. "Your mother burned them all."

James grimaced and exhaled a short cough of disgust but his wife just stared at Isobel.

"My mother did not wish to come to Dublin, did she?"

"No."

"And she does not want to see Miles?"

"No."

"Nor meet me – or any of us?"

"No. Coming to Dublin – wanting to visit Miles – wanting to meet you again – it was all your father's insisting."

Her mother nodded. "I see," she said crisply. "Thank you for telling me."

"Young John is eager to see Grandmamma Martha and Grandpapa James," Isobel continued brightly. "And the twins are becoming more alert every day. They both laughed at me when I had some trouble pushing the perambulator."

"I will come and see them tomorrow," her mother told her firmly.

"Good. I'm so sorry, Mother. I wanted your homecoming to be a happy one."

"Isobel, your grandparents' arrival in Dublin and what they did in the past is not your fault – nor yours, Alfie." Mrs Ellison took her cup and saucer from him, drank the rest of the coffee and Alfie placed the cup and saucer on a side table. "James and I shall try and digest this news and we will speak again tomorrow."

James Ellison was admitted to number 30 at half past nine the following morning just as Will and Isobel were leaving the breakfast room after a leisurely meal.

"Martha is enjoying breakfast in bed and Alfie has gone to meet a friend," he told them as Mary, their second house-parlourmaid, closed the front door and hung his hat and overcoat on the stand. "So I have called to speak to you both alone."

"Come into the morning room," Will said and he and James followed Isobel out of the hall. "Please, sit down," he added, gesturing to one of the reddish-brown leather armchairs and he and Isobel sat on the matching sofa.

"Thank you." James sat down and sighed. "Well, that was quite an exceptional homecoming yesterday," he began wryly. "No, don't apologise, Isobel. I knew from the moment you told me your grandfather was in the church that it would only mean trouble."

"How is Mother this morning?" she asked.

"Calmer. We talked for a long time after you left and she cried again but, as I said, she is calmer now. I have come to speak to you about Miles. His parents told everyone he died at a year old so it is likely he was baptised along with your mother and if there is a 'grave' there must have been a 'funeral' of some kind which means the baptism and burial will have been entered in the local parish registers. What else do you know?"

"Matron Rice told me the annual fee and Miles' servant's wages were always paid on time as well as an allowance for furniture, clothes, shoes and other sundries but that there was no other contact whatsoever with the Greenes," Isobel replied. "No-one but the hospital staff and we few know Miles is alive."

James nodded then turned to Will. "Both Martha and I would like to know if it is possible for Miles to leave Swift's Hospital and live in an ordinary home?"

"I asked Dr Harrison that," Will replied. "And the answer is that Miles likes everything tidy and in order and just so but, yes, he could live a happy life in a quiet home with some supervision."

"I'm glad. We hoped that would be the case."

"Are you sure, James?" Isobel asked. "It will be an enormous commitment."

"We're sure."

"The hospital will need written consent from Mr Greene regarding the transfer of Miles' care," Will said and James nodded. "As well as that, what is the legal position?" Will inquired. "As I said last evening, this will be Mr Greene's final Christmas. Can Miles inherit Greene Hall?"

"Yes, he can," James replied. "But that doesn't mean his father will leave the Greene Hall estate to him and, in my opinion, I don't think Miles should inherit it."

"Why not?" Isobel asked sharply. "Miles is my grandparents' only son."

"If he were to inherit property, Miles would be made a ward of court and his assets would be brought under the control of the court," James explained. "As well as that, anyone classed as a 'lunatic' is barred from making a will. So, in order to keep the matter out of the courts as much as possible, Miles needs a legal guardian – someone who will take care of his affairs – I would suggest Alfie."

"Why not you, James?"

"Alfie is a blood relation to Miles, he will qualify as a doctor in a few years' time and it is my opinion he should inherit the Green Hall estate from your grandfather. I will be happy to be on hand to provide legal advice, but Miles' guardian should be Alfie."

"In that case," she said. "You need to speak to my grandfather – without my grandmother present – and to Alfie."

"I will, as soon as possible. Your mother and I would also like to visit Miles and speak to Dr Harrison. I shall only be in the office tomorrow morning so if we were to go in the afternoon would the two of you be able to accompany us?"

"I have a couple of house calls to make," Will replied as Isobel nodded. "But, afterwards, I shall come to number 55."

"That's settled, then." James got to his feet. "I will leave you to enjoy your Sunday."

After luncheon, Will, Isobel, John and the twins made their way to St Stephen's Green to feed the ducks.

"Now, remember," Will said and John grinned.

"Only ducks can swim in the lake," they both proclaimed, Belle and Ben squealed with laughter and Will stared at them in astonishment.

"You thought I was exaggerating, didn't you?" Isobel teased.

"Well, just a bit," he admitted. "They are so alert now."

"They are, so be careful what you do or say in front of them. I had a little slip-up last week."

"Oh?"

She waved a hand dismissively. "Just some trouble with the perambulator. But I said something I shouldn't have and young John heard," she added in a low tone. "And I am amazed he hasn't repeated it."

"Give him time. He's more than likely saving it for an occasion to cause us the most possible embarrassment."

John fed the ducks then stood on the bank of the lake watching as they realised all the bread crusts were gone and swam away. Disappointed, he turned back to them.

"You will teach me how to swim?"

"Next summer, I promise," Will said. "I learned to swim at Seapoint. Isobel and I will take you, Ben and Belle there."

"Next summer?" John protested in dismay.

"Remember how cold the water in the lake was last week?" Will asked and the boy nodded. "Well, the sea will be very cold, too, at this time of year. So, next summer." John nodded and Will gave him a grin. "Good."

"Can I be taught how to swim, too?" Isobel asked. "Or is it boys only?"

"Oh, I don't know." Will pulled an overly indecisive expression and glanced at John. "What do you think? Shall we allow girls as well?"

"Yes – Isobel and Belle."

"Belle will be too young – even next summer – but Isobel will be taught to swim, too," he said, giving her a wink.

Isobel was shown into number 55's morning room at just after three o'clock the following afternoon. The room was empty and she turned to the butler with a frown.

"Is my mother not at home?"

"Mrs Ellison – and then Mr Ellison – have gone to call upon Mr Greene," Gorman told her. "Mr Stevens is upstairs in the library."

"Oh, I see. Thank you."

The butler closed the door after him and Isobel grimaced

as she went to the window, wishing her mother had not called to number 7 so soon. Hearing voices in the hall, she glanced at the door as it opened and Alfie came in.

"Why didn't you go with Mother and then James to number 7?" she asked.

"Because until James asked me – and then we asked Gorman – where Mother was, we didn't realise she had gone out," he replied. "I thought it best that James go after her to number 7. We had been discussing Miles. James has asked me to become Miles' legal guardian. I had expected for it to be James but he explained why he should not. And why it should be me."

"You sound as if you don't want to do it."

"I will do it—" Alfie stopped abruptly and spread his hands helplessly. "But James has told me he wants the Greene Hall estate to pass to me and not Miles when the time comes. Yes, it would be better not to have Miles be made a ward of court but, even so, I can't help but think the Greene Hall estate should be his – not mine."

"Alfie, we shall all be on hand to help and advise you."

"Isobel, I will never be married – I will never have a son…"

"And neither will Miles."

"But, unlike Miles, I shall be expected to marry and – when I don't – my bachelor status will be commented on."

"You will be a doctor with a busy Dublin practice with no time for marriage. There are plenty of bachelor doctors—"

"Who probably all have a 'secret friend' as I do."

Two cabs stopped outside and Will got out of the first. Seeing her at the window, he smiled and she waited for him to be shown into the room.

"Mother and James are at number 7," she told him before he could ask where they were and he rolled his eyes before peering past both her and Alfie at the street. "Have you asked the cabmen to wait?"

"Yes, and I hope your mother won't stay too long – not because of the cabs – but because seeing your mother again will be upsetting for your grandfather. I wish she hadn't called on him without my being present and I wish she hadn't called on him until after visiting Miles."

"Mother went first without telling James and I and James had to follow her," Alfie explained and Will swore under his breath. "Is Mother going be too emotional for Miles?" Alfie added. "Especially as Miles needs a quiet home?"

"I need to speak to James and – oh – there they are now."

Her mother and James were crossing the street, her mother waving her hands in the air in an agitated manner as she spoke to him while James simply shook his head before stopping and holding his arms out from his sides then letting them drop.

"Let's go outside." Will opened the door and then the front door for her. "James?" he called as the three of them left the house and James held up a hand to acknowledge him.

"I'm sorry, Will, but Martha took it upon herself to call to number 7, despite my having told her to wait until this evening."

"Do I need to call on Mr Greene?" Will asked.

"No, he is as well as can be expected. Despite having to deal with the unexpected caller."

"My father was delighted to see me," Mrs Ellison announced proudly.

"Did you or he mention Miles?" Isobel inquired.

"I had to," her mother replied and Isobel's heart sank. "James told me the hospital requires written consent from my father for Miles to come and live here – which I now have," she continued triumphantly, holding up an envelope.

"Did you see Grandmother?" Isobel added as Will opened the door of the first cab and James helped his wife inside and she sat down.

"Mother was 'resting'. Whether she does or does not wish to see me is entirely up to her but Father – oh, Will – that contraption – the face mask – the oxygen cylinder…"

"Your father needs it," Will replied. "To be blunt, Martha, your father cannot now live without inhaling oxygen and he must not be upset or agitated unnecessarily and I would have preferred that you had not called on him this first time without my being present."

Mrs Ellison flushed at Will's stern tone but raised her chin defensively. "So James told me – but he is my father – I had to visit him."

"And he is my patient – and I am trying to ensure he receives the best of care – please consider his needs in future and not your own."

Taking Isobel's arm, they went to the second cab and she climbed inside followed by Alfie. Will was the last to get in, he closed the door and both cabs left the square. They sat in silence until the two cabs stopped outside St Patrick's Hospital and the porter escorted them to Dr Harrison's office. Introductions were made, extra chairs were provided then they got down to business.

"Providing Miles with a home will be a huge commitment," Dr Harrison said, reading Mr Greene's letter of consent and nodding his thanks to her mother. "He needs stability, peace and quiet – and a routine. Are you able to provide him with all of those things?"

"Miles will have his own bedroom and it will house all the furniture and belongings he possesses here," Mrs Ellison replied. "Number 55 is large and there is also a rear garden and a private garden for the residents of the square."

"Miles must not leave the house unaccompanied," Dr Harrison told her. "The rear garden, yes, provided he cannot leave it. Your servants must be made aware of this."

"Yes, of course."

"You must also expect Miles to spend a great deal of time in his bedroom at first but he must also come here once per week so I can monitor him. It will be made clear to him that this will be a visit only."

"I don't understand?" Mrs Ellison frowned.

"Kind as Mrs Fitzgerald has been to visit him, Miles is always of the opinion that she will not return," Dr Harrison explained.

Isobel bit her lips. "But each time I assured him I would come back."

"Many other patients have been assured of a return visit which has not happened. Please do not be upset, Mrs Fitzgerald, Miles will need to build up a great deal of trust with all of you."

"Of course," she replied and Dr Harrison nodded.

"When can Miles leave here?" her mother asked. "And what possessions does he have?"

"As well as his clothes and furniture, Miles is inordinately fond of books which his servant, Peter, purchases for him," Dr Harrison replied. "So, whenever you can transport Miles, his clothes, his furniture and his books. He has managed to amass quite a collection. You will need to acquire a second bookcase for his bedroom."

"We shall," James spoke up. "May I ask if Miles ever becomes emotional?"

"Yes, he can be emotional. At times Miles struggles to express himself and he becomes frustrated – never angry or violent – he cries instead. It doesn't happen often as we generally know what Miles is attempting to say, so it happens more often than not with new patients he encounters. It will happen with you all, so you will need to be prepared."

"Might I suggest late Friday afternoon?" Will asked. "It will mean that James, Alfie and I shall be on hand over the weekend to ensure Miles settles in."

"Friday it is. Now, shall we go upstairs and introduce Miles to Mrs Ellison?"

It would be too much to expect her mother to remain composed but as she walked along the gallery Isobel hoped her mother wouldn't frighten poor Miles all the same. Dr Harrison opened the door to the apartment and she went in first. Miles glanced up from a book in first surprise and then delight when he recognised her.

"Isobel." He closed the book and got up from his seat at the desk. "How lovely of you to visit me again."

"This is a special visit, Miles," she said as her mother then James, Alfie, Will and lastly Dr Harrison came into the room.

"Oh?" Miles eyed them all nervously.

"Do you remember what I said on my first visit here? I told you how you are my mother's brother – that you are my uncle."

"Yes, that's right."

"Well, this," she clasped her mother's hand and led her forward, "is my mother – and she is your sister."

"Your twin sister." Mrs Ellison reached up and touched Miles' bearded cheek. "I am Martha."

"Why haven't you visited me before?"

"We—" Her mother faltered. "We were told—" She tried again and Isobel leapt in.

"We truly did not know you were here until the day before Will, Alfie and I visited you for the first time."

"My name is James Ellison," James said and held out a hand. "I am married to Martha."

"So, you are my… brother-in-law?" Miles asked hesitantly and shook his hand.

"That's right."

"Do you live on..?" Miles turned back to the desk and pulled a sheet of notepaper towards him. "Fitzwilliam Square?"

"Yes, I do," James replied and Miles nodded, picking up a pen and dipping the nib into a pot of ink.

"I have been writing it all down," Miles explained as he scribbled something at the bottom of the sheet. "I don't want to forget."

"You won't need to write it all down soon," Dr Harrison told him with a smile and Miles put the pen down and straightened up.

"Why not?"

"Because." His sister lifted his hand and kissed it. "James, Alfie and I would like you to come and live with us at number 55 Fitzwilliam Square."

Miles stared at her in silence for a moment. "Truly?" he asked quietly, hardly daring to believe it.

"Truly," Mrs Ellison replied. "You will have a bedroom all to yourself and we shall buy a—" she glanced at Miles' extensive library, "another extremely large bookcase for all your books."

Isobel gasped as Miles turned away, covering his face with his hands. He sobbed uncontrollably and she guided him to his desk chair. Sitting him down, she knelt at his side.

"It will be on Friday – in four days' time," she assured him. "The bedroom needs to be prepared for you and all your books packed here so they can be transported to Fitzwilliam Square. I shall come and visit you before then."

"Promise?"

"I promise," she replied and kissed his cheek.

"Dr Harrison?" Hearing her mother's voice shake, Isobel glanced at her as they returned to the porter who was to show them out of the hospital grounds. "You told us Miles doesn't often get very emotional."

"Those were tears of relief, Mrs Ellison," Dr Harrison replied. "Miles now knows what it is like to be wanted. He will soon have a home and – most important of all – he will soon be part of a family."

Chapter Three

After house calls on Tuesday afternoon, Will and Isobel walked to Pimlico in the Liberties. Dr David Powell, Will's colleague from the Merrion Street Upper medical practice, also took surgery in rooms on the ground floor of a tenement house on Wednesday evenings and Will was surprised to see the waiting room door ajar. He put his head around it and, to his relief, heard David's voice in the adjoining room so he closed the door and they went upstairs to call on his former housekeeper Mrs Bell.

"We're on our way to see Pat Callaghan to hire him and his cart and then to engage Frank Millar and his carriage," Will explained as Mrs Bell invited them into her kitchen. "But we couldn't pass by without visiting you. How are you?"

"Ah, sure, I'm grand and I'm delighted to see you both. Why do you need to hire Pat and the cart and Frank and the carriage?" she inquired. "You're not moving from the big house, are you?"

"No, we're not. You'd better sit down, it's rather a long story."

They sat at the kitchen table and Miles' story was told to an incredulous Mrs Bell.

"And he'll be living with Mr and Mrs Ellison and your brother, not his parents?" she asked Isobel.

"Miles needs peace and quiet," Isobel explained. "So our house with young children wouldn't have suited him and my grandmother refuses to acknowledge him so he cannot live with her and Grandfather either."

"That's shocking – his own mother."

"I'm stubborn, my mother can be stubborn but my grandmother appears to be the most stubborn of us all and – as well as Miles – she doesn't wish to meet my mother again either."

"That must make your mother very sad."

"Yes, it does," Isobel replied. "But I think she is resigned to the fact now. Grandmother and I have had 'words' and she now knows she cannot insult me without a likewise response."

"I'm glad to hear it. And your grandparents are from Co Mayo? My parents were Mayo people."

"I didn't know that." Will smiled. "Yes, Miles' parents are Lewis and Matilda Greene of Greene Hall. It is near to Westport."

Mrs Bell clapped her hands to her cheeks, startling him. "Lewis Greene of Greene Hall? The Lord save us all – the awful stories my mother used to tell about him and his land agent."

"Such as?" he asked cautiously, exchanging a wary glance with Isobel.

"Ah, no." Mrs Bell recovered quickly and gave them a bright smile. "It's all long in the past."

"Please, Mrs Bell," Isobel persisted and the older woman grimaced.

"Well, my parents were tenants on the Greene Hall estate…"

"And?"

"And you probably think the Great Famine was the only famine there ever was, but there were many others – when the crops were poor – or when there were harsh winters – and, according to Mammy, there could be very harsh winters out in the west."

"Galway winters can be very harsh," Isobel said. "There were at least three winters when I received a telegram at school from Mother telling me to spend Christmas there as it was too dangerous for me to attempt to travel home."

"Your mother was right. Well, my parents' first home was a two-roomed cottage on one acre of peat bog where they had to grow enough food to feed themselves and the family they would have. During that first year of their marriage, it rained so much the potato crop rotted in the ground. Once their store of food was gone, they spent all the money Daddy was earning from labouring on buying food which meant they had no money left over to pay the rent. So, on Lewis Greene's instructions, the land agent evicted them. Lewis Greene was young, he had recently inherited the estate and he wanted to make his mark and show his tenants he wasn't to be trifled with."

Will felt Isobel tense. "What happened to them?" she asked.

"Their parents' couldn't take them in, even though Mammy was expecting. So, they left Co Mayo and walked to Dublin." Mrs Bell smiled sadly. "They were country people. Living in a city didn't suit them. Both died well before their time and, to their dying day, they never forgave

Lewis Greene for turning them out of their home."

Isobel exhaled a long breath. "I'm sorry," she said simply.

"Listen to me, Isobel." Mrs Bell reached across the table and held her hands. "You have nothing to be sorry for. Your mother, step-father and brother are putting right an awful wrong by giving poor Miles a home. Now," Mrs Bell added brightly. "Tell me how John and the two babbies are?"

"They are very well, thank you," Will replied. "John will be four in January and rarely stops talking now, and Ben and Belle are laughing at their parents already."

"Ah, bless their hearts. Give the three of them my love."

"Thank you, Mrs Bell, we shall."

On their way out of the tenement house, they went into the waiting room where David was locking the surgery door and he turned to them in surprise.

"Just passing?" he teased.

"We were, actually." Will gave him a grin. "Has Alfie mentioned his uncle to you?"

"Miles Greene? Yes, he has." David sighed. "The poor chap. To be locked away like that by his own parents…"

"Well, Miles isn't going to be locked away for much longer. He is moving to number 55 on Friday and Isobel and I are going to hire Pat Callaghan and his cart to transport all of Miles' belongings."

"I'm so glad."

"How are things here?" Will asked.

"Fine, thanks, I've just made a list of a few items in the medicine cupboard which need replenishing so I can purchase them and bring them with me tomorrow," he replied, glancing at Isobel as she shook her head angrily. "Is everything all right?"

"I should have known," she raged and David's eyebrows shot up. "I should have known that a couple capable of discarding their son wouldn't hesitate for a moment in evicting a young couple who are trying to ensure they don't starve."

"We've just discovered Isobel's grandfather had Mrs Bell's parents evicted from their cottage and one acre of land in Co Mayo," Will explained.

"Good God."

"I'm sorry for shouting." Isobel squeezed David's arm.

"Many of my patients in Brown Street – and many of the patients here – either came to Dublin from the countryside themselves or are descended from people who came," Will informed her. "From what I was told, you would be hard pressed to find a landlord anywhere in Ireland who hadn't evicted tenants from their estate. I'm not making excuses for them," he continued as Isobel opened her mouth to argue. "It's just the way it was – and we both read the newspapers – so we know many evictions are still taking place – these past few winters have been very harsh in more ways than one."

"And many landlords live in England and never see their tenants," David added. "I was at school with a boy called Henry Cunningham whose father rented the largest house and farm on the estate – well over one hundred acres – and yet the family never saw their landlord – only his land agent who was a deeply unpleasant character by all accounts and ruled the estate with an iron fist in his employer's absence. It's not right but I'm afraid it is the way it is – for now."

"Are you a Land Leaguer?" Will asked.

"I wouldn't say that – and I know that as tenants, Henry's family and Mrs Bell's family were at completely opposite ends of the scale – but I try to keep up with what the Land League are doing as something badly needs to change for all tenants."

Half an hour later, Will and Isobel were seated in Miles' parlour surrounded by five tea chests full of books.

"...And Pat Callaghan will transport your belongings to number 55 in as many trips as is needed," Will told him. "And Isobel, Alfie and I shall call for you in a carriage which belongs to the brother of a cabman I usually engage. Frank's carriage is larger than George's cab so we can all travel to number 55 together. We will be here at five o'clock on Friday."

"Five o'clock," Miles repeated with a firm nod.

"And your bedroom is almost ready," Isobel said with a smile.

"Almost ready?"

"A huge bookcase is being delivered on Thursday and then all that is left is for you to decide where you would like it and the other furniture to be situated," she explained and his face broke into a grin.

"Thank you. You are being so kind."

"We are all looking forward to you living at number 55."

"So am I, but I cannot help but feel a little frightened," he said, peering down at his hands. "I cannot remember living anywhere else but here."

"You will have all your furniture and books around you," Will reminded him. "There will always be someone in the house – day and night – and Isobel and I live just across the square. If you are unsure of anything – just ask any of us."

"I shall, thank you."

On Friday afternoon while Will and Alfie spoke with Dr Harrison, Pat Callaghan and Peter O'Connor – Miles' personal servant – carried the tea chests full of books out of St Patrick's Hospital to the cart for its fourth and final trip to number 55.

Returning to Miles' apartment, Peter confided to Isobel that as each year had passed and Mr and Mrs Greene promptly paid the fee, his wages and Miles' allowance, he wished they had come to take their son home instead.

"Where does Miles believe the money comes from?" she asked in a low voice.

"Miles believes his parents are dead and that it comes from his inheritance. Dr Harrison and I have discussed the matter and we agreed that Miles should continue with that belief. Will you now tell him the truth?"

"Yes, in due course, but I'm afraid his mother still won't meet Miles," Isobel said. "However, his father shall meet Miles when he is well enough."

"I am glad to hear that. I often wondered if Miles would ever meet either or both of his parents again."

"Thank you for everything you have done with Miles."

"You are very welcome, Mrs Fitzgerald."

"What will you do now and what will become of this apartment?"

"I am to become the servant to one of the other chamber-boarders and this apartment will not stand empty for long, Mrs Fitzgerald. Nothing left behind?" he called to Miles, who was standing at his bedroom window.

"No, nothing," he replied and joined them.

"Good," she said. "Well, I think we should go downstairs. The carriage is waiting and the cart is fully loaded with the last of all your books."

"Are you not coming to see me off, Peter?" Miles asked as the other man hesitated.

"No, I'll say goodbye here." Peter held out a hand. "Goodbye, Miles, and good luck."

Miles shook Peter's hand then gave him a hug. "Thank you," he whispered before taking a long last look around the apartment, clasping Isobel's outstretched hand and leaving it for the last time.

Downstairs at the hospital's main door, Will, Alfie and Dr Harrison were waiting for them.

"All set, Miles?" Dr Harrison asked.

"Yes, I am."

"Well." Dr Harrison shook his hand. "Visits only from now on."

"Yes."

"And I will see you next week."

"Yes. Thank you."

"Not at all, Miles."

Isobel climbed into the carriage and Miles eyed all the tea chests on the cart before joining her and Alfie and Will followed him. As the carriage passed through the gates, Miles inhaled and exhaled a deep breath. Catching Alfie's eye, she wagged a finger towards the window, silently telling her brother to point some landmarks out to Miles to calm him a little.

"This is Bow Lane," Alfie announced. "And we are turning onto James' Street now and that is St James' Church of Ireland on the left and we shall see St James' Catholic Church shortly on the right."

"This is now Thomas Street," Will continued a couple of minutes later. "And that is the Guinness Brewery over there on the right."

Miles peered intently out of the window as the carriage travelled through the bustling streets, marvelling at the other carriages, cabs, outside cars, carts and people until Isobel patted his hand.

"We are now on St Stephen's Green. In the centre is a park which has a lake with lots of ducks."

"Ducks?" he repeated and gazed out of the window again.

"We can bring you to see them if you would like?" she offered and Alfie shot her a sharp glance.

"I would, Isobel, thank you," Miles replied and turned his attention to the streets once more.

As the cab turned a corner, she patted his hand again. "This is Fitzwilliam Square," she said softly. "Home."

"Look." Alfie pointed as the carriage stopped outside number 55 and Miles peered out as the Ellisons waved from the front door. "They've been waiting for us," he said as Frank Millar opened the carriage door, helped her out and Miles reached for her hand as he stepped onto the pavement.

"Miles." Her mother hurried down the steps with James behind her and hugged him tightly. "Welcome to your new home."

"Thank you," he replied and shook James' hand. "Isobel, where do you and Will live?" he asked.

"Over there." She pointed across the square. "At number 30 – it's not far at all."

"No, it isn't."

"Come inside." Her mother took Miles' hand and he was led up the steps and into the hall.

"Thank you, Frank," she called and he touched his bowler hat in reply. "And thank you, too, Pat," she added as he handed tea chests to Will, Alfie and James who went inside with them. "Miles was concerned his books might have got wet if it rained."

"We were lucky with the weather, Mrs Fitzgerald," he said as the Ellison's footman and two house-parlourmaids came outside to assist. "It's going to rain any minute now."

"Hand me that smaller tea chest, please, Pat," she instructed and he passed it to her. "Thank you." She set it down beside the others in the hall and went into the morning room.

"...And your bedroom is on the second floor, complete with new bookcase," her mother was telling Miles. "The fire was lit just after luncheon, your furniture has been carried up there and all your books will be brought there as well and you can arrange them to your liking."

"Thank you. You are all being so very kind."

"Are you hungry?" she asked.

"Yes, I am, but I usually have my dinner at six o'clock."

"So do we and it is ten minutes to six," his sister replied and Miles nodded. "You must tell me what you like and do not like to eat."

"Thank you, I shall."

"We have just enough time to show you your room."

"And then Will and I must go," Isobel said.

"Go?" Miles turned to her in clear dismay.

"Our own meal will be ready soon, too," she explained. "And you must have time to yourself to settle in."

They all went upstairs and her mother opened the door to the large bedroom at the front of the house. Some of the tea chests had been placed beside the bookcases but Miles wound his way past the bed, wardrobe, armchairs, desk, dining table and chairs, went to the window and looked out over the square.

"You can choose where you would like the furniture to

be placed," she reminded him and he turned back to them.

"Thank you, Isobel," he said. "I like this room very much."

"I am so glad," Mrs Ellison replied. "We shall have our dinner now."

"And Will and I shall call to see you tomorrow," she said and they left the bedroom and went downstairs.

"Isobel?" Alfie ran along the hall as Gorman opened the front door and he went with her and Will out onto the steps. "In the carriage – why did you not invite Miles to go to St Stephen's Green with you and the children on Sunday?"

"Because young John is not quite four years old and Miles is a grown man. I don't want Miles to unintentionally frighten John."

"I agree with Isobel," Will said. "For now, John, Ben and Belle will be taken to St Stephen's Green as usual on Sunday afternoons and Miles will be taken there – perhaps on a weekday – but only after he has settled in here."

After dinner, Isobel expressed milk for Belle and Ben and Will helped her to feed them before John was put to bed and read a chapter of *Alice's Adventures in Wonderland*. John and the twins were kissed goodnight and Will went downstairs with Isobel to the morning room.

"I hope Miles will be happy at number 55," she said, resting her head on his shoulder as they settled on the sofa with the *Freeman's Journal* and *The Irish Times*.

"He seemed delighted with his bedroom and we have all made him welcome."

"How long before he can be introduced to his father?"

"I will call to number 7 tomorrow morning and—" He

stopped abruptly and they got up as the door opened and Zaineb came in, pulling a handkerchief from her sleeve.

"I'm sorry to disturb you, Dr Fitzgerald, Mrs Fitzgerald," she began in a shaky voice and paused to blow her nose. "But there is a Mrs Greene at the front door demanding to speak with both of you."

Demanding. Will rolled his eyes.

"What did she say to you, Zaineb?" Isobel asked gently.

"Mrs Greene referred to the colour of my skin and I would prefer not to repeat her exact words, Mrs Fitzgerald," the maid replied and Isobel threw him a furious glance.

"I think it would be best if I spoke to Mrs Greene alone, Isobel," he said. "Bring Zaineb to the servants' hall and stay there until I come for you."

Putting an arm around Zaineb's shoulders, Isobel guided her out of the room. Will followed but turned to the front door. Isobel's grandmother was pulling off her black gloves and laying them on the hall table beside his medical bag but was still wearing a black velvet cloak and he could only hope it was because she did not intend to stay long.

"Mrs Greene." He greeted her in a curt tone. "How may I be of assistance?"

Without replying, she swept past him and into the morning room. Wearily, he went after her and closed the door.

"I saw," she said, her voice trembling with anger. "I saw you all this afternoon. How dare you – how dare you remove Miles from the asylum without his parents' permission."

"We had his father's permission to remove Miles from St Patrick's Hospital," he replied and her brown eyes widened. Clearly, her husband had not informed her. "Dr Harrison, the medical superintendent, told me Miles could have lived with you perfectly well all his life at Greene Hall and not be tucked away at St Patrick's Hospital at all."

Mrs Greene tensed. "Miles was beginning to frighten Martha – I could not have that."

"Well, Miles does not frighten her now and he will live at number 55 except for a weekly monitoring visit to Dr Harrison."

"This move was your wife's doing, I suppose?" she asked.

"It was a decision made by all of us, Mrs Greene."

"But your wife seems intent on rescuing as many waifs and strays as possible."

"John is now a happy little boy and Miles will be happy living at number 55. As for Zaineb, I would thank you never to make derogatory comments about her appearance again."

"She is—"

"An excellent house-parlourmaid and a valued member of our household," he snapped. "If you insult Zaineb again – or any of our servants – I will have no choice but to ask you not to call to this house in future. Now, is there anything else?"

"When will you be attending to my husband next? You have not called to him in the past few days."

"Your husband was comfortable and had enough oxygen to last some days. I will call again tomorrow morning. You came here alone – shall I accompany you back to number 7?" he asked as politely as he could.

"No, thank you, I am quite capable of walking there by myself," she replied crisply. "You may see me out now."

Biting his tongue, Will opened the door for her and followed her along the hall as she picked up her gloves from the table and waited for him to open the front door. She passed him without a word of thanks and he just resisted the urge to slam the door after her.

He went straight down the steps to the servants' hall and was relieved to find Zaineb laughing at something Isobel had just said. They all looked expectantly at him and he smiled.

"Mrs Greene has returned to number 7," he said and they relaxed. "If Mrs Greene insults you again, Zaineb – or any of you – please, inform Mrs Dillon, my wife or myself and she will be instructed not to call here in future. Are you all right, Zaineb?" he added and she nodded.

"I am now, thank you, Dr Fitzgerald."

"I'm glad."

"I think a cup of tea is in order." Mrs Dillon went to the solid fuel range in the kitchen and lifted the kettle onto the hot plate.

"An excellent idea," Will said as a bell jangled.

"It's the front door, Dr Fitzgerald," Mary told him as the bell jangled again. And again.

"I will answer it," he replied and went up the steps to the hall, hoping Mrs Greene hadn't returned. Opening the door, he found Alfie gasping for breath on the steps. "What is it?" he demanded. "Is it Miles?"

Alfie shook his head. "It's Grandfather. He's turned up at number 55 wearing nothing but his nightshirt and he's collapsed in the hall."

"Isobel?" Will roared over his shoulder before turning back to Alfie. "Go to number 7 and fetch the oxygen cylinder, tube and face mask. Your grandmother has just called here so please tell her where her husband is. Isobel and I will go straight to number 55."

"What is it?" Isobel asked, joining him in the hall as Alfie turned and ran down the steps to the pavement.

"Your grandfather has collapsed in the hall of number 55," he said, grabbing his medical bag from the table and taking her hand.

They ran around the Fitzwilliam Square garden. Number 55's front door was wide open and he could hear Martha Ellison sobbing.

"See to your mother and try and quieten her," he told Isobel as they went up the steps and into the hall.

James, Martha and her lady's maid, May, were crouching down around Mr Greene who was lying unconscious and wheezing on his back with a frock coat draped over him. They straightened up on seeing them and Isobel put an arm around her mother's shoulders. Dropping to his knees on the cold flagstone floor, Will put his medical bag to one side, noting how Mr Greene's toenails were a grey-blue colour and he lifted the frock coat a little. Mr Greene's fingernails were also grey-blue and Will grimaced and replaced it.

"Did Mr Greene hit his head when he fell?" he asked.

"No," James replied. "Gorman caught him as he fell, laid him down and draped his frock coat over him."

"Good. Where is Miles?"

"In his bedroom shelving his books."

"He needs to be kept there so he isn't upset."

"Yes, of course." James turned to the footman who was standing at the bottom of the steps to the servants' hall. "Vincent, please go to Mr Miles' bedroom and assist him with his books – put more coal on the fire – help him to arrange the furniture – just keep him there until someone comes for you."

"Yes, Mr Ellison."

Will opened his medical bag and lifted out a thermometer as Vincent ran up the stairs two steps at a time. Opening Mr Greene's mouth, he placed it under the tongue and took out his pocket watch. There was silence as he waited three minutes before removing the thermometer. It read just under ninety-five degrees Fahrenheit – mild hypothermia.

"Where the hell is Alfie?" he demanded as much to himself as to the others.

"I'm here," Alfie replied as he came inside, put the oxygen cylinder down and passed Will the face mask. "Grandmother is on her way here," he added, kneeling down as Will placed the face mask over Mr Greene's nose and mouth at an angle.

"I need a bed prepared for him, the fire lit in the room and he will need hot water bottles – as many as you can find," he said and May shot a glance at Mrs Ellison who held out her hands helplessly.

"But Miles can't be moved from his room—" Martha began.

"Grandfather can have mine," Alfie said, his mother squeezed his shoulders gratefully and May ran down the steps to the servants' hall while Isobel ran up the stairs. "I'll sleep in what was the nursery for the present. I'll help you carry Grandfather upstairs, Will."

"No." Mrs Greene stood in the front doorway and Martha gave a little cry on seeing her mother for the first time in a quarter of a century. "I insist you bring my husband back to number 7 at once."

"Your husband is not to be carried back out into the

cold," Will stated adamantly and she flinched. "If you are coming inside, Mrs Greene, close the door."

She did as she was told and watched as May ran upstairs, her arms laden with bed linen and Dora, one of the house-parlourmaids, followed with a bucket of coal and another bucket containing kindling.

"Will he live, Dr Fitzgerald?" she asked, her voice shaking.

"As with his previous collapse, his temperature needs to be raised slowly and his breathing eased."

"Please tell me he will live?"

"Alfie," he said instead of answering. "Take Mr Greene's ankles. James, could you carry the oxygen cylinder, please?"

James picked up the oxygen cylinder and, acutely aware they were leaving Martha and her mother alone in the hall, Will and Alfie began a slow progress up the stairs with James one step ahead of them. Would it have been easier to bring Mr Greene back to number 7, he wondered as they reached the first-floor landing and Gorman and Mrs Reilly, the cook-housekeeper, passed them each carrying two hot water bottles. No, he decided, able to feel just how cold the elderly man was through the nightshirt.

By the time they reached the second floor, Mr Greene felt as cold and heavy as lead. Isobel held the bedroom door open and Will and Alfie laid Mr Greene in the freshly-made single bed. The hot water bottles were placed around him, the frock coat returned to Gorman and Isobel pulled up the bedcovers. Will took the oxygen cylinder from James and stood it on the floor beside the bed as Mr Greene groaned, opened his eyes and shivered.

"You are in bed in Alfie's room at number 55 Fitzwilliam Square," Will told him, lifting off the face mask.

"Cold," he whispered through chattering teeth.

"The fire is being lit and the room will soon be warm," Will assured him, glancing at Dora on her knees at the hearth. "Could you bring up some warm milk, please," he asked Mrs Reilly. "Warm – not hot." She, May and Gorman left the bedroom and Will turned back to Mr Greene. "You need to warm up slowly," he said, replacing the face mask at an angle again. "And Miles will be here when you are well enough to meet him."

Mr Greene nodded and Will gently squeezed his shoulder.

May was surprisingly quick to return with a glass of warm milk. "Milk was being heated for cocoa," she explained as Will took it from her.

"Thank you. Alfie, can you help me, please?"

The two of them raised Mr Greene into a sitting position, the face mask lifted off and Will held the glass to his lips.

"Drink it slowly," he instructed and Mr Greene sipped the milk until the glass was empty. "Good. Do you feel any warmer?" Mr Greene nodded, they laid him down and Will replaced the face mask at an angle. "Rest, and I will be back soon."

"What else can be done?" Mrs Greene asked as Martha tailed her mother into the bedroom and Will doubted if she had even acknowledged her daughter, never mind spoken to her, judging by Martha's pained expression.

"Nothing," he replied. "We wait and hope your husband's temperature rises. Would you like to sit with him, Mrs Greene?"

"Yes, I would," she replied and Alfie carried the chair from his desk near the window to the bedside. "Is there anything I can do?"

"Please, keep the door closed – Miles is next door," he said, gesturing to the neighbouring bedroom.

Without even glancing in that direction, Mrs Greene went to the chair and sat down.

"I will return shortly to take your husband's temperature again," he added and ushered everyone from the room.

"Will he live?" Martha asked him quietly on the landing.

"Your father has mild hypothermia and his temperature must be raised slowly. As for Miles, I think he should come downstairs with us to the morning room."

"I'll fetch him." Isobel went to his bedroom door, knocked and went inside. A few moments later, she emerged along with Miles and Vincent. "Miles has decided to continue shelving his books tomorrow," she announced with a forced smile.

"Good." James extended a hand towards the stairs and Isobel and her mother went down the steps with Dora, Miles and Vincent following them. "Is Mr Greene going to die?" he added quietly, catching Will's arm.

"No, he won't die, but this must not happen again. Mr Greene cannot be trusted to remain in bed when his wife's back is turned and I cannot be on hand all day, every day. I am going to recommend to Mrs Greene that a nurse be engaged and if she refuses – or if the nurse cannot successfully supervise Mr Greene – then, I shall have no choice but to admit Mr Greene to a hospital. It is the last thing I would wish to do," he went on as James' eyes widened, "given how we have just brought his son home from one, but if this happens again, Mr Greene will die."

"You had better recommend a few nurses so Mrs Greene may choose one to her liking."

"She isn't going to like the prospect, no matter how many nurses I recommend but I'll speak to her tomorrow."

Downstairs in the morning room, May was placing a tea tray on a side table and Martha was instructing her to bring some tea upstairs to Mrs Greene.

"And could more milk be warmed for Mr Greene, please, May?" he added and the maid bobbed up and down before going out. "Martha, as I was telling James, I am going to recommend that a nurse be engaged."

"I agree," she replied. "He needs someone to watch over him."

"Who does?" Miles asked curiously.

"A neighbour who isn't very well," Isobel told him, lifting the teapot. "Do you take milk and sugar in your tea?"

"Just milk, thank you. Can I help?"

"That's very kind. I'll pour the tea and if you could add a little milk to them all and then one spoon of sugar in one cup for Alfie."

"I have a sweet tooth." Alfie gave Miles a grin.

Will accepted a cup and saucer from Miles, stirred the tea then went to the window and pulled the curtain aside. For a healthy person, the distance between number 7 and number 55 was relatively short but for Mr Greene in his state of health and in his bare feet... What determination he has to see his son. Will shook his head and let the curtain drop back into place.

"Alfie," he said, putting his cup and saucer on a side table. "May I speak with you in private?" They went out to the hall and Will nodded to the stairs. "I'll go on up, can you bring the warm milk?"

"Yes, of course."

Will picked up his medical bag, went upstairs and straight into the bedroom where the coal fire was now blazing in the hearth. Mrs Greene had been stroking her sleeping husband's hair but stopped abruptly and threw him a glare.

"Can you not knock, Dr Fitzgerald?"

"I must take your husband's temperature again," Will said and Mr Greene opened his eyes. Will lifted off the face mask, repeated the procedure and, to his relief, the thermometer read just over ninety-six degrees Fahrenheit. "Your temperature has risen, Mr Greene, but it needs to rise further. Alfie is bringing up some more warm milk for you."

Mr Greene nodded, Will replaced the face mask and returned the thermometer to his medical bag.

"What should my husband's temperature be?" Mrs Greene asked.

"Approximately ninety-eight degrees Fahrenheit. It is currently just over ninety-six. I would like to see it reach ninety-seven degrees and the milk will help. When it does, you should go home, Mrs Greene."

"No, absolutely not—" she began but Will held up a hand and she stopped speaking.

"It is getting late, your husband needs to rest and so do you," he said, deciding to be blunt. "You look exhausted, Mrs Greene. Another half an hour and, then, someone will escort you back to number 7. Ah, the warm milk," he continued as the door opened and Alfie came in carrying a glass of milk and placed it on the bedside table.

They eased Mr Greene forward, placed the pillows at his back and laid him against them. Will removed the face mask once more, Alfie passed the glass to Mrs Greene and she helped her husband to take a sip.

"I really don't think I should go home," she began again and her husband sighed.

"Listen to the doctor, Tilda. Go home. Sleep. Come back tomorrow morning."

"I will sit with Grandfather," Alfie told her and Will glanced at him in surprise. "As long as I have a more comfortable chair. There's one in the next bedroom."

"Thank you, Alfie," Will said, opening the door. "We'll carry it in while your grandfather is drinking the milk."

They went out onto the landing and into Miles' bedroom. Lifting two tea chests out of their way, they went to a yellow and white padded bedroom chair.

"Grandfather and Miles must be kept apart until it is explained to Miles that his parents are alive, that they sent him to St Patrick's Hospital and why one of them now wishes to see him," Alfie said. "And that his other parent doesn't wish to see him – and probably never will."

"Your grandfather won't be moved back to number 7 for a few days so we'll leave telling Miles for as long as possible. Miles needs to settle in here first and be supervised at all times."

"Yes, I agree," Alfie replied. "I'll speak to Mother and James about that and I'll supervise Grandfather."

"That's very good of you but you can't sleep in this chair for the next few nights. It's only a little better than the one in your bedroom."

"We'll bring a mattress down from the nursery and I'll sleep on it," Alfie decided, lighting the oil lamp on Miles' desk and picking it up.

Will followed Alfie up the stairs to the third floor. What

had once been the nursery was now being used as a storeroom for various odds and ends of furniture. In one of the bedrooms, Alfie lifted a dust sheet from the single bed and they hauled the mattress off the frame. It was heavy and awkward to carry, especially with the added complication of an oil lamp, so they slid it back down the stairs and into Alfie's bedroom.

"Alfie shall sleep here and this is more comfortable than a chair," Will explained to the Greenes as the mattress was laid down in a corner.

"I'll put this back and I'll go and find some bed linen," Alfie added and left the room with the oil lamp.

Will went to the bed as Mr Greene finished the milk and his wife placed the glass on the bedside table.

"There is more colour in your face and fingernails."

"Is that a good sign?" Mr Greene asked.

"Yes, it is. Your finger and toenails were a grey-blue colour."

"Are you not going to scold me for what I did?"

"Do I need to?" Will replied and Mr Greene shook his head. "Well, what I do need to tell you is that you will not be meeting Miles tonight – or tomorrow – you need to rest and Miles needs to adjust to living here. Please do not try to seek him out yourself as Alfie will stop you from leaving this room – do I make myself clear?"

"Perfectly."

"It also must be explained to Miles that his parents are alive and that you wish to meet him – and that his mother does not," Will went on, glancing at Mrs Greene, who immediately looked away.

"Who will do that?"

"All of us – although it was Isobel who explained to Miles

who we were on our first visit to Swift's Hospital."

"I would rather it was his sister," Mrs Greene said. "I would rather it was Martha."

"Have you spoken to her?" Will asked. "Made her aware of your wishes?" Mrs Greene looked away again, giving Will his answer and Will turned back to her husband. "We shall all speak with Miles."

"Thank you."

Will took Mr Greene's temperature again and nodded to himself. "Ninety-seven degrees Fahrenheit," he said and Mrs Greene exhaled an audible sigh of relief. "This must not happen again, Mr Greene."

"It won't."

"Good," he said and replaced the face mask. "Mrs Greene, your husband needs to rest now. I will be back in the morning." Picking up his medical bag, he went out onto the landing and saw Alfie coming up the stairs carrying sheets, blankets and a pillow. "Your grandfather's temperature is now ninety-seven degrees and Isobel and I will escort your grandmother home."

"Thank you, Will," Alfie replied, knocked briefly at his bedroom door and went inside.

A couple of moments later, Mrs Greene came out and Will extended a hand to the stairs. In the hall, he halted and gestured towards the morning room.

"I'll just fetch Isobel." He went inside, closed the door and they all looked at him anxiously. "There is nothing to worry about and I will call again in the morning. Isobel?"

"Goodnight, Miles," she said and kissed his cheek. "I hope you sleep well."

"You'll be back tomorrow?"

"I will, I promise," she said and both she and James went with Will out to the hall.

"I'm now satisfied with Mr Greene's temperature," he told them. "Alfie will stay with him – we slid a mattress down to his bedroom from the third floor."

"Thank you for all you've done this evening, Will."

"Not at all, James. Isobel and I will escort Mrs Greene home. Goodnight."

The three of them walked to number 7 in silence and Will rang the front doorbell.

"You have my grateful thanks for your assistance this evening, Dr Fitzgerald," Mrs Greene said crisply as Knox opened the door and she continued on into the hall before Will could reply.

"Knox?" he whispered as the butler began to close the door. "Does Mrs Greene like sherry?"

"Yes, she does."

"Please, pour her a glass – a large glass – and tell her I recommended it."

"Yes, Dr Fitzgerald," he said and shut the door.

Isobel began to laugh as they went down the steps to the pavement and he turned to her in surprise.

"That was quite an honour for you," she said, reaching up to kiss his lips. "I expect the number of people my grandmother has either thanked or paid a compliment to can be counted on the fingers of one hand."

"Yes, I think you're right," he replied with a grin and took her hand. "Let's go home."

Isobel opened her eyes, lifted her head and peered through the twilight at the clock on the mantelpiece. A quarter to eight. She exhaled a little groan and laid her head down again, hearing Will chuckle.

"Fifteen more minutes," he told her and she snuggled up to him. "I'll escort your grandmother to number 55 after breakfast, assess your grandfather and I'll try to be back here by the time Father arrives to visit the children. After luncheon, we'll go to Grafton Street for coffee and call to number 55 on our way home. Then, this evening, we shall retire early to bed and that will be our Christmas Eve Saturday."

"So, we will have some time to ourselves?"

"As I said before, I insist on it," he said, trying to lower her nightdress.

"Wait a moment." Sitting up, she pulled it over her head and threw it to the foot of the bed. She lay down, smiling as his eyes followed her breasts. But, instead of leaning over and kissing them, he simply raised himself onto an elbow and stared at her. "What is it?" she asked.

"We need to discuss something."

"Oh?"

"Whether we want more children."

"Oh."

"Isobel, I'm going to be completely honest with you – I don't – we have a son and a daughter and John. I almost lost you when you were giving birth and—"

Reaching up, she held her fingers against his lips. "I don't either," she whispered, lifting her fingers away. "I am content with Ben, Belle and young John."

"Honestly?" he asked anxiously, his brown eyes searching her face.

"Honestly," she replied and he slumped a little with relief. "I was going to discuss it with you over Christmas if you hadn't mentioned it by then. So, you had better order many, many more boxes of condoms." He laughed, rolled onto his back and she leant over him. "I am so happy with my life here at number 30," she said softly. "All twelve of us."

That made him laugh again. "I love you, Mrs Fitzgerald," he said and she lay down with her head on his chest.

An hour later, she saw Will out herself and went upstairs to the nursery. Young John was seated at the square table enjoying his usual breakfast of a soft boiled egg with toast 'soldiers'.

"Grandfather is visiting you and your cousins today," she told him, kissing the top of his head and he gave her an eggy grin. "So, I'll help Bridget to feed the twins while you finish your egg."

Ben and Belle gurgled happily as she went into the children's bedroom, leant into the cradles and gave them noisy kisses.

"They definitely recognise you, Mrs Fitzgerald." Bridget handed her a bottle and Isobel sat down beside the cradles with Ben in the crook of her left arm. He sucked strongly on the teat and she watched as Bridget sat on the other bedroom chair with Belle who sucked equally hard on the teat of her bottle. "I've never known such happy babies."

"They are very jolly babies and you should have seen my husband's face when they suddenly laughed at him."

"They love their outings to St Stephen's Green."

"Yes, they do. Let's just hope they don't ever take it into their heads to try and become a duck, like their cousin."

"Are you really going to teach Master John to swim?" Bridget asked. "He mentioned something but I wasn't sure whether to believe him."

"Yes, my husband is going to teach both Master John and I to swim next summer. Master John for safety's sake and I would quite like to learn, too."

"And the twins?"

"Yes, when they are older. Can you swim?"

"Yes, I can," a male voice replied and she smiled at Will's father standing in the doorway holding his namesake by the hand. "And to be able to swim is a very useful knowledge to have."

"I agree. There," she said, putting the bottle on the top of the chest of drawers and winding Ben. "All gone." Ben burped loudly and she laughed. "You enjoyed that and Grandfather is here to see you."

"The two of them have grown," he said and his eldest grandson tugged at his hand. "And you have as well young sir. Where is Will?"

"At number 55," she said. "He'll be back soon."

"Nothing wrong, I hope?"

"Not with Miles. I'll tell you later."

"Can we go to the gardens, Isobel?" young John asked. "Florrie says it isn't raining."

"Would you like a stroll?" Isobel asked her father-in-law who smiled and nodded.

"Yes, a stroll will be very pleasant."

"John, go and put your hat, overcoat and gloves on," she instructed his grandson. "And we shall wrap Ben and Belle up nice and warm."

Ten minutes later, Isobel was unlocking and opening one of the gates to the gardens in the centre of the square and Will's father pushed the perambulator onto the path.

"Keep to where we can see you," she called after young John as he ran onto the lawn.

"I will," he shouted back at them.

"What has happened at number 55?" his grandfather asked her.

"While my grandmother called to number 30 to berate Will and us all for removing Miles from Swift's Hospital, my grandfather walked to number 55 wearing nothing but his nightshirt wanting to see Miles and he collapsed in the hall with mild hypothermia."

"Good grief. How is he now?"

"As well as can be expected," she replied. "He was carried to Alfie's bedroom and his temperature rose satisfactorily but Alfie is having to sleep on a mattress on the floor to ensure Grandfather won't attempt to see Miles before we have spoken with him."

"And how is your grandmother?"

"Not happy. But I suspect she never is. She steadfastly refuses to reacquaint herself with Miles or my mother."

"Your mother, too?" he said and she nodded.

"My grandmother will never forgive Mother for marrying my father. Poor James, I have to say, is coping remarkably well with all this. How are you, John?" she asked suddenly and he smiled.

"I am well enough, thank you. The *Journal of Irish Medicine* keeps me busy during the week and I very much look forward to these Saturday visits."

"Do you ever see Diana Wingfield?" she added, suddenly thinking of Fred Simpson's maternal aunt. "I told her I would call to her and invite her to call here but," she shrugged helplessly, "I simply haven't had the time."

"I call to her every week. She understands how busy you are."

"Thank you. Please give her my regards."

"I shall," he replied and they turned, hearing the gate to the gardens opening and closing. "Ah, here is Will."

"Zaineb said you were all here," he said and kissed her cheek. "Father." They shook hands. "Your grandfather is much improved," he told her before she could ask. "Despite he and Alfie talking long into the night."

"Was that wise of them?" she asked. "You said Grandfather needed rest."

"They had the opportunity to talk so they took it. Your grandfather is sleeping now. Where's John?"

"He's over—" she began, pointing to the lawn, but he was nowhere to be seen. "John," she whispered furiously.

"Go," Will's father said and grasped the handle of the perambulator. "I'd wager the lad's up a tree," he called after them as they ran across the lawn to the trees which stood around the perimeter of the gardens.

He was right. Young John was sitting on a branch about six feet from the ground with an apprehensive expression on his face. Now he had climbed up the tree, he didn't know how he was going to get down again.

"So." Will peered up at him and the boy gave him a half-hearted wave. "Trying to be a monkey now, are we?"

"A monkey?"

"The tree-climbing," she elaborated and John made an 'oh' face.

"Except," Will continued. "From what I have read, monkeys generally only climb trees they are certain of being able to climb down again."

"Only climb trees when someone can see you," she added and the boy nodded.

"Come on, then." Will reached up for him and John slid off the branch and into his arms. "You must plan ahead."

"Yes."

They rejoined Will's father and the twins and Will set the boy down on the path.

"Trying to be a monkey this time," he explained.

"Ah," his father replied.

"I'm going to have to invent eyes in the back of my head," she said as young John ran onto the lawn again.

"He needs to use up his energy," his grandfather said. "Edward and Will were exactly the same." He gazed at the boy for a few moments before turning back to them. "Someone should bring Miles here for walks."

"James and Martha are going to show him number 55's garden this afternoon," Will told him. "It has to be a gradual process. There is so much for Miles to take in."

"Yes, there is," he replied and they strolled leisurely around the gardens, his grandson running in and out of the trees and finding 'treasure' beneath one of them.

"Look," he cried, holding up a penny. "May I keep it, please?"

"I don't see why not," she replied and he jumped up and down with delight. "What would you like to purchase with it?"

"Fud," he replied immediately, put the coin in his overcoat pocket and sped off across the lawn.

"Fud?" Will's father inquired and she smiled.

"Fudge," she explained. "Sarah brought him some last week – oh, no – rain – John?" she called to the boy, feeling drops on her cheeks.

"I hate rain," he declared as they left the gardens.

"I'm not too fond of it either," she said, taking his hand before crossing the street to number 30 and going up the steps. Opening the front door, they stood to one side while Will and his father carried the perambulator into the hall. "But if there was no more rain, nothing would grow," she added, smiling at Zaineb as the house-parlourmaid left the breakfast room.

Will went with his father into the morning room and she picked Belle up, Zaineb took Ben and they followed young John upstairs to the nursery. The boy ran into the children's bedroom, pulling off his hat, overcoat and gloves, dumped them on his bed then ran back out to the nursery and across the room to the window.

"It's raining very hard," he informed her over his shoulder. "And – look – there's someone standing under the tree I climbed up. I think they're going to get very wet."

With Belle still in her arms, Isobel went to the window. The rain was now pelting against the glass but she could see a female figure dressed in bottle green huddled under the tree. Her grandmother had worn a dress of the same colour the previous day and she quickly looked around for Zaineb who was passing Ben to Florrie.

"Zaineb, please run downstairs and tell my husband Mrs Greene is standing under John's tree – he'll understand."

"Yes, Mrs Fitzgerald."

Isobel turned back to the window and soon saw Will running across the street, putting up his black umbrella.

"Who is Mrs Greene?" John asked curiously.

"A new neighbour. Bridget, can I give you Belle? I must go downstairs and assist my husband."

She kissed Belle's cheek and passed her to Bridget before

kissing Ben's cheek then the top of John's head. Taking a towel from the chest of drawers in the children's bedroom, she left the nursery. Hurrying down the stairs, she reached the hall just as Will was opening the front door and helping her cloakless and hatless grandmother inside. She took the umbrella from him and handed him the towel. Placing the umbrella in the cast iron stand to drip, she closed the front door on the rain and followed them into the morning room.

Mrs Greene sat down in the armchair closest to the fire, Will draped the towel around her shoulders then went to the decanters and poured a glass of brandy. He held out the glass to her and she glanced up at him in surprise.

"It is far too early in the day for alcohol, Dr Fitzgerald."

"You are cold, it is brandy, and I would like you to drink it."

"Are both your grandparents determined to die of hypothermia, Isobel?" Will's father whispered as her grandmother stubbornly shook her head, sending droplets of water flying in all directions from her grey hair which was so wet and heavy it was starting to escape its pins. "Mrs Greene," he added in a normal tone and nodded a greeting to her. "If you remember what I told you when I called to number 7, I am a retired doctor, and I agree with Will that you should drink the brandy."

"I do remember – oh, very well," she said, taking the glass and sipping the contents.

"What were you doing out in the rain?" Isobel asked, trying to keep her voice neutral and not sound as if she were scolding her grandmother.

"I—" Mrs Greene paused to wipe away a bead of water from her cheek with a corner of the towel. "I called to number 55 to see my husband but I was told he was asleep and that you," she threw Will a glare, "had left instructions he was not to be disturbed – by anyone. I did not wish to return to number 7 immediately, so I followed a gentleman and his dog into the gardens. Unfortunately, it began to rain and I took shelter."

Under a tree with no leaves and wearing neither a cloak nor a hat, Isobel finished silently.

"You will stay for luncheon," she said. "And, then, we shall escort you home. Please, excuse me and I will let Mrs Dillon know."

She left the room, went down the steps to the servants' hall and into the kitchen. Mrs Dillon was at the range replacing the lid on a large saucepan before wiping her hands on her apron.

"I'm sorry for the very short notice, Mrs Dillon," she said as the housekeeper gave her a smile. "But there will be one extra for luncheon."

"It is vegetable soup and soda bread for luncheon today and there is plenty, Mrs Fitzgerald. I can serve now if you would like?"

"Thank you, yes. I would also be grateful if Gerald could call to number 7 and tell the servants there that Mrs Greene is here and that when she returns she will need a change of clothes and for her hair to be attended to."

"Yes, Mrs Fitzgerald."

"Thank you, Mrs Dillon."

She went back to the morning room and found her grandmother nodding at something Will's father had just said.

"…So you must look after yourself as well. Listen to Will and heed his advice."

"Thank you, I shall."

"Shall we go into the breakfast room?" she suggested. "Mrs Dillon is about to serve. We don't have very elaborate luncheons here. I hope you like vegetable soup?" she asked her grandmother as Will opened the door for them.

"I do."

"Good," she said and guided her along the hall and into the breakfast room where an extra place setting had been quickly added.

Mrs Greene ate just quickly enough for Isobel to know her grandmother had been hungry and she reached for the lid of the soup tureen and lifted it off again.

"Would you like some more?" she offered and Mrs Greene shook her head.

"Thank you but, no. The soup was excellent. Delicious, in fact."

"You are eating properly, Mrs Greene?" Will asked and her grandmother gave him a sharp glance as Isobel replaced the lid. "You must not forgo meals while your husband is at number 55."

"I had no appetite for breakfast, that is all."

"May I suggest porridge for your breakfast tomorrow?" John smiled at her from across the table. "It is both filling and nourishing and I enjoy it very much with some honey."

"Honey?" Her eyebrows rose. "I haven't tasted honey for a long time. I shall instruct the cook."

"Good. May I escort you back to number 7?" he offered as they rose from the table and Will opened the door. "On Saturday afternoons, Will and Isobel go out for coffee."

"Out for coffee?"

"We have so little time alone together these days," Isobel

explained, following her grandmother out to the hall, "that we walk to Grafton Street, have coffee, and either browse the shops or go to a museum or gallery."

"That sounds very pleasant." Mrs Greene pulled the towel from around her shoulders and handed it to Will. "Thank you for rescuing me from the rain, Dr Fitzgerald. And for the luncheon, Isobel."

"You're welcome," she replied while Mary helped Will's father with his overcoat and passed him his hat. "Thank you, John," she said as he took Mrs Greene's arm.

"Not at all, Isobel."

"Mrs Greene, I shall be calling to number 55 to examine your husband this evening," Will told her. "If you would like, I can escort you there and arrange for someone to escort you home later?"

"That is very kind, thank you."

"Shall we say seven o'clock?" he added and Mrs Greene nodded as Mary opened the front door.

"Seven o'clock. Good afternoon."

Mary closed the door after them and turned. "Shall help you with your hats and coats, Mrs Fitzgerald?"

"Thank you, Mary, but we can manage," she said and the maid went into the breakfast room to begin clearing the table. "I know it's still raining," she added to Will, "but if we don't go now we never will."

Half an hour later, they were seated at a window table in the Grafton Street café and Will was pouring their coffee. Despite the persistent rain, the street was busy with last minute Christmas shoppers carrying parcels and packages of all shapes and sizes.

"So John saw someone standing under the tree?" he clarified, putting the coffee pot down and Isobel nodded. "Do you think Mrs Greene did it deliberately? To get wet, I mean? She was a little too eager in accepting my help."

"No, I don't think it was deliberate," she replied, adding milk and sugar to both cups and stirring them. "She is simply lost without her husband. Since Mother left home to marry Father, it has just been her and Grandfather. And now he is dying and she is terrified at the prospect of being left alone."

"Unless your grandmother changes her attitude towards your mother and – to a lesser degree, Miles because he will never be able to look after her – she will be left alone because I meant what I said, Isobel, this will be your grandfather's last Christmas."

"Someone is going to have to sit her down very soon and spell that out to her."

"Someone – you mean me?" he asked.

"You should be there but it will probably be me," she said in a weary tone. "In the meantime, I would like to enjoy this cup of coffee and our afternoon out together."

"I would, too." He smiled, touched her cup with his and took a sip of the delicious strong coffee. "Where shall we go after this?"

"To find young John a book with lots of duck pictures?" she suggested and he laughed.

"A quest for a duck picture book it is."

The search took most of the afternoon but it kept their minds off Mr and Mrs Greene. They walked back to Fitzwilliam Square as dusk fell with a book containing some beautiful paintings of ducks and two painted wooden ducks – a drake and his wife.

After dinner, they fed the twins then presented the book and the drake to John while he was on his way to bed, deciding to wrap the drake's wife and give her to him in the morning along with his other presents.

"You'll have to think of a name for him," Will said, standing the drake beside John's favourite toy Mr Effalump Elephant on the bedside table.

"I will – thank you."

"And no dirty hands on the book," Isobel added as John climbed into bed.

"I'll wash them before I look at it."

"Good boy," she said, hugging and kissing him.

"Goodnight." Will kissed the top of his head, John lay down and Will pulled the bedcovers up. "Sleep well and in the morning we'll see if Father Christmas called during the night."

Will crouched down beside the twins' cradles and ran a hand over Belle's head and then Ben's. Belle already had a good growth of dark hair which was beginning to curl. Ben's hair was also thick and dark, but it was straight.

"It is ten minutes to seven," Isobel whispered in his ear.

"They will have our hair," he said softly. "And they are beginning to look very different from each other now."

"We'll see how like us they are when they start to eat solid food. Shall Ben dislike swede like his father and will Belle turn her nose up at sprouts as I do?"

He kissed each twin before straightening up and kissing Isobel's cheek. "Mother used to ask Mrs Porter, our cook-housekeeper, to hide pieces of swede amongst the mashed carrot we were fed. Edward would never notice and gobble it all down, but I always did – the colours were different – it used to exasperate poor Mother no end."

"You didn't pick all the pieces out, did you?"

"Yes, I did," he replied and smiled as Isobel gave Bridget a mock-weary glance.

"In that case, we have a lot to look forward to," she said to the maid. "I'm coming with you," she continued to him. "I'd like to see how Miles is."

Mrs Greene, her hair dry and tidy and wearing a chocolate brown dress, turned to Isobel in surprise as Will greeted her in the hall of number 7. She had not expected Isobel to have accompanied him.

"I hope you enjoyed your coffee outing," she said as Ida assisted her with a velvet cloak and hat, both in chocolate brown to match the dress.

"We did, thank you," Isobel replied. "We then browed some bookshops and managed to avoid most of the rain."

"Bookshops?" Mrs Greene echoed. "When do you find the time to read?"

"We bought a book for my nephew, John," Will explained. "He loves ducks and this book contains some lovely paintings of them for him to look at until he can read."

"Your father told me you wish to send the boy to Mr Allen's School for Boys on St Stephen's Green."

"Yes, and then he will attend Wesley College which is also on St Stephen's Green. As will Ben."

"And your daughter? Will she attend Cheltenham Ladies College like her mother?"

"Isobel and I will have to discuss where Belle will be educated. Alexandra College, perhaps. Now, shall we go?"

At number 55, he followed Mrs Greene upstairs while

Isobel was shown into the morning room. Mr Greene was reading a newspaper but closed and folded it and put it to one side as they went into the bedroom. Mrs Greene kissed her husband's forehead then sat down beside the bed and watched as Will made his examination.

"How long did you sleep for?" Mrs Greene asked and Mr Greene lowered the face mask.

"From eleven this morning until luncheon at one and then from two o'clock until about four. I am very much rested."

"Well, sleep tonight," Will told him. "Alfie needs his rest, too. He has to get an inordinate amount of information from those into here," he added, gesturing to the textbooks on the desk then tapping the side of his head with a forefinger, indicating his brain.

"Did you find it difficult?" Mr Greene asked and Will smiled.

"I had always wanted to become a doctor so I never found it a chore. Plus, I was at Trinity College with my two best friends, so we would help and test each other."

"Where are they now?"

"Jerry has a medical practice in London."

"And where is your other friend?" Mr Greene prompted and Will closed his eyes for a moment.

"Fred died," he said quietly, hoping he could trust his voice. "A few months ago. I'm sorry – it was very sudden and it's still rather raw. Like me, Alfie has wanted to be nothing else but a doctor," he went on in a forced bright tone, "despite his father wanting him to enter the church, and we are all delighted he is now a medical student."

"Last night, he told me how his father treated all of

them," Mr Greene said and shook his head. "The rows, the beatings, the treatment of Isobel when she told her father of her seduction and pregnancy… If only I had known but I did not," he went on sadly, inadvertently confirming Will's suspicions that Mrs Greene had kept Martha's letters and the inquiries made in Ballybeg from her husband. "And when I would read of Edmund Stevens' progress up through the ranks of the Church of Ireland, I assumed – stupidly and wrongly – that he and his family were happy."

Will glanced at Mrs Greene but she was staring intently at her hands. "Alfie is happy to finally be at Trinity College," he said. "Martha is now happily married to James, and Isobel and I are happily married, too. But," he went on firmly and Mrs Greene's head jerked up. "You need to be reunited with your children, Mrs Greene – both of them."

"Dr Fitzgerald is right, Tilda," her husband told her. "You are going to need the children – all the family – when I'm gone."

His wife burst into tears and Mr Greene reached out and held her hands. He gave Will a nod, silently asking him to leave them alone to discuss the matter and Will returned one.

"I will ask someone to escort Mrs Greene to number 7 in about an hour," he said quietly. "I will call again early tomorrow morning and, all being well, you shall be escorted back to number 7 so you will be settled before you enjoy Christmas dinner."

Picking up his medical bag from the bedside table, he went out onto the landing, closed the door and blew out his cheeks.

He went downstairs, left the medical bag on the hall

table, then went into the morning room. Isobel and Miles were at the window, where she was pointing at something outside in the lamp-lit darkness.

"Isobel, that discussion we had in the café this afternoon," he began and she turned. "I have just saved you from having to implement it."

Her eyes widened. "How?"

"The opportunity to mention what we discussed arose," he replied and James frowned at their cryptic conversation. "So I took it."

"Oh, I am so glad." Isobel laughed in clear relief. "How was it taken?"

"She was upset, which is natural, but her husband is comforting her and I am hoping he will convince her to do what is right." Isobel nodded and Will smiled at her uncle. "Are you settling in well, Miles?"

"I am, thank you. I have been shown the house from top to bottom – and the garden and mews – they are huge."

"They are," Alfie agreed. He was seated at one end of the sofa so, standing behind it, Will pulled his handkerchief from his trouser pocket, blew his nose and 'accidentally' dropped it on the floor.

"Can you escort your grandmother back to number 7 in an hour?" he whispered as he bent down to pick it up and Alfie nodded. "Actually," he continued and Alfie twisted around in his seat. "Please, follow me out to the hall." Alfie nodded again and Will straightened up, returning the handkerchief to his pocket.

They left the room as Isobel suggested another cup of tea and a mince pie to Miles and a few moments later, James joined them.

"What is it?" the solicitor asked. "Has Mr Greene's health deteriorated?"

"No, not at all," Will replied. "His health is stable, but I have been firm with Mrs Greene and I stated that she needs to be reunited with her children."

"I see," James replied cautiously. "But there is something else, isn't there?"

"Mr Greene can be moved back to number 7 in the morning. It is only a short distance but he must not walk it. We need to borrow a bath chair until I recommend to him that one is purchased."

"A bath chair?" James pulled a perplexed expression. "I'm afraid I don't know anyone who possesses one."

"I do," Alfie announced. "A friend acquired one for a prank. And, as far as I know, he still has it."

"Could you fetch it tonight?" Will asked.

"I'll try. It won't fit in a cab but, with a bit of luck, I'll get it onto an outside car. I'll get my hat and overcoat," he said and ran up the stairs.

"And I will escort Mrs Greene home shortly," James added.

"Thank you."

They returned to the morning room and Isobel got up from an armchair.

"It's time for Will and I to go home," she told Miles. "But we shall see you and Mother, James and Alfie tomorrow."

"I am very much looking forward to Christmas Day."

"Good. And, believe it or not, our cook-housekeeper Mrs Dillon is very much looking forward to roasting a huge goose for us all. She doesn't cater for large parties very often. Goodnight," she called to her mother and step-father then took Will's hand and they went out to the hall.

"Alfie has gone in search of a bath chair so your grandfather can be wheeled to number 7 in the morning," he told her. "I suspect David is the friend he mentioned who has one."

"Poor Alfie – having to try and transport a bath chair across Dublin on Christmas Eve."

"He'll be glad of the opportunity to see David. Let's go home, wrap the other duck, then go to bed. We're going to have a busy day tomorrow."

Chapter Four

They were up early on Christmas morning and at just after half past seven, Isobel and Will went upstairs to the nursery and into the children's bedroom. Young John was crawling to the foot of his bed, his dark eyes bulging as he saw the full Christmas pillowcase 'stocking' hanging on the bed frame.

"Happy Christmas, John, Father Christmas has been, I see," she said, lifting the pillowcase onto the bed and they sat down on either side of the boy as he reached inside. "What has he brought you?"

"A duck," he cried, pulling out and holding up a wooden drake painted green and black, its wings attached to the body with springs.

"This duck 'flies'." Will gave John a grin. "Waggle him up and down – good – see the way the springs make the wings move?" he asked and John nodded. "He can be hung on a length of string from a hook on the ceiling and you can make him 'fly'. What else is in there?" he inquired and the boy delved into the pillowcase again.

"More building blocks, a box of crayons and drawing paper and two oranges."

"Goodness me, all that was very good of Father

Christmas, wasn't it?"

"Yes, it was. Thank you, Father Christmas."

"Shall we see what presents he has for Belle and Ben?" she asked and John climbed off the bed, they went to the twins' cradles and she and Will sat Belle and Ben up.

"Large stuffed drakes." Will extracted a green and black drake from each pillowcase. He passed one to Ben, who immediately attempted to put the drake's head in his mouth. Belle went for the webbed feet of her drake and Will smiled. "Clever Father Christmas knew wooden toys wouldn't be suitable for them."

"Why not?" John asked curiously.

"Because they are starting to grow their first teeth," Will explained. "That's why they are putting everything they touch in their mouths at present."

"Did I do it?"

"Yes, you probably did," Isobel replied and held out a hand. "Come with me, and I'll help you get dressed."

"Am I really going to eat my dinner at the grown-ups table today?" he asked her eagerly.

"Yes, you are and everyone will be in their going out to dinner clothes," she said and the boy eyed her favourite deep red evening dress and Will's white tie and tails. "The drawing room and dining room have been opened up for today and Grandmamma Martha and Grandpapa James, Grandmother and Grandfather, Alfie and Miles are coming here."

"Who is Miles?"

"Sit on the bed and Will and I shall tell you."

John climbed onto his bed and they sat on either side of him again.

"Miles Greene is Grandmamma Martha's brother," she said. "He has come to live with her and Grandpapa James and Alfie."

"Is he going to live with them forever?"

"Yes, he is. He loves reading, so you must tell him about the book on ducks you received yesterday."

"I will."

"Good boy. Let's dress you now," she added, getting off the bed and retrieving a vest and socks, shirt and tie, waistcoat, morning coat and short trousers from the chest of drawers, followed by John's boots from underneath it. "Will and I are going to have breakfast shortly and yours will be brought up here very soon. When you've eaten, I'll bring you to the drawing room."

Ten minutes later, Will hugged her to him as they went downstairs and into the breakfast room. "Christmas Day is off to a good start," he said. "Once your grandfather is safely back at number 7, I can really start to enjoy the day."

He left for number 55 straight after their meal and Isobel went down the steps to the servants' hall and into the kitchen where Mrs Dillon was lifting an enormous goose into a copper roasting pan.

"That must be the biggest goose in Dublin," she said and the cook-housekeeper smiled.

"I was lucky to spot this bird, Mrs Fitzgerald. The butcher wanted to sell me a much smaller one."

"Master John is very much looking forward to dinner with the grown-ups."

"What did Father Christmas bring him?"

"Another wooden duck which 'flies'," she replied and Mrs Dillon chuckled. "When my husband returns, we'll give

Master John our presents. We're determined he will enjoy his first Christmas Day at number 30."

She went upstairs to the drawing room, decorated with sprigs of holly and ivy, and across the room to the window. The sky was grey but, thankfully, it wasn't raining. About to turn away, she was astonished to see Will and Alfie approaching.

"You cannot have moved Grandfather already?" she asked, hurrying downstairs.

"We have," Will replied as Alfie closed the front door and they hung their hats and overcoats on the stand. "Alfie had him out of bed and dressed when I got to number 55. The slowest part was carrying him downstairs to the bath chair in the hall. It was plain sailing after that."

"Was David the friend Will said you mentioned having a bath chair?" she asked Alfie as he straightened his white bow tie.

"Yes, but he wasn't at his rooms, so I went to Trinity College and managed to locate one and this chair is a little less battered than David's."

"Did moving Grandfather take a lot out of him?"

"It did," Will replied. "But he has been instructed to rest in bed until dinner is served. He can then be wheeled into the breakfast room in the bath chair and eat at the table with your grandmother. A bath chair will give him the freedom of the ground floor of number 7 and he agrees that a new bath chair should be purchased for him. He also agreed with my recommendation that he engage a nurse and he is leaving the task of selecting some candidates in my capable hands, as he put it."

"Did you speak to Grandmother?" she added and he shook his head.

"No, we did not see her at all. Your grandfather said she was still mulling over my request."

"Oh, for goodness sake," she snapped. "Grandmother either wants to be reunited with Mother and Miles again or she doesn't. There is no middle ground."

"Allow them to enjoy their last Christmas Day together," Will said and extended a hand to the stairs. "Let's give John our presents before everyone arrives from church."

"Miles accompanied Mother and James to church?"

"Mother wanted to as it's Christmas Day," Alfie told her, "but James and I persuaded her otherwise as he might find the large congregation overwhelming. He's in his bedroom, shall I go and fetch him now?"

"Yes, do. It will be better for young John and Miles to be introduced while it is still quiet here."

Lifting his hat and overcoat down from the stand, Alfie left the house and Isobel and Will went upstairs to the nursery. Carrying young John to the drawing room, Will set him down on his feet just inside the door and Isobel smiled as the boy ran out into the middle of the floor then climbed onto the sofa gazing wide-eyed at the pale gold wallpaper and at the sofa and two armchairs upholstered in burgundy silk satin.

"This room is huge," he cried.

"Yes, it is the main entertaining room in the house," she told him. "Come and see the dining room and how beautiful the table is laid and decorated."

Will opened the double doors which linked the two rooms and John slid off the sofa, gasping at the shining silver-plated cutlery, glittering glassware and more sprigs of holly and ivy on the Irish linen tablecloth.

"You will be sitting here," she said, placing her hands on the back of the chair beside hers. "Will sits at the head of the table, you and shall I sit here at the other end and you shall sit on a cushion so you can see everyone."

"We have some presents for you," Will added. "Come and open them."

Their presents were stacked beside the drawing room fireplace. They knelt down on the hearth rug and passed him the first.

"Another duck," he proclaimed in delight, ripping all the paper off and holding up the speckled brown wife of the wooden drake they had given him the previous evening.

"Mrs Drake." Will laughed. "She will look well with Mr Drake and Mr Effalump Elephant and Mr Drake-with-springs. We also bought you some sensible presents," he went on as John put the duck down and he handed the boy a second, much larger present. "We hope you like them," he said and John put the present down on the rug and pulled the paper off. "A morning coat, waistcoat and short trousers and a woollen overcoat which we think looks very grown-up."

"Thank you." John threw an arm around both of them and hugged them to him. "This is the bestest Christmas ever."

"You are very welcome," she said, hearing a knock and the door opening. Alfie ushered Miles, looking very smart in white tie and tails, into the room and they got to their feet. "Happy Christmas, Miles," she said and kissed his cheek. "Sit down and meet John." Miles sat on the sofa and Will led the curious boy forward.

"John is my nephew," Will explained. "He lives with us.

John, remember we told you that Miles is Grandmamma Martha's brother?"

"Yes," John replied, held out a hand and Miles shook it. "Do you like ducks?"

"I don't know," he replied. "I haven't actually seen one."

"There are lots in St Stephen's Green."

"I look forward to seeing them there."

"Will and I have a present for you," she said and passed it to him.

Miles set the present down beside him on the sofa before carefully unwrapping it and she smiled as his eyes bulged on seeing the set of Thomas Hardy novels bound in brown leather.

"This is," he began, covering his face with his hands. "Too much."

"No," she said softly as John stared at Miles in bewilderment. Will quickly led the boy to a window while she extracted a handkerchief from Miles' trouser pocket. Crouching down in front of him, she lowered his hands, dried his eyes and returned the handkerchief to his pocket. "This novel," she continued, laying a hand on top of it. "Is called *Far From The Madding Crowd* and I read it as a girl and I enjoyed it very much. You'll enjoy the others as well and they'll look very grand on your bookshelves."

"Thank you."

"Isobel?" Twisting around, she saw Will's mother dressed in pale pink and with her arms full of presents, being shown into the room by Zaineb.

"Happy Christmas, Sarah," she said, straightening up as Will went to his mother and kissed her cheek before taking the presents from her and placing them alongside the others next to the fireplace. "Miles," she added and he got to his feet, "this is Will's mother, Mrs Sarah Fitzgerald. Sarah, this is Miles Greene."

"I am very pleased to meet you, Miles," Sarah said shaking his hand warmly.

"And I'm delighted to meet you, Mrs Fitzgerald."

"I hope you're settling into number 55?"

"Yes, I am, thank you."

"Happy Christmas, Grandmother." John gave her a grin and she bent down and kissed him on both cheeks.

"Happy Christmas, John. Now, I know you love ducks, so when I saw this," she said, gesturing to a large, flat, present, "I knew it would be a perfect present for you. Perhaps, you should open it, Will."

"More presents," John squealed as Will lifted it up and unwrapped it, revealing a framed portrait of many different breeds of ducks. "Ducks – thank you, Grandmother."

"That will look wonderful on the nursery wall," Isobel said with a smile and kissed Sarah's cheek in thanks.

"And this one is for you, Miles," Sarah added, reaching for the present and passing it to him. "Will and Isobel told me you were a bibliophile."

"Thank you," he said, carefully unwrapping the present and lifting out a book bound in green leather.

"It is a history of Dublin. I hope you like history, Miles?"

"I do. Thank you very much, Mrs Fitzgerald."

"History, eh?" Will's father, also carrying presents, was shown into the room by Mary and Sarah tensed. "It's just as well I spotted these, then." He passed one to Miles and another to his grandson before handing the rest to Will. "A history of Ireland with plenty of illustrations for John and a history of Ireland with much fewer illustrations for Miles."

"Thank you, Grandfather." The boy couldn't quite keep the disappointment out of his voice as he slowly unwrapped it rather than simply ripping the paper off and Isobel had to smother a laugh.

"Thank you, sir." By contrast, Miles both looked and sounded delighted.

"You are both very welcome. Ah." He turned as they heard voices on the landing. "That sounds like your mother and James, Isobel."

It was, and they were shown into the room, both with presents in their arms.

"Happy Christmas, all." Mrs Ellison was resplendent in a new mauve dress and a gold pendant Isobel hadn't seen before hung around her neck – most likely a gift from James. "I have presents from James and myself and Alfie. May I put them with the others, Isobel?"

"Yes, of course. Happy Christmas." Isobel kissed them both and her mother placed the presents beside the fireplace. "Would everyone like some mulled wine?" she asked, extending a hand to a punchbowl beside the decanters.

There were general murmurings of agreement so she and Will served the wine and passed the glasses around.

The next two hours were spent chatting and distributing the presents until Zaineb announced that dinner was served.

Everyone applauded and young John's eyes bulged when Mrs Dillon carried the roast goose on a platter into the dining room and placed it on the table in front of Will.

"Are gooses just like big ducks?" the boy asked and craned his neck to observe Will carving the bird and putting a slice of meat on a plate for him.

"Yes, I suppose they are, and the plural of goose is geese,

and geese don't quack," he added while John's plate was passed to Isobel so she could cut the meat up for him and add some vegetables and gravy. "They honk."

It was an exceptional meal and everyone complimented Mrs Dillon as the ladies retired to the drawing room leaving the gentlemen to enjoy a glass of port.

"Does Will have to attend to Mr Greene later?" Sarah asked as she and Isobel went to a window and looked out over the square.

"No, not unless he is called for. Alfie has borrowed a bath chair but one is to be purchased for Grandfather so he isn't confined to bed."

"Miles appears to be coping very well."

"Yes, he is. I did worry whether today would be overwhelming for him but he is enjoying himself. And so is young John, despite the history book."

"A history book for a child." Sarah rolled her eyes. "Whatever was his grandfather thinking?"

"I'll see just how dull it is," Isobel replied with a smile. "It can always be put away until he is older. I wouldn't want him to be put off history."

"He is four in January, when are you going to start him at school?"

"Not for a while yet. I don't want him to think we are sending him away."

"But, Isobel, he won't be boarding."

"No, but even so."

"You and Will have done wonders with him – thank you. Have you introduced Miles to the twins?"

"Not yet. Will and I shall bring him to the nursery in a little while."

When the gentlemen left the dining room, she followed Will to the drinks tray and watched as he poured whiskey into five glasses.

"Would you like some brandy?" he inquired as Miles sat down in an armchair and began to examine his presents.

"Not yet, thank you," she replied. "You and I should introduce Miles to Ben and Belle now."

Will nodded and gently laid a hand on Miles' shoulder. "Come with us, Miles. Isobel and I would like you to meet two little people. Alfie, could you pass the whiskeys around, please?"

They went upstairs to the nursery and Isobel introduced Miles to Florrie and Bridget before leading him into the children's bedroom and to the cradles where Belle and Ben were fast asleep lying on their backs.

"This is our daughter, Belle, and this is our son, Ben. They are five months old."

"And twins?" he asked.

"Yes, they are. Just like you and Mother."

"What relation am I to them?"

"You are their grand uncle."

"Will they have to call me grand uncle?" he asked.

"Not if you don't want them to. Alfie is quite happy just being Alfie."

"Good," he replied with clear relief. "I am Miles – just Miles."

"Just Miles, it is."

"When will John have his own bedroom?" Miles asked, glancing around the room. "Out of the nursery, I mean?"

"When he is a little older," Will replied. "At the moment, it is easier here for him and the twins. Are you happy with your room?"

"Oh, yes." Miles grinned suddenly. "Very much so. When I'm not reading, I like to sit at the window and—" He hesitated. "Watch people going by or walking in the garden in the centre of the square," he finished in an embarrassed mumble.

"There is nothing wrong with that," she replied. "I like to watch people, too."

"Keep a look-out for number 13's dog," Will told him with a wink. "It's white and it looks like a small sheep being taken for a walk."

Miles went to the window and glanced around the square then peered down to the garden.

"Those elderly people really shouldn't be outside on a day like this," he murmured, pressing the tip of his right forefinger against the glass. "It's far too cold and soon it will be getting dark."

Isobel stood beside him and looked to where he pointed. Through the bare branches of the trees, she could see his mother pushing his father in a bath chair along one of the paths. A rug was draped over Mr Greene's knees but, even so, it really wasn't the weather for him to be out of number 7 for any length of time.

"Will," she said in a neutral tone and he came to them.

"Do you know that couple?" Miles asked curiously.

"I am the gentleman's doctor," Will replied. "I'll keep an eye on them to make sure they don't stay out – no," he gasped and she clapped a hand to her mouth as Mrs Greene collapsed onto the path beside the bath chair.

Will exchanged a horrified glance with Isobel. "Keep Miles here," he insisted quietly and she nodded.

"Miles, come and see John's ducks," she said in a shaky voice as Will ran out of the nursery.

"Father – Alfie – James," he roared as he thundered down the stairs to the first floor.

Alfie opened the drawing room door and James and Will's father stood behind him in the doorway. "What is it, Will? Is it Miles?"

"No. Come with me." He continued on downstairs to the hall, the three men following him and he took the key to the garden gate from the drawer of the hall table. "Mrs Greene has collapsed," he said, hauling open the front door and running down the steps to the pavement.

They crossed the street, he unlocked and opened the gate and they dashed across the lawn. Mr Greene was on his hands and knees beside his wife. Kneeling beside them, Will felt Mrs Greene's wrist for a pulse. Nothing. Undoing the buttons of her matching purple cloak and dress, he pulled them open and felt her neck for a pulse. Nothing.

"An acute myocardial infarction," his father whispered, bending down briefly. "There's nothing you could have done."

"Is my wife dead, Dr Fitzgerald?" Mr Greene asked and Will twisted around to face him, noting that the Greenes had left number 7 without the oxygen cylinder.

"Yes, she is. I'm so very sorry."

"I was to go first, not Tilda," Mr Greene said quietly, leaning over his wife and kissing her forehead.

"Alfie, please, bring your grandfather to number 30 and then fetch the oxygen cylinder, tube and face mask from number 7."

"I don't want to leave Tilda here," Mr Greene added, beginning to wheeze.

"Your wife will not be left alone," Will assured him as Alfie helped his grandfather to his feet and sat him down in the bath chair. "She will be brought to number 30 as well."

Mr Greene gave him a brief nod and Alfie wheeled him away.

Will got to his feet seeing James Ellison's ashen face. "Go back to the house, James."

"No – I – I want to help."

"Very well. Someone is going to have to fetch an undertaker."

"Will, it's Christmas Day…"

"I'll go and fetch John Dalton," his father announced and Will gave him a grateful pat on the back. "I'll get my hat and overcoat and I'll be on my way."

Will watched him walk across the lawn towards the gate before turning back to James. It was the first time he had seen the solicitor utterly unnerved. It wasn't simply Mrs Greene's body lying at his feet but the knowledge that soon he was going to have to break the news of his mother-in-law's death to her daughter – his wife of less than a month.

"Was it a stroke?"

"A massive heart attack."

"Did she die without suffering, Will? Martha will ask."

"Intense pain and then death. It was quick, I didn't see her even clutch her chest before she fell."

"You saw it happen?" James demanded incredulously.

"Yes. From the nursery window. Go inside, James, you're shivering."

"So are you," James replied and Will looked down at his trembling hands.

"I don't want to leave her alone. Go inside and when

Alfie comes back send him out here. We'll bring her into the breakfast room so please ask that the gas lamps are lit and the table is cleared."

James returned to the house and Will gazed up at the grey sky. Dusk was falling and he took out his pocket watch. It was four o'clock. It would be dark soon and all he needed now was for it to start raining.

"Will?" He jumped hearing Isobel's voice and put his watch back in his waistcoat pocket as she hurried toward him wearing her black and white coat and carrying his overcoat. "Put this on." She helped him with the overcoat before peering down at her grandmother. "James said a heart attack."

"Yes – a huge one to have killed her so quickly. It's possible she was dead before she even fell."

"My father died the same way," she murmured. "Alfie found him in his study. This will resurrect bad memories."

"Where are your mother and Miles?" he asked as she crouched down and did up Mrs Greene's dress and cloak buttons.

"Mother is still in the drawing room and Miles is still in the nursery," she replied, straightening up. "I didn't know what to do with Miles as I didn't want to bring him back to the drawing room and run the risk of Mother upsetting him. I carried young John to the nursery and Miles is looking through the duck book with him. Florrie is supervising them and Bridget is with the twins. James is going to bring Mother into the dining room and break the news to her and your mother will be on hand to comfort her."

"Thank you, but your mother is not to come out here, Isobel."

"James won't allow her to see Grandmother like this."

"Good."

"Now, what do we do?" she asked quietly and he put an arm around her and kissed her temple.

"We take matters one at a time. First, Father has gone for John Dalton. Second, Gerald and I will carry Mrs Greene into the breakfast room. Third, John Dalton will attend to Mrs Greene and she will be placed in a coffin."

"I meant about my grandfather, Will. He cannot live alone. He desperately needs a live-in nurse."

"I will move into number 7 until you engage one," Alfie said and they both turned, not having heard him approach. "But one must be found before lectures resume in the new year."

"Thank you, Alfie," he replied. "Please send Gerald out here to assist me."

"Gerald?" Alfie repeated with a frown and glanced at Isobel. "Yes, Father died of a colossal heart attack, too, but there is really no need to protect me. I'll take Grandmother's ankles."

The gas lamps had been lit in the hall and Mrs Dillon held the front door open as Mrs Greene was carried into the house and laid on the breakfast room table.

"Mr Greene is in the morning room, Dr Fitzgerald," the housekeeper said as he and Alfie left the room and the door was closed. "Mary is lighting the fire and I have just given Mr Greene a glass of brandy. I hope that was the right thing to do."

"It was," Will replied. "Thank you. My father and the undertaker will arrive shortly, I hope. Until then, please do not allow anyone to enter this room."

"I won't, Dr Fitzgerald. Would you like some tea to be brought to the drawing room, Mrs Fitzgerald?"

"Yes, please, Mrs Dillon," Isobel replied, before turning to him. "I must go to Mother."

He squeezed her arm and she picked up her skirts and ran up the stairs. Following Alfie into the morning room, he found Mr Greene seated in the bath chair beside the fireplace watching Mary as she placed some small pieces of coal amongst the blazing kindling.

"Your wife is in the breakfast room next door," he said, lifting the oxygen cylinder, tube and face mask from where they had been left on the seat of one of the armchairs and put the cylinder on the floor next to the bath chair. "And the undertaker is on his way here."

"The undertaker? Who?"

"John Dalton of Dalton and Sons. He buried Mr Henderson – your daughter's second husband – and—"

"And he will not bury my wife," Mr Greene interrupted firmly. "At least, not in Dublin. Tilda will be buried in Co Mayo with the Greene family in the graveyard at Ballyglas Parish Church."

Will glanced at Alfie, who pulled an awkward expression. "Inhale the oxygen," he said softly and passed Mr Greene the face mask.

"I mean it," Mr Greene added. "Tilda will be buried with the Greene family and I don't care how much it costs to bring her there."

"Inhale the oxygen," Will repeated and Mr Greene raised the face mask to his nose and mouth. Hearing voices in the hall, Will opened the door and left the room. "Mr Dalton," he said, closing the door behind him and shaking the undertaker's hand. "Thank you for coming on Christmas Day."

"Your grandmother-in-law?"

"Yes," he replied and gave his father a grateful smile. "Mrs Matilda Greene. And," he lowered his voice, "Lewis Greene, her husband, is in there." He gestured to the morning room and Mr Dalton nodded.

"I have brought an oak coffin. Your father said Mr Greene would want only the best."

"Thank you." Will opened the door to the breakfast room and was about to follow the two men inside when Alfie tapped him on the shoulder.

"Will, Grandfather insists on speaking to Mr Dalton – now."

Will sighed. "Mr Dalton?"

They went into the morning room and the undertaker expressed his sympathies to Mr Greene who bade him sit down in an armchair.

"Mr Dalton," he began as the undertaker sat down. "I have told Dr Fitzgerald this and I am telling you now, too. My wife will be buried in the graveyard at Ballyglas Parish Church. Ballyglas is near to Westport in Co Mayo and I don't care how much it costs to bring her there."

"If those are your wishes I shall, of course, abide by them, Mr Greene. I have never been to Co Mayo," Mr Dalton admitted. "But some years ago, I did liase with Andrew Hill of Hill and Sons in Westport regarding a client whose last wish was to be buried in the town of his birth. Mr Hill met the coffin at Westport Station and he took charge of matters from there on. If Westport is the nearest railway station to Ballyglas, I can do so again?" he offered and Mr Greene nodded.

"It is and, please, do."

"I shall liase with Mr Hill, Mr Greene, and I shall also have a death notice published in *The Irish Times*," Mr Dalton confirmed. "Is there a Co Mayo newspaper I should also send a notice to?"

"Please, send a notice to the *Connaught Telegraph*."

"Of course. I have an oak coffin in the hearse, Mr Greene. If you would prefer another..?"

"Does it have brass handles?"

"It does," Mr Dalton replied. "And silk cushioned lining. It is the finest coffin I possess."

"Very well."

"Do you have a preference for a dress for your wife?"

"The dress my wife was wearing today was her best. Did it get wet?" he asked, turning to Will.

"No, nor dirty," Will replied. "Where would you prefer the coffin to be placed at number 7?"

"On the hall table and if my wife's lady's maid, Ida, could then attend to my wife's hair? My wife was always very proud of her hair."

"Of course. Please, excuse us," Will said and he went outside with Mr Dalton to the hearse. The oak coffin was brought to the breakfast room and they laid Mrs Greene in it.

"I shall have to attach the lid in order to transport the coffin to number 7," the undertaker said, picking up the lid and screwing it in place.

Alfie and Mr Dalton placed the coffin in the hearse and Will had to quickly close the front door before he and his father could follow them when he saw Isobel coming down the stairs arm-in-arm with her mother and go into the morning room.

They walked behind the hearse to number 7. Knox, furiously blinking back tears, admitted them to the house and in the hall, the undertaker made sure the mahogany table was sturdy enough before Will and Alfie placed the heavy oak coffin on it.

"May we speak to Ida, please?" Will asked the butler as Mr Dalton unscrewed the coffin lid but left it in place.

"I am here, Dr Fitzgerald." A shaken Ida came up the steps from the servants' hall wringing her hands.

"Mr Greene has requested that his wife's hair be attended to but if you would prefer not to just say so," Will told her gently and she glanced at the coffin.

"I will do it," she said with a wobbly smile. "I helped to dress my grandmother for her viewing and wake. Mrs Greene has – had – beautiful hair. I will tidy her hair and make it beautiful again."

"Thank you, Ida," he replied and Mr Dalton lifted off the lid and passed it to Alfie who stood it in a corner. "Her daughter – my mother-in-law – will want to view her this evening."

"Mrs Greene did not wish to be reunited with her daughter – nor her son," Ida spoke up bravely. "I heard her say so this afternoon. Mr Greene begged her to change her mind but she wouldn't have it. They rowed, but Mr Greene backed down first and suggested a breath of air in the garden," she concluded miserably, turned away and hurried up the stairs.

"I'll complete a medical certificate and call to see you tomorrow," Will told Mr Dalton. "We shall all have discussed the funeral by then."

Knox saw the undertaker out and Will's father went to

the front door and shook the butler's hand in sympathy.

"Will, Alfie," he called. "The maid seems competent, let's leave her to do her work and return to number 30."

Isobel and Sarah twisted around on the drawing room sofa as Mrs Ellison emerged stunned from the dining room clutching James' hand. Isobel quickly moved along the sofa and he sat her mother down in between them, went to the decanters and poured a large brandy. Isobel put an arm around her mother's shoulders but Mrs Ellison was too shocked to notice.

"Where is my Father?" she asked suddenly.

"In the morning room," James replied, holding out the brandy glass. "Drink this."

"No, I must go to him." Her mother got up, almost stumbled and Isobel lunged forward to grasp her arm.

"I'll bring you to him, Mother."

Isobel escorted her downstairs and along the hall, glancing at the front door as Will closed it, so her mother wouldn't see what appeared to be a fine oak coffin being placed in the hearse. They went into the morning room and Mrs Ellison sank to her knees on the hearth rug, laying her cheek on her father's lap and finally bursting into tears.

Isobel went to the drinks tray, poured a glass of brandy and knelt down beside her mother and her grandfather's bath chair.

"Mother," she said softly, stroking her hair. "Drink this." Mrs Ellison just shook her head and Isobel sighed. "Grandfather has drunk some brandy and I would like you to do the same."

"No."

"Mother, if you do not drink this brandy, I will ask James to bring you home."

That made her mother raise her head. "Isobel, you wouldn't."

"You are distressing Grandfather. He doesn't need you crying like this, he needs you to be strong. So, drink this brandy – now, please."

Her mother wiped her eyes with her fingers then accepted the glass and drained it in two gulps. Isobel took it, squeezed her mother's shoulder in thanks then got up and returned the glass to the drinks tray.

"Have you eaten?" she asked her grandfather and he nodded.

"Your grandmother and I began our Christmas dinner at precisely one o'clock. The goose was delicious," he added sadly and raised the face mask to his nose and mouth. He inhaled and lowered the mask. "I have informed the undertaker that your grandmother will be buried in Ballyglas and I don't care how much it costs to bring her there."

Isobel fought to hide a frown. Could a funeral in Co Mayo be arranged from this distance away? And when would the trains be running again?

"I will be sending Knox back to Greene Hall – if not tomorrow – then the next day," her grandfather continued. "The house will be opened up and Knox will meet with the Reverend Barber in Ballyglas and request that the funeral be held as soon as possible. Once a date has been set, I shall notify Mr Dalton who shall send a telegram to Andrew Hill, who is an undertaker in Westport. Once those arrangements are in place, I shall bring Tilda home to Co Mayo."

"You are not going anywhere without a nurse," Isobel

told him and he looked up at her impassively.

"You had better find one quickly, then, hadn't you?"

"Father—" her mother began but he raised a hand to silence her.

"Where is Miles?"

"Upstairs in the nursery with young John," Isobel replied.

"Young John?" he inquired before nodding to himself. "Oh, yes, the orphan boy. Fetch Miles, will you?"

"No," she said simply and he glanced up at her again.

"Isobel, I came to Dublin to see my children. My daughter is beside me and I wish to see my son before I return home."

"Miles did not know your wife and he does not know you – so, no – I will not fetch him."

"Isobel," her mother scolded but she ignored her.

"Miles needs to be sat down and told about you and your wife in a patient and calm manner. And Miles will ask why he was sent away from Greene Hall. He will ask why he was put in St Patrick's Hospital. How should he be answered?"

"With the truth," her grandfather replied matter-of-factly. "That at the time an asylum was the best place for him."

"But it wasn't. We were told Miles—"

"Isobel." Her mother got to her feet. "This is neither the time nor the place."

"Then, when and where is, Mother?" she demanded.

"Tomorrow, Isobel," Will answered and she spun around and saw him standing in the doorway. "Miles will be told about his parents later this evening and he will meet his father in the morning. Mr Greene," he looked past her, "you will be accompanied back to number 7 later. Martha, if you wish to view your mother, you may do so then."

"Yes," she replied in a shaky voice. "Thank you, Will."

"Not at all. Now, please excuse me."

He turned away and Isobel followed him out to the hall, closing the morning room door firmly behind her.

"What happened?" Alfie asked while Will shrugged off his overcoat and passed it to his father who hung it on the stand. "We could hear raised voices."

"Grandfather wants Grandmother to be buried in Ballyglas," she said as they went up the stairs. "Grandfather is sending Knox to Greene Hall as soon as possible to start the funeral arrangements and Will must find a nurse quickly because Grandfather is going home regardless of whether one has been found."

Alfie and Will's father continued on into the drawing room to join James and Sarah, but Will halted on the landing and sighed. "A nurse will be found. But one who is suitable. A nurse will not be engaged quickly simply because she is immediately available."

"I don't think you made that clear enough to Grandfather," she said and he gave her a weary glance.

"My parents won't walk back to number 67 together so I need to escort them both there myself," he said. "Afterwards, I'll go to the practice house and complete a medical certificate so Mrs Greene's death can be registered as soon as possible. When I return, we'll escort your grandfather, mother and James to number 7. Then—" He grimaced. "You and I shall speak to Miles."

She went on upstairs to the nursery where young John was seated at the table finishing a slice of goose which had been cut up into squares and a fascinated Miles watched at the door to the children's bedroom as Florrie and Bridget bottle-fed Ben and Belle. Looking at her watch, she exhaled a long sigh, it was a quarter to seven already.

"It is almost your bed-time," she said and John's face fell.

"Must I go to bed, Isobel?"

"Yes. Eat those last few squares, go into the bedroom and see how far you get undressing yourself." To her relief, the boy did as he was told and she went to the rug, picked up the duck book and placed it on the table. "Did he enjoy the book?" she asked Miles.

"We looked at the paintings in the first three chapters and I read the descriptions to him then John wanted to play with his new wooden ducks. I have enjoyed the day very much, Isobel, thank you."

I'm afraid it is far from over yet, she told him silently but smiled. "I'll help young John to bed, I won't be long."

In the children's bedroom, the boy had got as far as unbuttoning his morning coat and she busied herself for the next few minutes in taking off his clothes and helping him into his blue and white striped nightshirt.

"Soon you'll be able to manage all by yourself," she said, assisting Bridget and Florrie in changing the twins' nappies and he gave her a grin.

"I can undo buttons now," he announced proudly. "But doing them up is harder."

"Practice makes perfect," Florrie said.

"I'll practice, I promise."

"And then we'll make a start on tying bootlaces," she added as she placed the soiled nappies in the laundry basket in a corner of the room before opening the bedroom door.

"Would you like to help us tuck young John into bed?" she asked Miles who was seated at the nursery table flicking through the duck book.

"I would," he replied, closing the book and getting to his feet. "Thank you, Isobel."

"May we tuck John into bed, too?" Sarah asked, peering around the door from the landing.

"Yes, of course, come in," she said and Sarah, followed by Will and then his father and Alfie came into the nursery.

Young John was climbing into bed as they joined them in the bedroom. "Sleep tight," Sarah said softly and kissed his cheek.

"Goodnight, young man." John's namesake gave him a hug then made way for Miles.

"Goodnight, John." Miles held out a hand and the boy shook it.

"Goodnight Miles. Thank you for reading to me."

"I enjoyed it very much."

"Well, I am already looking forward to Christmas Day next year," Alfie proclaimed, ruffling young John's hair and Isobel nodded to herself. So was she. So was everyone present. "I shall see you very soon, John."

"Did you enjoy today?" Will asked and young John grinned again as he snuggled down under the bedcovers.

"Yes, I did. Thank you."

"You're very welcome, John," she replied, kissing his forehead. "We're so glad."

"Goodnight and sleep well," Will said and kissed his cheek. "Come and see the twins," he added to his parents, Alfie and Miles and they gathered around the cradles.

"Oh, look at them," Sarah whispered in delight as she

bent down and kissed first Ben and then Belle. "Their first Christmas and they are utterly oblivious to it."

"Next year will be fun," her husband said drolly.

"I should go home now, it's been a long day," Sarah continued as if her husband hadn't spoken and walked to the door, opened it and left the bedroom.

"Merry Christmas little ones." Will's father kissed the twins then straightened up and went after his wife.

"I'll try not to be too long," Will told her and followed his father from the room.

"Let's go downstairs," she said to Alfie, taking Miles' hand. "Goodnight," she added to Bridget, Florrie and young John. "I shall see you in the morning."

"Where are Martha and James?" Miles asked as they went into the empty drawing room.

"They are having a breath of fresh air in the garden," Alfie lied in a light tone. "May I show Miles your books?" he asked her, gesturing towards the bookcase. "While you go and find them?" he added with a wink and she gave him a grateful nod and a smile.

In the morning room, her mother was seated in one of the armchairs beside Mr Greene in the bath chair holding his hand, while James was standing at the window with his back to them.

"Are any of you hungry?" she asked. "Or would like some tea or coffee and mince pies?"

All three shook their heads and Isobel went to the window, hoping Will really wouldn't be too long. She had planned for an enjoyable Christmas Day but now she simply wanted the day to be over and done with. She gazed out at the dimly-lit square until James touched her hand. Will was climbing the steps to the front door and she turned and left the room just as Will stepped into the hall, taking off his hat.

"Alfie is upstairs with Miles," she said, lifting her coat down from the stand and pulling it on.

"Good," he replied and she assisted her mother with her cloak and hat as James wheeled his father-in-law out of the morning room.

Will helped James into his overcoat, passed their hats to her and she held the front door open while they carried the bath chair out of the house and down the steps. Her mother followed and Isobel was the last to leave, closing the door behind her.

They quickly made their way to number 7 in the bitter cold and Knox answered the doorbell. The bath chair was carried up the steps, into the hall and Isobel hung Will and James' hats on the stand. On seeing the coffin on the hall table, Mrs Ellison reached out and clutched Isobel's hand so tightly she had to bite back a yelp as her mother's fingernails dug painfully into her palm.

"Martha?" Mr Greene heaved himself out of the bath chair and held out his hand. Releasing Isobel, her mother grasped it and they walked slowly along the hall to the coffin. "Your mother would never admit it," he said as Mrs Ellison began to weep, "but I know she was comforted by the knowledge you were happily married at last and that you had given Miles a home."

Isobel shot Will and James a sharp glance, not believing that for a second. Will shook his head, silently telling her not to comment, and she raised her eyes to the ceiling as she massaged her palm.

"Come outside for a moment, please, James," Will

murmured, lifting his hat down from the stand before opening the front door and the two men left the house.

"Mother," she said as softly as she could and Mrs Ellison turned a tearful face towards her. "Will and I must go home now. James will escort you back to number 55 when Alfie comes here and once we have spoken to Miles we will walk him home."

"When?"

"I don't know. We need to be patient with Miles."

Her mother nodded, turned back to the coffin and Isobel went out and down the steps to the pavement.

"...We have absolutely no idea how he will take the news," Will was telling James. "But we will sit with him for as long as it takes for him to fully understand."

"Thank you, Will," James replied. "And thank you, Isobel. It had been a delightful day."

"Yes, it had," she said, reaching up and kissing his cheek.

Will took her hand and they walked back to number 30. They hung up their hats and coats then went upstairs to the drawing room.

"Ah, here they are." Alfie put a book back on a shelf. "Miles is impressed with your library of books."

"I built up quite a collection when I lived alone in Brown Street," Will said. "These days, I read *The Irish Times* – and the *Freeman's Journal*, too – much to my father's disgust but I believe we should all read as widely as possible."

"I agree," Alfie replied. "Well, I must be off, Miles. Will and Isobel will see you home in a little while," he explained as a frowning Miles opened his mouth to wonder why Alfie wasn't bringing him home immediately. "There is no need to see me out, Isobel, I know the way."

"We shall call tomorrow." Isobel gave him a hug and

Will shook his hand. "Let's sit down, Miles," she said as Alfie went out and closed the door behind him.

Miles sat on the sofa, she sat beside him and Will pulled over an armchair.

"What's the matter?" Miles asked them both anxiously.

"I need to ask you something," she began and he nodded. "What were you told about your mother and father?"

"Nothing," he replied. "My parents are both dead, aren't they?"

She exchanged a glance with Will before reaching for Miles' hands. "Your father is alive but I'm afraid your mother died today."

"Today? Where is my father?"

"He has rented a house here on the square – number 7," she explained. "Alfie has gone there to stay with him until a nurse can be engaged."

"A nurse – why?"

"Your father is very ill," Will replied. "He has lung disease and he needs looking after."

They paused to allow him to digest the news. Miles stared down at his hands for a few moments before raising his head.

"My father and mother didn't want me, did they?" he asked.

"They thought St Patrick's Hospital would be the best place for you," Will told him gently.

"But it wasn't the best place, was it? If it was, I would still be there, wouldn't I?"

"No, it wasn't the best place," she said. "Which is why once Will, Alfie and I plus Mother and James knew you were there, we arranged for you to move to number 55 as quickly as possible."

"You didn't know I was there, did you?"

"No, we didn't."

"Were you told I was dead?" he added.

"Mother was told you had died when you were a year old," she whispered. "So, Alfie and I grew up thinking it, too. But we are all so happy that you are alive."

"All? Was my mother – and is my father – happy that I am no longer dead to everyone?"

"Miles, your father is dying," Will said. "And he knows he is dying. It was his decision to come to Dublin—"

"From where?"

"Co Mayo – near to Westport on the west coast. Your parents' home is called Greene Hall. You and Martha were born there. Your father wanted to come to Dublin and be reunited with both you and Martha."

"Why Martha, too?"

"Because my mother was estranged from your parents for twenty-five years," she told him. "Mother married my father against their wishes."

"Will, you said it was my father's decision to come to Dublin. Did my mother not want to?"

"No."

"Was my mother reunited with Martha before she died?"

"No."

"Because she died – or because she did not want to?"

"She did not want to," Isobel replied. "She never forgave Mother for leaving Greene Hall and marrying my father. Your mother and my mother saw each other briefly at number 55 a couple of days ago but your mother did not acknowledge mine."

Miles pursed his lips. "My mother did not want to be

reunited with me either, did she, Isobel?"

"No. But your father has been reunited with Mother and he also wants to be reunited with you."

"Only because he is dying and is full of guilt," Miles responded savagely. "Up to now, I have been dead to him. Well, he may have been reunited with Martha but he will not be reunited with me."

"If that is what you want," she said.

"It is. Where is my mother?" he asked. "If she only died today, then, where is she now?"

"She is at number 7," Will told him. "An undertaker came with a coffin—"

"On Christmas Day?"

"My father knows Mr Dalton, the undertaker. Mr Dalton came here with a coffin, your mother was laid in the coffin and she was brought to number 7. Martha and James are there now and Alfie will live with your father at number 7 until a nurse is engaged."

"Where will my mother be buried?"

"Your father wants her to be buried in Co Mayo."

"When will that happen?"

"We don't know yet," she replied. "We haven't been able to plan anything because it is Christmas Day."

"Thank you for telling me. It must have been difficult for you both."

"It was," she admitted. "But because there have been far too many lies told over the years. You needed to know the truth about your mother and your father, no matter how painful it is."

"My mother must have known I was now living with Martha, James and Alfie."

"Yes, she did know and she was very angry with us. She continued to believe the best place for you was St Patrick's Hospital but Dr Harrison and all of us believed otherwise."

"Thank you," he whispered, blinking back tears.

"We are your family, Miles," she assured him. "Will and I, and young John, Belle and Ben, and Mother, James and Alfie – plus Will's parents – John and Sarah – all of us are so happy you are now living at number 55."

"I like living there very much."

"I'm glad."

"But there is no shame in changing your mind about wishing to meet your father," Will said. "Think about it."

"He truly is dying?" Miles asked and Will nodded.

"Yes. This will be his last Christmas Day."

"Was my mother also dying?"

"No. Your mother's death was completely unexpected. Your father said he always expected to die first."

"Is there anything else you would like to ask?" she said and Miles shook his head.

"Not at the moment."

"Well, if you do have other questions, please don't be afraid to ask any of us. We won't lie to you."

"Thank you, Isobel. Can I go home now, please, I'm tired."

"Yes, of course. And, Miles?" she added as they got up. "Mother will be extremely upset. Deep down, she hoped she would be reunited with your mother but, tonight, she has viewed her laid out in a coffin."

"I understand."

"Good. Let's fetch your hat and coat."

They escorted Miles to number 55 and found James

alone in the morning room standing in front of the fireplace staring at the glowing coals.

"Martha is exhausted and has gone to bed," he said, turning away from the fire. "Are you tired, too, Miles?"

"Yes, I am. Isobel and Will have told me about my mother and father."

"Good. I'm relieved you know now. When would you like to meet your father?"

"I do not wish to meet him at any time," Miles replied firmly and James shot her and then Will an astonished glance.

"But didn't Isobel and Will explain—"

"James, I know he is dying but he shut me away for over forty years. I assumed I had no family. Well, he has no son – and if you would all excuse me – I am going to bed."

Miles left the room and James let his arms fall to his sides helplessly.

"James, give him time to fully digest all of this and—" she began.

"We don't have time," he interrupted irritably. "Knox is leaving for Greene Hall on the first train to Westport in the morning. The rest of the servants at number 7 are being given a weeks' notice tomorrow and Alfie has been asked to call on the landlord and give a week's notice on the house – also tomorrow."

Will exhaled a loud sigh but James continued before he could speak.

"Mr Greene has asked Martha, Alfie and I to travel with him to Co Mayo for the funeral and stay at Greene Hall. He is also going to ask you both. The question now arises – what about Miles? If he refuses to come to Co Mayo with us, he cannot stay here alone – even for a few days."

"I can't go to Greene Hall for a few days," she said. "I can't leave the twins and young John for that length of time. I can travel there for the day of the funeral but I can't stay overnight."

"Surgery resumes on Tuesday, so I can't stay overnight either so we'll call to number 7 on our way home and speak to Knox regarding the time of the funeral," Will replied. "And, if Miles refuses to come to Co Mayo, Isobel and I shall have him to stay at number 30 while you are away."

"Thank you. We won't be staying long – two or three days at most – but I suspect that after the funeral, Martha will be intent on visiting her father as often as she can. I can't always accompany her and I do not want her to travel alone."

"I could ask my mother to accompany her?" Will suggested and James' face brightened. "Two ladies travelling together is respectable enough."

"Yes, it is. If she would agree, I would be most grateful. Regarding a nurse, how quickly can you engage one? Especially at this time of year."

"I shall call on Eva, the practice secretary," Will replied. "Quite often nurses in need of employment send their letters of recommendation to her in the hope she will know of a patient who needs assistance. Eva will know of a reputable nurse seeking employment. But that is for tomorrow," he added and opened the door. "Go to bed, James, you look exhausted, we'll see ourselves out."

"I hate to say it, Will, but we all do. Goodnight."

Will woke with a jump and reached out to turn the oil lamp up a little so he could look at the clock on the mantelpiece.

Only half past one. He felt as though he had been asleep for hours. Reaching out to turn the lamp down again, Isobel stirred.

"I don't want to get up yet," she murmured and buried her face in his neck.

"You don't have to get up for another six and a half hours."

"Good," was the muffled reply and he kissed her hair. She lifted her head back and he kissed her lips. "I love you."

"I love you, too," he replied and kissed her again and again, feeling her hand slide under his nightshirt.

He adored her touch, just as much as she adored touching him and he rested his forehead against hers as she stroked him to full hardness. Rolling over, he opened the drawer of his bedside table and lifted a condom out of the red box. Taking off his nightshirt, he slid the condom on before rolling back to face her and she pulled her nightdress off. He began to caress her – her skin was like silk – feeling the weight of her full breasts as he licked her nipples and slid a hand between her legs.

She was ready and she straddled him before lowering herself onto him. They both sighed and exchanged a smile as their hips moved in rhythm. Sitting up and pulling at her lips with his, he ran his hands up and down her back. Then, with a change in her breathing and the small moans he loved so much, he knew she was at the edge. They went over together, he met her spasms with his own and she trembled in his arms as their climaxes ebbed away. Smoothing hair off her face, he gently kissed her lips.

"Sleepy?" he asked and she nodded. She climbed off him and he disposed of the condom. "Want your nightdress?"

"No."

"Good." They lay down and she curved her body back against his. "I love you," he whispered but received no answer. She was asleep. He closed his eyes and slept, too.

When he woke, she leant over and kissed the tip of his nose. "Good morning."

"You are startlingly cheerful for…" He lifted his head to look at the clock. "Ten minutes before eight in the morning."

"Yes, I am."

"Dare I ask why?" he teased.

"Middle of the night sexual relations with my husband," she said with a laugh. "I woke up and I wondered if it had been a dream but then I saw your drawer was still open and I realised it had been real."

He smiled. "Today—"

"Doesn't begin for another nine minutes," she said and he relented, kissing her instead. When the clock showed eight o'clock, she groaned. "You were about to say about today..?"

"After breakfast, I'll go and see Eva and any nurses she recommends I'll interview at the practice house as soon as it is possible," he told her. "The final say will, of course, go to your grandfather. But I hope to have one or, perhaps, two nurses for him to interview and choose from in the next day or two. I simply can't do it more quickly than that."

She got out of bed, went to her wardrobe and hung her black dress and a new black woollen three-quarter length coat on the front. Opening the door of Will's wardrobe, she lifted out his own loathed mourning attire – his best frock coat, waistcoat and trousers and a black cravat.

"It's time to get dressed," she said and he threw back the

covers on his side of the bed with a sigh and went to the chest of drawers.

Eva Bannister had never married and lived with her widowed sister in Longwood Avenue, a quiet street off the South Circular Road. Will had not been to her home before and a young maid showed him into the parlour where Eva was reading seated beside the fire in an armchair upholstered in pale blue floral damask.

"Dr Fitzgerald?" Eva put the book to one side and got up in clear surprise, pulling a white woollen shawl from her shoulders and lying it over the back of the chair.

"I'm terribly sorry to be calling on St Stephen's Day, Eva, but I'm afraid this is a professional call."

"Please, take a seat," she said, smoothing her hands down the skirt of her bottle-green dress before sitting down again. "Delia is visiting a neighbour."

Thanking her, Will sat on the sofa and related the events of the previous day.

"…So I need to find a nurse for Mr Greene as quickly as possible and one who will not mind a move to Co Mayo and I don't have the time to place a newspaper advertisement," he concluded. "Is there anyone you could recommend?" he asked, hoping he didn't sound too desperate.

"Yes," Eva replied slowly. "I think there is."

"Is it a nurse who handed a letter of recommendation into the practice?"

"Actually, no," she said, reaching for the rope and ringing for the maid. "Our maid's sister was a house-parlourmaid in Kingstown. Her employer, Mr Tyrrell, died last week and, from what Joan told Anne, his nurse trained at St Thomas' Hospital in London."

"At the training school for nurses founded by Florence Nightingale?" Will asked in surprise.

"Yes – ah, Anne," she added as the maid came into the parlour. "The nurse your sister mentioned to you, has she left the house in Kingstown yet?"

"Yes, Miss Bannister," Anne replied and Will's heart sank. "The house was closed up the day after the funeral. Joan has gone home until she finds another position and, as it was so near to Christmas, Nurse Barton has taken temporary lodgings there, too."

"Where do your family live, Anne?" Will asked.

"Tripoli, Dr Fitzgerald. It's in the Liberties."

"I know it well. I'd like to call and speak with Nurse Barton."

"Ask for the Flanagans."

"I will. Thank you, Anne."

"You're welcome, Dr Fitzgerald."

"I'll go now, Eva," he said and they got to their feet. "Thank you, and I am sorry for spoiling—"

"Don't be sorry, Dr Fitzgerald," she replied. "If I'm honest, I always find St Stephen's Day rather dull and I am happy to have been of assistance."

"Thank you, Eva. I must cancel my surgery on the day of the funeral but I'll discuss it with you and Dr Powell tomorrow."

Hailing a cab on the South Circular Road, Will instructed the cabman to bring him to Tripoli. He got out halfway along the street, paid the fare and asked two boys playing marbles on the pavement for the Flanagans.

"The Flanagans live in a room on the second floor," the older of the two boys told him, pointing to a dilapidated tenement house directly across the street. "First door on the landing," he added and Will gave him a penny before crossing the street, taking off his hat and going into the hallway.

He climbed the rickety stairs and a girl aged about eighteen answered his knock.

"My name is Dr Will Fitzgerald," he began and she quickly invited him inside as a group of children ran squealing along the landing and down the stairs. "I'd like to speak with Nurse Barton if it's convenient," he continued, glancing around the room which was divided into living and sleeping quarters by a white sheet draped over a clothes line then at a boy of about ten seated at the head of a large and well-scrubbed kitchen table.

"I am Barbara Barton." A handsome dark-haired woman somewhere in her early-to-mid-forties and dressed in grey came out from behind the sheet. "Are you in need of a nurse?" she asked in a light Scottish accent.

"I'll take Michael next door so you can talk in private," the girl said and ushered the boy out onto the landing.

"Thank you, Joan," Nurse Barton replied and closed the door after them.

"Yes, I am in need of a nurse." Will shook her hand. "My name is Dr Will Fitzgerald and I am seeking a nurse for my wife's grandfather."

"Shall we sit down and I will tell you my history."

They sat opposite each other at the table and Nurse Barton clasped her hands in front of her.

"I was born in Edinburgh and I am an only child. My late father was a schoolmaster and he hoped I would follow him into teaching but I was fascinated with the stories which came back from the Crimea about Florence Nightingale so I trained to be a nurse at the training school she founded at St Thomas' Hospital in London."

"Why come to Ireland?" Will asked.

"My late mother was Irish," she explained. "I nursed her until she died, then I decided to try for a fresh start here in Ireland and I found a position as nurse to Mr Tyrrell, a bachelor solicitor who had suffered a cerebral haemorrhage. He died last week and the servants and I vacated the house on Christmas Eve. I was very lucky that Joan's parents agreed to give me temporary board and lodgings here. What is the nature of your grandfather-in-law's illness?" she inquired.

"Chronic lung disease," Will replied. "I have him inhaling pure oxygen but he has a few months left at best. His bed is now downstairs in the morning room but he is not confined to bed just yet, so a bath chair has been borrowed for him until one can be purchased."

"Is he married or is he a widower?"

"A widower – his wife died unexpectedly yesterday afternoon," Will told her. "And he wishes for her to be buried near to his home not far from Westport in Co Mayo. Once he returns to Co Mayo, he will not leave. So a condition of the position is that you would have to be agreeable with a move there."

"My mother was from Co Mayo," she said. "The town of Ballina."

"Mr Greene's home is called Greene Hall. There is a village nearby called Ballyglas but I know nothing of its size."

"You have never been there, Dr Fitzgerald?"

"No. But from what I have been told, the house is large. There are plenty of servants and my wife's mother intends to visit regularly. You would not be completely isolated."

"Where would be the nearest large town or railway station?"

"Westport," he replied and grimaced. "I'm afraid I have never been there either."

"Westport," she mused, got up and went behind the sheet, returning with a bundle of documents which she placed on the table.

"My baptism certificate, my school reports and my nursing certificate. Sadly, I don't have a letter of recommendation from an employer because, as I said, Mr Tyrrell died last week but I do have one from my mother's parish priest – he spent a great deal of time in our home while Mother was ill."

The recommendation was glowing and Will leafed through the certificates and reports until he came to a medical degree, a medical licence and a midwifery licence and his head jerked up in astonishment.

"You're also a doctor," he said and her jaw dropped. She had clearly not intended for him to see the degree and licences.

"Yes, I am. While I was a nursing student, I attended some classes with the medical students. I sat at the very back so I would not be seen. I was encouraged to continue my studies and so I nursed while studying privately and I obtained a certificate in anatomy and physiology. I continued my studies at the London School of Medicine for Women and at the Royal Free Hospital but I was awarded an M.D. in 1879 from the University of Bern in Switzerland. I then qualified as a Licentiate of the King and Queen's College of Physicians of Ireland here in Dublin and

I was registered with the General Medical Council."

"So why on earth are you not practising medicine?" he asked and her shoulders slumped.

"I had returned to the Royal Free Hospital and I stupidly entered into a relationship with a fellow doctor. Not only that, he was married and his father in-law-was one of the hospital's governors. So after only two months, I was dismissed with no letter of recommendation and told in no uncertain terms that women are not fit to practise medicine. But what I said to you before was the truth. My mother fell ill shortly after I was dismissed and, following her death, I decided to return to Ireland and make a fresh start here and I found the position as nurse to Mr Tyrrell in Kingstown."

"If it were my decision, I would offer you the position immediately," he said and her face lit up. "But," he continued and her face fell. "The final decision lies with Mr Greene."

"Of course, Dr Fitzgerald, and I would very much like to be considered for this position. When may I meet with Mr Greene so he may appraise me?"

"Eight o'clock tomorrow morning at number 7 Fitzwilliam Square," he replied. "I do apologise for the early hour but my surgery resumes at nine o'clock and I would rather yourself and Mr Greene met as soon as possible because he is already making plans to return to Co Mayo."

"I understand, Dr Fitzgerald. Eight o'clock it is."

"Will you practise medicine in the future?" he asked and she sighed.

"I would very much like to. I can only hope that, in time, attitudes to women doctors will change."

Will left the tenement house and put on his hat, deciding

to call to see Mrs Bell while he was nearby. He strolled along the street to the tenement house on Pimlico reflecting on how straightforward his six years at Trinity College had been in comparison to Barbara Barton's journey to becoming a doctor and he also hoped attitudes would change in time.

Mrs Bell opened the door to her rooms and stared at him in first shock and then relief. Then, to his surprise, she pushed him back out onto the landing.

"Come with me, Dr Fitzgerald," she said and, puzzled, he followed her to the top of the stairs. "I have Jimmy with me," she explained, turning to face him. "And I don't want him to hear this."

"What's happened?"

"Maura, Jimmy's mammy, died on Christmas Eve. Cancer of the breast."

Will closed his eyes for a moment. Jimmy Donnelly, his former messenger boy, had never known his father as he had died when Jimmy was a baby. Jimmy's mother had never remarried and, as far as Will knew, Maura's only living relative was a brother who had emigrated to New York many years ago.

"Dr Powell was very kind but there was nothing he could do. Jimmy will now live with me," Mrs Bell continued softly but firmly.

"Can you afford to have him live with you?" Will asked, hoping he wouldn't offend her.

"Jimmy needs to find work so, tomorrow, we're away to Guinness' to see about a job for him at the brewery as a stable lad. I'll find him something – we'll be grand. What brings you to these parts?"

"I think – I hope – I have just found a nurse for Mr

Greene. His wife died yesterday."

Mrs Bell was silent for a few seconds. "I'd be lying to you, Dr Fitzgerald, if I said I was sorry to hear that," she told him quietly.

"I know," he said. "Mrs Greene died still refusing to be reunited with both her children. Isobel and I had to sit Miles down yesterday evening and explain to him that his mother was dead and had not wanted to see him again and that his father is dying and does want to see him again."

"How did he react?" she asked.

"Angrily. He doesn't want to meet his father."

"Do you think he'll change his mind?" she added and Will grimaced.

"I honestly don't know and Mr Greene is bringing his wife back to Co Mayo to be buried in the next day or two and he won't be returning to Dublin."

"I can't blame Miles for being angry, Dr Fitzgerald."

"Neither can I," he replied. "But I don't want him to regret his decision later."

"How is Isobel?"

"Putting a brave face on it all. It was our first Christmas with Belle, Ben and John and instead of it being a wonderful day it was awful. What did you and Jimmy do yesterday? It must have been awful for you, too."

"We went to Mass and I cooked a chicken for the dinner. Despite the day that was in it, we had a lot of callers in the afternoon and evening. Maura was a good woman and well liked. She'll be missed," Mrs Bell finished sadly.

"When is the funeral?" he asked.

"The day after tomorrow at St Catherine's Church on Meath Street. I asked Dr Powell if Maura's coffin could lie downstairs in the surgery waiting room and he agreed. I didn't want it up here with Jimmy so upset. She'll be buried in Mount Jerome Cemetery."

"I'm sorry, Mrs Bell, but I don't think I can attend."

"I know you can't, you'll have Mrs Greene's funeral to go to."

"So I want to give you this." Delving into his trouser pocket, he took out all the coins. He had three shillings, a thrupenny bit and two pennies which weren't enough and he put them back. Opening his overcoat, Will pulled his wallet out of the inside pocket. Extracting a sovereign, he put it in her hand. "Towards the cost of the funeral."

"I can't take this." She put the gold coin back in his hand. "People have contributed towards it and—"

"Mrs Bell, please." He dropped the sovereign into the pocket of her white apron. "Let me contribute, too. Now, do you have a pen and ink and some notepaper?" he asked before she could protest again.

"I do. Why?"

"I'd like to write Jimmy a letter of recommendation for Guinness' Brewery," he said and her face broke into a wide smile.

"Bless you, Dr Fitzgerald. Come along inside."

The boy was sitting at the kitchen table and glanced up impassively as Will pulled out a chair and sat next to him.

"Mrs Bell has just told me about your mammy," he said softly. "I'm so sorry, Jimmy."

"How can a lump kill a person, Doctor?"

"The lump – the cancer – spreads to other parts of the body."

"It's horrible."

"Yes, it is. Thank you," he said as Mrs Bell placed a pen, a bottle of ink and a sheet of notepaper down in front of him. "Mrs Bell says you are going to see about a job in Guinness' tomorrow so I'm going to write you a letter of recommendation."

"A what?"

"It's when someone who knows you states that you are trustworthy and punctual and so on," he explained as both Jimmy and Mrs Bell watched while he dipped the nib into the ink and wrote:

30 Fitzwilliam Square
Dublin

To Whom It May Concern,
I have known James Donnelly for the past six years. During that time, I employed him as a messenger boy and I found him to be trustworthy and a good timekeeper and he was always well-mannered, tidy and willing.
I would have no hesitation in recommending James Donnelly for any position he may apply for.
William Fitzgerald M.D.

"There," he said, pushing the sheet of notepaper away. "Let the ink dry."

"What does it say?" Jimmy asked.

"That you're a good lad," Will replied, getting up from the table. "And I think Guinness' would be eejits not to employ you," he added with a wink and Jimmy responded with a smile. "I'll call again soon. The very best of luck tomorrow."

Mrs Bell went with him out onto the landing and squeezed his arm. "Thank you. That was the first time he smiled."

"I meant every word."

"I know you did. How are Ben, Belle and John?"

"Very well, thank you. Despite what happened, John enjoyed Christmas Day very much. The twins slept through it all but, as my father said, there will be fun and games next Christmas. Goodbye, Mrs Bell." He kissed her cheek then hurried down the stairs and out of the tenement house.

Isobel was admitted to number 55 at a quarter to eight in the morning. Nurse Barton was due at number 7 in fifteen minutes and, on Will's instructions, Isobel had to ensure Mrs Ellison did not call there and get in the way or, at worst, interfere. Her mother, James and Miles were on their way into the breakfast room so she followed them and joined James at the sideboard.

"I must leave for the office in less than an hour," he whispered.

"I'll take charge of Mother," she whispered back and he squeezed her hand in thanks.

"Would you like some coffee?" he offered in a normal tone, lifting the coffee pot.

"Yes, please," she replied, watched him pour and added milk and sugar.

"How long will the appraisal take, Isobel?" her mother asked and she picked up her cup and saucer before turning to face her.

"I don't know. Will said he would call if it had ended

before he has to leave for the practice house. We simply must be patient."

Leaving them to their meal, she brought her coffee into the morning room. To her surprise, she found Alfie sitting on the sofa, balancing a cup on one knee and a book on the other.

"Am I disturbing you?" she asked.

"No, not at all." He closed the book and put it on a side table. "I was determined to read something not medically-related over Christmas but events have conspired against me and I am only on page ten." Getting up, he carried his cup to the window. "I came back so Grandfather, Will and the prospective nurse could discuss matters in private."

"From what Will told me last night, the nurse sounds ideal," she said. "I just hope Grandfather likes her."

"So do I." He drained the cup and placed it on a saucer on the side table beside the book. "I doubt if there is time for Will to begin searching for another one."

Will was shown into the morning room at twenty minutes to nine and they both got up from the sofa.

"Where is everyone?" he asked her, glancing around the room.

"Still at breakfast. We didn't know how long you would be."

"Shall I fetch them?" Alfie offered and Will smiled and nodded. "I won't be long," he said as he went out.

"Your grandfather has engaged Nurse Barton," Will told her and she flung her arms around him in delight. "And I've just told her about Miles," he added, kissing her temple and they waited for the others to assemble in the room.

"Well, Will?" Mrs Ellison asked anxiously as they hurried

into the morning room a couple of minutes later and he motioned for her to sit down on the sofa.

"Firstly, Mr Greene has engaged Nurse Barbara Barton," he announced and they all exhaled an audible sigh of relief. "And she has returned to her lodgings to collect her trunk. Secondly, a telegram from Knox has just been delivered. Mrs Greene's funeral will take place at two o'clock tomorrow afternoon at Ballyglas Church of Ireland church with burial immediately afterwards in the adjoining graveyard."

"Two o'clock," Mrs Ellison repeated, nodding to herself.

"I had told Knox it would be impossible for Isobel and I to stay at Greene Hall overnight so the time has been arranged in order for us to travel to Ballyglas, attend the funeral and burial, and return to Dublin on the same day."

"It shall be a long day for you both," Mrs Ellison commented.

"It shall," Will replied. "But it is the only way Isobel and I can attend the funeral. Miles," he added. "There is something I need to ask you. Do you wish to travel to Ballyglas with us and attend your mother's funeral?"

Poor Miles looked startled as they all turned to him.

"I don't know... I know I should... but I am still so..." He tailed off and Isobel went to him and kissed his cheek.

"You have all of today to consider it," she told him. "I will come and see you this evening."

"Thank you."

"I won't be home for luncheon, Isobel," Will said and she turned to him. "Knox has requested the time of our arrival in order that the Greene Hall carriage can be sent to meet us at Westport Station so, as well as surgery and house calls, I must go to Broadstone Station and call to see Mr

Dalton and make preparations for tomorrow. I'll call here later and update you all," he told the others before kissing her forehead and leaving the room.

"I must go and purchase a bath chair," Alfie declared. "The one I borrowed needs to go back to Trinity College as soon as possible. James, may I share a cab with you as far as Westmoreland Street?" he asked as James kissed his wife's cheek.

"Of course, you may," he replied with a smile. "Good day to you, Isobel," he said and they went out to the hall.

"Will you and Miles come to number 30, Mother?" she asked and Miles' face lit up. "We'll bring young John and the twins out to the gardens." It will keep your mind off the funeral for a while, she added silently.

"That would be lovely, Isobel. I will ask May for my hat, cloak and gloves and Miles' overcoat and hat. I shall be with you in five minutes."

Will arrived back at number 30 just after four o'clock and came into the morning room still wearing his overcoat.

"I won't sit down," he said by way of a greeting as she closed and folded *The Irish Times* and put it to one side. "If I do, I won't get up again. I've been to Broadstone Station to confirm the times of the trains to and from Westport. I then called on Mr Dalton and a hearse will arrive at number 7 at half past six in the morning to convey Mrs Greene's coffin to the station in time for the first Westport train of the day."

"Just the hearse?" she queried, getting to her feet. "We shall need Mr Dalton's carriage, too."

"For us all to be comfortable and to carry all the trunks and a bath chair, we shall need two cabs as well as a carriage," Will replied. "So I have told Mr Dalton his carriage is not required. I'll engage George Millar and two of his brothers instead to bring us to Broadstone Station in the morning. Come with me now?" he asked, holding the door open for her. "And we'll call on Mrs Bell to see if Jimmy got the job in Guinness'."

"Is George Millar a wise choice?" she inquired, walking out to the hall. "He'll either be still drunk at that time of the morning or exceptionally hung-over."

"His wife is a matter-of-fact woman. If she thinks half past six in the morning is out of the question, she'll tell me."

"Very well," she conceded, lifting her coat down from the stand. "Grandmother's death notice has been published in *The Irish Times*."

"Yes, I saw it," he said. "Mr Dalton showed me a copy. As well as sending the death notice to the newspapers yesterday, Mr Dalton sent a telegram to Hill and Sons, a firm of undertakers in Westport, informing Mr Hill of Mrs Greene's death, that her funeral will be held in the next day or two and requesting that he convey Mrs Greene's coffin from Westport Station to Ballyglas," he continued, helping her with her coat. "Another telegram was sent today advising Mr Hill of the date and time of the funeral and of our arrival. I then returned to Broadstone Station and I purchased first class tickets for us all – including Miles in case he comes with us – and passage for Mrs Greene's coffin, the trunks and a bath chair in the guard's van. Afterwards, I called to Mr Dalton again and a telegram from Mr Hill had just been delivered confirming that his hearse and carriage would meet our train tomorrow."

"Did you reply to Knox's telegram?" she asked, putting on her hat.

"I did, telling him the time of our arrival so the Greene Hall carriage can also be sent to meet us at Westport Station. I also wrote to Dr Bourke informing him of Mrs Greene's death, Mr Greene's return to Greene Hall and that a nurse has been engaged. I made him aware of the state of Mr Greene's health and I requested that he call to Greene Hall as soon as possible. My surgery tomorrow has been cancelled and David will see my most urgent patients and carry out my most urgent house calls. And if there is anything else, I am too tired to think of it," he concluded with a wry smile, lifting his hat down from the stand and she reached up and kissed his lips before he opened the front door.

"Mother, Miles and I spent the morning with the children in the gardens," she said as they walked out of Fitzwilliam Square. "And watching young John, I couldn't help but think of poor Jimmy. How old is he now?"

"Almost twelve. He really should be in school – he's a bright lad – but he's had to earn whatever money he can to supplement what little his mother was earning selling second-hand clothes. If he could get a job in Guinness' and earn a regular wage, it would be wonderful for him – and for Mrs Bell."

They met a surprisingly sober but very pale George Millar in the stable to the rear of his rooms in a tenement house a few doors along from Mrs Bell's home on Pimlico.

"I've had the 'fluenza," he explained, touching his bowler hat to her. "Maggie's been looking after the horse for me. This is the first day I've been out 'o me bed in a week."

Has anyone had an enjoyable Christmas, she wondered.

"Are you well enough to work?" Will asked.

"As long as I don't eat or drink anything, I am."

"Even if you don't feel like eating, you still need to drink something or you'll become dehydrated. I'd advise boiled water."

"Water?" George looked incredulous and she smothered a laugh.

"Boiled water, George. Then, some warm milk. Then, some porridge. Start eating again gradually."

"I'll do that and, thank you, Dr Fitzgerald."

"Not at all," he replied. "My wife and I have called because we need to hire your cab, Albert's cab and Frank's carriage to take seven of us – possibly eight – to Broadstone Station early tomorrow morning. There will be a number of trunks and a bath chair to be transported as well. We're bringing my wife's grandmother back to Co Mayo to be buried."

"Oh, I'm sorry for your loss, Mrs Fitzgerald," he said, touching his hat to her again.

"Thank you, Mr Millar," she replied with a weak smile.

"Half past six at number 55 Fitzwilliam Square, please, George," Will instructed him. "And then on to number 7 Fitzwilliam Square. There will be a hearse outside number 7."

"We'll be there, Dr Fitzgerald."

"Thank you, George." Will shook his hand. "And, remember – boiled water."

Mrs Bell opened her door to them wearing the fine black bombazine dress and black hat adorned with white silk roses she had worn to their wedding. Relief was written all over her face as she welcomed them and invited them into the kitchen.

"We're just back from Guinness'," she said, pulling a pin

out of the hat and putting them both down on the table.

"Good news?" Will asked with a smile.

"Jimmy?" Mrs Bell prompted and they turned to the boy who looked very smart in a brown morning coat and short trousers, white shirt and black tie and well-polished black boots.

"I start on Monday."

"And it was all down to Dr Fitzgerald's letter of recommendation," Mrs Bell added.

"I'm sure it was all down to the management at Guinness' meeting a very bright lad." Will held out a hand and the boy shook it. "Well done, Jimmy."

"Thank you, Dr Fitzgerald."

"Congratulations, Jimmy," she said.

"Thank you, Mrs Fitzgerald. I'll go and fetch some water," he said, picking up an empty enamel bucket and going out onto the landing.

"He's relieved but nervous," Mrs Bell explained. "He knows his childhood – such as it was – is over now."

"May I go and speak to him?" she asked suddenly.

"Of course you can. Go down the stairs and turn to your left."

Isobel followed Mrs Bell's directions and went out to a large cobbled yard where Jimmy was at a water pump, pumping the handle up and down. Water sloshed into the bucket and she waited until it was full before speaking.

"I was very nervous before I started working as a parlourmaid," she said and the boy looked up at her in astonishment.

"A parlourmaid, Mrs Fitzgerald? When Mrs Bell told me you'd been a maid, I thought she meant a lady's maid."

"I was a lady's maid for a short time," she told him. "But, before that, I was a parlourmaid. I knew it would be very hard work – and it was – but I was happy and I was earning a regular wage. If there are any problems at the brewery please don't keep them to yourself, will you? If there is someone there you can speak to, then do. If there isn't – please speak to Mrs Bell."

"I will. You were really a parlourmaid, Mrs Fitzgerald?"

She nodded. "I could never have become a cook because I simply can't cook, but dusting and polishing and beating the rugs and setting and clearing the table and answering the front door – I've done all that – I'm not afraid of hard work. My husband and I have servants now but I would never ask any of them to do something I wouldn't be prepared to do myself. Except to cook, of course," she added, pulling a comical expression and Jimmy smiled sadly.

"Mammy was a good cook."

"What did she cook for you?"

"Boxty. It was lovely straight out of the frying pan with lots of butter melting on it."

"I haven't had boxty since I was a little girl. Our cook-housekeeper used to make it for my brother and I," she said, omitting the fact that her father had put a stop to it not wanting his children to be fed 'peasant food' made primarily from potatoes. "And, yes, it was delicious with butter melting on it. What else did your mammy cook for you?"

"Coddle," he replied immediately and she frowned. "It's a kind of a soup-stew with potatoes, bacon and sausages," he explained. "Mammy used to put onions in it, too. I miss her," he whispered, sitting down beside the bucket with his face in his hands.

Without hesitation, she sat on the cobbles, put an arm around him and the boy sobbed on her shoulder.

"Don't ever be ashamed to cry," she whispered. "She was your mammy and you will always love her and miss her. I'll tell you a little story," she continued and he raised his head. "The reason I'm wearing black is because my grandmother died on Christmas Day. But I only met her for the first time a few weeks ago so I hardly knew her. Now she is dead and I can't mourn her because I didn't know her well enough. You are so very lucky that you have so many good memories of your mammy."

"Is your mammy still alive?"

"Yes, she is but, like me, she is not a good cook. So, you are very lucky that your mammy cooked delicious meals for you."

"Do you have children?"

"My husband and I have twins – a boy and a girl – and my husband's nephew also lives with us. I'd like to cook for them, but it would have to be something very easy," she said and Jimmy smiled.

"There you are," Will called from the back door. "Mrs Bell needs the water to make a pot of tea."

"Jimmy was telling me about the delicious meals his mammy cooked for him," she said as Will came to them and helped her to her feet. "Boxty and coddle."

"Mrs Bell made coddle for me quite regularly," he said. "It was something she could leave to simmer on the range and it would be cooked and delicious by the time I would return home from my rounds. I don't think I've ever had boxty."

"I'll have to mention it to Mrs Dillon, then," she said, as

Will picked up the bucket and they went inside. "Because both Jimmy and I agree that hot boxty with butter melting on it is absolutely delicious."

They called to number 55 on their way home and were met by a grim-faced James in the morning room.

"Miles has told Martha and I that he does not wish to meet his father and is not coming to Co Mayo with us," he said. "Martha is disappointed and upset and has gone to her room but we must respect Miles' decision. Can we take you up on your offer of him staying at number 30 while we are away?"

"Of course," she replied. "I'll ask that a guest bedroom be prepared and Miles can keep young John company tomorrow. I don't particularly like the idea of placing him in the nursery but Florrie and Bridget will be on hand to supervise and I will ask Mrs Dillon to look in on them regularly, too."

"Is he in his room, James?" Will asked.

"Yes, he is. I think he is rather afraid of what you might say. Especially after Martha's reaction."

"We'll go upstairs and set his mind at rest," she said.

"Alfie has bought a second-hand bath chair," James added. "It has just been delivered and is in excellent condition for a second-hand one. Are we all set for tomorrow?"

"We are," Will replied before relating his toing and froing between Mr Dalton and Broadstone Station earlier in the day to the solicitor. "And George, Albert and Frank Millar will bring us to the station in the morning," he concluded.

"Thank you, Will," James said and shook his hand.

"Not at all," he replied, opening the door for her.

Miles was standing at his bedroom window and gave them a nervous little smile as they went in and Will closed the door.

"I'm staying here, Isobel," he said.

"James has told us. We're not angry—"

"But Martha is. She wants me to meet our father before he leaves. I will not."

"Mother is grieving for your mother. You did not know her and you are not grieving and that is not your fault," she assured him. "Mother, James and Alfie will be in Co Mayo for a few days but Will and I shall only be away for one day. We don't want you to be alone here for the few days so you shall stay at number 30 and you can spend tomorrow with young John, Belle and Ben and Florrie and Bridget. You could bring a book suitable for John and read to him?"

To her relief, Miles nodded. "I would like that very much."

"Good. One of us will call for you in the morning."

"We're not angry, Miles," Will told him. "So don't feel uneasy about your decision."

"I won't. Thank you for being so understanding."

Returning to the morning room, they updated James.

"Now Isobel and I must tell Mr Greene," Will finished and exchanged a grimace with James. "We shall see you in the morning."

A rather glum Ida admitted them to number 7, took Will's hat from him and hung it on the stand.

"Ida, my husband has told me you have been given a week's notice."

"Yes, Mrs Fitzgerald."

"Do you have a letter of recommendation?"

"No, I don't. Mr Knox said he would ask Mr Greene to write ones for all of us when he is settled back in Greene Hall but…"

I need one now, Isobel finished silently.

"Call to number 30 and I will write a letter of recommendation for you – and for any of the other servants who need one," she said and the young woman's face brightened.

"Thank you, Mrs Fitzgerald," Ida replied gratefully, turning as a dark-haired woman in her forties dressed in grey came down the stairs. "That is very kind of you."

"You're welcome."

"Just a moment, Ida," Will called after her as the maid went to open the morning room door. "We can manage, thank you."

Ida bobbed a curtsey and went down the steps to the servants' hall.

"Isobel," he said. "May I present Nurse Barbara Barton. Nurse Barton, may I present my wife, Isobel."

"I'm very pleased to meet you, Nurse Barton," Isobel said, shaking her hand.

"And I you, Mrs Fitzgerald."

"May we have a quick word with you before we join Mr Greene?" Will extended a hand and they walked along the hall to the breakfast room door. "I'm afraid Mr Greene's son, Miles, will not be accompanying us to Co Mayo tomorrow."

"Had they been reunited?" the nurse asked.

"No," she replied. "And I don't think they will ever meet again now."

They went into the morning room where Mr Greene was sitting up in the bed which had been placed in the alcove between the fireplace and the window. He folded the newspaper on his lap, took a breath of oxygen and waited expectantly for one of them to speak. Bracing herself, Isobel went to the bed and lifted one of his hands.

"There is no easy way to tell you this, Grandfather, but Miles will not be coming to Co Mayo with us tomorrow," she said and Mr Greene shook off her hand before glancing out of the window.

"Will Miles meet me before we leave?" he asked, despite knowing the answer.

"No, he won't," she told him quietly and Mr Greene nodded.

"Tilda and I should never have come to Dublin – I should never have insisted we come to Dublin."

"You were reunited with Mother."

"It was my dearest wish that I see Miles again before I die. Can you not persuade him?" Mr Greene inquired, turning back to her. "From what your husband tells me, Miles likes and trusts you very much."

"Miles has had time to consider," she said. "And I will not persuade him because strange as it may seem to you, Miles does have a mind of his own," she added and heard a sharp intake of breath from Nurse Barton.

Her grandfather pursed his lips and smiled humourlessly. "And he is stubborn. Please, look after him?" he asked the smile vanishing.

"We will," she replied and he gave her a firm nod of thanks. "Goodnight to you Grandfather, Nurse Barton." She went out to the hall with Will following her and squeezed her eyes shut for a moment. "My mother is never to know that Miles was the priority all along," she said as

Will reached for his hat and opened the front door for her.

"She won't."

"I think I shocked Nurse Barton," she murmured as they walked back to number 30.

"I think it will take a great deal more than you speaking your mind to shock Nurse Barton," he said, lifting her hand and kissing it.

"After dinner, we'll speak to the servants about Miles and kiss the children goodnight, then we'll go to bed. Tomorrow is going to be an extremely long day."

Chapter Five

They got up at five o'clock in the morning and while Will washed, shaved and dressed, Isobel expressed milk for the twins before washing and dressing and he followed her upstairs to the nursery. Having said goodbye to John the previous evening, they left the boy to sleep and kissed Belle and Ben.

"When I've eaten, I'll bring Mr Miles here," he told Florrie and Bridget. "Please remember what I said last night and supervise him at all times. Mr Miles is a grown man but he thinks like a fifteen-year-old boy."

"Yes, Dr Fitzgerald," Florrie replied.

Despite the early hour, they ate a hearty breakfast then Will went to the stand in the hall. Shrugging his overcoat on, he slipped a scarf around his neck and put a pair of gloves in the overcoat's pockets. Reaching for his hat, he left the house and hurried around the garden to number 55. Four trunks – one large and three small – stood near the front door and Alfie nodded a greeting as he came down the stairs with Miles behind him.

"Guess which trunk is Mother's?" he asked drolly and Will smiled. "Well, Miles, enjoy your stay at number 30 and

I shall see you again in a few days' time."

"I will," Miles replied, picking up one of the small trunks. "Thank you."

"Alfie, when the cabs and carriage arrive, make sure the bath chair is tied to the roof of George Millar's cab and the trunks are tied to the roofs of the other cab and the carriage and to the carriage's luggage rack," Will said and Alfie gave him a puzzled stare.

"Why?"

"The bath chair will slow George down a bit," he explained and Alfie replied with a grin.

"I chose *Gulliver's Travels*," Miles told Will as they walked to number 30.

"By Jonathan Swift."

"Yes."

"John will enjoy you reading it to him very much. My mother read it to my brother and I when we were small."

"Did your father not read to you and your brother?" Miles asked.

"No," he realised after a short pause. "He never did."

"Miles." Isobel greeted them in the hall and kissed her uncle's cheek. "Young John is still asleep. He gets up at eight o'clock and he has a soft boiled egg and toast 'soldiers' for his breakfast. A pot of tea will also be brought up to the nursery for Florrie, Bridget and yourself."

"I won't wake him, I promise."

"Thank you, Miles," Will replied. "See you sometime late this evening."

Isobel escorted Miles upstairs and returned a few minutes later wearing her small black tricorn hat, her new black woollen three-quarter length coat and a long black woollen scarf wound around her neck.

"We're dressed for the North Pole but I still hope we're going to be warm enough." Pulling on some black gloves, she gave him a little smile. "I'm ready. Let's get this day over and done with."

The hearse, cabs and carriage were stopping outside number 7 as they approached. Will passed his hat to Isobel and she joined her mother, James and Alfie at the bottom of the steps while he went into the hall. Nurse Barton and Mr Greene were standing at the coffin and Mr Greene bent and kissed it before it was borne outside to the hearse.

Will picked up the oxygen cylinder, tube and face mask and left the house as Nurse Barton helped Mr Greene down the steps and into the carriage. She got in and sat beside him and Will stood the oxygen cylinder at her feet and passed her the face mask. Mr and Mrs Greene and Nurse Barton's large trunks were then carried out of the house and one was tied to the carriage's luggage rack and the other two were tied to the roof.

Lastly, the bath chair was wheeled out and Alfie, Albert and Frank lifted it onto the roof of George's cab and held on to it while George threw ropes over the chair and secured it in place. The bath chair would receive some strange looks so Will tapped James' arm.

"You and Martha go in the carriage with Nurse Barton and Mr Greene. Isobel and I will go in one cab and Alfie will go in the other."

"Thank you, Will."

He waited for them all to get in before nodding to the driver of the hearse. He climbed into the cab, closed the door and the procession left Fitzwilliam Square.

At Broadstone Station, the coffin was carried straight to the guard's van while the bath chair and six trunks were untied and lifted down from the cabs and carriage. Mr Greene was wheeled along the platform to the first class carriage, helped into a compartment and the bath chair and trunks were stored next to the coffin.

"Thank you." Will paid George, Albert and Frank before tipping the three men plus the hearse driver generously. "How are you getting on with the boiled water, George?"

"Well enough, Dr Fitzgerald. I think I'll try milk tomorrow. Good morning to you, and thank you."

To Will's relief, their compartment was warm and he sat down between Isobel and Alfie. Martha gave a little cry as the train juddered and began to move and Will exchanged a weary glance with Isobel. This was going to be a long journey.

Mr Greene didn't speak, despite being asked continuously if he were comfortable. The train crossed the River Shannon at Athlone and as they travelled further into Connaught, Will stared out of the window in dismay as dawn broke and it began to pour with rain.

When the train pulled into Westport Station it was still raining. Will and Alfie carried the coffin to the hearse with Isobel and her mother following them while James and the station porter dealt with the bath chair and six trunks. As Alfie returned to the train to assist Nurse Barton with Mr Greene, Will saw to his shock that only one carriage had come for them.

"My wife and I are returning to Dublin immediately after the burial," he informed the coachman, as he helped Isobel and her mother inside before having to adjust his hat so the rainwater dripped from the brim down his back rather than in front of his face and down his chest. "We were expecting two carriages. Can another carriage be sent to the church to bring us back here, please?"

"This is the only carriage at Greene Hall, sir, and these are the only two horses."

"Is there someone else who could bring my wife and I back here?" he added, glancing at a man with a horse and trap, the only other vehicle waiting outside the station. "We were expecting Mr Hill's carriage, too," he continued, turning to the undertaker who was closing the door of his hearse.

"Mr Hill's carriage is away for repairs, sir."

"Is there anyone in Ballyglas, then?" Will inquired, not believing him for a second.

"There's no-one in the village with a vehicle to hire, sir."

The coachman was being deliberately unhelpful and Will fought to control his temper.

"Right, well, we'll hire the man and his trap here, then," he said and went to point to them, only to see the horse and trap trotting away.

Beg someone at the funeral to bring you both back here, he told himself as Nurse Barton approached wheeling the bath chair with Alfie behind her carrying the oxygen cylinder, tube and face mask. Both the coachman and the undertaker stared at the bath chair in consternation. Neither had any rope so while Mr Greene was helped into the carriage, Will went back onto the platform and purchased two lengths of rope from the station master.

Three of the large trunks were tied to the carriage's luggage rack and the fourth was handed inside. Alfie then clambered onto the roof and as the coachman and undertaker simply stood back and watched, Will, James and the porter passed the bath chair up to him. The chair was covered with some Hessian sacks which would provide a little shelter from the rain and it was secured to the roof with the remaining rope.

"I'm terribly sorry my carriage is not available today, Dr Fitzgerald, it needs new springs," Mr Hill explained to Will who forced a smile. "I'll ask someone to bring you and your wife back here, don't you worry."

As long as we're not carried here in the back of the blasted hearse, I don't care who brings us, Will thought. He nodded his thanks to the undertaker who returned to the hearse and he tipped the porter as Alfie got down from the roof and followed the coachman up to his seat. Will passed one of the two small trunks to Alfie to hold on his lap before opening the carriage door. James, Nurse Barton, Mr Greene, Isobel and Martha plus the oxygen cylinder were squeezed inside with Nurse Barton's trunk on hers and James' laps and Will gestured to the coachman's seat.

"Alfie is sitting up top here and I'll sit alongside Mr Hill on the hearse," he said and closed the door.

He handed the second small trunk to the undertaker, climbed up to the seat and sat beside him. Quickly pulling his gloves on, he took the trunk back from Mr Hill and balanced it on his knees. The hearse and carriage set off through the picturesque town and out into the countryside which looked as sodden as he felt. Some low-lying parts of the road were flooded and the hearse and the carriage were forced to pass through the water at a walking pace. Will squinted up at the grey sky as the rain continued to beat down. He couldn't get at his pocket watch but he didn't need it to tell him this was taking far longer than he had anticipated.

What seemed like an age passed in silence until Mr Hill cleared his throat as the hearse and carriage entered a village.

"This is Ballyglas," he said simply.

Single-storey thatched dwellings stood on each side of the wide street except for one two-storey building with a slate roof and *J. Healy* written above the door. It was possibly the post office, a shop or a public house. Although Will reflected, it could well be all three together as some men and women came out to watch the small procession, blessing themselves as the hearse went past.

The hearse and carriage halted at a plain church with a tall spire just outside the village. The mourners were waiting for them, lined up in the rain along the gravel path which ran from the road up to the church door and Will rolled his eyes. Couldn't they have waited inside? The funeral hadn't even begun and he was wet, cold and starting to get very irritated.

Mr Greene, accompanied by Nurse Barton holding the oxygen cylinder and face mask and with Isobel and her mother following them greeted each person individually while Will, Alfie, James and the three other pallbearers stood at the rear of the hearse. Why can't Mr Greene do this afterwards so Isobel and I can leave, Will raged and, to pass the time, he approached the undertaker.

"Mr Hill, could you please inquire if any of the mourners would be willing to take my wife and I back to Westport?" he asked, pointing to the four carriages and at least ten horses and traps standing on both sides of the road. "We must catch the last train of the day back to Dublin."

"I'll certainly ask for you, Dr Fitzgerald."

"Thank you."

When, finally, Mr Greene and the ladies went into the church, the coffin was carried inside. Will sat in the front pew beside Isobel, reached for her hand and squeezed it.

"You're freezing," she whispered during the first hymn. "And I thought I was cold."

"The sooner we are back on the train to Dublin the better."

By the time the pallbearers carried the coffin out of the church and across the soggy graveyard, dusk was falling and Will had lost all contact with his feet. The Greene family graves were separated from the rest of the graveyard by a cast iron fence and gate. The coffin was placed beside the open grave which had a couple of inches of muddy water in the bottom and Will went and stood between Isobel and Alfie.

As the coffin was being lowered into the grave, Isobel suddenly grabbed his hand and he looked at the headstone she was nodding to.

IN LOVING MEMORY OF
MILES WALKER GREENE
SON OF LEWIS AND MATILDA GREENE
OF GREENE HALL
DIED 12th FEBRUARY 1836
AGED 1 YEAR

Good God, it was the grave Martha had mentioned. Had she seen it? Leaning slightly forward, he peered along the line but Isobel's mother was sobbing into a sodden handkerchief.

Straightening up again, he felt Isobel's hand slip from his. She covered her face with both hands and he quickly put an arm around her as she rested her head against his shoulder.

"Take me home," she whispered. "I want to go home now."

"We're going home," he replied softly as Alfie nudged him. The other mourners were beginning to stare but he simply stared back stony-faced and their attention quickly returned to the coffin. "We're going home," he repeated and she nodded.

"Isobel?" Alfie asked as the burial service ended and the mourners began to leave the graveside. "What is it?"

"Look." She gestured to the headstone and Alfie stared at it in disbelief. "I overheard two women talking as I went into the church. 'Mrs Greene is with her son now, God love her'." She shook her head in clear disgust. "Someone needs to take a sledgehammer to that bloody awful thing."

"Let me go and speak to Mr Hill again," Will said. "And see who has agreed to take us back to Westport."

The undertaker was standing at the rear of the hearse and grimaced as Will approached.

"I'm sorry, Dr Fitzgerald, but no-one is travelling to Westport today."

"I am willing to compensate them for their time," Will assured him.

"That's very good of you, but no-one is travelling to Westport today."

"The coachman told me there was no-one in Ballyglas with a vehicle to hire. Was he telling me the truth?"

"Partly," Mr Hill replied, irritating Will even more. "There is a man in the village with a horse and outside car for hire but he will not hire them to you, Dr Fitzgerald."

"Because of my connection to the Greenes?" Will demanded. "Because the Greenes are not liked?"

"Yes, Dr Fitzgerald."

"All these 'mourners' are here simply because they feel they have to be, aren't they? That's why they all lined up outside the church so Mr Greene could see and greet each and every one of them and know they had attended the funeral."

"That is correct. If there were only one of you, I'd carry you up top on the hearse again, but…" The undertaker tailed off and gave Isobel, standing at the graveyard gate with Alfie, a sympathetic smile. "Stay at Greene Hall tonight, Dr Fitzgerald, and Mulloy will bring you to Westport in good time for the first train in the morning."

"Oh, will he?" Will's patience finally gave way. "I have to take surgery in Dublin in the morning – I—"

"Even if someone were to bring you now, with the weather and the state of the roads and that it will be dark soon, by the time you arrive in Westport, you will have missed the last train," Mr Hill interrupted and Will swore under his breath as he realised the other man was right. "Mulloy will bring you to the station in the morning."

"Where is the nearest telegraph office, Mr Hill? If I am to be forced to miss surgery, I must inform a colleague."

"The nearest telegraph office is in Westport," the undertaker replied and Will exhaled a humourless laugh. "My advice to you, Dr Fitzgerald, is to stay at Greene Hall tonight and return to Dublin in the morning – all of you."

Will returned to Isobel and Alfie and brought them a little way up the road away from the village out of anyone else's hearing.

"We're going to miss the train," he said and, wide-eyed, Isobel clapped a hand to her mouth. "No-one will take us to Westport and no-one will hire a vehicle to us. We are all hated here – guilty by our association to Mr and Mrs Greene. Mr Hill has advised all of us to stay at Greene Hall tonight and return to Dublin in the morning."

"Will?" James called and Will beckoned the solicitor to come to them, repeating what he had just said. "We are not staying at Greene Hall – not if we are hated this much," James stated firmly. "I shall tell Mr Greene and instruct the coachman and undertaker to take us all back to Westport. We shall spend the night in a hotel there."

"Ben and Belle don't have enough milk," Isobel whimpered as James walked away.

"Powdered milk will suffice for tonight," he said.

"It will have to suffice because we are stranded in this awful – awful place – and now it's getting dark – and what about young John and Miles?"

"Florrie and Bridget and Mrs Dillon will cope," he assured her as the three of them jumped, hearing raised voices.

"Don't be a bloody fool," James was shouting at his father-in-law. "Don't you remember what happened to the Earl of Leitrim?" he demanded. "He was shot dead," he added and Isobel's mother burst into tears.

"Christ," Will whispered and they hurried back along the road to the graveyard gate.

"This bloody fool won't come with us," James roared at them then turned back to Mr Greene. "I've been polite up to now – far too bloody polite – but this is too much. I have tolerated you ruining the wedding day – I have tolerated your wife refusing to be reunited with mine – I have tolerated the infernal journey here – and this atrocious weather – but this is too much. You are returning to Dublin with us and that is final – I am not having your murder by a Land Leaguer on my conscience."

"No," Mr Greene replied quietly yet firmly. "I want to die in the house I was born in. I have earned the hatred of my son – my tenantry's hatred for me is nothing compared to that. If one of them shoots me – so be it. Either way, I will be with Tilda soon."

James threw Will a furious yet helpless glance and Will nodded wearily before turning away to speak to the undertaker. They were going to Greene Hall.

It was almost dark and still pouring with rain when the hearse and carriage stopped outside Greene Hall. Will got down from the hearse, took the small trunk from Mr Hill and put it on the gravel drive.

"Won't you come inside?" he asked the undertaker.

"I must return to Westport, Dr Fitzgerald. I have a funeral in the morning."

"Thank you for your assistance today, Mr Hill," he said, reaching up and shaking his hand.

"Not at all, Dr Fitzgerald, and I am sorry for this inconvenience."

The hearse pulled away down the drive and Will glanced up at the three-storey house while Alfie and Mulloy climbed down from the carriage coachman's seat. The front door opened and two men hurried down the steps, one carrying an oil lamp and an umbrella.

"Knox." Will greeted the butler as civilly as he could and nodded to the footman. "I'm afraid my wife and I have been forced to miss the last train," he said, opening the carriage door and accepting Nurse Barton's trunk from James and placing it beside the small trunk.

"I'm sorry to hear that, Dr Fitzgerald. Two rooms will be prepared for you."

"We don't need two rooms, Knox," Isobel called as she got out on the other side of the carriage and assisted her mother. "One room will be enough, thank you."

"One room, Mrs Fitzgerald," the butler confirmed and Isobel followed her mother inside. "Leave the trunks, Dr Fitzgerald. Seamus and Mulloy will see to them."

"Thank you," he said gratefully. "I would like a word with you in private, Knox," he added as James and Nurse Barton got out. "Once we are all settled."

"Of course, Dr Fitzgerald."

"Oh, and we have acquired a bath chair for Mr Greene. It is on the roof of the carriage and is wet through."

"The fire has been lit in the hall. The bath chair can be stood in front of it to dry."

"Thank you. Go on inside with Isobel and Martha," he said to James as Knox hurried back into the house. "I'll assist Nurse Barton and Alfie with Mr Greene."

Mr Greene was helped out of the carriage and with Will and Alfie each holding an arm and Nurse Barton bringing up the rear carrying the oxygen cylinder, tube and face mask, Mr Greene was guided slowly up the steps and into a square high-ceilinged entrance hall.

"I thought I would never set foot inside this house again," Martha said, pulling off her gloves and laying them on a round table then gazing around the hall as if she could not quite believe her eyes.

"Mr Greene's library has been prepared for him and a bed and nightclothes carried downstairs, Dr Fitzgerald," the butler said, taking Will's hat and then Alfie's before opening a door to the left of a large sandstone chimney piece. "Dinner will be served in half an hour and a room will be prepared for yourself and Mrs Fitzgerald."

"Thank you, Knox," he replied.

The library was small with only one outside wall and would be easily kept warm. Mr Greene was helped to undress and dressed in a nightshirt and dressing gown. He got into the single bed which had been placed in a space possibly once occupied by a writing desk along the wall opposite the fireplace. The oxygen cylinder was stood on the floor beside the bed and bedside table and Mr Greene accepted the face mask from Nurse Barton and inhaled as deeply as he could.

"It is wonderful to be home," he said, lowering the face mask and peering around the room at the floor-to-ceiling bookcases laden with leather-bound volumes. "Let me rest now before dinner."

"I'll ask that your dinner be brought here to you on a tray," Nurse Barton told him carrying a large oil lamp from a side table to the bedside table and he nodded.

"Very well. Go – all of you – and change your clothes."

They went out to the hall and as Will and Alfie peeled off their heavy, saturated overcoats, Will could hear shouts and a door slamming upstairs. James had evidently just told his wife that, whether she liked it or not, they were returning to Dublin first thing in the morning and they were leaving her father behind.

"We all need to discuss our stay here – in private – and

before dinner, if possible," Will said. "That includes you, Nurse Barton," he added, lowering his voice as two maids, one blonde, one dark-haired, approached and bobbed a quick curtsey.

"May I take your hat and cloak, madam, and your overcoats, sirs, and Grainné will show you to your rooms," the dark-haired maid said.

"Thank you," Will replied and he and Alfie waited for Nurse Barton to take off her black hat and unbutton her black cloak and hand them over before passing their overcoats and scarves to the maid.

"My name is Nurse Barton," she informed the maid. "Might I speak to the cook regarding Mr Greene's meals?"

"Of course, Nurse Barton," the maid replied and extended a hand to a green baize door at the far end of the inner hall. "Please, come with me."

"Thank you," she replied and they left the hall.

Will and Alfie followed Grainné up the stairs and she showed Will into the first bedroom on the right. The room was lit by a single oil lamp on one of the bedside tables and the furniture was large, plain, dark mahogany which only added to the gloomy atmosphere. Isobel was standing in front of a fire which had only just been lit, hugging herself in an effort to keep warm.

"Are you wet through?" she asked as he opened the door a couple of inches and saw Alfie being shown into the bedroom opposite.

"Yes, and so is Alfie," he replied, closing the door then lifting a chair from a corner of the room and standing it beside her with its back to the fire. Slipping his damp frock coat off, he hung it over the back. "What about you?"

"No, only my hat, scarf and coat are wet but I wasn't out in the rain for as long as you. I absolutely hate being stranded here," she said, walking to the window and pulling the curtain aside.

"Isobel – don't." He quickly dragged her away and she grabbed his shoulders, staring up at him in astonishment.

"Are we in danger, here, Will?"

"No, I don't believe we are, but we are in a landlord's house – a landlord who is hated for miles around – so we must be cautious." She nodded and he put his arms around her. "I'm sorry," he murmured into her hair. "This is awful. We should never have come to Co Mayo. Poor James has just told your mother she is only staying one night and we are returning to Dublin without her father."

"What about Nurse Barton?"

"It is to be left entirely up to her whether she wishes to stay here and I won't think any less of her if she chooses not to," he said, hearing a knock at the door. "Yes?" he called and James came in carrying a pair of shoes and some clothes.

"I hope these fit you, Will," James said, laying the shoes, a nightshirt, tailcoat, waistcoat, trousers, shirt, collar, white tie, socks and drawers on the double bed. "Alfie and I have only one change of clothes with us."

"Thank you, James."

"Not at all. Alfie is changing out of his wet clothes, too. We shall see you downstairs shortly," he said, went out and closed the door after him.

Will got changed while Isobel stood the metal spark guard and his shoes in front of the fire, draped his damp clothes on some coat hangers from the wardrobe and hung them from the mantelpiece to dry. James was a slighter man than Will and the shirt and collar, waistcoat and tailcoat were a little tight but the clothes were dry and he gave her a satisfied smile.

"Let's go downstairs," he said.

They joined Alfie and Nurse Barton in the huge drawing room and a few minutes later, the Ellisons came in. Martha's eyes were red and puffy but she was calm as she sat down on one of two sofas upholstered in russet coloured velvet.

"I believe it would be best for us all to leave here first thing in the morning," Will began. "But as Mr Greene refuses to leave, I have a question for Nurse Barton. Do you wish to return to Dublin with us or remain here at Greene Hall?"

"I wish to stay with Mr Greene, Dr Fitzgerald," she replied firmly.

"I must mention this to you, Nurse Barton, Mr Greene is not liked here and neither was his wife."

"I understand that Dr Fitzgerald, and I am grateful for your concern but I still wish to stay here with Mr Greene. I can ride – both side-saddle and astride – and I can drive a horse and trap so the unwillingness of the coachman or – indeed, anyone here – will not prevent me from travelling to Ballyglas or further afield."

"Are you absolutely sure?" Will asked, having to be certain.

"I am. I shall write to you with weekly reports on Mr Greene's health and post the reports in Ballyglas myself on my afternoon off. My mother was a Mayo woman," she said, glancing at Martha. "She was very resourceful. I am resourceful, too."

Will couldn't help but smile. "Thank you, Nurse Barton."

"If there is anything you need and which you cannot buy in either Ballyglas or Westport, add it in a separate note to me and tell me where to send it to if there are difficulties with the post reaching here," Isobel told her and she nodded.

"I shall, Mrs Fitzgerald, thank you."

"Good," Isobel said as the door opened and the butler came in.

"Dinner is served and two trays have been brought to the library for Mr Greene and Nurse Barton."

"Thank you, Mr Knox," the nurse replied.

"Come here to the drawing room when Mr Greene is asleep," Will told her.

"I shall, thank you."

The meal of vegetable soup, followed by roast pork with potatoes, cabbage and carrots and a dessert of sherry trifle was delicious and when Isobel and her mother returned to the drawing room, Will sat back in his seat and drained his glass of wine.

"I'm exhausted, furious, frustrated but – thankfully – dry," he said and Alfie lifted his glass in agreement.

"I must apologise to Mr Greene." James poured himself some port. "I don't lose my temper often but this afternoon I was furious, too."

"I need to speak to Knox," Will said, getting up from the dining table and ringing the bell. "Before I'm too exhausted to think coherently. Excuse me," he added and left the dining room.

He gazed up at the exquisite rococo plasterwork panels of swirling foliage which decorated the walls of the inner hall then at the heavy green velvet curtains which hung in the archway which led to the entrance hall. The servants had done their best but nothing could disguise the faded grandeur in the house. The folds of the curtains exposed to daylight were several shades lighter and where the curtains touched the stone flagged floor, the edges were frayed.

"You rang, Dr Fitzgerald?" The butler approached and halted at the foot of the stairs.

"Why did you not warn me as to the level of animosity my family and I would be subjected to before we travelled here?" Will asked.

"I assumed you knew what to expect, Dr Fitzgerald," Knox replied. "Mr Parnell's policy of social ostracism has been reported on in the newspapers at great length and in great detail."

"Those reports detailed the events on the Earl of Erne's estate at Lough Mask – his land agent, Captain Boycott, leaving as a result of being ostracised because he refused to lower rents and was carrying out evictions – there were no reports of anything similar occurring in this locality. Is the Land League now targeting Mr Greene, his land agent and anyone associated with the Greene Hall estate?"

"Yes, it is, but I have made it known Mr Greene is dying so the ostracism will not be to the same extent as on the Earl of Erne's estate. When you return to Dublin we will all live very quietly here and we shall simply have to endure certain minor inconveniences."

"I can only hope they are minor." Will gave him a grim smile. "Because the events of today may seem trivial but my wife and I have very young children who need our care and I shall not be able to take surgery in the morning so missing our train is a rather large inconvenience. The coachman didn't shun us, exactly, but he could not have been more unhelpful. And I don't believe for one minute that Mr Hill's carriage is away for repairs."

"Mulloy has to tread very carefully, Dr Fitzgerald. He has to show the Land League he is in favour of abolishing landlordism. He also has a wife and eight children to support. Being unhelpful – and publically unhelpful to you – was the only way he knew how. The same applies to Mr Hill. You will catch the morning train to Dublin, Dr Fitzgerald, I can assure you of that."

I shall believe it when I am seated on the train, Will told himself but nodded to placate the butler.

"Nurse Barton shall remain here with Mr Greene," Will said. "She will post a weekly report on the state of Mr Greene's health to me. If you believe she should not travel to Ballyglas alone each week, please have the footman accompany her."

"I shall accompany Nurse Barton to Ballyglas – or to Westport – if need be."

"Thank you. I have informed Dr Bourke that Mr Greene is returning from Dublin and that a nurse has been engaged and I requested that he call here. Mr Greene has only months to live, those months must be made as comfortable for him as possible."

"They will be, Dr Fitzgerald," Knox replied as the library door opened, Nurse Barton came out and closed it quietly behind her.

"Oh." She jumped, seeing them standing at the stairs.

"Thank you, Knox." Will shook the butler's hand then smiled at her. "May I speak with you before you go to the drawing room?"

"Yes, of course," she said and he waited for Knox to leave them before continuing.

"Has Mr Greene settled into his library-come-bedroom?"

"He has," she replied. "He told me it is the cosiest room in the house and it is true. He did not quite finish his meal – the portions were a little too large – I must speak with Mrs Cleary, the cook, again and explain that Mr Greene's appetite is now very small."

"Mrs Ellison will want to be here in Mr Greene's final days and then attend his funeral. If the Land League campaign – no matter how intense or lenient it is – has not abated in this locality, please inform me and she will not travel here."

"I shall."

"And if you wish to return to Dublin, you are most welcome to stay at number 30 until you find another position."

"That is extremely kind of you, Dr Fitzgerald, thank you."

"Not at all. Would you send my wife out here, please, then join the gentlemen in the dining room? I'm afraid my wife must break the news to her mother that it is likely once she leaves here tomorrow, she will not see her father again – alive or dead."

Five minutes later, Isobel returned to the drawing room and fought to hide a grimace as Mrs Ellison looked at her expectantly.

"Mother, when we leave for Dublin in the morning, there is a high probability you will not come back here," she began at once.

"Until…" Mrs Ellison tailed off, unable to put her father's impending death into words.

"No," she said softly but firmly. "Unless the Land League is no longer active in this locality, you cannot return here to be with Grandfather when he dies nor attend his funeral. You must not draw attention to the estate and make matters even more difficult for, not just its servants, but everyone who lives or works on it. Tomorrow, you will need to say goodbye to him for the last time."

"No." It came out in a squeak. "We have just been reunited – I refuse to completely abandon him now."

"Mother, you must not come back here with matters the way they are."

"We should never have come here."

"No, we shouldn't have but we are here and we must deal with the consequences. I am sorry," she said, sitting down beside her on the sofa and holding her hands as her mother cried. "I was always curious about the house you were born and grew up in and, despite the circumstances, I am glad I have now seen it."

"I called it my prison." Her mother gave her a wobbly smile, pulled a handkerchief from her sleeve and dried her eyes. "But I was happy here, despite being cut off from the rest of the world. I was ten years old when the Great Famine began and I was utterly oblivious to the people dying of starvation, being evicted from their homes and land, leaving the estate forever – just beyond those trees." She made a vague gesture towards the front of the house. "Just as I was utterly oblivious to the fact that my brother – my twin – was alive and locked away in a hospital for the insane. Little wonder I ran away to marry the very first man who turned my head."

"But now you are married to James and he loves you very much."

"Yes, he does, but he was so angry today, Isobel."

"So was Will. So was I. We were wet and cold and we were – and are – worried about the children and about Miles."

"You have extremely competent nursery maids."

But I should be in the nursery now, Isobel raged silently, feeding my babies and kissing young John goodnight.

"Yes, we do," she managed to reply calmly. "We're very lucky. And Will was very fortunate to find Nurse Barton. She will provide your father with exemplary care but tomorrow morning you must say goodbye to him."

"He is my father... we lost so much time... I wanted him to tell you about his parents and Mother's parents... Now, he never will. Look up there on the mantelpiece."

Isobel got up and stood on the hearth rug. On the mantelpiece were three photographs. The first was of her grandparents standing unsmiling and ramrod-straight, taken in the very early days of photography. The second was of an elderly woman with snow-white hair, while the third photograph made her gasp. If it wasn't for the army uniform, clean-shaven face and shorter hair, the man could have been Miles.

"Who is this?" she asked, pointing to him and Mrs Ellison looked past her.

"My mother's younger brother, Alexander Walker. Goodness, how like Miles, he is. That photograph was taken in London just before he departed for the Crimea. He did not return. Beside him is your grandfather's mother on the occasion of her eightieth birthday. My maternal grandparents refused to be photographed but Eleanor was fearless. That is her aged twenty-one."

Her mother motioned to the chimney breast and Isobel glanced up at a portrait of her great-grandmother. She clapped a hand to her mouth as brown eyes which could have been her own stared down at her. Little wonder her grandfather's eyes had widened when he saw her for the first time in St Peter's Church. Eleanor's hair was auburn but those eyes...

"She was a widow for fifty years and lived to the age of ninety-one," Mrs Ellison continued.

"Fifty years?" Isobel repeated.

"Her husband, Henry, died of consumption aged forty-five," her mother explained. "Oh, there are so many stories you should know."

"When we return home, write them all down so they are not forgotten," she said and Mrs Ellison nodded.

"This house is not yet a century old but coming back here, it seems far older than that. Everything appears faded... paler... diminished... it was all so very bright and vibrant when I was young. It is as if my parents simply did not care anymore... both their children were gone... What will happen to this house... when the time comes..?"

"I don't know, but I am sure Grandfather has made a will."

"They are our ancestors," her mother went on, pointing to the painting and photographs. "I don't want their faces – their history – to disappear or—" she shuddered, "for people to come into this house and destroy them all out of envy and spite."

"I shall mention it to James and he will discuss with Knox the possibility of hiding them all somewhere."

"I thought this would be the first of many visits," Mrs

Ellison said with a sad little smile.

"Let me speak to James and then you can bring me on – not quite a candle-lit tour of the house – but a lamp-lit one. Yes?"

"Yes."

"I won't be long." Isobel went out to the entrance hall, finding Will, Alfie and James peering up at a portrait of a gentleman in a grey wig hanging above the sandstone chimney piece. "Mother is afraid people will come into the house and destroy the paintings and photographs when Grandfather dies. I am rather afraid that may happen before then. Can the portraits be taken down and hidden and the landscape paintings I saw upstairs hung in their place?"

"Yes, that's a good idea," Will replied.

"I'll go and ask Knox for a ladder," Alfie said and left the hall.

"How is your mother?" James asked.

"Upset. She assumed this would be the first of many visits here. Is Nurse Barton with my grandfather?"

"Yes, she is."

"Thank you." Isobel went to the library door, knocked lightly and the nurse opened it. "Is my grandfather awake?" she asked and Nurse Barton nodded and held the door open for her. "Thank you. Mother has been showing me the photographs and the portrait in the drawing room," she told Mr Greene as she went into the warm room and he smiled.

"You have your great-grandmother's eyes."

"I saw that," she replied, sitting on the edge of the bed. "Mother and I are worried that the photographs and the portraits may be damaged—"

"Or looted?"

"Yes. We are going to take the portraits down and replace them with landscapes. Where would you recommend we hide them and the photographs?"

"You should bring them all back to Dublin. What purpose do they serve here now?"

The thought of removing them all from the house made her feel very uneasy. "If we did that, I would feel as if we were the ones looting them."

"Please take them," he begged, squeezing her hands tightly. "I need to know they are all in a safe place."

"Very well."

"Good. There are ten portraits in the house. Two are small and will fit with all the photographs in a trunk – ask Knox to find one for you. I also want you to take all your grandmother's jewellery. Knox will show you where the jewellery cases are. Nothing can make you more beautiful than you already are, Isobel, but promise me you will wear the jewels?"

"I promise."

"Good. Now, send your mother here to me."

"Before I do, there is something I need to show you. Let me fetch it." She went to the drawing room, lifted the photograph of Alexander Walker down from the mantelpiece and returned to the library. "Mother told me he was Grandmother's brother," she said, placing the photograph in his hands.

"His name was Alexander. He died in the Crimea."

"If you can picture him in your mind with a beard and slightly longer hair, he is Miles."

"My son has a beard?"

"Yes, he does. And a very kind smile. He loves books and reading."

Mr Greene lifted her hand and kissed. "Thank you. I can see my son in my head. Now, go and find the jewellery."

She went out and put her head around the drawing room door. "Grandfather would like to see you, Mother."

As Mrs Ellison hurried to the library, Alfie climbed a ladder and lifted the portrait of the grey-wigged gentleman down from above the chimney piece in the entrance hall.

"He was Mr Greene's grandfather, Laurence Greene," Knox explained to her. "He had this house built in 1795."

"My grandfather wants us to take all the portraits, the photographs and my grandmother's jewels back to Dublin with us," she said and they all stared at her in astonishment.

"All of them?" Will asked and she nodded.

"Two small portraits and the photographs will fit in a trunk and the remainder of the portraits will need to be wrapped in... sheets?" She turned to Knox with a questioning expression and he nodded. "Grandfather says you will find a trunk and bring me to the jewellery."

"Of course." The butler went to a rope and pulled it before lighting an oil lamp. "Ask the maid for sheets and pillowcases, Mr Ellison. As many as she can find."

"Thank you, I will, and I shall retrieve all the photographs," James replied. "Isobel, the jewellery cases can be put in my trunk and Alfie's – we didn't bring half as many clothes as your mother," he added and she couldn't help but smile.

She accompanied the butler up the stairs and into a bedroom at the back of the house dominated by more large and ugly dark mahogany furniture including a huge double bed with carved headboard.

"This was Mrs Greene's bedroom," Knox said and went

to the dressing table. He put the lamp down, opened the drawers and began to lift out jewellery cases. He stacked them on the top before straightening up. "There is a miniature portrait in Mr Greene's bedroom which you should also take. Please, follow me, Mrs Fitzgerald."

She picked up the cases, took one quick look around the room, before following him across the landing and into another bedroom with furniture just as oppressive. The miniature was of her grandmother as a young woman and stood on a stand on the bedside table.

"Grandfather should keep this," she said as Knox passed it to her. "We cannot leave him with nothing. I'll take the stand, too."

"Of course. Please, excuse me while I find a trunk."

She packed the jewellery cases between layers of clothes in Alfie and James' trunks then went out onto the landing with the miniature and stand hearing feet coming down the stairs from the third floor.

"How long have you been butler here?" she asked as Knox balanced a large brown leather trunk on the banister rail for a moment.

"Twenty years, Mrs Fitzgerald."

"Has this house always been so—" She fought for a suitable word and failed. "Sad?"

"Yes," he replied simply. "It is a house with few visitors. Sad is a very apt description."

Downstairs in the entrance hall, Will and James were wrapping the last large portrait in a sheet and Knox placed the trunk on the round table. She put the miniature and stand to one side and set to work wrapping the small portraits and the photographs in pillowcases and handing them to Alfie who packed them tightly together in the trunk so they wouldn't be jostled about while in transit and be damaged.

"These portraits can't be tied to the roof of the carriage like the bath chair," James told Will. "What if it rains again?"

"We'll get them inside somehow." Will stacked the portrait with seven others against the wall near the front door. "Even if we have to sit with them on our laps. What have you there?" he asked her, nodding to the miniature on the table beside the trunk.

"It's Grandmother and it must be left with Grandfather," she replied and showed it to him and then to James and Alfie before knocking at the library door again. "Please, give this to Grandfather," she said as her mother opened the door and she passed the miniature and the stand to her. "Everything else is safely wrapped and packed."

"Mother." Mrs Ellison fought back more tears as she smiled at the miniature. "Thank you, Isobel. Father is going to rest for a little while so I will bring you on a tour of the house shortly."

The door closed and she returned to Will. "Mother is going to bring me on a tour of the house," she said. "I didn't know what else to suggest to keep her calm but I am genuinely interested in viewing it with her. Go with James and Alfie, join Nurse Barton in the drawing room and sit down," she added, kissing his lips. "You look exhausted."

"I will and I am."

He went with Alfie and James into the drawing room and she gazed at the landscape painting of a mountain now hanging above the chimney piece.

"It's Croagh Patrick," her mother told her, closing the

library door. "The holy mountain. The clouds were so low today it wasn't visible. I wanted to climb it when I was young but I wasn't allowed and I never will now."

"Never say never. You came home when you thought you would never set foot in this house again. Knox brought me to both Grandmother and Grandfather's bedrooms – show me yours?" she asked and picked up a small oil lamp from the round table.

"Yes," her mother replied with a smile and they went upstairs. Halfway along the landing, Mrs Ellison opened a door. "I haven't been in this room for almost twenty-six years," she said as they went in and Isobel glanced around the large bedroom. The furniture was also mahogany but not as dark and gloomy as in her grandparents' rooms. A doll with a china face and blonde hair in ringlets lay on a single bed propped against the pillows and her mother lifted it up. "Dolly. I never called her anything else. Mother thought it was a common name and wanted me to name her Victoria or something equally grand but I would not." Bringing the doll with her, Mrs Ellison left the room and Isobel followed.

"Will you show me the nursery?" she asked and her mother led her back to the stairs.

They climbed the rather steep steps to the third floor and Isobel opened a door to a large room with three rooms off it. The nursery was icy-cold and empty of furniture except for a table and four chairs in the centre of the floor.

"The middle door over there was my bedroom until I reached the age of twelve," her mother explained. "The bedroom to its left was Nanny's and the bedroom on the right was my nursery maid's."

"What is your earliest memory?"

"Can I remember Miles being here, you mean?" Mrs Ellison inquired and Isobel nodded. "I have wracked my brain time and again but I simply cannot remember him. Even being here now hasn't stirred any fresh memories. I wish I could remember him but there is nothing, I'm sorry."

"You have nothing to be sorry for."

"My first memory is of looking out of the window and watching Father and Mother leaving in the carriage. I don't know where they were going but I remember I cried because I thought they were not coming back. I was alone here with Nanny for a great deal of my childhood and then with my governess when this room became the school room. I was determined my children would not be as isolated as I was and would attend the best schools possible. And you both did," she said and Isobel waited for her to confess how that had been achieved but Mrs Ellison did not continue.

"Thank you." Isobel hugged and kissed her then held the door open. "Let's go downstairs." Taking her mother's hand, they returned to the entrance hall. "Sit with Grandfather, if you wish."

"I shall."

She waited for her mother to go into the library before opening the door to the drawing room and going inside. Will was placing a log on the fire and she closed the door and stood in front of the hearth to warm herself.

"We were in the nursery and it was freezing up there," she explained. "And Mother can't remember Miles being here at all."

"That's not surprising," Will said. "My first memory is from when I was about three years old."

"Is your mother calm?" James asked.

"For now, yes," she replied. "But tomorrow morning will be very difficult." For her and for all of us, she added silently.

As they had another very early start, they all retired to bed at ten o'clock. To her relief, their bedroom had warmed and Will's clothes were drying well. After undressing, she sat naked on the bed and held her full and tender breasts in her hands. She needed to express some milk but how?

"Into a chamber pot," Will said as if having read her mind and pulled one out from under the bed. "Are your breasts painful?" he asked, passing it to her.

"They ache. Oh, Will, how do I do this?" she moaned, balancing the cold chamber pot on her lap.

"Gently press down on each of them," he instructed and she laid the palm of a hand on a breast and pressed downwards. Milk squirted out of a nipple and into the chamber pot. "That's it – good – keep pressing."

"Well, this is a first," she said wryly as she continued and he bent and kissed her forehead.

"Are you going to wear that monstrosity?" he asked, pointing to one of her mother's overly-fussy cotton and lace nightdresses which had been left on the chair.

"No," she replied with a smile. "Are you going to wear James' nightshirt?"

"No, so cuddle up to me." He added two logs to the fire then got into bed and watched as she expressed the last of the milk and returned the chamber pot to its home under the bed. "Feel better?"

"Much better." She climbed in beside him. "But we can't be home soon enough."

Alfie knocked at their door at just after five o'clock in the morning and, with a groan, Will turned up the oil lamp. He shaved using Alfie's razor and within fifteen minutes they were washed and dressed. While he returned James' clothes and helped to carry the trunks downstairs, she went to the dining room. A huge array of breakfast dishes were laid out on the sideboard and she helped herself to some porridge and coffee before glancing at the door as her mother came into the room.

"Some porridge?" she suggested and Mrs Ellison's face contorted in disgust at the thought. "You must eat something, Mother. There is scrambled egg?"

"Very well."

"Good." She served her mother the scrambled egg and some coffee before sitting down with her own meal.

"The trunks are at the front door and it has stopped raining," Will announced as he came in followed by James and Alfie and they helped themselves to bacon, egg, sausage, toast and coffee. "Where is Nurse Barton?" he asked as he sat opposite her.

"I haven't seen her, she must be with Grandfather."

"I can't eat," Mrs Ellison declared in a shaking voice then got up from the table and ran from the room.

James immediately went to go after his wife but Isobel laid a hand on his arm.

"Don't, James. Let her go to her father. When we have eaten, we will need to escort her from the house by force."

James grimaced and, while they ate, she heard the carriage pulling around to the front of the house. The front door opened and voices echoed around the entrance hall followed by a guffaw.

"Someone is glad we are leaving," James murmured. "I just hope they are careful with the trunks."

"We cannot disguise the paintings," she said. "But we must not act as though there is anything of great value in the trunks. Excuse me while I say goodbye to Grandfather."

The three men stood while she left the room. Nurse Barton was waiting discreetly in the hall watching the trunks being carried out of the house and nodded to Isobel as she went into the library. Her mother was seated by the bed, clasping her father's hands.

"The trunks are being brought out to the carriage." Isobel walked around the bed and sat on the edge. "So I must say goodbye."

"You are a beautiful woman, Isobel," Mr Greene told her. "A strong and beautiful woman and I am glad I met you."

"I am glad I met you as well," she replied truthfully. "And I will tell my children about their great-grandfather."

"That all you saw was an old man who wheezed instead of breathed."

"There are the photographs. And the paintings. They won't only hear about the old man and Mother will tell them about you, too."

"Good," he said, patting her hands. "Your mother is upset," he added in a whisper as if Mrs Ellison couldn't hear them. "She doesn't want to leave me here. But she must."

"I know she must."

"Take her home now, Isobel," he instructed and her mother gave a little cry. "She has a husband, children, grandchildren and brother and she needs to be with them."

"I'll take her home." Isobel got up and kissed her grandfather's cheek.

"Look after her. And look after my son."

"I will, I promise," she said and he turned to his daughter.

"You know you must go now, Martha," he said and tears began to spill down Mrs Ellison's cheeks. "I love you little girlie," he continued and she flung her arms around his neck. "Give me a kiss and go now, Martha."

Her mother's arms slid from his neck and she kissed him on both cheeks and then on his forehead. "I love you, Father," she told him in a voice hoarse with emotion and Isobel squeezed his hands before leading her mother from the room. As she closed the door, her grandfather gave her a smile and blew her a kiss.

Knox, the footman and two maids assisted them with their cloak, coat, overcoats, hats, scarves and gloves. Taking one last glance around the entrance and inner halls – wishing she'd had the opportunity to view Greene Hall in daylight – Isobel led her weeping mother out of the house as Will, Alfie and James went to the library. Helping her mother into the carriage, she heard feet behind her on the gravel. She closed the carriage door and Nurse Barton held out a hand.

"Goodbye, Mrs Fitzgerald."

"Goodbye, and thank you, Nurse Barton." Isobel shook her hand. "And I meant what I said. If there is anything I can send you from Dublin just write."

"That is very kind, thank you," the nurse replied and went back into the house.

Standing back from the carriage, Isobel gazed up at the three-storey house. The columns of the balustrade around the roof were visible against the night sky and she wondered if the Atlantic Ocean could be seen from up there. Opening the carriage door, she vowed she would come back one day and find out.

"Stand the paintings against the carriage and get inside," Knox instructed as he, James, Alfie and Will approached each carrying two paintings with the footman behind them holding up an oil lamp. "And I'll pass them to you."

She climbed into the carriage and sat beside her mother. Will squeezed onto the seat beside them, James and Alfie sat opposite and the butler passed the portraits to them one at a time.

"Goodbye, Knox," Will called. "Thank you – and all the servants – for all your hard work."

"Goodbye, Dr Fitzgerald." Knox closed the carriage door, raised a hand and the carriage set off down the drive.

It was a long, dark journey to Westport with the silence only broken by her mother's sniffs. The carriage halted outside the station and Mulloy jumped down and opened the door. The portraits were passed out to him, he stood them against the carriage and the five of them got out. By the sounds of screeching, puffing and hissing, their train was waiting at the platform.

"I'll purchase our tickets," Will told her. "And we'll bring the portraits into the compartment."

The four men carried the portraits away and Will and Mulloy returned as she and her mother waited by the carriage, not wanting to leave the four trunks unattended. The trunks were placed in the guard's van and she escorted her mother onto the train while Will spoke briefly to the coachman.

"We both apologised for yesterday," he said as he came into the compartment and slammed the door closed. "Mulloy has to be seen being uncivil to the gentry and I wasn't used to being classed and treated as gentry."

"I've never been referred to as gentry before either," she replied. "A few months ago, I overheard someone in the Fitzwilliam Square gardens referring to 'those families who are in the professions' in a very derogatory tone."

As the train chugged out of the station, her mother exhaled a long, shaky breath. Isobel held one of her hands and James the other, but Mrs Ellison simply stared at her reflection in the window, blinking furiously.

Isobel had always thought the train journey from Galway to Dublin long, but the journey from Westport seemed endless. They were all exhausted and exchanged very few words. Dawn broke and gradually the countryside came into view. When the train finally halted in Broadstone Station, she simply closed her eyes in silent relief.

Two cabs conveyed them to Fitzwilliam Square and the trunks and paintings were carried into the hall of number 55.

"I will bring Miles back as soon as I have apologised to him, to young John and kissed the twins," she told James. "Perhaps, Mother should go and lie down?" she added, glancing at Will.

"Yes," he said. "And if something to eat and drink could be brought up to her."

"I'm not hungry," her mother protested feebly.

"You still need to eat and drink," Will advised her gently. "You were going to have scrambled egg for breakfast. Would you like some now? And some tea?"

"Very well," Mrs Ellison replied, Will nodded to Gorman and the butler returned to the servants' hall.

As James helped his wife up the stairs, Will caught Alfie's arm.

"After we've checked on Miles and the children, I'm going to call to the practice house and apologise to Eva and David. If David has started his house calls, I'll put a note through the door at Westland Row to tell him we're back."

"Thank you, I don't know when I'm going to get a chance to see him. Miles is going to need looking after."

"If Miles is upset, I'll calm him before bringing him back here," she said and Alfie gave her a grateful smile. "See you later."

"I feel as though I never want to leave Dublin again," Will commented as they walked around the gardens and up the steps to number 30. He opened the front door for her and Mrs Dillon came hurrying down the stairs.

"Oh, Doctor, Mrs Fitzgerald, thank goodness you're back."

"We're terribly sorry, Mrs Dillon." Will closed the door, took off his hat and hung it on the stand. "We were deliberately made to miss the train yesterday. How are Mr Miles and the children?"

"Master John is very upset," the housekeeper replied, confirming what Isobel had feared. "When he woke up this morning and you still weren't back he became hysterical so I sent Gerald to Merrion Square to ask that his grandmother come. Mrs Fitzgerald senior has been here since nine o'clock this morning but she simply cannot calm him. The poor lad thinks you are never coming back. Mr Miles is trying to comfort him, but it is clear he is upset, too."

"Thank you, Mrs Dillon." Picking up her skirts, Isobel ran up the stairs, hearing not only Will following her, but screams and cries from the nursery. She threw open the door and saw her mother-in-law leading young John out of the children's bedroom. "John," she said softly and the boy turned a tearful face towards them.

They knelt down as John raced across the floor and all but flung himself at them, putting his arms around both of them.

"Where were you?" the little boy demanded, sobbing so much it gave him the hic-ups. "Thought you weren't coming home."

"We missed the train," she said, kissing his wet cheeks. "And we couldn't get to a telegraph office to send a telegram. We're so sorry," she added, pulling a handkerchief from a sleeve and wiping his eyes. "We would never go off and leave you – never."

"Come to me." Will lifted him up and John put his arms around his neck, clinging to him for dear life. "Miles," he added and her uncle closed a book and got up from the table. "We're sorry."

"We were very worried," he said and she almost smiled at the understatement.

"We really are sorry." She gave him a hug and a kiss. "Where we went to in Co Mayo was very isolated – we didn't like being stranded but there was nothing we could do."

"Mother." Will bent and kissed her cheek. "Thank you for coming."

"Not at all," Sarah replied and Isobel could see and hear her relief.

She squeezed Sarah's hand gratefully and went into the children's bedroom. "How are they?" she asked Bridget as she bent over the twins' cradles and kissed them.

"They've drunk the milk substitute with no complaints, Mrs Fitzgerald," the maid replied, stifling a yawn. "Their last feed was an hour ago. Florrie would like to speak to you about Master John, though," she added in a whisper and Isobel nodded.

She went into the maids' bedroom, Florrie followed and shut the door. Like Bridget, the poor young woman looked worn out.

"Mrs Dillon said Master John was hysterical," Isobel began and Florrie rubbed her forehead.

"He was, Mrs Fitzgerald, I've never seen him like it. I couldn't calm him, Bridget couldn't calm him, Mr Miles couldn't calm him – even his grandmother couldn't calm him. He was so upset he wet himself and he's never done that before."

"We missed the train – we were deliberately made to miss the train."

"I told him it was probably that but he was sure you were both never coming back."

"I'll keep him with me this afternoon and then I shall get him back into the everyday routine – dinner – and bed. Mrs Dillon said Mr Miles is upset, too."

"He is but he is better at hiding it. We thought it best that he sleep up here last night so we carried my bed out to the nursery and I shared Bridget's bed in here."

"My husband and I should never have gone to Co Mayo – it was awful for everyone. Thank you for coping so well."

"We didn't cope very well at all, Mrs Fitzgerald," Florrie admitted miserably. "I hope we don't have to start all over again with Master John."

"We'll go back to his routine this evening and take matters from there."

"Yes, Mrs Fitzgerald."

They left the bedroom and she reached up and kissed John's cheek. He was still clinging to Will and she sincerely hoped Florrie wasn't right.

The five of them went downstairs to the morning room and the housekeeper carried in some tea and a mountain of sandwiches.

"Oh, Mrs Dillon, you are wonderful, thank you," Will cried.

"I thought you'd be peckish, Dr Fitzgerald," she said, putting the tray on a side table.

"We had breakfast before six o'clock this morning and we've had nothing to eat since."

"We had some of Mrs Dillon's vegetable soup for luncheon," Miles said, sitting down in one of the armchairs. "It was delicious."

"Thank you, Mr Miles, I'm delighted you enjoyed it," she replied and left the room.

"Did you enjoy the soup, too?" Isobel asked John, lifting him onto the sofa and she and his grandmother sat on either side of him.

"I didn't want any."

"Well, how about one of these?" Reaching for a ham sandwich, Isobel passed it to him. He bit into it and Will ruffled the boy's hair before sitting down with a little groan of contentment in the other armchair.

"Help yourself to a sandwich, Miles." Will's mother lifted up the plate and he chose one while Isobel poured the tea.

"After a cup of tea and a few sandwiches, I need to go out," Will told John and the boy's face fell. "Because Isobel and I are very late back, I missed surgery this morning so I need to go and apologise to Eva and to Dr Powell and call on some patients. But Isobel will be here with you and Miles and I will be back in time to help you get ready for bed this evening."

"Promise?" John asked.

"I promise. What happened yesterday to Isobel and I was utterly out of our control and we are so sorry you were upset. You are our little boy and we would never leave you and we would never leave Ben and Belle. Grandmamma Martha, Grandpapa James and Alfie would never leave Miles either. We just got stuck in Co Mayo – it won't happen again."

"All right."

After devouring four sandwiches and gulping down a cup of tea, Will reluctantly heaved himself out of the armchair.

"I must go. May I walk you back to Merrion Square, Mother?" he asked and she nodded, getting to her feet.

"Thank you, Will."

"Sarah, thank you so much for coming." Isobel stood up and gave her a hug. "We shall see you very soon."

"You shall." His mother bent and kissed John's cheek as the boy reached for another sandwich and bit into it. "Goodbye, John. Goodbye, Miles."

His mouth full, John just waved, but Miles got up and shook her hand.

"Goodbye, Mrs Fitzgerald. Thank you for coming and keeping us company."

Will glanced at his mother as they walked out of Fitzwilliam Square. She was quiet and he passed his medical bag to his left hand before taking her arm.

"I'm sorry," she said and patted his hand. "But I didn't

realise quite how much John adores you both until this morning. I have never witnessed a child behave so hysterically. He truly thought you had abandoned him."

"And now some of his trust in us has been eroded. Poor John. I was absolutely furious when I realised we would miss the train. It's been a long time since I've been quite so angry. Or wet."

"Was it terrible?" she asked.

"Yes, it was. Leaving Mr Greene there was very difficult. Naturally, Isobel's mother was the most upset."

"Would you like me to call on Martha in the next day or two?"

"I would, Mother, thank you."

"Will the nurse cope, do you think?"

"Yes, she is very competent," he replied. "It is just that there is a dying man, his nurse and his servants in a huge house miles from the nearest telegraph office with the Land League campaign in progress."

"Were you in danger – will they be in danger?"

"No, the campaigners appear to be obeying Mr Parnell's policy of social ostracism but it was still best that we leave. We were all but shunned yesterday – only one carriage came to Westport Station for us – the coachman and the undertaker had to be seen being as uncooperative towards us as possible – and no-one at the funeral would bring Isobel and I back to the station. We spent most of last evening removing valuable family portraits from the walls for fear of them being damaged or looted."

"Good gracious me. Where did you hide them?"

"We didn't. Mr Greene insisted we bring them back to Dublin, along with all the photographs and his wife's jewellery. I didn't like doing any of that," he admitted. "It was as if we were the ones doing the looting. They are all now at number 55."

Outside number 67, his mother kissed his cheek.

"There is no need to see me inside. I will call soon to number 30 – and to number 55. Retire to bed early this evening, you look tired."

"I am exhausted," he told her with a little smile. "Goodbye, Mother, and thank you."

He hurried on to Merrion Street Upper and found Eva at the filing cabinet in the practice house office lifting out some patient files.

"I'm sorry," he said, hanging his hat on the stand as she put the files down on her desk. "Isobel and I were forced to miss the train and there is no telegraph office in the village."

"Dr Powell and I wondered if that had been the case. You've only just missed him, he insisted on seeing all the patients and he will carry out your most urgent house calls as well as his own."

"That's good of him. I'll do the remainder of my house calls. Are there any others?"

"No, Dr Fitzgerald," she said. "But Dr Powell has left you some notes regarding your patients."

"Thank you, Eva."

He went upstairs to his surgery and read the notes before scribbling a short message to David. He slid the sheet of notepaper into an envelope and sealed it, wrote David's name on the front and dropped it into his medical bag.

"Will Nurse Barton stay in Co Mayo, Dr Fitzgerald?" Eva asked as he returned to the office and lifted his hat from the stand.

"She says she will. Nurse Barton and Mr Greene are in no danger. All the campaigning in the locality is non-violent at present."

"I'm very relieved to hear that. Good day to you, Dr Fitzgerald."

After completing his house calls, Will walked to Westland Row. Turning off Lincoln Place, he saw a man across the street standing on the steps of the Georgian terraced house David had rooms in. Thinking it was David, Will was about to call out a greeting when he spotted David approaching from the direction of the railway station. Will's eyes widened as the first man took off his hat and shook David's hand. It was his father. David opened the front door and the two men went inside.

Pushing his hat to the back of his head, Will waited until light appeared in a room on the first floor and a figure closed the curtains. Should he even try and contemplate why his father was meeting David in his home? As far as he was aware, his father had never met David socially anywhere, never mind in David's rooms. Will closed his eyes for a moment. He was worn out. Go home, he told himself, and worry about Father tomorrow. Hailing a cab, he travelled back to number 30.

Isobel was upstairs in the nursery sitting on the red rug with John and they were playing with the train set while Florrie was lifting his empty dinner plate, dessert dish and glass onto a tray. The boy was pushing his locomotive and carriages around the track and Will got down on his hands and knees, relieved to see John was calm and smiling.

"That is just like the train Isobel and I travelled on to and from Westport," he said as the boy yawned. "Tired?"

"Yes."

"So are Isobel and I. We're going to have our dinner soon and then we shall be having an early night, too."

"Let's get you ready for bed." Isobel got to her feet and held out a hand. Without a word of protest, John took it and they went into the children's bedroom.

"How has Master John been?" he asked Florrie.

"Very quiet, Dr Fitzgerald. It's clear Master John is extremely relieved to have you and Mrs Fitzgerald back. Bridget and I will check on him regularly in case he has nightmares."

"Thank you, Florrie." He dismantled the train set, placed it in the wooden toy box and went into the bedroom. Isobel was putting John's clothes away in the chest of drawers and Bridget was changing the twins' nappies. "We are so sorry you were so upset today," he said as the boy climbed into bed. "Do you feel better now?"

"Yes," John replied.

"Good. Isobel and I will see you in the morning."

"Promise?"

"We promise," Isobel replied, sitting on the bed and hugging him. "What happened to us was something we could do nothing about and we hope it never happens again." She kissed both his cheeks and he lay down. "Night-night, John," she said then kissed Belle and Ben goodnight.

"Sleep tight, John." Will kissed the boy's and the twins' foreheads. "Goodnight, Bridget," he added and he followed Isobel from the bedroom. "Master John is calm," he told Florrie. "And tired. Hopefully, he'll have a peaceful night. Goodnight."

They went to bed straight after dinner and, in their

bedroom, he shrugged off his frock coat before sitting on the bed and groaning with sheer exhaustion.

"I walked to Westland Row with a note of apology for David," he said as Isobel sat down at the dressing table and extracted the pins from her hair. "And I saw him meet with my father and they went into his rooms."

"Your father?" she asked, staring at him in the mirror with clear suspicion. "At David's rooms? He's never met with David before, never mind at his rooms."

"Perhaps, David is submitting a piece to the *Journal of Irish Medicine*," he said, knowing it sounded feeble.

"I doubt that very much. Your father does not have the highest opinion of David. Even if it were the case, David would be going to your father's office at the *Journal*, and not your father going to David's rooms."

"Let's bide our time and see if either of them mention something. Don't say anything to Alfie, please?"

"I won't. Is David happy at the practice?" she asked, shaking her hair loose.

"Yes, he is. He has said often enough that he is very grateful for the opportunity to work at the practice. He interacts well with patients and he and Eva get on well, too. After what happened between Fred and Eva, I have made a point of keeping an eye on how well David and Eva work together. I haven't seen anything to give me cause for concern. Let's just wait and see."

Before Will left for surgery in the morning, the two of them went upstairs to the nursery. To Isobel's relief, young John was tucking into a soft boiled egg with toast 'soldiers' and she kissed the top of his head.

"Did you sleep well?" she asked and he nodded. Sitting beside him, Florrie nodded, too, and she smiled in reply. "Will has to take surgery now and I am going to call on Grandmamma Martha," she told the boy. "Would you like to come with me?" John's face brightened and she pointed to the egg. "Finish that, I'll see Will out and then we'll go."

"I'll be back for luncheon." Will ruffled his hair. "How are Ben and Belle?"

"Ben burped very loudly after drinking his milk."

"Very loudly?" she asked.

"It was so loud Bridget laughed. And Belle laughed, too."

"Dear me." Will went into the children's bedroom and picked Ben up. "You are embarrassing Bridget, your sister and your cousin, you know?" he told Ben, who just stared back impassively. "We shall have to see how you fare burp-wise with mashed carrot."

Ben laughed suddenly, startling him, and Isobel, John and the two maids roared with laughter.

"I see," Will continued lightly. "So that is what you think of mashed carrot, is it? Well, I'll have you know mashed carrot is delicious — when pieces of swede haven't been surreptitiously added to it, of course. Let's see if you laugh with derision when you taste some this evening." Smiling, he kissed Ben's cheek and laid him down in the cradle. "Goodbye, little man. Goodbye, little miss." He kissed Belle's forehead and they let the nursery and went downstairs to the hall.

"Back to our everyday routine," she said, helping him with his overcoat then passing his medical bag and hat to him. "Keep a secret eye on David," she added, opening the front door.

"I will – reluctantly," he replied, kissing her lips. "I hope it was nothing but where my father is concerned, it rarely is nothing."

She closed the door after him, went back upstairs and ten minutes later, she and young John were admitted to number 55. Alfie was coming down the stairs and, along the hall, she could hear her mother and James' voices in the breakfast room.

"We're all up extremely late this morning," Alfie explained. "Come and have a cup of coffee with us."

"May I have some milk, please?" John asked and Alfie grinned.

"Of course you can. Come with me to the kitchen and I'll ask for some."

She went into the breakfast room, walked around the table and kissed her mother's cheek.

"Thank you, Isobel, but you need not fuss. Father wished to remain at Greene Hall and I must respect his decision."

Isobel glanced at James, seated at the head of the table buttering a slice of toast and squeezed his shoulder. He returned a smile and she sat down beside her mother.

"Where are the paintings?" she asked.

"In the morning room," Mrs Ellison replied. "I thought that this morning we could discuss who shall have each painting."

"Yes, of course. They will look very grand in our drawing rooms."

"You are going to hide yours away in a room you rarely use?" her mother asked in dismay.

"Until you or Grandfather write down your family history, I simply don't know who any of the people in the paintings are and, if I'm perfectly honest, I don't particularly want dead people staring down at Will and I in our morning room. The drawing room is huge and a more suitable location. I did think it would be best if you were to keep the portraits of people you actually knew, such as your grandmother, and Will and I could take the portraits of the earlier Greenes. Is that agreeable to you?"

"Yes, very much so." Mrs Ellison chuckled as Alfie ushered young John sporting a milk moustache into the room and Isobel pulled out the chair next to hers. "Isobel." Her mother held out a napkin and she lifted John on to the chair, took the napkin and wiped his mouth.

"Some coffee, Isobel?" Alfie offered, sitting down beside Miles and gesturing to the coffee pot.

"Yes, please," she said, watched as he poured and accepted the cup and saucer from him. "Thank you. Have you looked at the jewellery, Mother?" she asked, adding milk and sugar to the coffee and stirring it while Alfie poured a cup of coffee for himself.

"No, I haven't," Mrs Ellison replied. "I would like to delay it for a little while. I remember Mother wearing the jewellery and…" She tailed off and James patted her hand.

"Of course," Isobel said softly. "Perhaps, you should invest in a safe?"

"I shall purchase a safe today," James announced and she nodded.

"I had thought," her mother began again tentatively as Isobel sipped her coffee. "That tomorrow evening, we could all assemble here at seven o'clock for a New Year's Eve dinner party – Will's parents included. As much as we all enjoyed Mrs Dillon's excellent Christmas dinner, the dreadful events of the afternoon marred the entire day. I propose roast pork and a trifle for dessert and that we not dress in mourning attire."

"That is an excellent idea, Mother."

"Will there be cracking on the roast pork, Grandmamma?" John asked.

"I shall request that the pork have a considerable covering of skin for crackling, John," Mrs Ellison replied.

"Thank you."

"Well." Alfie drained his cup, set it on its saucer and got up from the table. "I propose that while Mother and Isobel are looking at past generations of Greenes and James is purchasing a safe, Miles, John and I wrap up warm and have a breath of air in the garden."

The three of them left the room and Isobel turned to her mother. "How is Miles?" she asked. "He hasn't uttered a word."

"I'm afraid I upset him last night," Mrs Ellison admitted. "I was distressed and I deeply regret it now."

"I think we should put dividing the paintings between us off for now and that you, Miles, John and I walk to number 67 and see if Sarah is at home. John will enjoy the walk, Miles will see more of Dublin and Alfie can continue with his novel."

"Isobel is right," James said. "Spend some time with Miles. I know the type of safe I wish to purchase so I will be home in time for luncheon."

"Very well." His wife rose from the table and Isobel and James got up. "It will be pleasant to see Sarah again. I shall go and ask for my hat, cloak and gloves."

Mrs Ellison went out to the hall and Isobel grabbed

James' arm. "What happened last night?"

"Your mother hasn't forgiven Miles for not wanting to meet his father and for not coming with us to Greene Hall," James explained. "Perhaps, she never will, but at least she knows she spoke too harshly to Miles. She did apologise and she knows to choose her words more carefully in future."

"John was hysterical when Will and I returned home yesterday. He's calm now but his trust in us has definitely lessened."

"Poor little lad."

"Miles was upset, too, but managed to hide it better. Mother being angry with him won't have helped. Go and purchase a safe and we will see you later."

Holding young John's hand, she glanced at her mother and Miles as they walked to Merrion Square. Mrs Ellison, in an effort to make amends, had linked her arm through her brother's and was pointing to a rag and bone man rattling past them on his horse and cart.

Luckily, Sarah Fitzgerald was at home and Tess showed them into the morning room.

"How lovely to see you." Sarah put a periodical to one side, got up from the sofa and kissed them all. "Do sit down."

"We were in need of a walk," Isobel said as they sat, catching her mother-in-law's eye and Sarah gave her a brief nod of understanding. "And John has never been to the house Will was born in." And his father, she added silently and Sarah stared at the rug for a few moments, clearly also thinking of Edward. "Miles was eager to see more of Dublin, too."

"We saw a rag and bone man," he said. "His cart was

piled high with all sorts."

"I probably shouldn't admit to this, but I do enjoy browsing in junk shops," Sarah said and laughed kindly as Isobel's mother stared at her in surprise.

"You go alone?"

"Yes, I do. You are most welcome to accompany me the next time I go. I rarely purchase anything but some of the items people discard simply astonish me. Some tea?"

"Thank you, but we have just risen from the breakfast table," Mrs Ellison said. "We all needed to lie abed a little longer this morning."

"I understand," Sarah replied. "And I also enjoy browsing in second-hand bookshops. I am compiling quite a library," she added, sweeping an arm towards a bookcase in a corner. Miles' face lit up and she smiled. "You are most welcome to browse, Miles."

"Thank you, Mrs Fitzgerald," he said, getting up and, a moment later, John slid off Isobel's lap and went to one of the windows.

"Look, Isobel," the boy cried, pointing at something and she joined him as her mother invited his grandparents to the New Year's Eve dinner party. "The gardens are huge – even bigger than Fuzwillan Square."

"Yes, Merrion Square is considerably larger than Fitzwilliam Square."

"Well, is your husband at home?" Mrs Ellison asked a little irritably, Sarah having not wanted to mention the dinner party to her husband herself.

"My husband is not at home," Sarah replied. "I don't know where he is – I heard him go out at a ridiculous hour this morning and it cannot be to the *Journal* – the next issue won't be published until the first week of January."

"In that case, I shall ask Isobel or Will to invite him. I would very much like for you both to be there – we are all family after all."

"Yes, we are. I'm sorry for snapping, Martha, it's simply that this is the first Christmas and New Year I have been 'alone', so to speak, and I used to so much enjoy receiving a long letter from Edward. We have both suffered great losses this year," Sarah finished sadly and Mrs Ellison clasped her hands.

"Great losses and wonderful additions to our family," she said and they gazed at young John and Miles. "Christmas is over and it was awful for all of us. Please call to number 55, Sarah? We each need a friend. I am snapping at people, too. I was horrible to poor Miles last evening. Please call, and we can snap at each other and no-one else?" she asked with a little smile and Sarah laughed and gave her a hug.

"I would be very happy to, thank you, Martha. What have you found over there, Miles?"

"An atlas," he replied, turning away from the bookcase and holding it up. "It has beautiful maps."

"You don't have an atlas, do you, Miles?" Isobel asked, leading young John away from the window and lifting him onto Sarah's lap.

"No, I don't," he replied. "I never really saw the need for one."

"Well, you shall have one – a late Christmas present."

"That is very kind, thank you." Miles smiled as she heard the front door close.

"That must be John," she said. "I'll invite him to the dinner party. Excuse me."

She went out to the hall and Will's father glanced at her in surprise as he passed his hat and overcoat to Tess.

"Isobel?"

"Mother, young John, Miles and I came for a walk. Miles is admiring Sarah's atlas."

"Sarah used to look up where Edward was stationed. She always felt happier knowing exactly where he was, even though it was thousands of miles away." He gave her a sad smile. "Come upstairs."

"Thank you."

They went up the stairs to the drawing room, now John's living room-come-dining room. The double doors to what had been the dining room and was now his bedroom were closed.

"You haven't been here since the transformation," he said. "It is not so much of a transformation, I suppose. At least not in this room. The dining table doesn't look so out of place in here, does it?"

"No, not at all. The room is big enough to accommodate it."

"The living arrangement is working extremely well – no-one suspects a thing. If I have to meet with someone, I ask them to come to my office at the *Journal*."

Except for David Powell, she added silently. Why?

"And I have rejoined the Trinity Club. I had left, as after Nicholas, Fred and Maria's deaths I didn't feel like socialising, but Jim Harvey brought me there for dinner and he persuaded me to renew my membership. We now have dinner there one evening per week because I need to keep myself busy and occupied socially."

"Well, here is a date for your diary," she said. "Tomorrow

evening. Mother has decided to hold a New Year's Eve dinner party and both Sarah and yourself are invited. Christmas was – well – Christmas and Mother believes we need to – not so much try again – but have an evening we can all enjoy and not wear mourning attire. Will you come? Half past six for seven?"

"I would be delighted to, thank you. Was the trip to Co Mayo awful?"

"Yes," she replied at once. "Greene Hall is like a mausoleum and Mother hated having to leave Grandfather there. I must admit, I did, too."

"The nurse Will found is capable, though?"

"Oh, yes, very. Grandfather will receive excellent care from Nurse Barton. It is just that with the Land League's campaign of social ostracism, we cannot risk visiting Greene Hall again and making life even more difficult for everyone who lives on the estate so Mother had to say goodbye to her father for the last time."

Will's father's face contorted in sympathy. "I overheard Sarah telling Tess that both John and Miles were very upset."

"Young John thought Will and I were never coming home and he has lost a certain amount of trust in us. Miles was upset, too, but managed to hide it better."

"I wasn't at home when the footman came for us, otherwise I would have gone to number 30 as well."

"Young John and Miles have both been reassured again and again and this morning Alfie took them out to number 55's garden – they both love the garden – and Mother and I have taken them for a walk here."

"Is Alfie good with Miles?" Will's father asked.

"Alfie is good with both Miles and young John. Alfie has

great patience with them and he loves being 'an uncle of sorts' to John."

"John will inherit this house one day. Will Alfie inherit Greene Hall?" he added.

"James thinks so."

"It will be a huge responsibility for Alfie, especially as he is still a student."

"James will be on hand to offer Alfie advice when the time comes. Your namesake is very impressed with the size of the Merrion Square gardens," she continued, changing the subject. "I will bring both him and Miles to explore them soon."

"His father and uncle loved the gardens. Does Will ever mention Edward?" John asked suddenly and she hesitated before answering. "No. I can tell by your face that he does not. What about Fred?"

"Rarely," she said. "Fred's death is still very painful to him."

"It has been almost a year."

"On the anniversary we shall visit Fred's grave. Would you like to accompany us?"

"I—" He faltered and she reached out and held his hands. "I have not been to Mount Jerome Cemetery since Maria's burial…"

"If you decide to come, please tell Tess or Maura in case I do not see you."

"Thank you," he replied and she squeezed his hands before letting them go. "Tell me about your grandmother's funeral. I must admit I have never attended a country funeral."

"It was very wet with a lot of mourners. Well – I say,

mourners – they were mostly tenants on the Greene Hall estate who had to be seen to have attended the funeral. The Greene family graves are in a small enclosure in the graveyard. Miles' 'grave' is also in the enclosure," she added and John's eyes widened.

"Good God."

"It gave me a terrible shock," she admitted. "Mother said there was a grave but to actually see a headstone with his name inscribed on it was awful. Imagine if Miles had decided to come with us and saw his own grave?" she asked and John just shook his head. "Mother is angry he did not want to meet his father or come to Co Mayo but she did not see the headstone."

"Will you tell her you saw it?"

"Yes. I just have to choose a suitable moment – whenever that will be." She gave him a comical smile. "I'll tell her you are attending the dinner party. She will be happy we shall all be together. Will and I and the children shall see you tomorrow morning." Reaching up, she kissed his cheek. "Young John enjoys your weekly visits."

"So do I."

"And we shall see if Ben and Belle laugh at you. If they do, consider it a compliment."

An hour later, Isobel and young John returned to number 30. She hung her hat and coat on the stand in the hall and John scrambled up the stairs.

"Ida, the lady's maid from number 7 is here, Mrs Fitzgerald," Zaineb said, coming out of the breakfast room as she went to go after him.

"Oh, Ida – yes – I said I would write her a letter of recommendation. I'll be five minutes, Zaineb."

"Yes, Mrs Fitzgerald."

She accompanied John to the nursery then went back downstairs to the servants' hall. Ida was seated at the dining table trying not to stare at Zaineb but caught Isobel's eyes on her, flushed, and got to her feet.

"Mrs Fitzgerald."

"Good morning, Ida. Come with me, please. Zaineb is from London," she said as they went into the morning room and she sat at the writing desk. "Do sit down. Where were you born?"

"Thank you." The young woman chose the sofa. "I was born just outside the village of Ballyglas, Mrs Fitzgerald."

"But you're definitely staying here in Dublin?"

"Yes, I am, Mrs Fitzgerald. There are far more opportunities for me here."

That was true. "How long were you my grandmother's lady's maid?"

"Almost six years. I joined the household in January 1876"

"And your surname?"

"Joyce, Mrs Fitzgerald," Ida replied and Isobel nodded, writing almost the same letter of recommendation she had written for herself as Maisie Byrne and which had helped her to secure the position of parlourmaid in the Harvey household.

30 Fitzwilliam Square
Dublin

To Whom It May Concern,

Ida Joyce was lady's maid to my late grandmother, Matilda Greene, of Greene Hall, Ballyglas, Westport, Co Mayo from January 1876 to December 1881. During that time, she proved to be a hard worker and she was always polite, tidy, courteous and willing.

I would have no hesitation in recommending Ida Joyce for any future household position she may apply for.

Isobel Fitzgerald (Mrs)

"Ida, I wish I could tell you of someone looking for a lady's maid but, unfortunately, I cannot."

"The agency I'm going to register with opens again on the 2nd of January."

"What will you do until then and until you find another position?" Isobel asked, blotting the ink, before folding the letter and placing it in an envelope. "Where will you live?"

"Susan – the scullery maid – her family live on North King Street," Ida replied as Isobel got up and sat beside her on the sofa. "They have agreed that I can lodge with them."

"I'm glad. Here is the letter and the very best of luck to you."

"Thank you, Mrs Fitzgerald." Ida took the envelope. "I'm very grateful."

"What was it like being a servant at Greene Hall?" Isobel inquired and Ida squirmed. "I expect my grandmother was an exacting mistress."

"She was, Mrs Fitzgerald."

"Mrs Greene may have been my grandmother but I

barely knew her. I hope she wasn't cruel to you?"

Ida's gaze dropped to the envelope in her hands. "Mrs Greene expected only the very best from the servants," she said diplomatically.

"And Mr Greene?"

"Mr Greene's health has been failing for quite a while and Mrs Greene devoted all her time to him. Mr Knox and Mrs McKee, the housekeeper, manage the house and servants and a land agent manages the estate, the outdoor servants and the tenants."

"What is the land agent's name?"

"Christopher Dudley, Mrs Fitzgerald. He is an English gentleman like—" Ida stopped abruptly and grimaced.

"Like Captain Boycott who was the land agent on the Earl of Erne's estate?" Isobel prompted and Ida nodded. "The Boycott affair was reported on in the newspapers here as well. Is Mr Dudley as disliked as Captain Boycott was?"

"Yes, he is, Mrs Fitzgerald."

"How long has he been the land agent?"

"Since my grandfather's time, Mrs Fitzgerald. Mr Dudley is eighty-five now—"

"Eighty-five?" Isobel exclaimed and Ida nodded.

"And he is still as fit as a fiddle."

More's the pity. Isobel could almost hear the young woman silently adding the words.

"Was he land agent prior to the Great Famine?"

"Yes, Mrs Fitzgerald."

That meant Mr Dudley was more than likely responsible for evicting Mrs Bell's parents.

"Has Mr Dudley had a free rein since Mr Greene's health declined?"

"Mr Dudley has had a free rein for many, many years, Mrs Fitzgerald. Mr Greene loves his books and his interest in the management of the estate dwindled. Mrs Greene had more of an interest but Mr Dudley would never heed her…"

"Because she was a woman," Isobel finished. "What do you think should happen to the estate when Mr Greene dies?" she asked and Ida's blue eyes bulged.

"You're asking me that, Mrs Fitzgerald?"

"You've lived on the estate all your life, Ida. Surely there are improvements you would wish to see made?"

"Well…"

"Mr Dudley retiring for a start?" Isobel suggested and Ida nodded.

"And… well… the Land League want to bring about the end of landlordism…"

And so do I, Isobel silently concluded the sentence for her.

"How do you think that should happen?" she asked.

"Peacefully," Ida stated firmly. "I agree with Mr Parnell on that."

"One of the clauses in Mr Gladstone's land-reform bill is land purchase. The government will advance three-quarters of the purchase cost to be repaid over thirty-five years at a small rate of interest. Can the Greene Hall estate tenants afford to avail of it?"

"The majority of them won't be able to afford it, Mrs Fitzgerald," Ida replied and Isobel's heart sank. "They would still have to pay one quarter of the purchase cost and that amount is out of the reach of all but a few of the more well-off tenants."

"Another clause allows tenants to appeal for a reduction

in their rent in a Land Court so that may help."

"Yes, my father said he would be a fool not to try for a reduction in the rent."

"How long have your family lived near Ballyglas, Ida?"

"For hundreds of years, Mrs Fitzgerald. My father says the Joyces used to own the land once. Now, he lives in a rented cottage on five acres of rented land. I hope he will own them both one day."

Chapter Six

Will stared at his reflection in the wardrobe mirror as he shrugged on his tailcoat the following evening. His father had behaved as normal when he had come for his weekly visit to the children that morning. So what had the Westland Row meeting with David been about? Try as he might, he simply couldn't put it out of his head.

"Where is David spending New Year's Eve?" he whispered to Alfie as he followed Isobel and John into number 55's drawing room and the boy ran to his Grandmamma Martha for a kiss.

"At his rooms," Alfie replied with a grimace. "We had planned to go to the theatre but then Mother organised this dinner party and we had to cancel."

"Soon, your lives will return to a routine." Will tried to raise his spirits but it was clear Alfie was bitterly disappointed.

"I know, but I did want to spend more than a few minutes with him before I go back to Trinity College."

"Surprise him tomorrow?" Will suggested but Alfie was glancing towards the door.

"Here are your mother and father," he said and Will turned in surprise at his parents arriving together. James and

Martha greeted them warmly and Will smiled as his mother approached, wearing a striking purple dress. "You look magnificent, Mother," he said and kissed her cheek.

"Thank you. My cab and your father's cab arrived here at the same time," she said and he sighed. So they hadn't travelled together after all. "Still," she went on with a little smile, "it was ladies first and I was admitted to the house before him. You look wonderful, Isobel."

"Thank you, Sarah, you do, too," Isobel replied, smoothing a hand across the bodice of her favourite deep red dress.

"Are Ben and Belle enjoying eating solid food?"

"Belle loves carrot. Ben is taking a little time to adjust to it."

"He will adjust," Will said confidently. "Ben simply has a more discerning palate."

"Oh, so that is what slapping Bridget's hand away and sending the spoonful of carrot flying across the nursery at young John is called." Isobel laughed. "The carrot went into John's hair and he wasn't at all amused."

"But Ben was." Will grinned.

"Ben was what?" Will's father came to them and Will's mother moved away.

"Not too enamoured with mashed carrot," Will explained.

"Ah. Well, give Ben time, his father loved carrot. Once he had picked out all the pieces of swede with his fingers and dropped them on the floor, that is," he added slyly and Will rolled his eyes comically.

"John?" Isobel hurried after the boy as he climbed onto the sofa, grasped the back and began to bounce up and down.

"Has he overcome his hysterics?" Will's father asked.

"He's been calm and he's stopped asking Isobel and I to promise that we will see him later or in the morning. It was a setback we could have done without. Miles also seems to have recovered," he added, glancing across the room at Miles as he lifted a volume down from the bookcase and showed it to James.

"Miles looks very grand in his new white tie and tails."

"He does." Will smiled. "I think your namesake is a little jealous."

"White tie and tails do not go well with short trousers. I'm afraid my namesake is going to have to wait a few years. You mentioned you brought portraits back from Greene Hall?" his father added with a glance at the walls.

"Isobel and her mother haven't got around to dividing them up yet. Nor to looking at Mrs Greene's jewellery. Martha thought it was a little too soon and has suggested to Isobel that they wait a while."

"That was wise of her."

"The *Journal* offices reopen the day after tomorrow," Will commented.

"They do. I never thought I would say this after practising medicine for so long but I truly enjoy my work at the *Journal* and I'm happy you are now content at the practice."

"I am very happy having David at the practice. He is also gaining valuable experience in the Liberties."

"I do not know how he can practise medicine on opposite sides of the city."

"He is more than able," Will replied simply.

"Will you make his position permanent?"

"Offer him a partnership, you mean?" Will asked and his father nodded. "I haven't thought about it."

"It is almost a year since Fred died."

"I know it is," Will snapped and closed his eyes for a moment. "After what happened with Fred, I don't know if I want to go into partnership with anyone else and David is not thirty yet. I am content with the way things are for now."

"But, in time, you'll consider David?"

"I sincerely hope you are not suggesting Fred's memory will fade – I will never forget Fred – ever," he roared and everyone stared at him in astonishment. "I do apologise," he said quietly. "Excuse me."

He went out onto the landing and found himself trembling.

"Come with me." It was Isobel and she took his hand and led him up the stairs to the second floor. "What did he say to provoke you?" she asked softly.

"Father wanted to know if I will offer David a partnership," he said. "Perhaps that is what they met to discuss – whether I had mentioned the possibility. I haven't – and I don't think I will – I don't think I can."

"Has David said anything about a partnership? Or dropped any hints?" she inquired and he shook his head.

"No, not a thing. Everything at the practice has been as normal – there has been nothing to suggest David wishes to leave and join another practice. When is my father going to stop interfering?" he demanded, raising his gaze to the ceiling. "The practice is mine and I will run it as I see fit."

"Would you like to go home?" she offered.

"No. But thank you for asking." Lifting her hands, he bent his head and kissed them. "I miss Fred, that is all."

"We all miss Fred," she said. "And on his anniversary, you and I will go to Mount Jerome Cemetery with some porcelain flowers – I have seen some with a glass dome. There are no fresh flowers at this time of year and these will ensure his grave is always adorned."

Tears pricked his eyes and he blew out his cheeks in an effort to calm himself. "Thank you. I haven't been there since Maria's burial."

"Are you ready to go back downstairs?"

"In a moment." Taking her in his arms, he kissed her. "You always look stunning in that dress."

"And I do find you very handsome in white tie and tails," she said, straightening the bow tie then kissing his lips.

"Ahem." Both of them jumped and peered down the stairs at Alfie, who gave them a grin from the half landing. "Dinner is about to be served."

Taking her hand, they went downstairs and followed Alfie through the drawing room and into the dining room. They were seated opposite each other with John beside Isobel. Thankfully, John's grandfather was placed further along the table.

The onion soup followed by roast pork, carrots, parsnips and potatoes was delicious and John, in particular, enjoyed the crackling. The boy's dark eyes bulged when a huge fruit trifle was carried into the dining room and he devoured a dish-full and a small second helping.

"Lovely," he proclaimed before stifling a yawn.

Will pretended he hadn't seen the yawn but he would bring John home in a few minutes and he got up as Martha, his mother, Isobel, John and Miles retired to the drawing room.

"Come and join us at this end of the table," his father called and, reluctantly, Will moved three places along the table and accepted a glass of port from James. "Looking forward to starting back at Trinity College, Alfie?"

"Yes, I am. After this Christmas, going back will seem like a rest."

Will couldn't help but smile and James nodded.

"I am looking forward to settling into a routine as well. I simply haven't been able to since the wedding and now I must. Martha has resigned herself to the fact she will not see her father again and Isobel has been wonderful – bringing young John here – having Martha visit the twins – asking Sarah to call here – I simply cannot thank her enough for all she has done. And Miles has settled in so well it is as if he has lived here all his life. Again, I have Isobel – and you, Alfie – to thank for that."

Alfie raised his glass in reply. "But poor Will has had to try and maintain a routine all along – people do not stop being ill simply because it is Christmas."

"I have managed," he replied. "Just. I think we have all coped very well with the events of the past month. I sincerely hope 1882 is kinder to us all."

"Hear-hear," Alfie replied and clinked Will's glass with his.

"And now a young gentleman needs to be escorted home to bed," he said, draining his glass and getting up. "I saw him trying to hide a yawn. Excuse me."

He went into the drawing room and John stared at him in dismay, knowing immediately why he was there.

"It's not home-time already, is it?"

"Yes, it is. It's half past eight and you need to sleep off

the crackling and those bowls of trifle."

"The trifle was scrumptious," he declared.

"Yes, it was. Say goodnight and Happy New Year to everyone."

John went into the dining room then returned to the drawing room and shook Miles' hand and kissed and hugged the ladies before Will led him from the room.

"Is it really another year tomorrow?" the boy asked as they walked around the Fitzwilliam Square garden.

"Yes. Tomorrow will be the first day of January 1882 and you will be four years old later in the month."

"My birthday?" he asked eagerly.

"Yes, your fourth birthday."

"When are Ben and Belle's birthdays?"

"Not for a while yet – they will be a year old in July."

"How old are you?" John continued and Will smiled.

"I am thirty-two years old," he said and the boy stared up at him in awe. "Don't ask Isobel, Florrie or Bridget how old they are, will you? It's rude for a gentleman to ask a lady her age."

"All right," John replied and yawned.

"Good boy." They climbed the steps to number 30 and Will opened the front door. He carried John upstairs to the nursery and Florrie took the boy from him and gave John a kiss. "He's had crackling and trifle, amongst other things, and he now has an attack of the yawns."

Florrie chuckled. "The sooner you go to sleep, Master John, the sooner it will be the new year."

"Will says it is going to be 1882 and I'll be four."

"Four? Good gracious me."

He followed them into the children's bedroom and went

to the twins' cradles. Ben was asleep on his back with his mouth slightly open while Belle was also lying on her back but with her head turned to one side and her cheek resting in the palm of her tiny hand.

"They are very different now, Dr Fitzgerald." Bridget smiled at them. "And noticing more and more every day. Master John shows them his elephant and ducks and they laugh and try and reach out and grab them."

"We must buy them some more soft toys because they are going to be either thrown across the nursery or put in their mouths."

He kissed the twins' foreheads then turned to John and kissed his cheek. "Goodnight, John," he said. "Happy New Year. Isobel and I will see you in the morning. Goodnight, Florrie. Goodnight, Bridget. Happy New Year to you both," he added before returning to number 55 and accepting a glass of whiskey from Alfie.

"Don't take offence, Will." Alfie replaced the stopper on the decanter. "But I'm not in the humour for sitting here simply waiting for midnight."

"Charades, anyone?" Mrs Ellison suggested and Alfie shot Will a horrified glance.

By one minute to midnight, Will was aching to go home and go to bed. During a seemingly never-ending game of charades, they had exhausted songs, poems, novels and plays and Will had had enough. Still, he reflected, Martha had enjoyed herself so the evening hadn't been an utter waste of everyone's time.

They all sang *Auld Lang Syne* as the clock on the mantelpiece chimed midnight and as they sang, Will hoped it wouldn't be seen as extremely rude if he and Isobel were to leave in ten minutes' time.

"1882." His mother-in-law kissed his cheek. "Happy New Year, Will."

"Happy New Year to you, too, Martha." He pretended to stifle a yawn and she patted his hands.

"You are tired?"

"I'm afraid I am, yes. Tomorrow, Isobel, the children and I will have a relaxing day."

"Have you heard from Nurse Barton?" she added in a whisper.

"I hope to hear from her in the next few days. We agreed that she would send a weekly report on Mr Greene's health."

Mrs Ellison nodded, he squeezed her arm and looked around for Isobel. Catching her eye, he made a brief nod towards the door and she joined them.

"Isobel and I are going home now, Martha," he told her. "And a cab is due to come for Mother soon, too. Thank you for a very enjoyable evening," he said and saw Isobel fight to hide a smile. "Goodnight, all," he called. "Happy New Year."

They were shown out of the house and he stood on the pavement for a moment, inhaling and exhaling a deep breath.

"I'm not quite sure who looked the most bored," Isobel teased. "You or Alfie."

"Alfie wanted to be with David and I can't bear charades."

"Dare I ask for a New Year's kiss?" she asked and he gave her a grin.

"Happy New Year, Mrs Fitzgerald," he said and kissed her lips. "Let's go to bed."

Everyone gladly fell into a routine over the next few days and as Will went downstairs to breakfast on the Friday morning of the following week, Zaineb passed him a letter in the hall. Assuming it to be from Nurse Barton, he tore open the envelope before noticing the Dublin postmark and grimacing. He really should have heard from her by now. Pulling out a sheet of notepaper, he glanced at the signature. The letter was from Dr Harrison.

> *St Patrick's Hospital*
> *Bow Lane*
> *Dublin*
>
> *Dear Dr Fitzgerald,*
> *I would be grateful if you could come and see me in the next few days, ideally before Miles' next visit.*
> *Yours truly,*
> *Bertram Harrison*

Short and puzzling. Will put the letter in the inside pocket of his frock coat and went into the breakfast room.

At the practice house, he bid Eva a good morning and hung his hat and overcoat on the stand in the office.

"Are there any additional house calls I need to be aware of this afternoon?" he asked.

"Yes, Dr Fitzgerald, one. Could you please call to Mrs Jones?"

"Of course. Thank you, Eva."

That was settled, then. He had time to go to Swift's Hospital that afternoon.

He was shown into Dr Harrison's office just after four o'clock and the older man rose briefly from behind his desk and shook Will's hand.

"Thank you for coming so promptly. Please, sit down."

"Not at all." Will sat on one of two chairs in front of the desk. "Is there a problem with Miles?"

"Not so much of a problem now but a potential problem. Since his move to Fitzwilliam Square, Miles has been to see me three times. Each time, he has spoken of little else but your wife."

"My wife – and Mrs Ellison – bring Miles here each week. My wife spends a great deal of time with him."

"Yes, and therein lies the potential problem." Dr Harrison leant forward, clasping his hands in front of him on the desk. "Dr Fitzgerald, I am concerned Miles may be forming an inappropriate attachment to your wife," he said and Will's jaw dropped.

"What has Miles been saying about my wife?" Will asked slowly.

"How beautiful she is. How he enjoys her kissing his cheek. How he enjoys her bringing him for walks."

"They have never gone walking alone together – never. My wife and Mrs Ellison bring Miles for walks in the Fitzwilliam Square garden and they showed him St Stephen's Green for the first time last week. As for my wife kissing his cheek… my wife is demonstrative… she wants to make Miles feel loved and welcomed. I see now she may have gone too far."

"Dr Fitzgerald, I would suggest that for the time being your wife spends less time with Miles and that you – as well as I – make it abundantly clear that she is not only your wife but a close relative of his."

"Yes, of course, but my mother-in-law cannot bring Miles here alone each week. It is not that she is inept, she simply finds this hospital and the fact that Miles was all but abandoned in it very distressing."

"Is there no-one else who could accompany them?" Dr Harrison asked.

Will sighed and pondered the question for a moment. "My mother," he said. "I shall call and ask her."

"Good."

"Has Miles developed an attachment to anyone before?"

"I was made aware there was a nurse some years ago but she left to get married. Nothing untoward happened – the attachment was nipped in the bud."

"Would Miles ever act upon his feelings?"

"Miles admired the nurse from afar, Dr Fitzgerald. I believe your wife has nothing to fear from him but he needs to be told that this particular attachment is not appropriate. I would be grateful if you would speak to Miles before my next meeting with him."

Will walked to James' Street in search of a cab deep in thought. He needed to alert James and Alfie but should Martha be told as well and, most importantly, should he tell Isobel? Yes, he decided at once, he couldn't keep it from her. He was going to have to inform her mother, too, as Martha would wonder why Isobel wasn't visiting Miles as often.

"You looking for a cab, or what?" A voice made him jump and he realised he had been standing on the pavement with a hand in the air.

"Yes, I am." Instructing the cabman to bring him to number 8 Westmoreland Street, he got in.

Will had to wait outside James' office for a few minutes until the solicitor saw a client to the door and did a double-take.

"Will? Is there something wrong?"

"Do you have a few minutes?" Will inquired.

"Yes, come in," James replied, extending a hand into the office. "Take a seat," he added, they sat down and Will recounted his meeting with Dr Harrison.

"...So you are going to have to inform Martha, too," he concluded.

"Are you absolutely sure Isobel is in no danger from Miles?" James asked and Will nodded.

"According to Dr Harrison, Isobel is in no danger," he confirmed, getting to his feet. "I must go. I need to call on Mother before I go home. Please tell Martha and Alfie as soon as possible?"

"Yes, of course."

"Thank you, James. Once they know, I shall speak with Miles."

"One of us will advise you when you are free to do so – most likely tomorrow."

"I must admit I am not looking forward to it," he said and James gave him a sympathetic smile. "And please don't tell Martha this, but I'm getting worried about Nurse Barton. I haven't received a report from her. I'm going to write to her but have the letter delivered to the address of Dr Bourke in Westport and hope he brings it to her at Greene Hall."

Will was a little late arriving home and, hearing the front door close, Isobel went out to the hall hoping there was nothing wrong.

"I'm sorry." He kissed her lips. "I had to go and see both James and Mother."

"Oh? Why?"

"Is dinner ready?" he asked instead of answering.

"Yes, it is."

"Good. We'll eat first and then I'll tell you."

Half an hour later, they sat on the sofa in the morning room and she listened. When he finished, she got up and stood in front of the fire with her back to him.

"I truly had no idea."

"Isobel, none of us had. James is going to tell Alfie and your mother and I have just spoken to mine."

"Why your mother?" she asked, turning to face him.

"Because you shouldn't accompany Miles and your mother to Swift's Hospital for a while. My mother has agreed to instead."

"Do I have to keep away from Miles altogether?"

"No, but Dr Harrison advised that you not visit Miles as often. Tomorrow, I shall go to number 55 and speak to him."

"No," she said and Will frowned. "I shall."

"Isobel—"

"It must come from me, Will," she insisted. "I'll be gentle but firm if that makes any sense? Agreed?" she asked and he nodded.

Her heart was thumping as she walked with Will to number 55 after luncheon the following day and a net curtain twitched at the morning room window as they went up the steps to the front door. Gorman admitted them to the house and her mother, James and Alfie came out to the hall.

"This is most disturbing, Isobel," her mother said severely.

"I'm sorry."

"We haven't made a terrible mistake in having Miles live here, have we?" Mrs Ellison added in a hushed tone.

"No," she replied firmly. "Absolutely not. Any mistakes made have all been mine. I will speak with Miles and I will make him understand. And this is not a conversation we should be having in the hall. Where is Miles?"

"He has gone to the library," her mother replied shortly and returned to the morning room.

Isobel rolled her eyes and went up the stairs, Alfie and Will following her as far as the landing.

"We'll be waiting here," Will told her and she nodded.

Miles smiled at her in pleasant surprise as she went into the library and closed the door.

"Isobel, how lovely to see you." He waited for her to kiss his cheek and frowned when she didn't.

"Miles, I must speak to you on a serious matter. I like you very much. You are a kind and gentle man and I am so glad you are living here but—" Pausing, she took a deep breath before continuing. "No matter how much I like you, I will never love you – at least not in the way I think you would wish me to."

Miles flushed a deep red but she ploughed on.

"Miles, I am married to Will and he is the love of my life. If it were not for Will… well… let me just say, I am so happy I am his wife and the mother of his children and mother in all but name to young John. As well as that, nothing can alter the fact you are my mother's brother – my uncle – grand uncle to my children. Do you understand what I am saying to you, Miles?"

He gave her a sad smile. "I understand. I'm sorry, Isobel."

"For the next little while, Sarah shall accompany you and Mother on your weekly visits to St Patrick's Hospital."

"You do not wish to see me anymore?"

"I will still visit you, Miles, just not as often. Ben and Belle are eating solid foods now, Belle is attempting to crawl and I need to be with them more."

"I understand," he said again. "I am so grateful to you for all you have done for me that I appear to have mistaken gratitude for love."

"You are my favourite uncle," she said, omitting the fact he was her only uncle. "And a good friend. And I will visit you again soon, I promise."

"Will I ever find someone I can truly love?" he asked as she went to turn away. "Someone who will truly love me in return?"

She stared up at him, not knowing quite how to answer. "I don't know," she replied, deciding the truth would be best. "I thought no-one would ever love me but then I met Will. Miles, all I can say is do not assume it will never happen. Do not ever lose hope."

She squeezed his hands before leaving him standing forlornly at the window.

Will and Alfie were sitting on the stairs and got up as she left the library and closed the door behind her.

"Well?" Will asked anxiously.

"It is done. And he understands that he mistook gratitude for love."

Relief flooded into both their faces and she grabbed Alfie's arm as he went to go into the room.

"I'm sorry," she said, knowing the more time he now spent with Miles was less time to spend with David.

"It's not your fault."

"Yes, it is."

"Miles realises his mistake and knows where he stands now." Alfie kissed her cheek and went inside.

Downstairs in the morning room, James got up from an armchair and her mother turned in her seat at the writing desk.

"I have spoken with Miles," she announced. "And he understands. It seems to have been a case of him mistaking gratitude for love."

"Was he upset?" Mrs Ellison asked.

"Quiet, rather than upset. Alfie is with him now. Let me know how he is later, please?"

"I shall ask Alfie to call to you."

"Thank you and, Mother, please do not question or regret the decision to bring Miles to live here."

"But, Isobel, for him to think of you in such a way…"

"He acknowledges he was mistaken," she said and her mother nodded.

"Are you and Will going out for your Saturday afternoon together?" James asked brightly.

"Yes, we are."

"Enjoy yourselves," he said and she replied with a weak smile.

They left the house and walked in silence out of Fitzwilliam Square.

"We don't have to go if you don't feel like it," Will said and she stopped.

"I do want to go. I want to be away from here – if only for an afternoon."

"Good," he said softly. "I want to be alone with you – if only for an afternoon."

In the Grafton Street café, they sat at a window table and Will ordered a pot of coffee.

"Am I too..?" she began and grimaced. "I don't know… I wanted to be welcoming to Miles and I over-did it. He's not a little boy like young John. I went about it all wrong. Your mother really doesn't mind taking my place on Miles' visits to Swift's Hospital?"

"No, not at all. In fact, I think she is secretly glad to have the opportunity to not only be of help but to get out of the house. She has been rather wary of inviting friends and acquaintances to number 67 for fear of them wondering where Father is."

"Your father has rejoined the Trinity Club."

"Oh, good grief." Will rolled his eyes. "I was in the Trinity Club once with Jim Harvey. It was a dreadful place."

"Your father said he visits once per week. I suspect it is mainly to be seen socially but in a men-only club where no-one will ask where your mother is. Thank you." She smiled at the waitress who brought their coffee. "I think he has coped a little better with the separation than your mother so if a little good can come of this and your mother feels thankful she can be of use, then, I am glad."

Will nodded in agreement while he poured their coffee and she added milk and sugar to the cups.

"There is something else, isn't there?" she inquired as he stirred his coffee and took a sip.

"Yes, and your mother doesn't know this, but I haven't received a report from Nurse Barton. I was going to write to her via Dr Bourke in Westport on Monday but I think I will send her a telegram via him this afternoon."

They went to the nearest telegraph office and Will

decided to make the telegram a little cryptic but not too much so.

> *Happy New Year to all in Co Mayo. All well here.*
> *Write soon.*
> *W.F. M.D.*

"What do you think?" he asked her.

"It's fine. You've corresponded with Dr Bourke regarding Grandfather so it shouldn't be too difficult for him to work out who the W.F. M.D. is," she replied and he went to the counter. "I won't say anything about this," she said when he returned. "But Mother is bound to start asking questions soon."

"She did ask me just after midnight on New Year's Day but it was a little too soon to have received a report then."

"Let's just hope either Nurse Barton or Dr Bourke sends a reply. While we wait," she added, taking his arm. "Young John is four soon and we must plan his birthday. And Miles must be invited."

"Yes, of course, he must."

"If we were to have a very informal luncheon with all his favourite foods..?"

"Soft boiled egg and toast 'soldiers' followed by trifle, trifle and more trifle?" Will suggested and she laughed.

"The trifle, yes. I'll speak to Mrs Dillon."

"What can we buy him? It's so soon after Christmas."

"We could bring him to the Zoological Gardens as a birthday treat," she said and Will's face brightened.

"That is a wonderful idea and if we went on a Sunday all of us could go. I cannot remember when I was last at the Zoological Gardens."

"A Sunday it is." She smiled and they left the telegraph office.

It was Monday afternoon when a telegram for Will was delivered to number 30. She passed the envelope to him as soon as he came home. To their relief, the telegram was from Nurse Barton.

Happy New Year to you all from Co Mayo. All here as well as can be expected. Hope to enjoy a day out in Castlebar soon.
B.B.

"Good God," Isobel exclaimed. "Does the poor woman have to travel as far as Castlebar simply in order to make sure a letter gets to us?"

"It looks like it." Will folded the telegram and put it back in the envelope. "But it is a weight off my mind to have heard from her."

"Should I show it to Mother?"

"Yes, I don't see why not."

After dinner, they called to number 55 and Gorman admitted them to the house.

"Is Mr Miles in the morning room?" she asked.

"Mr Miles is in his room reading, Mrs Fitzgerald," the butler replied and opened the morning room door for them.

"Thank you, Gorman," she said. "There's no need to stand," she added quickly as James and Alfie went to get up from the armchairs and she went straight to the sofa and handed the telegram to her mother. "It's from Nurse Barton and was delivered this afternoon."

"'All here as well as can be expected'," her mother read aloud before giving Isobel and then Will a puzzled glance.

"I sent a rather cryptic telegram to Mr Greene's doctor

in Westport on Saturday," Will explained as Mrs Ellison passed the telegram to her husband. "I don't think any post is getting to or from Greene Hall."

"This has eased my mind considerably," James said, reading the telegram before handing it to Alfie. "I was getting quite concerned."

"Won't you sit down?" Her mother patted the seat of the sofa and Isobel shook her head. "Thank you, but it's young John's bedtime. We simply came with the telegram and to tell you we are going to have a very informal luncheon for him on his birthday and a trip to the Zoological Gardens on the nearest Sunday. You are all invited – Miles as well. How is he?" she asked tentatively.

"A little quiet," Alfie replied, passing the telegram to her. "But he'll love the trip to the Zoological Gardens. And I'll come, too. I've never been."

"Good. Well, we shall see you all soon. We'll see ourselves out."

A letter postmarked Castlebar arrived a week later. Will brought it into the breakfast room, sliced the envelope open with a knife and pulled out two sheets of notepaper.

Greene Hall
Ballyglas
Westport
Co Mayo

Dear Dr Fitzgerald,

As you can see from the postmark, this letter has been posted in Castlebar. There is no post to or from Greene Hall via the post office in Ballyglas and while I did consider the post office in Westport, I thought it more prudent to take a short railway journey to Castlebar and Mr Knox himself drove me to and from Westport Station in the carriage so as not to put Mr Mulloy in a difficult position.

It will be impossible for me to travel to Castlebar each week as the journey there and back takes the best part of a day but I shall travel there once per fortnight and post a report to you. Castlebar is a pleasant enough destination for a days' excursion.

Dr Bourke has been very kind. He called here to Greene Hall on the afternoon of the day you left. He next called with your telegram and two oxygen cylinders and he will continue to call once per week. He and I agree that Mr Greene's breathing is deteriorating. It is now a considerable effort for Mr Greene to move from the bed to the bath chair and vice versa but I will continue to move him for as long as he is able so as to prevent bed sores.

I wheel Mr Greene around the ground floor, which he enjoys very much. That the paintings, photographs and jewellery are now in safe hands is a huge weight off his mind. I also read the newspapers to him and play the piano in the drawing room. Mrs Greene used to play to him and both he and the servants enjoy the sound of music in the house.

I do not believe Mr Greene, myself or the servants are in any danger here as long as we all use our common sense. There are far larger estates for the Land League to target more harshly. My only concern was the postal issue but as it can be circumvented, it is no longer a problem and is trivial when compared to what occurred on the Earl of Erne's estate at Lough Mask.

And that concludes my report, Dr Fitzgerald. As I stated, please expect further reports from me every fortnight.

My kind regards to you and your wife and to your extended family.

Yours truly,
Barbara Barton

Will passed the letter to Isobel and waited until she put it down.

"Except for the inconvenience of having to travel to Castlebar to post a letter, all seems as it should be," she said. "Grandfather's health is declining, but we all know it would."

"Bring the letter to your mother after breakfast," he said and she nodded. "I may be a little late home this evening, I'm going to engage George Millar and his brothers for the visit to the Zoological Gardens on Sunday and afterwards call to Mrs Bell."

That afternoon, after completing house calls and hiring the Millar brothers' cabs and carriage, Will walked along Pimlico to Mrs Bell's rooms. His former housekeeper had just finished the washing and was hanging the last few items of clothing to dry on wooden rails which hung above the fireplace in her kitchen.

"How is Jimmy getting on at Guinness' Brewery?" he asked, pulling on the rope and hoisting the rails high above their heads. "Does he like it there?"

"I think he does," she replied while he wound the rope

around a hook to secure it. "This past month has been a lot to take in – his mammy dying – and him starting work in a place as big as Guinness'. But he knows he's lucky to have the job and he does love the horses."

"Good. And how are you?"

"Me?" she cried as they sat down at the table. "Sure, I'm grand, and I do enjoy having someone to look after again. I do miss Maura, though. Thirty-two years-old is no age to die."

"No, it isn't," he agreed quietly. "When is Jimmy's birthday?"

"The day before St Patrick's Day."

"Don't ask him directly, but try and find out what he would like as a present."

"I will, thank you."

"It's John's fourth birthday next week and on Sunday, all of us are going to the Zoological Gardens."

"I was there once many moons ago. They have lions, you know? Huge things. And their teeth – one of them yawned and – Mother of God – the size of them teeth."

Will smiled. "I haven't visited for many years. I was taken there with my brother. It will be strange that my next visit there will be with his son."

"You must miss your brother," Mrs Bell said sadly.

Which brother, Will asked himself. "I'm starting to," he admitted. "No matter where in the world he was, Edward would always write a long letter home at Christmas, and the lack of it this Christmas past…"

"Has John started to ask questions about him?"

"No. He sees Isobel and I as his mother and father, even though he doesn't call us that. It will be a few years yet before we can sit him down and tell him about Edward and the little we know about his mother."

"Poor child," Mrs Bell murmured.

"It's also Fred Simpson's first anniversary at the beginning of February. And I'm dreading it," he confessed. "Isobel and I are going to Mount Jerome Cemetery on the day – she's going to buy some porcelain flowers in a glass globe – or some such frightful ornament for his grave – and I'm really dreading the visit."

"If you cry, it is nothing to be ashamed of."

"I know. Both Edward and Fred's deaths were unexpected but Fred's death hit me the hardest. I expected Fred to always be there – does that sound ridiculous?" he asked and she shook her head.

"Not at all. He was the same age as you and he was your oldest friend."

"This year has gone so fast – Ben and Belle are being weaned onto solid foods already."

"Ah, bless their little hearts. And how is Isobel's uncle settling in?"

"Miles has settled in very well," Will replied. "But there are lessons we must all learn."

"Oh?"

"Miles was starting to form an attachment to Isobel – an attachment based on deep gratitude – but one which was inappropriate all the same – given the fact he is her uncle," he explained and Mrs Bell's eyes widened. "Dr Harrison at Swift's Hospital alerted me to it and I should have seen it myself – we should all have seen it. Isobel has admitted she treated Miles like John – as a child – we all did. But Miles is not almost four – he is a man in his forties – but a man who thinks like a fifteen-year-old boy."

"Have you had a word with Miles?"

"Isobel has and Dr Harrison has. From now on, Miles will be treated and spoken to as an adult."

"And his father?"

"I received a letter from Nurse Barton posted in Castlebar to get around the post office in Ballyglas refusing to deliver post to or accept post from Greene Hall. Mr Greene's health is deteriorating but we all knew it would. He is receiving the best of care from both Nurse Barton and a Dr Bourke in Westport."

"And you're happy with Dr Powell in the practice?"

"I am," he replied cautiously. "And he appears to have been well-accepted here?"

"Oh, yes. Some people were concerned with his age but I reminded them you were around his age when you came to Brown Street first. He was so good with poor Maura…" Mrs Bell tailed off and Will squeezed her hands.

"Let me know about a birthday present for Jimmy," he said, getting to his feet.

"I will. Thanks for calling, Dr Fitzgerald, I enjoy our chats."

"I do, too." He kissed her cheek and left her.

After luncheon on Sunday, the Millar brothers' cabs and carriage stopped outside the Zoological Gardens in the Phoenix Park. As Will got out of the cab, Isobel glanced up at the grey sky, hoping it wouldn't rain. She passed young John to him then followed, took the boy's hand and they smiled as he gazed at the thatched entrance lodge with awe.

"We could be a couple of hours," Will told George.

"There's no hurry, Dr Fitzgerald, I have a packet of smokes with me."

Will helped her mother and his mother out of the other cab then went to pay the entrance fee while James, Alfie, Miles and Will's father got out of the carriage.

"I want to see the lions," young John announced. "Will was told they have huge teeth."

"They eat raw meat," his grandfather said. "So they need to have big, sharp, teeth."

"What are you looking forward to seeing, Miles?" she asked, determined that he not be made feel left out.

"I have always been fascinated by giraffes. I never thought I would get an opportunity to see any."

Young John's jaw dropped when they all stopped at the lion house. To his delight, a male lion yawned, displaying a dazzling array of razor-sharp teeth.

"Very impressive." Alfie grinned. "And very clean."

"He gnaws on bones which keeps them both sharp and clean," Miles explained and Alfie nodded.

"I must try that myself."

Will's mother gave a little gasp at the giraffe enclosure when one raised its head to its full height. "Ungainly, yet graceful," she said. "How odd."

Miles remained silent and Isobel approached him a little warily.

"You said you found giraffes fascinating. Do you not like these giraffes?"

"Yes," he replied simply.

"But?" she prompted.

"I realise the purpose of a zoo is to show the general public birds and animals they otherwise would never see but—" He sighed. "None of them are free – and never will be free. I did wish to come but now I am here, I find this place very sad."

"We have seen over half the animals now and—"

"I shall not say anything to young John, I promise."

"Thank you," she said and squeezed his arm. "Perhaps, when young John is older, he may share your view."

"Do you?" he asked and she stared up at him.

"Most of these animals have never been free and don't know any different."

"In St Patrick's Hospital, I was the same – until you came. At least people didn't pay to come and view me like they do in London to the poor souls in Bedlam."

"You know of Bethlem Royal Hospital?" she asked in surprise.

"Indirectly. Some years ago, I overheard two doctors discussing the hospital. I will always be grateful to you for rescuing me," he added quietly and her eyes filled with tears.

"We brought you home – like we brought young John home – because you are part of our family and you always will be."

"What are you two whispering about?"

She hadn't heard Alfie approach and jumped.

"I will tell you later," Miles replied. "This is young John's afternoon. Shall we go on? I believe the reptile house is along this path."

Alfie shot her a puzzled glance as Miles walked away but she shook her head and they followed him.

On 26th January – young John's birthday – luncheon was planned for two o'clock, so Will could make three urgent house calls straight after surgery. Mrs Dillon was worth her weight in gold. In addition to the ham and cheese sandwiches, there were cold meats, devilled eggs, cheeses, soda bread and savoury biscuits. A gigantic fruit trifle followed and when they all retired to the drawing room, the housekeeper carried in a sponge cake in the shape of a number four.

Young John's eyes had bulged at the fruit trifle but he clapped both hands to his cheeks as the iced birthday cake was placed on a side table. Sliding off the sofa, he ran to Mrs Dillon and hugged her around the waist.

"Thank you, Mrs Dillon, it's huge," he cried in delight. "There is enough for everyone."

"There certainly is, Master John. Mrs Fitzgerald kindly instructed that there be enough for you, your guests and all the servants. You may have a slice when Mary and Zaineb bring the tea and a glass of milk shortly."

"Thank you, Mrs Dillon, I'm full of trifle."

"You are very welcome, Master John," she replied and began to cut the cake into slices.

"We really must divide the Greene portraits between us, Isobel," her mother said, glancing at a rather dull landscape hanging on the chimney breast. "They have sat in a corner of our morning room for far too long."

"Whenever you feel up to it, Mother."

"Tomorrow morning?" Mrs Ellison suggested and she nodded. "I'll ask Miles if he would like to see them, too. He may not, but he should be given the opportunity to refuse," her mother added and they got up from the sofa and walked to a window. "He didn't enjoy the visit to the Zoological Gardens last Sunday," Mrs Ellison continued quietly. "Alfie spoke to him and he later told me why. I am appalled. Bethlem Royal Hospital in London charges the public to view their patients?"

"Some of the wardens did," Isobel replied. "Whether they still do, I cannot say. Thankfully, according to Will's father, they never have at Swift's Hospital."

"I am very relieved to hear it. Does young John ever speak of the children's home?"

"No. And we do not mention it either."

"You and Will have done wonders with him. I hope we can all – not make Miles forget he was shut away – but help ensure it fades?"

"I hope so, too, Mother."

Isobel was admitted to number 55 at half past ten the next morning. Her mother and Miles were in the morning room and she smiled at the portraits which had been lined up on the floor leaning against the seat of the enormous sofa.

"Shall I ring for coffee before or after?" Mrs Ellison asked.

"After, please. It is still a little soon after breakfast. Miles?"

"I agree. After, please."

Miles stood the first portrait of a middle-aged man in a grey powdered wig on the seat of the sofa and Isobel turned to her mother.

"I am quite happy to do as what was suggested before," she said. "That Will and I take the 'wigged portraits' of earlier Greenes and you keep the portraits of Greenes you knew or knew of."

"Thank you," her mother replied and gestured to the portrait. "I'm afraid I don't know who this gentleman is so he may go to number 30."

Miles turned the portrait around and bent to read a label stuck to the back. "This is George Greene – 1700 to 1777."

"Hello, Georgie," she said cheekily and Miles laughed. "Next."

Next was the portrait of Eleanor Greene, her brown-eyed and auburn-haired great-grandmother and Mrs Ellison shook her head.

"She was beautiful. Even in old age, she was beautiful."

The next portrait placed on the sofa was of her great-grandfather, Henry Greene, and Miles stood back to view it.

"According to the label, he died at the age of forty-five."

"Eleanor never remarried," his sister told him. "And she lived to a great age."

They continued to inspect the portraits until two groups of four 'wigged' and six more recent Greenes stood against the wall near the door.

"On Grandfather's insistent instruction, we also took all the photographs and they are staying here." Isobel went to a box on the floor in a corner and picked it up. "I think you should see this one, Miles."

She set the box down on a side table before passing him the framed photograph of Alexander Walker and Miles' eyes widened.

"If I were clean-shaven, this man could be me."

"Alexander Walker was your mother's brother," she explained. "He was a soldier and died in the Crimea."

"May I keep this photograph and display it in my room?" he asked hesitantly and Isobel glanced at her mother.

"Of course you may," Mrs Ellison replied. "And, later, we shall put the other photographs and portraits on display – one or two in this room and the rest in the drawing room and library. Poor James must not be made feel as though there has been a sudden invasion of Greenes in the rooms we use most."

"No," Miles agreed. "I have enjoyed this morning very

much – it was a marvellous introduction to our ancestors, wasn't it, Isobel?" he asked and they exchanged a smile. "Some coffee would be very welcome now," he added and Isobel's mother went to the rope and rang for a servant.

Chapter Seven

On February 7th, the first anniversary of Fred's death, Will and Isobel took a cab to Mount Jerome Cemetery. Isobel had the flower globe she had purchased on her lap wrapped in her black fringed shawl. How the year had flown by. On the evening of that bittersweet day, Isobel had told him of her pregnancy and, oh, how he wished Fred could have seen Belle and Ben and been a godparent and 'uncle' to them and John.

They walked up the main avenue before turning off to the right for the Simpson graves. Two tall, plain headstones had recently been erected over Fred and baby Nicholas' grave, and that of Maria, Fred's mother and her husband Duncan Simpson.

"I should come here more often," he told Fred. "But, well, there is no excuse, except the fact that I miss you and I always will."

"We have something for you, Fred," Isobel added. "But, as I wrapped it before we came out, I regretted buying it."

"Oh?" Will frowned. "Why?"

"Because it's utterly hideous, isn't it?" she asked, pulling the shawl away and holding up the globe.

The porcelain roses were an unnatural shade of red and the globe's glass was so thick, it magnified them to an enormous degree.

"I'm afraid it is, yes," he replied and roared with sudden laughter. A moment or two later, both of them were laughing at Fred's graveside. "Let me put it on the grave, anyway, and give Fred a good old laugh."

"The shop did have a much nicer one with white roses," she said, as he took it from her and placed it near the headstone. "But this one seemed a little sturdier. I really should have purchased the other one."

"It doesn't matter," he said, straightening up and draping the shawl around her shoulders. "Thank you for making me laugh. I came here fully expecting to cry."

"We will come here every year – even when we are old and grey."

"Fred will be forever young – always thirty-one."

"Thirty-one is a good age, Will. Mature but still young."

"Yes, it is. I'm surprised Father didn't come with us."

"When I called to see your mother yesterday, I asked Tess if he had mentioned anything and she said no. Perhaps he wishes to come alone later."

"Perhaps," he agreed and shivered as an icy gust of wind blew into their faces. "Why is this cemetery always so cold?"

"Because we are never here in summer," she replied with a little smile.

"That is true," he said. "When did you last hear from Margaret?"

"The thank-you letter we received from Co Wicklow about a week after the children's christenings."

"I did think she would have come to Dublin for Fred and

Nicholas' first anniversaries."

"I thought she would, too, and I was expecting her to call to number 30 but…" Isobel tailed off and shrugged.

"Call to see Diana Wingfield?" he suggested. "She may have heard from Margaret at Christmas or more recently."

"I shall. I should have called to her long before this. I meant to call over Christmas – which must have been dreadful for her – but events put paid to my plans. I will ask her to call to number 30 as well and see the children."

"I can't help but wonder how things would have been if baby Nicholas and Fred had lived. They and Margaret would have been regular callers at number 30. Oh, how Fred would have laughed at our new collection of bewigged Greene gentlemen in the drawing room. He probably would have rehung all the portraits in order of greyness. Dark grey – not quite so dark grey – dirty white – and snow white."

"That is what I shall call them from now on," she said and he laughed again. "Young John is fascinated by them. He simply can't understand why a gentleman – who most likely had a perfectly reasonable head of hair – would wish to cover it all with an utterly disgusting wig which was probably infested with who-knows-what."

Another icy blast of wind blew into their faces and he took her hand.

"We'll go. And we won't leave it so long before we come back."

Walking to the practice house the next morning, Will made a detour to number 1 Ely Place Upper. To his pleasant surprise, all the shutters were open and a maid was cleaning the morning room window. Margaret must have found tenants at long last. He walked along Ely Place in the direction of Merrion Row, not sure if he were sad no Simpsons would ever live there again or relieved the house was reoccupied.

"There are tenants in the Simpson house," he told Eva as he hung his hat and overcoat on the stand in the office.

"I'm glad," she said with her usual forthrightness. "I didn't like seeing the house all shuttered-up."

"Neither did I."

"Did you go to Mount Jerome Cemetery yesterday?"

"Yes. I'm sorry, I just…" He tailed off and sighed.

"A year can seem a very short but also a very long time."

"Yes, it can." He gave her a little smile. "I'd better get on."

On his way home, he stood opposite number 1 Ely Place Upper again. The maid was now on the first floor, cleaning one of the drawing room windows. Good. After standing unoccupied for months, the house was receiving a thorough going-over.

"Tenants at last," Isobel mused as he told her while closing the morning room door. "I'm pleased," she added firmly. "Fred's estate must finally be settled. The house is lived-in again and Margaret has an income from it."

"Yes, I'm glad about that. It will give her an independence she has never had before."

"I called to Rutland Square today," she added. "But Diana Wingfield wasn't at home. I'll call again next week."

After dinner, he and Florrie helped John to bed while Isobel and Bridget fed Ben and Belle and changed their nappies. They kissed the children goodnight, he followed Isobel downstairs to the morning room and they settled on the sofa – Will with *The Irish Times* and Isobel with the

Freeman's Journal – which they would later swap. He read an article here and there but, then, his eyes were drawn to a short notice.

> *The engagement is announced between David Powell, M.D., only son of the late Cecil Powell and Mrs Powell of Trim, Co Meath, and Margaret Simpson, youngest daughter of the late Nicholas Dawson and Mrs Dawson of Dame Street, Dublin.*

Will read it again. And again. But it still made absolutely no sense to him.

"What is it?" Isobel murmured and he folded the newspaper, passed it to her and pointed to the notice. He felt her tense and she threw both newspapers down on the rug and got to her feet. "David and Margaret?" she demanded, her voice little more than a squeak.

"I don't understand it."

"But how can they marry – how can they? Oh, my God – Alfie…"

"Isobel – wait – stop," he commanded as she ran to the door. "How has Alfie been recently?"

"Does he know, you mean? Of course not – we would have noticed something. I'm going to number 55—"

"No, Isobel, I will see if he's there. If he is, I shall bring him here. Please, go upstairs and fetch my wallet in case he isn't."

He left the house without his hat or overcoat, hurried around the garden and rang number 55's front doorbell. Gorman opened the door and Will beckoned him out onto the steps.

"Please don't tell Mr and Mrs Ellison I have called, but I am looking for Mr Stevens."

"Mr Stevens has not yet returned home this evening, Dr Fitzgerald," the butler said and Will's heart sank. "Mrs Ellison is becoming rather concerned."

"Do you know if Mr Stevens had any plans for this evening?"

"No, Dr Fitzgerald, none as far as I am aware."

"I see. Thank you, Gorman."

The butler went back inside, Will turned away and took out his watch while racking his brains. It was half past seven. Where could Alfie be? Did he know about the engagement? If he did, could he have gone to Westland Row to confront David? Will grimaced and put his watch back in his waistcoat pocket. There was only one way to find out.

Returning to number 30, he called for Isobel before lifting their hats, her coat and his overcoat down from the stand.

"Alfie hasn't come home," he told her as she ran down the stairs. "So, you and I are going to Westland Row first and I'm bringing this just in case," he added, nodding to his medical bag.

Within five minutes, they had hailed a cab on Baggot Street Lower and were on their way. When the cab stopped on Westland Row, he turned to her.

"Stay here, I'll speak to David."

"But—"

"You'll have a chance to speak your mind to him some other time. Stay here." He got out of the cab carrying his medical bag and knocked at the front door. There was no reply so he hammered on the door with his fist. "Open up," he roared. "Now."

The door opened and a young man in his shirtsleeves glared at him. "Jesus – can a man not get any peace?"

"Is David Powell at home?"

"David?" The young man stared at him suspiciously.

"Well?" Will demanded before swearing under his breath and pushing past him.

He ran up the stairs two at a time and along the landing. The door to David's rooms was ajar and he went inside. Standing in the parlour doorway, his jaw dropped. The gas lamps on the walls illuminated a room which had been turned upside down. Every piece of furniture was either lying on its side or broken.

Walking along the hall to the bedroom, he saw that the double bed was intact but the bedcovers had been flung into a corner, the wardrobe toppled over onto its front and all the drawers of the chest of drawers pulled out and flung to the far side of the bed. The mirror, which had hung on a chain over the washstand was smashed, the jagged pieces glistening in the basin and on the rug.

In the kitchen, pots and pans were scattered across the floor and food had been thrown at the walls. The table was upturned and the four chairs left legless.

Returning to the hall, Will found the young man watching him warily from the door to the landing.

"What on earth happened here?" Will asked and he quickly looked away. "You must have heard – so tell me."

The young man sighed. "Someone hammered on the front door, like you did, shortly after six o'clock. I knew David was at home as I had seen him return, but he didn't answer the door, so I went downstairs and opened it. Alfie was standing on the steps and he looked – well – I have never seen a man look as he did. He pushed past me, like you did, and ran upstairs. The next thing I heard was them fighting and the furniture being destroyed."

"Then what happened?" Will prompted.

"David threw Alfie out – and, I mean, threw him out – he hauled Alfie down the stairs and threw him out onto the street. Both of them were bloody, sweating – swearing – the whole street and beyond must have heard. Alfie managed to get to his feet and stagger away. David went back upstairs but, only a matter of moments later, he went out and he hasn't come back."

"You said they were bloody – could you see any severe injuries?"

"Apart from their knuckles, not that I could see – and don't ask me where they are now because I don't know – and I don't care. If they want to fight over women – they can fecking-well do it somewhere else."

Will nodded. "Which way did they go?"

"Towards Lincoln Place."

"Thank you." Will ran down the stairs and out to the cab. Instructing the cabman to bring them to the practice house on Merrion Street Upper, he climbed inside and shut the door. "Alfie was here," he told Isobel, opening his medical bag and retrieving his keys. "He and David fought – everything in David's rooms is lying on the floor or smashed to pieces. Alfie left first and David shortly afterwards. Both of them are bleeding."

The cab stopped outside the practice house and Will jumped out. He helped Isobel onto the pavement before turning and halting abruptly. The front door was wide open and a bunch of keys had been dropped on the mat.

Picking them up, he stepped into the hall noting they were David's keys to the front door and to every room in the practice house. The office door was open, there was light in the room and he paused in the doorway returning his own set of keys to his medical bag. The oil lamp on Eva's desk was lit and he walked around it. The drawers were open and had been searched but everything else was as it should be.

Taking the lamp, he left the office. Isobel was standing at the front door and he passed his medical bag to her, held a finger to her lips and crept along the hall to the dispensary. The door was locked but he unlocked and opened it. None of the medicines had been touched so he closed and locked the door before trying the door of the waiting room. It was also locked but he unlocked and opened it as well, saw the room was deserted, closed and locked the door and went upstairs.

The doors to the three surgeries were ajar and Will went into the unused room first but the only things amiss were the empty desk drawers which had been pulled open. In his own surgery, the desk drawers had been opened and rummaged through and, in David's surgery, the drawers had been pulled out of the desk, placed on top and ransacked.

He hurried up the stairs to the second and third floors but found no-one there and returned to the first floor to lock the doors.

"It's safe, there's no-one here," he called to Isobel and she came upstairs. "This must have been Alfie. David wouldn't have needed to search everywhere."

"Has Alfie taken anything?" she asked and Will pursed his lips before realising what could be missing.

"The spare keys to the Pimlico surgery," he said and they went into David's surgery.

"You kept them here – the key to the medicine cupboard, too?" she cried while he lifted the contents out of the drawers and grimaced as he confirmed the three keys were gone. "For God's sake, Will, how could you be so reckless? Alfie has them now." She finished on a shaky whisper and clapped a hand to her mouth fighting back tears.

"Isobel." Clasping her hand, he kissed it. "David has keys, I have keys at number 30 and we agreed to keep a spare set here in David's desk. The spare set has always been secure up to now – Eva locks all the doors each evening before she leaves. Please go and instruct the cabman to take us to Pimlico by the most direct route while I lock up here."

Leaving the drawers and contents on David's desk, he locked the three surgery doors and that of the office. Extinguishing the oil lamp, he left it on a table in the hall before leaving the practice house and locking the front door behind him.

When the cab stopped on Pimlico, the first thing Will noticed was the waiting room and surgery were both in darkness. They got out and he hurried into the hall of the tenement house and tried the waiting room door, hearing feet on the stairs. It was locked and he went back outside, cupped his hands to the glass of each window but couldn't see a thing.

"Dr Fitzgerald?" Straightening up, he glanced at the front door. Jimmy was staring curiously at him and then at Isobel as she asked the cabman to wait for them. "What's the matter?"

"Have you seen anyone go into the waiting room, Jimmy?"

"I didn't see anyone go in, but I was carrying a bucket of

water inside not too long ago and I heard the door close. What's the matter?" he asked again. "Do you need to speak to Dr Powell?"

"Thank you, Jimmy. You can go back upstairs now."

"Upstairs?"

"Please, go upstairs, Jimmy."

"Yes, Dr Fitzgerald."

The boy turned and went inside and, hearing him climb the stairs, Will ran back to the waiting room door.

"I'm going to have to force the door," he said as Isobel joined him and she took his hat then stood back as he put a shoulder to it. The sturdy new door wouldn't give way so he tried again – nothing. He then tried with a foot but the door remained firm. "Damn it."

"Dr Fitzgerald?"

Mrs Bell was coming down the stairs and he tried with his foot again. The door crashed open but it was pitch black in the room.

"A lamp – I need a lamp."

"There's an oil lamp on the kitchen table," Mrs Bell told Isobel, who handed his hat to her and dashed up the stairs. "Isn't Dr Powell in there?"

"No," he replied, hearing Isobel return. "Thank you." Taking the lamp from her, he went into the waiting room. Apart from the chairs and stools, it was empty. Trying the handle of the surgery door, he found it locked and swore under his breath.

Passing the lamp back to Isobel, he kicked at the door. The brutal kick broke the lock and they went inside. The medicine cupboard was open and the spare keys, the oil lamp from the waiting room, a whiskey bottle with a quarter gone from it and an empty pill bottle were on the desk. Alfie, with dried blood on his face and hands, lay on the floor behind the desk curled into a foetal position. Giving a little cry, Isobel put the lamp on the desk and dropped to her knees beside her brother.

"He's alive," she stammered with two fingers on Alfie's neck.

Will knelt down, pressed his fingers to Alfie's neck and felt a slow but steady pulse.

"You're learning," he said, forcing a smile to calm her a little and she spluttered a mixture of a sob and a laugh. "Two tablespoons of salt dissolved in a mug of warm water and a bowl, please," he added at once to Mrs Bell. "We need to make him sick to bring up the pills – and please keep Jimmy up there – he must not see any of this."

Leaving his hat on the desk, Mrs Bell went out and Will peered at the pill bottle. Opium. Had it been full, half full or almost empty?

They hauled Alfie into a sitting position and Mrs Bell returned with a mug and a large baking bowl. Isobel held Alfie's shoulders, Mrs Bell the bowl and Will forced him to drink from the mug. Alfie's brown eyes flew open as he belched then lurched forward, vomiting noisily into the bowl. He hadn't eaten for some hours as there was very little in his stomach apart from the salt water, whiskey and pills. Judging by the amount in the bowl, the bottle had been all but full.

"Good," Will said as Alfie coughed and gasped for breath. "And now some more salt water – we have to be cruel to be kind."

For a second time, he forced Alfie to drink and put the

empty mug on the desk while Alfie retched and vomited then retched again a few seconds later. The third retch didn't produce any more pills and Will nodded to Mrs Bell, who put the bowl to one side.

"Alfie?" Will slapped his cheeks. "Alfie look at me." Shaking his head, Alfie squeezed his eyes shut and Will shook him. "Stay awake, Alfie," he commanded. "You are going to stay awake and you are coming home with us. Keep him awake and upright, Isobel, while I speak to Mrs Bell."

He lit the waiting room oil lamp, passed Mrs Bell's lamp to her then picked up the bowl and mug. Temporarily closing and bolting the tenement house's front door, he followed her outside to the pump in the rear yard and she held up the lamp while he disposed of the pills down a drain and washed out the mug and bowl.

"The man is Alfie Stevens, Isobel's brother," he explained. "And he discovered today that his lover is getting married."

"And she didn't tell him." Mrs Bell shook her head sadly.

"No – he – David Powell – didn't tell him," Will clarified quietly and her eyes widened. "The only people who know about Alfie and David are Isobel and I, my father – and now you."

"I won't say a word to a living soul, Dr Fitzgerald."

"Thank you. I will lock the medicine cupboard and bring the bunch of keys with me but the locks of both the waiting room and surgery doors need to be replaced urgently."

"I'll send Jimmy along to a locksmith at once."

"And when you receive the new keys, give them to me – not to David – I will come here for them in the next few days."

"Is this the end of the surgery here, Dr Fitzgerald?" she asked.

"I honestly can't say."

Mrs Bell nodded and took the bowl and mug from him. "Bring Alfie home. Jimmy and I will see to matters here."

"Thank you," he said, unbuttoning his overcoat and pulling his wallet out of the inside pocket. Extracting two half crowns, he passed them to her. "Take these."

"This is too much for two locks…"

"Please take them, Mrs Bell. I have enough change for the cabman."

They returned to the surgery finding Alfie leaning against the wall staring intently up at the ceiling. Isobel had found ointment in the medicine cupboard and had wiped the dried blood from Alfie's face and hands but his jaw was swollen and his knuckles were covered in scabs which had cracked and were bleeding again. Will put the ointment and the empty pill bottle back in the cupboard and lifted out some bandages before locking the door, putting the keys in his trouser pocket and winding the bandages around Alfie's hands. Isobel gave Mrs Bell a grateful hug while he helped Alfie to his feet. He nodded his thanks to Mrs Bell and they went outside to the cab.

With Alfie squashed between them to keep him upright, they travelled back to number 30 and as they went into the hall, Zaineb came downstairs carrying an empty coal scuttle and eyed Alfie in horror.

"My brother will be staying here for a few days," Isobel told her. "Can a guest bedroom be prepared for him, please?"

"Of course, Mrs Fitzgerald."

The maid hurried down the steps to the servants' hall and

they brought Alfie upstairs to the second floor. Will put an arm around Alfie's shoulders and they waited on the landing while Mrs Dillon and Mary hurried into the guest bedroom and Isobel helped them to light the gas lamps and make the bed before fetching one of Will's nightshirts. When the ladies left the room, Will led Alfie inside. He undressed Alfie, dressed him in the nightshirt then got him into bed. Alfie didn't utter a single word throughout the entire process and Will sat on the edge of the bed.

"I read the engagement notice in *The Irish Times* just before half past seven this evening," he said. "I didn't know a thing about it and I hadn't suspected a thing." He waited for a response but Alfie simply fixed his eyes on the chimney breast. "Is David injured, Alfie? I went to Westland Row and I know you two fought. Is he hurt?"

Alfie didn't reply and Will sighed. He went out onto the landing and Isobel grabbed his hands as Zaineb went into the bedroom with matches, kindling and coal.

"Has he spoken?"

"No, and I need you to sit with him while I go to number 55 and lie to your mother."

Gorman admitted Will to the house, showed him into the morning room and Martha peered behind him, expecting Alfie to be there. When Alfie didn't appear and Gorman closed the door, she turned to Will in alarm and went to get up from the sofa but he quickly held up a hand to stop her.

"Alfie arrived at number 30 a short while ago complaining of stomach pains and he has been violently ill," he said, glancing around the room and spotting a pristine and unread copy of *The Irish Times* on a side table beside

James' armchair. "I have examined him and I would like to keep him at number 30 confined to bed for the next few days until this passes."

"What was it which made him ill?" Mrs Ellison asked with a puzzled glance at her husband and Miles. "We went ahead with dinner but, other than it, we have all eaten the same meals and none of us has fallen ill."

"It was boiled bacon and cabbage at a friend's home. The bacon may have been rancid. Whatever it was, it has made him quite ill. He is weak and feeling very sorry for himself."

"When may I see him?" she asked.

"Tomorrow, Martha. He needs to rest. Goodnight."

He saw himself out, crossed the street and walked around the Fitzwilliam Square garden, hoping he had been convincing. Approaching number 30, he saw the front door was wide open and quickened his pace. When Zaineb staggered out onto the steps and peered up and down the street, a stricken expression on her face and her right hand clutching her left bicep, he began to run.

Isobel lifted a chair from a corner of the guest room, placed it beside the bed and sat down. Alfie was resting against the pillows, his eyes fixed on a point on the chimney breast opposite him. If he had lowered his gaze, he would have seen Zaineb setting and then lighting a fire in the hearth. Reaching out, Isobel laid a hand on one of his. Alfie's fingers were freezing and she rubbed each of them vigorously.

"The room will be warm soon," she said but she may as well have not been there.

"Can I bring up a hot drink for either of you, Mrs Fitzgerald?" Zaineb asked and Isobel hesitated before answering. Should Alfie drink anything? His stomach was empty and surely something easy on it wouldn't hurt?

"Some warm milk would be lovely, thank you, Zaineb."

The maid left the room and Isobel turned back to Alfie. The fire was crackling and spitting into life but he was still staring intently at the chimney breast.

"What did you say to David?" she asked. There was no response but she ploughed on nonetheless. "Will and I went to Westland Row first. He told me to stay in the cab and when he came back he was shocked. What happened there?" she pleaded. "What did you say to David?" Again, she received no response so she pretended to be angry. "You know what I'm like, Alfie. I'm going to damn-well stay here until you say something."

The fire began to spit loudly so she got up and prodded the kindling with the tongs and added a few more small lumps of coal from the scuttle.

"We will find out what happened – how this came about – honestly – David and Margaret – it's completely and utterly—"

Opening her eyes, she found herself sprawled face-down on the hearth rug. Lifting her head, the room spun around and she groaned. Hearing screams from downstairs, she tried to raise herself onto her hands and knees but her head was pounding and she fell to the floor.

Opening her eyes for a second time, she found herself lying on the bed, her head still pounding. Will was holding an oil lamp over her and easing her eyelids back with a thumb. She tried to blink, the light was making her eyes water and she forcibly squeezed them shut for a moment.

"Where's Alfie?" she asked and Will put the lamp on the bedside table. "Will, where is he?"

"Gone," he said and she tried to sit up. "Oh, no, you don't." He pushed her back down. "Alfie struck you across the back of the head with something – I don't know what it was – but you were unconscious for at least ten minutes, so I want you to stay there and rest."

"But—"

"You have been struck on the head so please do as you are told and allow me to attend to you, Isobel. Is your vision distorted?"

She blinked a few times. "No, it's clear. My head is thumping like nobody's business but I don't feel dizzy or lightheaded."

"That's good. Now, listen, Alfie has taken his clothes, shoes and wallet. Zaineb met him in the hall and she tried to stop him opening the front door but he pushed her aside and she fell against the stand. She'll have a bruised arm, other than that she is thankfully unharmed."

"I'm glad."

"I've sent Gerald to number 55 to escort your mother, James and Miles here and show them into the morning room," he continued. "What has happened this evening – and what brought it about – cannot be kept a secret any longer. Alfie has tried to kill himself and now he has attacked you and pushed Zaineb aside. He must be found – and found quickly – before he harms anyone else."

"David."

"Yes, David. Your mother will be upset, so once she has seen you, she must return to the morning room. James and I will try and find Alfie and David."

"If his rooms are uninhabitable, David has probably gone to Ely Place Upper – and Alfie, too."

"Yes. Isobel, please stay where you are."

"I'll stay here."

"Good." He kissed her forehead. "I've taken off your boots and removed all the pins from your hair, so please lie back and rest."

She nodded, winced and closed her eyes.

Will ran down the stairs to the hall as Gerald held the front door open for Martha, Miles and James.

"Thank you, Gerald." Opening the door to the morning room, Will ushered the three of them inside before the footman had a chance to take their hats, cloak and overcoats. "I'll come straight to the point," he said, closing the door and leaning back against it. "I lied to you earlier. Alfie was here but it was after Isobel and I had brought him here from the surgery on Pimlico where he had tried to take his own life."

Mrs Ellison clapped her hands to her cheeks but again Will quickly held up a hand before she could speak.

"Alfie was escorted upstairs to a guest bedroom and while I was with you at number 55 he attacked Isobel," he went on. "She was unconscious for a short time but I have examined her and she needs rest."

"But why?" James demanded. "What has caused this behaviour?"

"David Powell was Alfie's lover but David is now engaged-to-be-married to Margaret Simpson and Alfie knew nothing of it."

"Alfie's lover?" Martha shrieked. "No – no – no—"

"Alfie and David were lovers for a year and a half," Will went on, almost having to shout. "For obvious reasons, no-one could know."

"But you did," Mrs Ellison accused.

"Isobel and I found out purely by accident. Now, we must find Alfie before he and David come to blows again."

"Again?" James frowned.

"When Isobel and I read the engagement notice in *The Irish Times*, we went to David's rooms on Westland Row. Alfie had been there and he and David fought – the place was turned upside down. James, please come with me. Martha, you may look in on Isobel, then leave her to rest and rejoin Miles here – is that understood?"

Mrs Ellison nodded, Will squeezed her arm and opened the door for her. Gerald was waiting in the hall with his hat, overcoat and medical bag.

"Thank you," he said, taking them from him as Martha went upstairs. "Could you please ask Mrs Dillon to keep an eye on Mrs Ellison? If Mrs Ellison cannot remain calm, send for my mother. Actually – no," he decided. "I will send a cab to Merrion Square to bring my mother here. With my wife resting, Mrs Ellison needs someone else to be firm with her."

Will and James hurried out of Fitzwilliam Square, heading for number 1 Ely Place Upper. On Baggot Street Lower, Will stopped a cab, gave the cabman instructions and paid the fare.

"I cannot apologise for lying to you all," he said bluntly as they walked on.

"I don't expect you to apologise," James replied. "After what happened with Ronald, I perfectly understand. But Martha won't. Alfie is her son and he has kept this a secret from her all these years and she may never forgive him."

They went up the steps to number 1 and Will rang the front doorbell. To his surprise, Ida opened the door.

"Dr Fitzgerald?"

"I am looking for Mr Alfie Stevens and Dr David Powell, Ida," he said, taking off his hat. "Are they here or have they been here?"

"I—"

The young woman hesitated and Will peered over her shoulder, hearing voices in the morning room.

"I'm sorry, Ida, I must come in, this is urgent." He brushed past her, strode along the hall, pushed open the door to the morning room and went inside. Margaret and his father got up from the sofa and Will failed to control his temper on seeing him there.

"I knew it – I didn't want to admit it to myself – but I knew you were behind this. Where is David, Margaret? Your fiancé – where is he? Has Alfie been here looking for him?"

"Alfie has not been here," she said and he noted her grey-blue dress. Would he ever be able to accept the fact that soon she would no longer be Fred's widow but David's wife? "But David called here about two hours ago – Alfie attacked him in his rooms on Westland Row – David came here to tell me he was going home to his mother in Co Meath for a few days until this has blown over."

"Blown over?" Will echoed harshly. "This will never blow over. Alfie knew nothing about this – have you any idea what this has done to him? No, of course, you don't – you don't care one bit – to announce your engagement a year and a day after Fred died—"

"Will." His father addressed him sharply. "Do not bring Fred into this. David and Alfie are not here. Now, be on your way."

"One year and one day, Father."

"Your dear mother-in-law waited just over one year and one month after Ronald Henderson died to marry husband number three."

"Because Will's dear mother-in-law had been deeply hurt in the past and husband number three loves her and wished to marry her as soon as possible." James halted in the doorway and Will's father stared at him in consternation. "Dr Powell and Mrs Simpson's engagement is not a love match in any way – rather one of convenience – why?"

"David Powell is from a good family, is a good doctor and he will be a respectable husband for Margaret."

"Why?" James repeated. "Why does she need one?"

"She does not wish to be alone for the rest of her life," Margaret announced before Will's father could stop her.

Will felt James look at him briefly. "What parting gift did your husband leave you with, Mrs Simpson?" James continued and Margaret burst into tears.

"Enough," Will's father snapped but James ignored him.

"Something serious enough for you to marry a man who will never bed you."

"Get out, James," Will's father roared.

"Mrs Simpson, your fiancé has broken my step-son's heart. Alfie went through hell with his father – so did his mother and sister – and now Martha must try and understand what Alfie is and why he attempted suicide and Isobel must recover from being attacked by her brother."

"Alfie attempted suicide?" Will's father shot a shocked glance at him. "Is Isobel badly injured?"

"Alfie struck Isobel across the back of the head," Will replied. "She was unconscious for some minutes and is now resting. Earlier, Alfie consumed a bottle of opium pills and washed them down with a quarter of a bottle of *John Jameson*. A few more minutes and he would have been dead." His father wasn't going to be provoked into a guilty response and Will turned to James. "We're wasting time here."

They left the house and stood on the pavement. Where now? Would Alfie have gone back to Westland Row?

"Broadstone Station, James," he said suddenly. "Alfie's going to try and get to Greene Hall on the early morning train because he knows none of us will follow him there."

They hailed a cab on St Stephen's Green and travelled north across the city to the railway station. James asked the cabman to wait for them and they went onto the platform they had used departing for and returning from Westport.

"Look." James pointed to Alfie who was huddled on a bench barefoot, still wearing Will's nightshirt and clutching his clothes, shoes and wallet. "Thank God."

"Keep away from him," a male voice advised and a porter approached, gesturing to Alfie. "He tried to push me onto the tracks. Someone's gone to fetch a constable."

"There is no need for the police," Will replied. "We're here to bring him home."

"Home?" The porter both looked and sounded incredulous. "Look at him – look at the state of him – he needs to be locked up."

"Thank you," Will replied as politely as he could. "But we are here to bring him home. Where may we dress him?"

"In the waiting room." The porter nodded to a door a little further along the platform from Alfie. "I'll stand outside and make sure no-one goes in."

Will thanked the porter and he and James slowly approached Alfie. They sat on either side of him and Will put his medical bag down at his feet but Alfie simply continued to stare at a fixed point on the platform floor.

"You must be cold," James began and Alfie's head jerked up. He stared at James wide-eyed and James gave him a kind smile. "Shall we help you to get dressed?"

"No," he replied and looked away. "I might miss the train."

"Which train is that?"

"Westport."

"There's no train to Westport until early tomorrow morning."

"I can wait."

"Let us help you to get dressed, Alfie." James tried again and Alfie frowned.

"Do you know who we are, Alfie?" Will asked and he nodded. Will exchanged a relieved glance with James before gently touching one of the younger man's hands. The bandages were gone and the dark red scabs on the knuckles stood out in stark contrast to the skin which had a greyish hue. "You're very cold. Let James and I help you to dress. Your lips, fingernails and toenails are blue. You know what that means, don't you?"

"Yes."

"Alfie, will you allow us to help you get dressed?"

"I want to go to Greene Hall, Will. I need to get away – as far away from Dublin as I can."

"I need to look after you here in Dublin. I need to get you dressed and I need to get you warm and I need to look after Isobel, too."

"Isobel." Alfie bit his lips. "I hit her. She wouldn't stop talking and I hit her. I hit her with one of these." He glanced at his shoes. "I hit her… she fell onto the rug…"

"She was unconscious for approximately ten minutes and she is resting now."

"I'm sorry."

"Come with us and you can tell her you're sorry yourself."

"To number 30?"

"Yes. I would like you to stay at number 30 for a little while."

"A little while?"

"Yes. And I will go to Trinity College and tell them you are in bed with a bad cold."

"But I don't have a bad cold."

"You will have soon," Will replied and to his astonishment, Alfie began to laugh. Seconds later, the laughter turned to tears and Alfie covered his face with his hands. James quickly gathered up the clothes, shoes and wallet and Will put his arms around Alfie as he sobbed. "Cry," Will whispered. "That's it. Cry it all out."

Before long, the sobs turned to shivers and Will clasped Alfie's shoulders.

"James and I are going to bring you into the waiting room – just along there – and help you get dressed. Then, we're going to number 30."

Will helped him to his feet then had to grab his arm as Alfie stumbled and almost fell. Nodding his thanks to the porter for waiting at a discreet distance, Will picked up his medical bag and guided Alfie into the waiting room with James following them.

Alfie's feet were bleeding but Will put the socks on anyway wondering how far Alfie had walked before a cab would stop for him and he and James continued with the rest of the clothes – putting them on over the nightshirt – then, lastly, the shoes.

When they opened the door to the platform, a constable was waiting with the porter.

"I'm a doctor," Will said before the policeman could speak. "And he is coming home with me."

"Is he drunk?"

"No. Distressed, but not drunk. He is also very cold…" Will tailed off and the constable looked Alfie up and down before waving a hand in assent.

"Take him home."

"Thank you."

They walked out of the station to the waiting cab, James instructed the cabman to take them to 30 Fitzwilliam Square and they got in.

"Remember what we did for your grandfather each time he collapsed?" Will asked Alfie in an effort to keep him alert as the cab made its way back across the city.

"Yes."

"What did we do?" Will prompted.

"Warmed him slowly with hot water bottles placed not too close to him."

"Good. That is exactly what we shall do with you. I will bring you straight upstairs," he added, staring at James until the cab passed a street lamp and he saw James look at him and nod, agreeing that Martha must be kept away from her son until he was in bed and warm. "What would you like to eat? Some of Mrs Dillon's delicious vegetable soup?"

"Yes, please," Alfie replied and Will squeezed his arm.

At number 30, James paid and tipped the cabman then hurried into the house to reassure his wife. Will and Alfie followed him and Will rang the front doorbell before they went into the hall. Mrs Dillon came up the steps from the servants' hall and smiled.

"Hot water bottles and vegetable soup, Dr Fitzgerald?"

"Yes, please, Mrs Dillon."

They took their time climbing the stairs to the second floor and Will sat Alfie on a chair on the landing.

"I need to see if Isobel is well enough to be carried to our bedroom," he said, went into the guest room and she opened her eyes. "We found him," he whispered, putting his medical bag on the bedside table and she burst into tears. "He's very cold and his feet are bleeding," he added, crouching down beside the bed. "James and I found him on the Westport platform at Broadstone Station still wearing my nightshirt."

"Is he having a complete mental breakdown?" she asked, wiping the tears away with her fingers.

"I can only surmise that he is on the brink of one. We must all make sure he does not go over the edge."

"Yes."

"Did you sleep?" he asked.

"Yes. My head still hurts but it doesn't pound like it did before."

"Good. I'll carry you to our room and I want you to stay in bed tomorrow."

"But—" she began, her face creasing with dismay.

"Alfie hit you hard on the back of the head with a shoe, Isobel. You were unconscious for at least ten minutes. I take no chances with head injuries."

"Very well. But you will have to tell young John that I fell or something like that."

"I will. I'll ring for Mary to help you undress then I'll go and turn the bed down."

"No, Will, not Mary. Ask Mother to come up here. Helping me to bed will make her feel useful."

The gas lamps and fire had been lit, their bedroom was warm and he pulled the bedcovers down. Leaving the room, he saw the chair on the landing was vacant and he ran to the guest room, rolling his eyes in relief when he saw Alfie kneeling beside the bed.

"I'm so sorry, Isobel," he was saying through chattering teeth. "I think I went mad for a while. Are you all right?"

"A day in bed and I'll be fine. You're shivering so much, Alfie. Will, is Mrs Dillon bringing—"

"Everything is in hand," he assured her. "Let me carry you to our bed."

"Alfie," she said, grabbing his hands before Will could pick her up. "You are strong – do you hear me? You stood between Mother and I and Father so many times – let all of us help you to stay strong now."

Alfie just nodded, Isobel kissed his hands and Will lifted her up.

He carried her to their bedroom and laid her down in the bed.

"Don't stay awake for me," he said, kissing her lips and pulling the bedcovers up to her chin. "I don't know how long it will be before I come to bed."

Closing the door, he saw Mary and Zaineb at the top of the stairs, each maid carrying two hot water bottles.

"How is your arm, Zaineb?"

"It is a little bruised, Dr Fitzgerald. Thank you for asking but I am perfectly well."

"Good. You can leave the hot water bottles on the side table, thank you."

Zaineb put them on the table, went downstairs and Will took the other two hot water bottles from Mary.

"Could you ask Mrs Ellison to help my wife prepare for bed, please, Mary? Oh, and please ask Mrs Dillon to leave the soup here on the table."

"Yes, Dr Fitzgerald."

He went into the guest room and found Alfie sitting cross-legged on the rug in front of the fire gazing into the flames.

"Your soup will be here soon," he told him, placing the hot water bottles in the bed.

"I'm scared, Will," Alfie replied in a little voice, twisting around to look up at him. "I've never acted in that way before – I've never wanted to die before – am I going mad?"

"You are welcome to stay here for as long as you need," he said instead of answering. "Would you also consider something?"

"What?"

"That you speak to Dr Harrison. I can ask him to call here and he may be able to offer you some advice."

"I don't know – what if it gets out – that David and I were lovers – that I tried to take my own life? What if I get locked up like Miles? What if it prevents me from ever being able to practise medicine?"

"Alfie." Will knelt beside him. "You are not mad but I would advise you to speak to Dr Harrison. He won't be able to stop David from marrying Margaret and he won't be able to ease the hurt and betrayal you are feeling but he has the expertise I don't and everything you say to him will be held in the strictest confidence."

"Very well."

"Good. Now, who can I speak to at Trinity College? Someone must be informed you will not be attending lectures for a few days."

"Kenneth Fisher – he is in my year – he's a good friend – a confidante."

"I'll find him. Now, let me see to your hands and feet, fetch another nightshirt and help you to bed."

Ten minutes later, Will had just placed the other two hot water bottles around Alfie and pulled up the bedcovers when there was a soft knock at the door.

"The soup, Dr Fitzgerald," the housekeeper said.

"Thank you, Mrs Dillon," Will called, carried the tray into the bedroom and set it on Alfie's lap. "Eat," he said and squeezed Alfie's shoulder. "I'll be back shortly."

Martha was coming up the stairs as he closed the door. She gave him a wobbly smile and for the first time ever, he gave her a hug.

"Alfie is calm," he said. "He is lucid and he is eating."

"May I see him?"

"Wait until the morning, Martha. Come over after breakfast. He needs to eat and to rest and he does not know yet that you know."

"And Isobel?"

"I have instructed her to remain in bed tomorrow – simply as a precaution. In the morning, I shall go to the nursery and tell John she fell and hit her head."

"Yes, and your mother said she would call here in the morning and stay in the nursery with John and reassure him. Thank you for asking her to come and sit with Miles and I. Her presence made the waiting a little more bearable."

"Not at all. I shall walk her home now."

"Alfie will recover from this, won't he?" Martha asked quietly and he nodded.

"He will – with all our support. He knows he acted utterly out of character and it has scared him. The fact he understands that and cares what people might think of him is a good sign."

His mother was unusually silent as they walked along Fitzwilliam Street Upper. Then, she stopped abruptly and turned to him.

"I should have seen it – Alfie and David – I should have seen it – or suspected at the very least when you took David on at the practice despite him being less than a year qualified and especially when David was included as one of Belle's godparents—"

"Mother, I took David on at the practice because he is an excellent doctor and good with patients and, yes, he was included as one of Belle's godparents because he was Alfie's lover, but it was also because when she was born, I could not have managed without him."

"But you would not even have considered him for the practice if it were not for the fact he was Alfie's lover."

"That is true," he conceded. "But I could never – ever – have foreseen this."

"No," she replied with a sigh. "I really did not think your father could sink any lower in my estimation. He did not care one whit about poor Alfie in orchestrating this absurd engagement and how can David be so callous?"

"Money. Status. A home at number 1 Ely Place Upper. Plus the fact that to obtain all three, he need only marry Margaret and never bed her."

"Margaret would have had a rental income from the

house and be able to live comfortably and independently for the first time in her life."

"Father knows I have not offered – and I will not offer David a partnership – and I think he intends to set David up in practice – most likely at number 1."

"David will take clients away from your practice," she said and he shrugged helplessly.

"If they choose to follow David to his new practice, there is nothing I can do about that."

"And will you run the practice alone?"

"Yes, Mother. It is something I probably should have done all along."

"Can you cope?"

"I hope so. I shall have to sit down with Eva and try and even out the numbers presenting at surgery across the week. Friday is always busy because people either leave their coming until the last minute or do not want the weekend to pass without seeing a doctor," he explained.

"It has always been a multi-partner practice."

"Father only has himself to blame for this."

"Did you speak to him?" she asked and he gave her a humourless smile.

"I shouted mostly and you can only imagine what Isobel will say to him in due course. But, for now, my priorities are Isobel and Alfie and the practice."

Hearing a knock at the door, Isobel carefully rolled over in the bed as her mother came into the bedroom.

"It has been a long time since I helped you to bed," Mrs Ellison said, closing the door behind her.

"Many years," she agreed, throwing back the covers,

swinging her legs off the bed and slowly sitting up on the edge. "Ouch," she whispered, locating the lump on the back of her head and running her fingers over it.

"Does it hurt very much?" her mother asked.

"It is easing a little," she replied and couldn't help but smile as Mrs Ellison sat beside her brushing and then plaiting her hair realising it was at least ten years since her mother had last done so. "Mother, Will and I discovered Alfie and David were lovers by accident and we assured Alfie we wouldn't tell you."

"But I'm your mother," Mrs Ellison said in a hurt tone.

"Alfie asked us not to tell you," she said, undoing the jet buttons on the front of her mourning dress then easing herself off the bed and stepping out of it.

"Will says I may see Alfie in the morning. I dearly want to see him but I do not know what to say to him. When I was told the truth about Ronald, I did not have to face him…"

"Alfie is still Alfie," Isobel stated firmly, passing the dress to her mother.

"Had you any suspicions growing up that he had a fondness for men?" her mother asked tentatively, hanging the dress up in Isobel's wardrobe.

"Mother, we did not discuss, mention or even think of such things growing up," she said, opening the waistband of her small bustle frame and handing it to her mother followed by her corset, petticoat and chemise.

"That is true," Mrs Ellison replied.

"Come for breakfast?" she suggested brightly, stepping out of her drawers then rolling her stockings down her legs. "And you, Alfie and I shall eat our meals from trays in the guest room together."

To her relief, her mother nodded eagerly, taking the drawers and stockings from her and laying all the undergarments over the back of the bedroom chair before passing Isobel's nightdress to her. "I will, thank you."

"That is settled, then." Isobel pulled the nightdress over her head and got back into bed. "Eight o'clock."

"What I do not understand is why Dr Simpson's widow is marrying a man who will never love her." Mrs Ellison gave a puzzled little shrug. "She cannot be so starved for companionship, surely?"

"No, her mother is still alive and she also has a sister. You wished to marry again and, clearly, Margaret does, too. Go home to bed, Mother, you look exhausted. Alfie is safe here and we three will talk in the morning."

"Goodnight, Isobel." Mrs Ellison kissed her cheek. "Sleep well."

After her mother had gone, Isobel waited for five minutes before getting out of bed and putting her dressing gown and slippers on. She went out onto the landing and knocked at the guest room door before going inside. Alfie was sitting up in bed staring across the room at the fire and she was glad to see he had finished all the soup and the tray was on the bedside table.

"Mother has just put me to bed," she said and he turned to her. "But I had to come and see how you were before I went to sleep."

"Did Mother not wish to see me?" he asked.

"Yes," she replied, sitting on the edge of the bed. "But I persuaded her that in the morning would be best. The three of us will have breakfast on a tray in here. Would you like some more soup?" she added pointing to the tray.

"No, it was enough – and delicious – thank you."

"Are you warmer now?"

"Yes, much warmer – I'm sorry," he cried suddenly and she jumped. "Will wants to stop me going completely mad and ask Dr Harrison to come here to see me."

"I would be very surprised," she began carefully. "If Dr Harrison hasn't spoken with someone whose heart has been broken."

"How did you cope after James Shawcross abandoned you? After Father whipped you and threw you out? I know you did as I tried to do – you got away from home as far as you could."

"Like you, I was not thinking rationally," she admitted with a shudder, forcing Sally Maher's brothel in Monto and the six months of hell from her mind. "And I wish I'd had the chance to speak to someone like Dr Harrison but I would speak with Will and if it were not for him… It took a long time, but I did put James Shawcross behind me," she told him with a smile and Alfie returned a small one.

"Yes, you did," he whispered.

"I know people will say they understand – even though they don't – but I do – and I am your sister and I love you. I will always be here for you to talk to. Just please don't wallop me across the back of my head with a shoe if I talk too much."

That made Alfie's smile disappear and he burst into tears.

"I'm sorry I hurt you," he sobbed, resting his forehead on her shoulder.

"I know," she said softly, stroking his hair. "I won't mention it again. How did you find out about the engagement?" she asked and he drew back from her.

"I was waiting for a friend in Front Square at Trinity College and two students were standing nearby with a newspaper gossiping about Dr Simpson's widow being engaged-to-be-married to another doctor," he said, wiping his eyes on the sleeve of Will's nightshirt. "Then, one of them mentioned David and I grabbed the newspaper from them and—" Alfie broke off and inhaled and exhaled a shaky breath.

"I'm so sorry you found out in that way."

"Why?" he asked, spreading his hands helplessly. "I ran to David's rooms and I asked him why and he told me it was none of my business. I saw red and we fought and I managed to grab his keys to the practice house from the hall floor before he threw me out onto the street. We've been lovers for a year and a half and he tells me the engagement is none of my business and throws me out onto the street. I planned to go to the practice house so I could tend to my hands but, instead, I went to Margaret Simpson's home intending to confront her but, from across the street, I saw Will's father standing at one of the windows closing the curtains. Shortly afterwards, I saw David be admitted to the house and it was then I resolved to look for the keys to the Pimlico surgery and kill myself there because I realised the engagement must have been planned for weeks, if not, months behind my back. Oh, Isobel, why did Will's father arrange this engagement – why?"

"Will's father has been very close to the Simpson family all his life," she explained. "He and Duncan Simpson were best friends since their school days—"

"And now Will's father wants what is best for Fred's widow." Alfie shook his head in disgust. "And he thinks the best is David – a man who does not love her – who cannot love her. I think Will's father needs to speak with Dr Harrison more urgently than I do."

"Will's father will be receiving a piece of my mind as soon as I can leave this house."

"No, Isobel," Alfie snapped. "I can fight my own battles."

"But he will not heed you, Alfie. But he will heed me. Oh, John Fitzgerald knows well that I can choose when and when not to be a lady – and I will certainly not be one when I speak to him. He will no longer be welcome here – I will not have the children anywhere near a man who can cause so much suffering."

"What about Will? He and David cannot continue to work together at the practice."

"That is entirely up to Will but he certainly cannot trust David now." Reaching across the bed to the other bedside table for Alfie's pocket watch, she opened it and sighed. "It is very late but there is one last thing I must tell you."

"Oh?" he replied apprehensively."

"When you disappeared from here this evening, Will needed James' help in finding you. He could not lie anymore as to why you did what you did."

"James knows about David and I?" he asked and she nodded.

"As does Mother and Miles," she added and Alfie gazed up at the ceiling. "Mother was upset but I think it was also the fact that you had not told her—"

"How could I?" Alfie demanded savagely. "There were many times – hundreds of times – I was on the brink of telling her. When James Shawcross coerced me into leaving you alone with him. When Father threw you out. When

Father died. When Mother and I moved to Dublin. When I started at Trinity College. When I met David. But her reaction to the revelations about Ronald Henderson made me swear to myself never to tell her. Christ, Isobel, how am I going to face her now?"

"I will be with you. We will eat and then we will talk – all morning – if need be."

She slept deeply and dreamlessly and woke to an already shaved and dressed Will kissing her forehead.

"It's just after half past seven. How is your head?"

She reached for the lump and winced. "It only aches when I touch it."

"Don't touch it, then." He smiled and kissed her lips. "I'll look in on Alfie and tell John that you fell and hit your head then I must eat and then I must go. I need to speak to Eva. Try and rest as much as you can today."

Her mother hadn't plaited Isobel's hair tightly enough and it had come undone overnight, so she sat in front of the dressing table mirror and redid it. She expressed milk for the twins before washing and putting on a fresh nightdress. Shrugging on her dressing gown, she slipped her feet into her slippers and left the bedroom.

"Come in?" Alfie answered her knock a little hesitantly and she went into the guest room.

"How did you sleep?"

"I woke a few times not knowing where I was. Other than that, I slept well."

"I'm glad. There is warm water if you would like to wash?"

"I'd better, as Mother is coming. Am I allowed to shave, too?" he asked and she hesitated. "I'm not going to do anything stupid, Isobel, I swear."

"Very well," she replied and brought him one of Will's blades. "I'll be back in a few minutes, I need to go and see young John, Belle and Ben."

She went upstairs to the nursery with the twins' milk and the boy stared at her state of undress in surprise as she passed the milk to Bridget.

"Did Will tell you I fell over yesterday?" she asked and he nodded. "I tripped over a rug and banged my head – it was very silly of me – but these things happen. Feel the huge lump." Crouching down, she took his hand and guided it to the back of her head. "Can you feel it?"

"It's round."

"Yes, I suppose it is. Well, Will has instructed me to rest today. He says it is not serious but when someone bangs their head hard, it's not good for their head. So, I just wanted to tell you that I am all right but I must go back to bed after breakfast."

"Sleep well," he said and she smiled.

"Thank you, John, I shall."

Mrs Ellison was waiting on the second-floor landing as she came down the stairs from the nursery.

"Should you be going up and downstairs, Isobel?"

"Probably not but I had to bring milk to the twins and reassure young John." Taking her mother's arm, she led her to the window. "I told Alfie last night that you know."

"I see."

"Alfie will always be Alfie and we all should treat him as we always have done." Mrs Ellison nodded and Isobel took her hand and led her to the guest room. "Mother is here," she called, knocking at the door.

"Come in," Alfie replied and they went inside. He was standing in front of the fire wearing Will's dressing gown and slippers and let his arms drop to his sides. "I'm sorry," he said simply and their mother gave a little cry and hugged him tightly.

"You have nothing to be sorry for – nothing. You are my darling Alfie and you always will be. I have two extraordinary children. Isobel overcame her troubles and so will you."

"But I love David, Mother. I can't just stop loving him."

"It will take time but you will find love again." Releasing Alfie, Mrs Ellison clasped his clean-shaven cheeks in her hands. "And I shall be delighted to meet him."

Alfie's eyes widened and he exhaled a long breath. "Thank you, Mother," he whispered.

Will was exhausted and it was only five minutes before nine in the morning. It had been a quarter to three when he had got slowly into bed beside Isobel so as not to wake her. Eva was in the practice house office and he went in, closed the door on the patients making their way to the waiting room and put his medical bag on the floor.

"Eva, it is my belief that Dr Powell has left this practice and will not be returning," he said, deciding to come straight to the point.

Placing a stack of patient files down on her desk, she failed to hide her astonishment.

"I take it from your tone, Dr Fitzgerald, you were not aware of his intentions?"

"No, I was not," he replied, hanging his hat on the stand and shrugging off his overcoat. "Did you see yesterday's *Irish Times*?" he asked and she grimaced.

"I'm afraid that before I had time to read it, our copy was used to absorb one of my sister's elderly cat's 'accidents'."

"You would not have seen a notice announcing the engagement of David Powell to Margaret Simpson, then," he said as he hung his overcoat beside his hat.

It was a long time since he had seen Eva quite so astounded. "Dr Powell and Dr Simpson's widow? I don't believe it."

"I had to read the notice a number of times myself," he admitted.

"But it has barely been a year since poor Dr Simpson died… You knew nothing of a courtship?"

What courtship, Will asked silently but shook his head. "I knew nothing about either a courtship nor the engagement. At present, Dr Powell is in Co Meath with his mother and I don't know when he is returning to Dublin. Would you be so kind as to clear his desk and I shall deliver the contents to Ely Place Upper?"

"Yes, of course, but what will you do now?"

"Carry on alone. The practice may lose some patients to Dr Powell if he sets up in practice elsewhere but from now on I would be grateful if you could try and even out the patients presenting at surgery across each week?"

"Yes, Dr Fitzgerald. My goodness, I'm shocked."

"Eva, the patients must be told the truth – Dr Powell has decided to leave this practice of his own accord – and there has been absolutely no animosity between us in the past." That is not to say there will be none in the future, he added to himself as he picked up his medical bag.

"You always got on very well," Eva agreed. "Goodness me… well, I shall do my best to even out the patients, Dr Fitzgerald."

"Thank you, Eva," he said, left the office and, producing as bright a smile as he could manage, escorted his first patient upstairs to his surgery.

It was half past one before surgery ended and he returned wearily to the office.

"Tomorrow will be better, Dr Fitzgerald." Eva pointed to a list on her desk. "I have spoken with everyone who attended here today and I shall do the same tomorrow and so on and the non-urgent cases shall be evened out across each week."

"That will be an enormous help, thank you."

"Are you really going to carry on alone?" she asked. "I know it is none of my business but there have always been at least two doctors in this practice."

"I shall have to see how I cope, Eva."

On his way home, he went into Trinity College via the entrance on Lincoln Place and made his way to the School of Physic, as the medical school was known, in search of Kenneth Fisher. He was directed to rooms on the top floor of number 8 Front Square and a blond young man with a cigarette dangling from his lips answered Will's knock.

"Kenneth Fisher?" Will inquired.

"Yes?"

"My name is Will Fitzgerald. I am Alfie Stevens' brother-in-law."

"Is Alfie ill?" Kenneth asked anxiously, pulling the cigarette from his lips. "I was due to meet him at six o'clock yesterday evening but he didn't turn up and I haven't seen him today either."

"Alfie told me you were a good friend – a confidant – do we understand each other?" Will asked, meeting Kenneth's blue eyes, holding his gaze and the young man nodded.

"Come in," he said and Will went into a large sitting room and Kenneth closed the door. "Yes, I know about Alfie and David."

"Well, as of yesterday, Alfie and David are finished," Will said and Kenneth's jaw dropped. "David is engaged-to-be-married to a well-to-do widow."

"Engaged-to-be-married? David Powell? No?"

"Alfie knew nothing about the engagement and to say he is distraught would be an understatement."

"Good God, poor Alfie."

"Alfie is currently recuperating at my home – number 30 Fitzwilliam Square. He would greatly appreciate seeing a friendly face."

"I'll call this evening," Kenneth told him with a firm nod and stubbed out his cigarette in an ashtray balancing on the arm of a rather battered brown leather sofa. "In the meantime, I had better attend today's lectures. I'm usually the one copying Alfie's notes – not the other way around."

"Nothing ever changes here, does it?" Will couldn't help but smile.

"You're a former Trinity man?"

"I'm a former Trinity medical student and I had a friend who used to continually walk out of lectures too dull for him and then copy my notes."

"Did he ever graduate?" Kenneth asked curiously.

"He did. With flying colours."

"There's hope for me yet, then."

"There's always hope, Kenneth. Alfie will be delighted to see you for a chat this evening." He shook the younger man's hand warmly, Kenneth saw him out and Will walked back to Fitzwilliam Square.

After putting his head around their bedroom door and seeing Isobel asleep, Will sat down to a late luncheon before going out on house calls. Almost three hours later, and finding himself near the practice house, he went inside and found Eva still in the office.

"Go home, Eva," he said and she jumped.

"Oh, Dr Fitzgerald, you startled me. I've just finished clearing Dr Powell's desk. The contents are in that wooden box near the door."

"Thank you, I'll take it with me. The sooner we start afresh the better. It's almost dark, allow me to hail a cab for you."

A cab stopped for him outside the National Gallery on Merrion Square West. He helped Eva inside, waved her off then walked on to number 1 Ely Place Upper carrying his medical bag in his right hand and the box under his left arm. Putting his medical bag down, he left the box on the top step and rang the front doorbell. He picked up his medical bag, turned away and had just crossed the street when he heard his name being called.

"Will?" It was Margaret. "Will, don't go, please?"

"I have nothing polite to say to you, Margaret," he replied over his shoulder.

"Please, Will? Please come inside."

Sighing, he recrossed the street and went into the hall seeing Ida place the box on a table then scurry down the steps to the servants' hall.

"I asked for David's desk to be cleared as I assume he won't be returning to the Merrion Street Upper medical practice," he said. "Even if he did return, I would dismiss him, I do not wish to be in practice with a man I cannot trust."

"Please, come upstairs to the drawing room?" she asked, lifting the skirt of her burgundy-coloured dress.

"The drawing room?" Walking along the hall, he opened the morning room door. The room was empty. "Is this to be David's surgery or the waiting room?" he asked her.

"The surgery. Come upstairs."

"No, thank you, I don't intend to stay long," he replied and a flicker of irritation crossed her face. "I take it you still have not told your family you have syphilis? My father chose well. Having a husband a doctor and a man who will never bed you will be doubly convenient."

"It is none of your concern, Will," she snapped.

"If Ida is your new lady's maid, you need to tell her at the very least – Ida needs to be told, Margaret," he said, his voice rising as she opened her mouth, no doubt to argue the point.

"Very well."

"When do you and David intend to marry?"

"On Saturday, the 6th of May."

Marry in May, rue the day, he thought immediately.

"I know you shall never forgive me for this, Will," she continued. "But I did not want to be alone for the rest of my life and David and I are the same age…"

"Alfie may now be alone for the rest of his life – think on that." Returning to the front door, he went out leaving it wide open and strode back to number 30 relieved in a way he had made his feelings clear.

As he closed the front door, Zaineb came out of the breakfast room and picked up a tray with an envelope on it from the hall table.

"This telegram was delivered just after you left this afternoon, Dr Fitzgerald," she said and his heart sank as he put his medical bag on the table.

"I see. Thank you."

He hung his hat and overcoat on the stand then took the envelope, tore it open and pulled out the telegram.

Mr Greene passed peacefully away at eight o'clock this morning. Reverend Barber, Dr Bourke and I were at his bedside. Letter to follow. My sincere sympathies.
B.B.

"Forgive me, Will," Isobel said, coming down the stairs. "But if I do not get up now, I won't sleep a wink tonight. Grandfather is dead," she added, spotting the telegram in his hands and guessing immediately.

"Yes," he said, passed the telegram to her and she read it, her face creasing in sorrow.

"Poor Grandfather. Mother is going to be very distressed, especially after Alfie…"

"How is Alfie?"

"Mary has just shown Kenneth Fisher, a friend of Alfie's from Trinity College, into the guest room. He seems a cheerful chap so I have asked Mary to bring some tea and cake for Kenneth along with Alfie's dinner and we'll leave them to chat."

"How are you?" he asked.

"Much better, the lump is getting smaller – feel," she replied, turning her back to him and he sank his fingers into her hair, having to search for the swelling.

"It is smaller – good," he said and kissed the side of her neck. "Hungry?"

"I'm very hungry."

They went into the breakfast room and Will held her chair as she sat down.

"I sought out Kenneth in Trinity College this afternoon – he knows about Alfie and David," he told her, sitting down at the head of the table and her eyes widened.

"I didn't know anyone else knew. Kenneth must be extremely trustworthy. Will, I don't think Alfie should be told about Grandfather until the morning – unless Kenneth saw the telegram and mentions it."

"If Kenneth did see it, when Alfie tells him what happened yesterday he will know not to mention it," he replied as Zaineb came in with their meals. "Thank you, Zaineb."

The maid went out and closed the door and Isobel sat back in her chair. "Alfie's middle name may be Greene, but Miles is the last Greene now. I think we should tell Mother this evening. James will be able to comfort her a little and I shall call there again in the morning after we have told Alfie."

Will nodded, even though all he wanted to do was go straight to bed. They ate then wrapped up warm and walked to number 55. Gorman showed them into the morning room and Mrs Ellison took one look at their faces and all but threw the book she had been reading onto a side table.

"Is it Alfie?" she demanded, getting to her feet.

"Alfie is eating his dinner and chatting to a friend from Trinity College," Will assured her. "We are here because a telegram was delivered this afternoon…"

Martha sank back down onto the sofa. "My father is

dead," she whispered and Will passed her the telegram. "Oh, how I wish I could have been with him, too."

"You were reunited with him," Isobel said, sitting on the sofa and giving her mother a hug and a kiss. "Even if it was only for a short time. And he was so happy to see you again."

"Yes," Mrs Ellison replied quietly. "Should you be out of bed, Isobel?"

"I am quite well, Mother," she said. "I slept all afternoon and the lump on my head is much smaller now."

"I'm very happy to hear that."

Miles got up from an armchair and went to the window. Pulling back one of the curtains, he stared out at the street. Will followed him while James kissed the top of his wife's head before going to the decanters.

"Was I wrong not to want to meet my father?" Miles asked.

"That is not for me to judge," Will replied. "But he was greatly reassured that you were now living here."

"I'm glad."

"Miles?" his sister asked softly and Miles gave her a little smile.

"I am well," he said, walking around the sofa and kissing her cheek. "And I know you are grieving and I am sorry."

"I am comforted by the fact Father was so relieved you are living with us now."

"So Will has just told me," Miles told her and she nodded.

"The Land League campaign cannot last forever and, one day, I would like to show you where you were born."

"One day," Miles replied and she stood up and hugged him.

A letter postmarked Castlebar arrived the next morning. Bringing it into the breakfast room, Will slit the envelope open with a knife and pulled out two sheets of notepaper.

> *Greene Hall*
> *Ballyglas*
> *Westport*
> *Co Mayo*

Dear Dr Fitzgerald,

Please excuse my scrawl, Dr Bourke is to travel to Castlebar on business later today and I have asked him to send the telegram on my behalf and also to post this letter there so I am writing in a hurry so as not to delay him.

As I said in the telegram, Mr Greene passed away this morning. His end was peaceful. Over the past week, his breathing declined rapidly and the day before yesterday was the last time he was able to be moved from his bed to the bath chair and back again. He also knew he would not leave his bed again and so I helped him into his overcoat and slippers, put a blanket over his knees and we went outside. I wheeled him down the drive and back up to the house so he could look upon it for the final time. Then, I brought him inside and wheeled him through each room on the ground floor before returning him to his bed in the library.

I sent Mr Knox for Dr Bourke and Reverend Barber at six o'clock last evening and they and I sat with Mr Greene all night. Mr Greene slipped in and out of consciousness but passed peacefully away just after eight o'clock this morning. I must admit that I cried. I have dealt with death many times but knowing how he wished his life could have been different, how he wished he could have died surrounded by his wife and two children and how, instead, three strangers were at his bedside made me weep.

Mr Knox was assaulted by a man in Ballyglas village last week. Thankfully, he was not seriously injured. We think it was an isolated incident as, to my knowledge, no-one else has been attacked but I would advise you and your extended family not to attend Mr Greene's funeral. Nothing has been arranged yet but it may take place tomorrow. On his return to Westport, Dr Bourke will inform Mr Hill, the undertaker, who will liase with Reverend Barber. Dr Bourke will also inform Mr Anderson, who is Mr Greene's solicitor.

Mr Knox has spoken with Mr O'Connell, the gardener, who has some early daffodils in one of the glasshouses. Two wreaths will be made from them and I shall place them on Mr and Mrs Greene's graves. I shall also ask Mr Hill for some porcelain flowers to be placed on the graves when the daffodils fade so the graves are not left unadorned.

I have been paid until the end of the month. I shall remain at Greene Hall until the day after the funeral and then I shall put a portion of my funds aside and will travel a little. I have always wished to see my mother's birthplace in Ballina and view the graves of my grandparents. After that, I shall accept your kind offer of staying at number 30 Fitzwilliam Square while I seek another nursing position.

Again, my sincere sympathies to you and your extended family on your loss.

Yours truly,

Barbara Barton

Will put the letter down and Isobel gave him a curious stare.

"I mentioned to Nurse Barton that she would be welcome to stay here until she finds another position," he explained and passed the letter to her.

"Nurse Barton will be very welcome here," she murmured as she read. "I'll bring this letter to Mother once we've eaten, she will be reassured to know how wonderfully Nurse Barton cared for Grandfather in his final days."

"Do, and I'll reply to Nurse Barton today via Dr Bourke and ask her to inform us by telegram when she is returning to Dublin."

"Will." She folded the letter and put it back in the envelope. "I need to talk to you about your father. I do not want him here – I do not want him to ever set foot in this house again – I do not trust him and I do not want him anywhere near the children."

"I agree, but we tell John – what?" he asked, spreading his hands helplessly. "That his grandfather has a bad cold and won't be visiting him for a little while?"

"Something like that – Alfie?" she cried as the door opened and he came in. "Should you be up?"

"I'm not an invalid, Isobel," he chided gently. "But I shall take your advice, Will, and go to Swift's Hospital and speak to Dr Harrison. I will also be returning to Trinity College on Monday."

"That is a little soon," Will began but Alfie shook his head.

"Kenneth is going to keep an eye on me and he will accompany me to Swift's Hospital."

"I would have gone with you," Isobel said, sounding a little hurt.

"It is no secret when I tell you that Kenneth's father killed himself when Kenneth was fifteen," Alfie told them. "Kenneth says that if his father had the opportunity to speak with someone like Dr Harrison, he may still be alive today. He doesn't want the same to happen to me and I agree."

"Does Kenneth wish to pursue a career in psychiatry?" Will asked and Alfie shrugged.

"He doesn't know yet. I shall write to Dr Harrison this morning and ask to see him in a professional capacity."

"I'm glad." Isobel rose from her chair and kissed his cheek. "Did someone bring you your breakfast?"

"Thank you, yes, it was delicious. Now, if you don't mind, I would like to return to number 55 now and—"

"Before you go, please sit down." Will pointed to a chair and Alfie did as he was told. "I received a telegram yesterday afternoon and then a letter this morning from Nurse Barton," he said and Alfie sighed.

"Grandfather is dead."

"Yes. He died peacefully yesterday morning. I'm very sorry."

"Does Mother know?"

"We told her yesterday evening while you were talking to Kenneth," Isobel replied. "We thought it best not to tell you until this morning."

"Was she very upset?"

"Upset, but relieved she had been reunited with him. Miles has agreed that she will show him Greene Hall one day."

"The Greene Hall estate will come to me now, won't it?" Alfie asked quietly.

"James thinks so, yes."

"What on earth am I going to do with it? I don't want to be a landlord – especially the way matters are now."

"We will wait to hear from Grandfather's solicitor," Isobel told him." And he and James will advise you."

Alfie grimaced and went to get up but Will reached out and grabbed his hand.

"Wait a moment," he said and Alfie sank down onto his seat. "I asked Eva to clear David's desk yesterday and I delivered the contents to number 1. I spoke briefly to Margaret and she and David will marry on the 6th of May."

Alfie exhaled a shaky sigh. "I see."

"And he is setting up practice in the house."

"A wife, a house and a medical practice – lucky David," he said bitterly. "What will you do now – can you run the practice alone?"

"I would like to," Will replied. "But, even if some of David's patients follow him to his new practice, I don't know if I can. I will just have to see how I cope for now."

"I suppose he is also abandoning the Pimlico surgery?"

"I have excluded him from the Pimlico surgery," Will clarified. "Mrs Bell is seeing to having the locks replaced on both the waiting room and surgery doors and she will be giving the new keys to me, not to David. I must go there for them at the weekend and collect David's belongings. And I must advertise for his replacement."

"Write an advertisement and I will put copies up in Trinity College," Alfie said. "Most of the students have fathers, brothers, uncles and cousins who are doctors."

"But would they be willing to take on a practice in the Liberties?"

"You did. But we shall wait and see. Write an advertisement and bring it to me."

"I'll write it today." Will gave him a grin. "I'm very relieved you're going to see Dr Harrison and are looking to the future."

"What I did terrified me, Will. I never want to act in that way again."

Chapter Eight

Will's father was due on Saturday morning for his weekly visit to see his grandchildren and Isobel was determined he would not set foot inside number 30. At nine o'clock, the front doorbell rang and, heart thumping, she went to the door with Will. He opened it and his father stared at them both in surprise.

"May I come in?"

"No, you may not," Will replied and his father's eyebrows shot up. "You are no longer welcome in this house."

"You would prevent me from visiting my grandchildren?"

"You should have thought of the consequences when you meddled in other people's lives," Isobel told him and he infuriated her by roaring with laughter.

"Oh, don't be so overly-dramatic, Isobel."

"Overly-dramatic?" Will echoed then went to grab his father's collar but she pulled him back into the hall.

"Will – no. Go, John, and don't come back," she told him as she shut the door. Turning, they saw Zaineb standing wide-eyed on the steps to the servants' hall. "We're sorry you witnessed that, Zaineb," she said, ushering Will along the hall and opening the morning room door. He went inside, she closed it and approached the maid. "Dr John Fitzgerald is no longer welcome in this house," she announced. "Please do not admit him. And if he causes trouble, please call for my husband, myself or Gerald."

"Will he come back, Mrs Fitzgerald?" Zaineb asked, no doubt remembering how Mrs Greene had greeted her.

"I hope not, but he is stubborn."

Returning to the morning room, she found Will pacing the floor, his hands on his hips.

"Attacking your father would have got us nowhere," she said and he halted. "Denying him his visits to the children is enough."

"Yes," he conceded. "This afternoon, we shall walk to Pimlico. Mrs Bell needs to be able to tell people something about the surgery's future. She rarely bakes a cake, so we'll bring her one."

On their way, they stopped at a bakery and bought a large round fruit cake decorated with glazed cherries. Mrs Bell was delighted to see them and brought them into the kitchen thanking them for the cake and hanging the kettle over the fire.

"How is young Alfie?" she asked, lifting cups, saucers and side plates down from the dresser.

"A lot brighter," Will replied. "What he did terrified him – and I'm glad it did. As well as all of us, he has a friend from Trinity College who will keep an eye on him. It will take time but he will recover from this."

"Thank you for helping us and for being so calm," Isobel said, hugging Mrs Bell.

"Ah, now," the older woman protested modestly. "I've

never been so happy to see someone be sick in all me life," she added and Isobel couldn't help but laugh.

Will took the new keys from Mrs Bell, the three of them went downstairs and he unlocked the waiting room and surgery doors. Walking through the waiting room and into the surgery, Isobel shuddered as she remembered Alfie lying curled up on the floor behind the desk. Will squeezed her arm and began to empty the contents of the desk drawers into a small wooden crate.

"I have begun to advertise for Dr Powell's replacement," he told Mrs Bell.

"So, he isn't coming back?" she asked.

"He is starting his own medical practice from number 1 Ely Place Upper."

"Competing against your practice?" she added sharply.

"My practice has many competitors," Will replied. "As for this practice, yesterday, I placed advertisements in *The Irish Times* and the *Freeman's Journal* and Alfie will put copies of the advertisement up in Trinity College when he returns on Monday. I can't say how long it will take to find a doctor but you can tell people it is being dealt with. Are Maura's rooms still unoccupied?"

"They are," Mrs Bell replied. "You'd like the doctor to live here?"

"Preferably, yes." Will closed the drawers and picked up the crate. "But we'll just have to wait and see."

"Come upstairs for a cup of tea and some of that lovely-looking cake."

Isobel cut three thick slices of cake and put the remainder in a cake tin while Mrs Bell made a pot of tea.

"Jimmy will enjoy a slice later." Mrs Bell poured the tea

and passed her a cup and saucer. "He's settled in at the brewery – it took a few weeks – but he's settled at last."

"I'm glad. Please give him our best wishes?"

"I will, he'll be sorry to have missed you both."

When they sat down with their tea, Isobel added a little milk to their cups before reaching across the table and patting Mrs Bell's hands. "There is something you ought to know – my grandfather died at Greene Hall two days ago."

Mrs Bell was unusually silent and Isobel exchanged a glance with Will.

"So they are both dead now." Mrs Bell nodded to herself. "I cannot be sorry for your loss, Isobel. Lewis Greene caused so much misery to his tenants."

"I understand but I thought you deserved to know."

"And I'm grateful. What will happen to the Greene Hall estate now?"

"We are waiting to hear from Grandfather's solicitor but it is expected that Alfie will inherit the estate."

On Monday afternoon, Alfie called out a greeting to them as he crossed the street while Will was leaving number 30 to make house calls.

"I have just received a telegram from Mr Anderson, Grandfather's solicitor," he said. "Grandfather's funeral took place last Friday morning at eleven o'clock and Mr Anderson will be in Dublin tomorrow and he has asked if it is convenient to us all if he calls to number 55 at three o'clock to read Grandfather's will. Can you both be there?"

"I can," she replied immediately.

"I shall try and be there at three o'clock but I can't promise anything," Will replied and Alfie nodded.

"I'll send Mr Anderson a reply a little later on to confirm it."

"We also received a telegram this morning," she said. "Nurse Barton is returning to Dublin the day after tomorrow and she will be staying here at number 30 while she looks for another position."

"That's very good of you. I look forward to meeting her again. Now, I must hurry. I don't want to be late for my first lecture back."

"Let me walk part of the way to Trinity College with you?" Will offered and Alfie grinned.

Isobel, her mother, James, Alfie and Miles gathered in number 55's morning room the following afternoon. Will hadn't yet returned from house calls but they decided to proceed without him. The solicitor, Reginald Anderson, was a man in his late fifties whom, James discovered, had been two years ahead of him at Trinity College.

"It's a small world." Mr Anderson lifted the will out of a black leather despatch case and put the case on the floor beside the writing desk before turning to face them. "Before I begin, you should be aware that Mr Greene updated his will a week after his return to Greene Hall from Dublin. This is his will," he continued and cleared his throat.

> "'I, Lewis Greene of Greene Hall in the County of Mayo hereby revoke all former wills and testamentary dispositions made by me and declare this to be my last will and testament. I bequeath to my son Miles Greene all the books from my library at Greene Hall. I bequeath to my daughter Martha Ellison and her husband James Ellison the sum of fifteen thousand pounds on the condition that the sum is used to provide for the

maintenance and well-being of my son Miles Greene for the remainder of his life. I bequeath to my daughter Martha Ellison and to my granddaughter Isobel Fitzgerald all the portraits, photographic portraits and jewellery instructed by me to be removed from Greene Hall for safe keeping and to be divided between them as they see fit. I bequeath to my granddaughter Isobel Fitzgerald and her husband William Fitzgerald the sum of five thousand pounds to be used to educate Benjamin Fitzgerald and Isabella Fitzgerald my great-grandchildren and also their ward John Fitzgerald. I bequeath to my grandson Alfred Stevens the house and estate of Greene Hall including farms of land, houses, money and the contents of the house not already bequeathed. I hereby nominate and appoint Richard Bourke and Jeremiah Barber to be the executors of this my will. Given under my hand this 5th day of January One Thousand Eight Hundred and Eighty-Two ~ Lewis Greene ~ Signed and acknowledged in the presence of Reginald Anderson, solicitor, Westport and Simon Lowe, law clerk, Westport.'"

A long silence followed, broken only when Will was shown into the room, whispering his apologies for being late. Mr Anderson passed him the will and they waited for Will to read it. When he put the will down, he gave her an incredulous glance.

"Grandfather wishes to put his fortune to good use," she said, noting how Alfie, seated in an armchair, was staring intently at his hands.

"We shall all have some tea," her mother announced, her voice shaking a little as she got up from beside Isobel on the sofa and rang for a servant.

"Thank you." Mr Anderson took the will back from Will and returned it to his despatch case. "I have copies here for you all."

"Alfie?" Isobel went to him and crouched down beside his armchair.

"It is so much – the house – the estate…"

"Both Mr Anderson and I will be on hand to advise you." James laid a hand on Alfie's shoulder. "Can Knox and the other servants stay on in the house to ensure it won't stand empty?" he asked Mr Anderson. "Until a decision is made on its future?"

"That can be arranged," Mr Anderson replied.

The copies of the will were distributed and the tea was carried in. Mrs Ellison busied herself in serving it and accepting a cup and saucer from her mother, Isobel followed Miles to the window.

"Your father has been very generous," she said gently, passing the cup and saucer to him. "You will never want for anything and – all those books – there must be thousands of them."

"I cannot help but think I do not deserve to have such a huge amount of money spent on me," he replied sadly. "I refused to meet him."

"He was your father and he wanted to ensure you were provided for," she added and Miles nodded and she squeezed his hand before approaching Alfie.

"Can I suggest that your first actions as landlord of the Greene Hall estate are to instruct Mr Anderson to see that the land agent retires and to advertise for his replacement?"

"Why?" Alfie asked suspiciously.

"Because the current land agent is a Mr Dudley who is eighty-five. He is greatly disliked and he—"

"Who has told you this, Mrs Fitzgerald?" Mr Anderson asked sharply and they both turned to him.

"Someone who has knowledge of the estate," she replied, being deliberately vague. "Mr Dudley has been land agent since before the Great Famine, hasn't he?"

"That's right but he is still a fit and capable man."

"Alfie," she continued in a low voice, turning back to him. "Start afresh with a new land agent? One who is more sympathetic to the needs of the tenants? One who is more in tune to modern farming practices?"

"Is Mr Dudley very much disliked?" Alfie asked Mr Anderson over her shoulder.

"Yes, he is, Mr Stevens. But he has an unpopular job to do."

"Please ensure Mr Dudley retires and receives an adequate pension and then advertise for his replacement," Alfie instructed the solicitor. "I shall interview the applicants at Greene Hall."

Mr Anderson tensed and stared at Alfie stony-faced without responding.

"Have I not made myself clear enough, Mr Anderson?" Alfie asked him in a quiet yet firm tone.

"You have, Mr Stevens, and I shall do as you instruct," he replied with clear reluctance.

"Thank you, Mr Anderson. Would you like some tea?"

"No tea for me, thank you, Mr Stevens." Mr Anderson shut the lid of his despatch case and closed the lock with a loud snap. "I must be on my way to Broadstone Station."

Gorman showed Mr Anderson out of the room and as the door closed, Alfie turned to James with a grim expression.

"He must go, too. There must be other – more suitable – solicitors in Westport? No offence, James, but it would be better for me to appoint a local man to deal with matters regarding the estate."

"No offence taken, and I shall make some inquiries," James replied with a smile and slapped Alfie's shoulder. "He now knows you are not a man who can be taken for granted."

"I have inherited an estate I do not want, with tenants who will hate me simply for being their landlord – and an absentee landlord at that – but I want to do what is best for them. When I appoint a new land agent, I shall instruct him to assess all the rents paid by the tenants on the estate and have the findings delivered to Greene Hall for my appraisal. I have been reading up on Mr Gladstone's land-reform bill and if the tenants can have their rent reduced without them having to go to a Land Court – or purchase their farm over a set number of years – I shall be content."

"Good," James replied.

"I don't know what to do with the house, though," he added. "I will never live at Greene Hall. Mother, what if I were to find tenants for the house?" he asked. "Would strangers living there upset you?"

"I would like for the house to be lived in," she said. "And, if possible, that the servants retain their positions. Some have been there a very long time – since my time there – and that is an exceptionally long time ago."

"I shall try my best."

"Should you go to Greene Hall?" she asked tentatively.

"Grandmother and Grandfather are dead," he said gently, "and I want this to be a fresh start for the estate and, like I said, I want to do what is best for the tenants – and I want them to know it, too. So I must go there and make myself known to them and show them that I will not be a fully absentee landlord."

"Please, be careful."

"I promise," he told her and kissed her cheek before turning to them all. "I shall never be able to thank Will, Isobel and James enough for looking for me and saving my life. But a day or so in bed is not enough to recuperate so I want to announce that from tomorrow, I shall be visiting Dr Harrison at Swift's Hospital on a weekly basis. I don't know how long for – I simply want to ensure what happened will never happen again."

Mrs Ellison hugged and kissed him. "We are all very proud of you," she said softly.

"Thank you, Mother. And the only other person who knows is Kenneth Fisher. I would be grateful if it could stay that way."

As she saw Will off to the practice house in the morning, Isobel glanced at the wooden crate containing David's belongings from Pimlico which had sat on the floor under the hall table for the past few days. Will hadn't had time to bring them to number 1 and Nurse Barton would be arriving from Ballina that afternoon so, as she closed the front door, she made the decision to bring them there herself. It was about time she faced Margaret.

She received a few puzzled glances as she carried the

rather awkward crate to Ely Place Upper but she ignored them. Her arms were starting to ache as she went up the steps, balanced the crate against the wall of the house and rang the front doorbell. Ida opened the door and Isobel smiled.

"Ida, I have come to deliver the last of Dr Powell's belongings and to see Mrs Simpson."

"I will see if Mrs Simpson is at home, Mrs Fitzgerald."

"Ida, I don't know if you have heard," she added quickly before the young woman turned away. "But Mr Greene died last week. My brother has inherited the Greene Hall estate and will be making a number of changes. First and foremost – Mr Dudley is being replaced."

Ida's face lit up but her joy was short-lived as Margaret came down the stairs wearing a gorgeous russet-coloured dress which made Isobel feel exceedingly drab in her mourning attire. Four steps from the bottom, Margaret stopped abruptly and gave Isobel an icy gaze.

"Thank you, Ida. I shall deal with Mrs Fitzgerald."

Ida bobbed a curtsey and wisely hurried away in the direction of the servants' hall.

"David's belongings from Pimlico." Isobel held out the crate but Margaret made no effort to come down the remainder of the steps. "Very well," Isobel said crisply, stepping into the hall. Placing the crate on the floor, she gave it as good a shove across the tiles as she could manage with her boot. "This ends any connection between you and your fiancé and myself and Will."

She turned to go but Margaret ran down the steps, along the hall and pushed the front door closed.

"Please, Isobel, allow me to explain—"

"I don't want to hear your excuses, Margaret," she snapped. "What you, David and Will's father have done behind Alfie's back is utterly disgusting. You could have found tenants for this house and you could have lived quietly and independently for the first time in your life."

"I'm only twenty-six, Isobel." Dropping her voice, Margaret added, "I do not know how long I have to live – I do not wish to be alone – to have my family's pity."

"You still haven't told them you have syphilis, have you?" Isobel whispered fiercely. "Have you told your lady's maid – have you?" she demanded. "If Ida is going to attend to you, she needs to know."

"Will said something similar."

"Well, if you haven't taken any notice of him, you will take notice of me. If you do not inform Ida – I shall," she declared and Margaret's jaw dropped.

"You wouldn't dare?"

"Oh, yes, I would. Ida must be told and she must be given a choice of whether she wishes to stay in your service. It is about time you started considering other people's feelings," she said and an expression of offence crossed Margaret's face.

"Fred went with whores, Isobel. One of them gave him syphilis. He passed it on to me and to our child. Our child died and had to be cut out of me. I will never have another. Having been put through all that – and with just as bad to come – when my mind and body will disintegrate – it is about time I consider myself and my future."

"Your future with a man who will never love you and who only sees you as an easy route to a prestigious address, his own medical practice and an extremely profitable future," Isobel clarified. "And what will happen when he has to fulfil his sexual needs?" she asked and Margaret made a dismissive gesture with a hand.

"I don't care what happens, as long as he and Alfie are discreet."

"Alfie?" she whispered incredulously. "Alfie? Margaret, David has broken Alfie's heart. Alfie will never trust David nor allow David near him ever again. David may be a respectable husband for you but he is going to have to be very, very careful as to where he goes and who he fulfils his sexual needs with."

Margaret didn't respond and Isobel reached for the front door handle.

"John Fitzgerald is no longer welcome to call at number 30. I would thank you and David not to call on us either. Goodbye, Margaret. I can only wish you luck – you will be in great need of it."

Opening the front door, she went out and down the steps leaving it wide open.

She strode back to number 30 and slammed the front door, bringing the housekeeper out of the breakfast room in alarm.

"Have you ever wanted to shake some sense into someone, Mrs Dillon?" she inquired, pulling the pin from her hat and laying them both on the hall table.

"Many, many times, Mrs Fitzgerald," the older woman replied drolly and Isobel laughed. "The larger guest bedroom has been prepared."

"Thank you, and if the train journey from Ballina is as long and tiring as the journey from Westport, Nurse Barton will be in dire need of tea."

"The kettle shall be kept on the boil, Mrs Fitzgerald."

At four o'clock, Isobel heard the front door close then voices in the hall and she left the morning room. A large trunk stood beside the hall table and Zaineb was carrying a carpet bag up the stairs.

"You are very welcome to number 30." Isobel shook Nurse Barton's hand warmly. "Gerald, our footman, will bring your trunk upstairs shortly. I shall show you to your room."

"Thank you, Mrs Fitzgerald," the nurse replied and they followed Zaineb upstairs and into the guest bedroom at the front of the house.

"You may hear some strange noises," Isobel told her while Zaineb placed the carpet bag on the bedroom chair and added some coal to the fire. "The nursery is directly above this room and young John is playing with his wooden stream locomotive. Will built a tunnel with building blocks yesterday evening and John has been attempting to recreate it – with varying results."

Nurse Barton laughed. "This is a lovely room."

"Thank you. I'll leave you to settle in and I'll ask for some tea in a few minutes."

As she and Zaineb went downstairs, passing Gerald on the first-floor landing with the trunk, the maid gave her a smile.

"When I open the door to callers, Mrs Fitzgerald, I receive two reactions from people who do not know of my appearance," she explained. "They either stare – and make no secret of the fact they are staring. Or they stare for a moment and then try their best to hide it. Nurse Barton is the first caller to do neither."

"She has lived and nursed in London. I hope she is the first of many callers to do neither."

Isobel and Nurse Barton were enjoying a second cup of tea when the front door closed and a few moments later Will came into the morning room.

"Nurse Barton." He shook her hand. "It is very good to see you again."

"And you, Dr Fitzgerald. Thank you for allowing me to stay here, it is most kind of you and your wife."

"Please call us Will and Isobel?" she asked and the nurse smiled.

"I shall, thank you. And I am Barbara. I intend to place an advertisement in the Dublin newspapers, I shall not impose on you for long."

"You are not imposing on us at all," Isobel chided gently. "It is the least we can do. I read your letter to Will and you were so good with Grandfather."

"No matter how the tenants and local people viewed him, to me, Mr Greene was an elderly gentleman in the final days of a long life and I wished to ensure those final days were as comfortable as possible. Mr Knox and the other servants will now remain in the house as long as they are needed."

"Alfie has inherited the estate," Isobel told her. "And he has already begun to make changes. Mr Dudley will be replaced, as shall Mr Anderson," she added and Barbara looked visibly relieved.

"That will go a long way to easing tensions in the locality. Mr Dudley has been land agent – and hated – for such a long time. As for Mr Anderson, when he came to the house to update Mr Greene's will, he was extremely rude to both

Mr Knox and myself. Everyone on the estate will welcome a fresh start."

"Alfie intends to be firm but fair."

"I'm glad to hear that, Isobel."

"How are you coping?" she asked Will as he sat down in one of the armchairs with a little groan. "Unfortunately, Barbara, Will is in need of two doctors."

"Two?" Barbara turned to him in surprise.

"Dr Powell has left the Merrion Street Upper practice and my former practice in the Liberties in order to set up in medical practice on his own," he explained. "It was very sudden and I must admit I am struggling to cope at the practice house. I advertised to fill the position in the Liberties and I received six letters of application which I have narrowed down to two. I haven't advertised for the position at my own practice yet," he added and Isobel frowned as Barbara stared down at her hands. "If I have not found a replacement for Dr Powell in the next few days, then, I must."

Isobel shot Will a puzzled glance while Barbara remained silent but he gave her a brief shake of his head and she didn't pursue it.

When dinner was announced and they went into the breakfast room, Barbara still hadn't spoken. But, as they sat down at the table and Zaineb and Mary carried their plates in, Barbara exhaled a little sigh.

"Isobel, there is something you do not know about me," she said, nodding her thanks to Zaineb as the maid put a plate with two slices of succulent roast beef on it down in front of her. "Your husband found out by accident when I passed him more documents than I should have when I showed him my baptism certificate, school reports, nursing certificate and letter of recommendation from my mother's parish priest."

"Oh?" she replied apprehensively as Mary put a plate down in front of her and then another in front of Will. "Thank you, Mary, thank you, Zaineb," she said and the maids left the room.

"I am a doctor, Isobel, as well as a nurse, and I am licensed to practise medicine."

Isobel's jaw dropped. "So, why are you not practising medicine?" she asked before adding quickly, "if it is confidential, then, I completely understand."

"I was dismissed from the Royal Free Hospital in London for entering into a relationship with a fellow doctor. With no letter of recommendation from the hospital and considerable debts, I fell back on my nursing training and, after my mother's death, I moved to Dublin to start afresh and I found a position as nurse to a solicitor in Kingstown."

"Will, if you want to speak to Barbara alone, I can eat in the morning room?" she said but he shook his head.

"It was entirely up to Barbara whether she wished to tell you," he said. "Now that she has, I would like to put this to her," he went on and turned to Barbara. "Would you consider joining the Merrion Street Upper medical practice? You do not have to give me an answer at once but the offer is there."

"Dr Fitzgerald – Will – I was laughed at many times in London when I introduced myself as Dr Barton. I can only assume I shall be a laughing stock in Dublin, too."

"I understand you have not been in general practice before but…"

"I could be broken in gently?" Barbara suggested and Will smiled.

"There will be talk," he said. "And derision. But you are an excellent nurse. I believe you can be an excellent doctor as well."

Isobel looked eagerly from Will to Barbara as she awaited the older woman's response.

"May I consider it for a day or two, Will?" Barbara asked and Isobel's heart sank.

"Of course you may. I would be interested to hear your views on the two main candidates for my former practice in the Liberties. One is a gentleman recently returned from Australia and used to 'roughing it', as he put it. But Pimlico is not the Australian outback and the waiting room, surgery and the rooms he could live in are very respectable."

"I would be happy to help in any way I can," Barbara replied and Isobel lifted the lids off the serving dishes and they began their meal.

Will was grateful to Isobel for not mentioning the offer in front of Barbara at any point during the evening or at breakfast the next morning. She did confess to him privately as they lay in bed how a female doctor in the practice would be a wonderful addition and left it at that. The decision was entirely up to Barbara and all they could do now was wait.

Eva had worked wonders and he saw his last patient to the surgery door at five minutes to one. Putting the letters of application from the two main candidates for the Liberties practice in his medical bag so he could discuss them later with Barbara, he left his surgery and went downstairs to the office.

"If I haven't secured a replacement for Dr Powell in the next two days, I shall advertise," he told Eva. "I have made an offer to someone and I have given them time to consider it."

"I'm glad, Dr Fitzgerald. I know you said you wished to carry on alone but…"

"I cannot," he finished and she nodded sympathetically.

"Have you spoken to Dr Powell at all?"

"I haven't seen him, Eva. He may still be in Co Meath. My wife and I have each called to number 1 and both times he wasn't there. Whether he 'wasn't at home' or he really wasn't at home, I cannot say."

"There has been talk, Dr Fitzgerald."

"I'd have been astonished if there had not been talk, Eva. What is being said?"

"That you and Dr Powell fought and that you threw him out of the practice house."

"I see," he replied dryly. "And what did we fight over?" he added and Eva grimaced.

"Your wife, Dr Fitzgerald."

Will didn't quite know whether to be furious or to roar with laughter.

"Of course, it is ridiculous," Eva went on quickly. "Especially with Dr Powell engaged-to-be-married to Mrs Simpson. I have dispelled the rumours as best I can."

"Thank you, Eva. Have we lost any patients?"

"We haven't lost any. But I have heard that Dr Powell does not begin in practice until Monday."

"So I must try and have a doctor in place by then," he said. "I shall do my best."

When he returned to number 30 from house calls that

afternoon, Zaineb informed him that Mrs Fitzgerald and Nurse Barton had just come in from a walk in the Fitzwilliam Square garden with the children. Mrs Fitzgerald had gone upstairs to the nursery and Nurse Barton was in the morning room so he joined Barbara and they went through the two letters of application. She read the letters twice before putting them down.

"The gentleman returning from Australia," she said and he gave her a relieved grin.

"I hoped you would choose him. The other applicant seems a little too… snooty."

Barbara chuckled. "I'm afraid he does. I didn't live in the Liberties for long but it certainly came across to me as a unique locality you either accept the way it is or not at all."

"The Liberties certainly opened my eyes while I lived and practised there," he said. "I'll write to Dr O'Brien straight away and invite him for interview. I hope he comes across as well in person as he does on paper."

"Will, before you do, I have thought of nothing else but your offer. It would be utterly foolish of me to turn it down. I would be delighted to accept, as long as I can truly be broken in gently."

He roared with delighted laughter and shook her hand. "You shall start on Monday and be broken in gently, I promise. Thank you, Barbara. Let's tell Isobel and then walk to the practice house."

They went upstairs to the nursery. Isobel was on the rug with John, Florrie and the train set and she gave them an expectant smile.

"Barbara has agreed to join the practice," Will announced and Isobel gave a squeal of joy.

"Oh, Barbara, that is wonderful news." Getting to her feet, she gave Barbara a hug. "Nurse Barton is now Dr Barton," she explained to a puzzled John. "Dr Barton is going to be working with Will at the practice."

"But you're a lady?" he said and Isobel crouched down.

"There are lady doctors now and there's nothing wrong with that."

"No," he conceded a little unsurely, glancing at Florrie.

"I would be very happy to have a lady doctor attend to me, Master John. It will be nice for people to have a choice."

"Yes," he replied more firmly and peered up at Barbara. "Good afternoon, Dr Barton."

"And, good afternoon again to you, John," she said with a smile. "I must find lodgings now," she added to Will.

"Actually, in the hope you would accept Will's offer, I have been thinking about that," Isobel said mysteriously. "Wait a moment," she continued and kissed John's cheek. "We need to go out," she told the boy, "but Will and I shall be back in time to tuck you up in bed."

Isobel kissed John's cheek again, they went downstairs to the hall and she turned to them.

"When I last called to the practice house, Eva was reminiscing about the time she lived there when she first became practice secretary and how lucky she was to have had a kitchen, a parlour and two bedrooms and that she only had to go downstairs to what had once been the scullery for water and to a newly-installed privy…" She tailed off as Will began to smile.

"The four rooms on the second floor have been used for storage purposes for years," he said. "Old patient files – old furniture – you name it – but with a thorough clearout and the rooms decorated, some new furniture and a kitchen range for heating and cooking, the rooms would be ideal for you," he told Barbara whose face lit up. "Let's go there and make some plans."

Twenty minutes later, they were standing in the room above his surgery surrounded by furniture no longer fit for purpose. It was at the front of the practice house and Eva had used it as a parlour. The room next door, which Eva had used as a kitchen, was full of boxes of patient files and a table and four chairs. The two bedrooms contained a mixture of yet more patient files and old dining chairs relegated from the waiting room.

"I'll ask Eva to go through the files," he said. "She'll know which can be disposed of or moved up to the top floor."

"Are these four rooms enough for you?" Isobel asked Barbara, who nodded vigorously.

"There is only myself – and they are perfect – completely private and yet with the surgery only downstairs."

"That is settled, then." Will smiled. "I shall engage a chimney sweep, the decorators we used at number 30 and write to Dr O'Brien – he is the candidate I want to interview for the practice in the Liberties," he explained to Isobel.

"You write to Dr O'Brien now so the letter goes in the last post. Barbara and I shall do the rest."

He gave her a grateful nod and saw them out before going upstairs to his surgery and writing the letter. Sitting back in his chair, he ran a hand across his jaw, content that at last matters seemed to be falling into place. He posted the letter then returned to the practice house and spent an hour carrying the patient files downstairs to the office and stacking the furniture on the landing for when a rag and bone man would next pass by.

The four rooms now empty, he walked through them. They were light and airy and if the decorators were as competent here as they had been at number 30, Barbara would be very comfortable in her new home.

He walked back to number 30 and heard laughter in the morning room as he hung his hat and overcoat on the stand. Isobel came out to the hall a few moments later and kissed his lips.

"You can expect the chimney sweep at the practice house at nine o'clock tomorrow morning and the decorators at eleven o'clock," she said triumphantly. "We also engaged a firm to install a front doorbell who will work in conjunction with the decorators."

"Tomorrow? How did you manage that?" he asked but she just tapped the side of her nose mischievously and he laughed.

"We also found a second-hand kitchen range in excellent condition and we are visiting a furniture warehouse in the morning."

He told Eva before surgery the next day and, to his relief, the practice secretary clapped her hands in pure delight.

"Oh, Dr Fitzgerald, you need not have looked so terribly worried. I'm absolutely thrilled – a female doctor – how wonderful."

"And if it were not for you, I would never have discovered her. Now, in Dr Barton's own words, she would like to be broken in gently so she won't be offended if you assign some ladies to her."

"And some of our more broad-minded gentlemen?" Eva asked and he smiled.

"Yes, I think she would take offence if all her patients were female."

"Oh, I never thought I'd see the day."

"My father will be furious," he added bluntly, repeating exactly what he had said to Isobel the previous evening as they got ready for bed. But he was ready for a confrontation if his father took his displeasure out on him. "So please be prepared, Eva, he may come here."

"I shall be prepared, Dr Fitzgerald, and I will make Dr Barton very welcome on Monday."

"Thank you, Eva. Now, if the Dr O'Brien I have invited for interview is suitable for the Liberties practice, my life may return to a normal pattern at last."

Barbara returned to number 30 on Monday evening and, to Isobel's relief, gave her a broad grin as they went into the morning room. Barbara had been quiet at luncheon, simply mentioning how Eva had welcomed her warmly to the practice. Isobel hadn't wanted to press her for more details, hoping Barbara was waiting for her first day to be over before commenting further. It proved to be the case as they sat on the sofa and Barbara happily related that her first surgery and house calls had passed without any derision whatsoever from her new patients.

Will arrived home shortly afterwards announcing that after interviewing Dr O'Brien at the practice house, they went to Pimlico to inspect the waiting room and surgery and he had engaged him. Dr O'Brien was introduced to Mrs Bell and he also rented the rooms Jimmy and his mother, Maura, had lived in and would begin in practice on Wednesday.

Isobel sighed contentedly as she got into bed that night

and snuggled up to Will. For the first time in weeks – months, even – she was happy and relaxed. Ben and Belle were adjusting well to solid food and young John no longer looked panic-stricken when told she or Will were going out. Decoration of the four rooms on the second floor of the practice house was well underway and the kitchen range and the serviceable furniture Barbara had chosen on Friday were to be delivered in a few days' time.

"Ida called to the servants' hall this afternoon and asked to speak to me in private," she said. "Margaret has told her she has syphilis and gave her the option of staying or finding another position with a glowing letter of recommendation."

Will's eyebrows rose. "Wonders will never cease. Is Ida staying with Margaret?"

"Yes, she is."

"Then, she is a brave young woman. To go from being your grandmother's lady's maid to Margaret's... It won't be easy for her, especially when Margaret's symptoms begin to present themselves."

"I've told Ida if she is in need of any help or advice then she is to call to us here," she said and he nodded. "What can you tell me about Dr O'Brien?" she added.

"His name is Robert O'Brien – known as Bob – he is forty-seven and he was born on Tripoli in the Liberties. He and his parents emigrated to Australia when he was ten."

"Why come back to rainy old Dublin?"

"His wife eloped with another man," Will replied. "After she left him, he told me Australia didn't seem quite so sunny anymore. Having said that, he's a jolly and to-the-point chap and he and Mrs Bell liked each other. He told me he will probably look to rent a house eventually but the rooms would suffice for now."

"Dare I say it, but I think matters have settled at last."

"I hope so," he murmured sleepily. "But my father hasn't heard about the 'lady doctor' yet."

"And you're expecting him to turn up here?"

"He'd have a nerve to turn up here. I'm expecting him to come to the practice house first thing tomorrow morning. He'll be livid. His protégé may be many things, but David isn't a woman."

"When I last spoke to your mother, she said she usually hears your father going out and coming in but these last few weeks he must have been leaving and returning home at all hours because she has heard nothing."

"Does she seem happy?" Will asked suddenly and she felt him shrug. "Happy is the wrong word… Is she more content? I haven't seen near enough of her over the past few weeks."

"She said the same about you. Which is why I shall ask her tomorrow to now come to number 30 on Saturday mornings and stay to luncheon."

"Thank you," he replied and she felt him kiss the top of her head.

Tess showed Isobel into Sarah's morning room at eleven o'clock the next morning and Will's ageless mother, wearing a striking sapphire blue dress, smiled at her in delight.

"Isobel, how lovely to see you. Please, sit down and tell me if what I have been hearing is true and that Nurse Barton is actually a doctor and she has replaced David Powell at the practice?"

"It is all true." Isobel laughed as she sat next to Sarah on the sofa. "And, from next Monday, Barbara will be living in the four rooms above the surgeries."

"John will be furious. I heard David Powell started in his new practice yesterday and a female doctor will eclipse him entirely."

"Will is expecting his father to come to the practice house this morning. I would be very surprised if John wasn't there at nine o'clock on the dot," she said and her mother-in-law grimaced.

"Poor Will."

"Will can cope with his father. I just hope there isn't too much of a scene. He was saying last night how he hasn't seen very much of you recently so I have come to ask whether you can change the morning you visit the children from Wednesday to Saturday?"

Sarah was silent for a few moments. "Young John will expect to see his grandfather on Saturday mornings, not me."

"Young John has been told his grandfather is unwell and will not be visiting him for a little while."

"Unwell with a 'bad cold'?" Sarah asked sharply and Isobel stared at her in surprise. "Isobel," Sarah began again calmly. "No matter what we think of my husband, any disagreement we have with him is between us and him – the children should not be involved."

"I do not want him near them," she said firmly and Sarah gave a little shrug.

"Very well. I simply wished to give you my opinion."

"And I am grateful for it but matters shall remain as they are. Sarah, I don't wish to fall out with you as well."

"You won't, Isobel. As well as being my daughter-in-law, you are one of my dearest friends and one of the most forthright people I know."

"You are quite forthright yourself," she said and Sarah laughed.

"I shall be fifty-eight this year. I haven't reached such a grand old age without being plain-spoken every now and again."

"A grand old age?" Isobel echoed. "That is nonsense – you are still young and you always look wonderful."

"And quite often I wonder why I bother," Sarah said sadly, smoothing a hand down the skirt of her dress. "At first, I dressed myself up to show to John what he has all but lost but we have not seen each other since your mother's New Year's Eve dinner party and now I dress simply to please myself. Oh, how I wish I could divorce him and move on with my life. I detest feeling so free and yet so trapped. You won't tell Will any of this, will you?" she added anxiously and Isobel shook her head.

"Not if you don't wish me to. Come to number 30 on Saturday mornings so Will can see you, too?"

"Thank you, I shall."

"Good. I must introduce you to Barbara and when she moves into the rooms in the practice house she will be glad of some callers and Mother greatly appreciates you accompanying her and Miles to Swift's Hospital each week."

"Miles appears to have overcome his attachment to you. How has he reacted to his father's death?"

"He inherited all of Grandfather's books and Mother and James were left an enormous sum of money to ensure he wants for nothing for the rest of his life. But because he refused to meet his father, Miles thinks he doesn't deserve any of it."

"Poor Miles." Sarah's face contorted in sympathy.

"I've tried to reassure him but he's been very quiet. The past couple of months have been a lot for him to take in. I'll keep reassuring him, it's all I can do."

"And how is Alfie?" Sarah asked softly and Isobel fought back tears. Would she ever rid her mind of the sight of her brother lying curled up on the Pimlico surgery floor?

"Oh, Sarah, I thought he was dead," she whispered. "He consumed an entire bottle of opium pills and washed them down with whiskey and I thought he was dead. He has been so strong over the years but this…" She tailed off, pulled a handkerchief from her sleeve and wiped her eyes. "And that is why I don't want Will's father anywhere near the children – I will never trust him again – never." She finished on a shout and Sarah nodded.

"I understand."

"I'm sorry for shouting," she said and gave Sarah a wobbly smile. "Alfie is recovering and he shall overcome this. He didn't allow our father to get the better of him and he won't allow Will's father to get the better of him either."

Will and Barbara had just arrived at the practice house when an exasperated-looking Eva came out of the office.

"I have just turned a journalist away," she said and Barbara's eyes widened in alarm. "You needn't worry, Dr Barton, I told him I had heard that a doctor recently returned from Australia had set up practice in the Liberties."

Barbara exhaled a sigh of relief and Will gave Eva a grin but it faded as, over her shoulder, he saw his father accompanying some patients inside and closing the front door behind him.

"Please, go upstairs to your surgery," he instructed Barbara in a low tone. "You'll hear raised voices but please stay there," he added and she did as she was told.

The patients were agog, recognising Dr John Fitzgerald and knowing he hadn't called to pay his son the compliments of the morning.

His father walked past without acknowledging any of them, went straight up the stairs and Will turned to Eva.

"I'll try and make this as short as possible," he said, before following his father and closing his surgery door.

"A woman," his father said by way of a greeting.

"A highly-qualified doctor with a licence to practise medicine from the College of Physicians," Will clarified, putting his hat and medical bag on the desk.

"Are you determined to make this practice the laughing stock of Dublin?"

"Be careful, Father, you almost sound as if you care. I thought David Powell's new practice was your main concern these days."

"This practice has been in the Fitzgerald family—"

"For over a hundred years. Yes, Father, I know. Which is why I have seen fit to move with the times. There is no reason whatsoever why women cannot practise medicine. Now, you have had your say and Dr Barton and I have surgeries to take."

"Dr Barton." His father almost spat out the words as he walked to the door.

"How is David Powell's practice progressing?" Will inquired and his father gave him a suspicious glance.

"Your wife called to number 1 last week," he replied without answering the question. "Threatening Margaret and barring her and David from your home as well."

"And?"

"You see nothing wrong in your wife making threats?" his father asked. "Telling Margaret if she did not inform her lady's maid of her illness then she would," he continued in a low tone.

"Syphilis is not just an illness, as you well know," Will whispered fiercely. "Margaret is not behaving responsibly. I'm glad Isobel laid down the law to her because Margaret's lady's maid deserved to know. Margaret's family ought to know, too."

"No. Her mother and sister would die of shame."

"Does Margaret not ask why you have taken such an interest in her well-being and future?"

"All she knows is that I was Fred's godfather and, as Duncan and David's father are both dead, I am being on hand to provide what little service I can."

"Little service." Will rolled his eyes. Tell that to Alfie, he added silently. "Good God, she is self-centred and naïve."

"She is my daughter-in-law and I shall do what is best for her."

"So is Isobel and because of your meddling, her brother tried to take his own life. Alfie is recovering well, thank you for asking," he added sarcastically when he received no reply. "Now, I really must get on." He opened the door and his father walked out.

Will went straight along the landing and into Barbara's surgery and she got up from behind the desk.

"Will, if it is easier—"

"My father has had his say," Will interrupted firmly but calmly before she could finish. "We will never agree on female doctors but I run this practice now." She nodded and he smiled. "Let's begin surgery."

Alfie, brandishing a periodical, was shown into number 30's morning room a week later.

"I saw you walking home from house calls, Will, and I thought you ought to see this."

Getting up from beside Isobel on the sofa and taking the periodical from him, Will saw it was the latest edition of the *Journal of Irish Medicine*.

"Read the editorial," Alfie told him and Will opened the *Journal* and glanced at a column on the left-hand side of page two.

Women Doctors – Cure or Curse? The editorial asked and Will walked to the window. He stood there, having to pause and either shake his head or roll his eyes every few lines.

"Bloody hell," he finally exploded, closed the *Journal* and threw it onto the sofa. "Father has actually brought up the women have smaller brains subject," he said as Isobel reached for it. "He thinks the practice will be a laughing stock – well, when people read that rubbish – the *Journal* certainly will be."

"More copies than usual were circulating around the School of Physic," Alfie explained. "And Kenneth showed one to me."

"And the general consensus is?" Will asked and Alfie grimaced.

"That the *Journal* is now a laughing stock and many of its contributors are furious. There is a rumour that your father may be replaced as editor if he doesn't write something with less archaic views in next month's issue."

"I hope Barbara doesn't see this." Isobel lay the *Journal*

on her lap. "It is not just insulting to women in general but to her, personally, as well."

"I think I should show it to her first thing in the morning all the same," he said. "If there is so much controversy, I don't want her to see it by accident."

"Yes, you're right," Isobel conceded. "Can we keep this copy, Alfie?"

"Of course you can – I certainly don't want to be seen with it," he added with a grin. "How is Dr Barton settling into the practice house?" he asked.

"Very well," Will replied. "The rooms look wonderful. How are you, Alfie?"

"I'm getting there. Wherever there is, slowly but surely. Dr Harrison is helping a great deal."

"We're here if you need anything – you know that?" Will reminded him and Alfie replied with a grateful smile.

The following morning, Barbara stood at the window in her surgery and read the editorial in silence before turning to face Will with a combination of hurt and indignation in her eyes.

"I had to show it to you," he said, hearing a knock at the door. "My father may be dismissed because of it. Yes?" he called and Eva came in.

"Mr Alfie Stevens has just called, Dr Fitzgerald. He was in a hurry to get to a lecture and couldn't stop. He says he knows you take this newspaper but he asked me to show you this piece as you otherwise won't see it until this evening."

"Thank you, Eva." He took the folded newspaper from her and smiled as he read an article marked with a large X. "Someone at the *Freeman's Journal* has taken issue with Father's 'antiquated and misogynistic' editorial in the

Journal of Irish Medicine. This will leave Father even more irate as he believes the *Freeman's Journal* is only fit for one thing."

"I really did not wish or expect to cause such a fuss, Will." Barbara sat down behind her desk with a sigh. "But if this fuss can encourage other determined women to even consider going into medicine then, I shall do my best to carry on regardless. I have faced far worse difficulties than this and I have overcome them all."

Chapter Nine

Isobel couldn't help but laugh as Will passed the March edition of the *Journal of Irish Medicine* to her and she read the editorial. His father had done a complete about-turn in order to keep his position as editor.

"You should have this framed," she said, handing it back to him.

"I was thinking that – both editorials side-by-side."

"Your father must be both humiliated and furious."

"He's lucky to still have a job. Alfie told me some contributors still aren't happy so Father is going to have to watch his step very carefully from now on. He should have known better than to use his position as editor to rant and rave. Walk with me to Pimlico later?" he asked. "It's Jimmy's birthday soon and I want to ask Mrs Bell what we can buy him. If Bob is in the surgery, I'll introduce you."

Dr O'Brien was sweeping the waiting room floor in his shirtsleeves but leant his broom against the wall and shook Will's hand with gusto. He had a rugged face with straight brown hair greying at his temples and hazel eyes.

"Bob, may I introduce my wife, Isobel?" Will said and she held out a hand.

"I'm very pleased to meet you, Dr O'Brien."

"Call me Bob, Mrs Fitzgerald," he replied in a strong Australian accent and gallantly kissed her hand.

"I am Isobel. Are you settling in?" she asked and he gave her a grin as he lifted a black morning coat from the back of a chair and shrugged it on.

"I certainly am, thank you. It's like I've never been away. I was born just up the street in Tripoli and it's hardly changed in thirty-seven years."

"Will you come to luncheon tomorrow, Bob? I'd like to hear all about Australia."

"I would be delighted to, thank you. Would you like to visit Australia one day?"

"I considered it once," she admitted and felt Will glance at her. "But I'm happy living here in Dublin. One o'clock at number 30 Fitzwilliam Square. You can meet Dr Barbara Barton, she has been in practice with Will for just over a month. I have also managed to gather together Will's mother, my mother and step-father, my uncle and my brother," she said, omitting the fact that another reason for the meal was for Sarah to be at number 30 and not at home alone on her wedding anniversary.

"I won't be intruding on the gathering?" Bob asked anxiously.

"No, not at all. The more the merrier."

"Then, one o'clock it is."

She and Will went upstairs and he reminded Mrs Bell about Jimmy's birthday.

"Yes, I've been thinking about what you can buy him as a present, Dr Fitzgerald. He's about to burst out of his boots. I can almost watch him grow these days and he'll be delighted with a good pair o' boots from the market."

"It's his thirteenth birthday, so please bring him to the best boot maker you know of and have a pair made for him." Will put a sovereign on the kitchen table and Mrs Bell's eyes bulged.

"But, Dr Fitzgerald, Jimmy's never had a new pair o' boots – he'll ruin them."

"Ask the boot maker to show him how to polish the boots until they shine. If they're cleaned and polished regularly, they won't crack and they'll last longer."

Isobel smiled as Mrs Bell reached up and kissed Will's cheek.

"I'll do that and, thank you. When you said Jimmy was a bright lad, you were right. A gentleman from Guinness' came to see me about enrolling him in evening school. I told him I'd think about it. Jimmy's eager but going to school after a long day at the brewery will be awful tiring for him."

"It will but if Jimmy has the chance to learn to read and write, he should jump at it."

"Dr O'Brien said exactly the same thing. He didn't learn to read and write until he got to Australia. I'll agree to it," she added firmly. "Jimmy deserves the chance to prove himself. Now, sit yourself down, Dr Fitzgerald, and we'll have a cup of tea."

Isobel helped Mrs Bell to make the tea and when they sat at the kitchen table, she reached out and squeezed the older woman's hands.

"Alfie has inherited the Greene Hall estate," she said.

"How is he and what is he going to do with it?"

"He is recovering well, thank you, and he is going to do his best for the tenants. Mr Dudley, the land agent, has retired, the position has been advertised and Alfie shall interview the applicants shortly."

"Mr Dudley?" Mrs Bell repeated sharply. "A Mr Dudley was the land agent in my parents' time. Is this man his son?"

"No, Mr Dudley is the man who evicted your parents," Isobel told her gently and Mrs Bell sat back in her chair shaking her head. "He is eighty-five now and greatly disliked. When the new land agent is appointed, he will assess all the rents paid by the tenants on the estate and deliver the findings to Greene Hall for Alfie's appraisal. If the rents can be reduced, they will be, and if some tenants can afford to purchase their farms over a set number of years, then that shall also be arranged."

To her surprise, Mrs Bell's eyes filled with tears. To her knowledge, she had never seen her cry before.

"If only Mammy and Daddy had either of those opportunities. Alfie is a good man, Isobel, and you tell him that from me."

Bob was late for luncheon the next day. It was five minutes past one and Isobel wondered if they should begin without him. If he hadn't arrived by a quarter past, they would, she decided. Sarah was in good form, laughing at something Barbara had just said. Whether it was forced or genuine, Isobel couldn't quite decide.

At thirteen minutes past one, Zaineb showed Bob into the morning room and he held his hands up.

"I can't apologise enough, Isobel. I was just about to leave when I had to put five stitches in a little boy's knee."

"How is he?" she asked and Bob smiled.

"Perfectly well and delighted to hear he will have a small scar to show off to his friends."

Introductions were made and they went into the breakfast room where they feasted on onion soup, followed by roast lamb and steamed vegetables and chocolate mousse for dessert.

"You have an exceptional cook, Isobel." Bob smiled his appreciation at her.

"Are you cooking for yourself?" Barbara asked and he rolled his eyes comically.

"Apart from dinner – which I eat with Mrs Bell and Jimmy – yes, I am, and I have a lot to learn."

"You've never been married?" Isobel's mother asked.

"My wife left me for a man with ten thousand sheep," he replied matter-of-factly and Mrs Ellison's eyebrows shot up. "I simply couldn't compete with that many animals, I've never even owned a dog."

"I'm sorry to hear that – about your wife, I mean," her mother said and he laughed kindly.

"Thank you, but I've quite recovered from the loss of her and I am very happy with my life back here in Dublin. I left as an illiterate ten-year-old boy and I've returned a forty-seven-year-old doctor. Australia was good to me but it was time to come home."

"I hope you will be as successful in the Liberties as Will was," Sarah said. "He learned a lot there – matured there – and I'm very proud of him."

"Mrs Bell has been telling me about Will's time in Brown Street," Bob replied. "To start and maintain a medical practice from nothing is impressive."

"If it wasn't for Mrs Bell, I'd have been back living in number 67 within three months," Will said and Bob nodded.

"She's a wonderful woman. To take Jimmy in after his mother died – not many people would have done that. And Jimmy is starting evening school on Monday," Bob added. "And I'm so pleased for him."

"So are we." Will smiled. "Once he learns the three R's, he could go far in Guinness'."

"And you're a medical student?" Bob asked Alfie.

"Yes, I am."

"Do you want to go into general practice or specialise?"

"General practice but I have a friend who has just decided to go into psychiatry."

"Kenneth?" Will asked and Alfie nodded. "Give him my good wishes."

"I shall, thank you, Will," Alfie replied then turned and gestured to Miles. "This man here has, I would think, the largest personal collection of books in Dublin. You name a subject, Miles has a book on it."

"The Australian Outback?" Bob suggested and Miles grinned.

"I have a book on Ayers Rock and one on kangaroos."

"Kangaroos?" Mrs Ellison echoed. "Good gracious me."

"It is one of the books I inherited from Father," Miles explained and she made an 'ah' face. "I also found a book of his on various breeds of ducks. Young John might enjoy it when he is older because – and this is probably the wrong expression to use – the prose is rather dry."

"And I'm just a dull old solicitor," James announced drolly and they all laughed.

"There is nothing at all dull about you, my dear," his wife protested and squeezed his hand.

"Mother and James are newly-weds," Isobel explained to

Bob. "They married last December and, shortly afterwards, Miles came to live at number 55 from St Patrick's Hospital. After a very busy few months, we are really only catching our breaths now."

"You have my congratulations." Bob nodded across the table to the Ellisons. "And I hope you are very happy in your new home, Miles. I also hope Dr Barton paves the way for many more women to enter the various branches of medicine."

"Hear – hear," Will called and Barbara flushed.

"I hope so, too," she said. "And not just medicine, women have much to contribute to many professions – including the law."

"I agree," James replied. "There are many laws which could benefit from a woman's assessment and revision."

Isobel saw Sarah look down at her hands and could almost hear her say silently, 'especially the laws surrounding divorce'.

"Isobel, my heartiest compliments to Mrs Dillon, the luncheon was delicious," James said, placing his napkin on the table beside his dessert dish. "But, I'm afraid, some of us must return to work."

They all rose from the table and she ushered her mother, Sarah and Miles into the morning room before returning to the hall to see James, Alfie and the three doctors out.

"Fitzwilliam Square is beautiful," Bob proclaimed, gazing across the street at the gardens from the front doorstep.

"It is," she replied. "No matter what the season is. We're very lucky to live here. Do call again, Bob."

"I will, thank you," he said and waved with his hat as he went down the steps.

"I like him," she whispered to the others. "I hope he does well in the Liberties."

"Thank you for a wonderful luncheon, Isobel." Barbara kissed her cheek. "Call to the practice house one evening?"

"I'll call in the next few days, I promise. James." She gave him a hug and a kiss. "Thank you for coming."

"Please send your mother and Miles home well before six o'clock?" he asked. "Alfie and I have arranged that we eat early as we are going to the Gaiety Theatre to see a performance by the Compton Comedy Company. It's a surprise."

"I won't say a thing," she assured him. "Alfie." She gave him a bright smile. "The Compton Comedy Company?"

"Dr Harrison recommended an evening at the theatre to me and suggested I bring Miles, too. So I mentioned it to James and all four of us are going."

"Enjoy yourselves," she said.

"We certainly shall."

"A kiss for your husband?" Will asked with a grin and she reached up and kissed his cheek. "Look after Mother," he whispered at the same time and she nodded. "See you later," he added as he followed the others down the steps and she closed the front door.

All five of them walked out of Fitzwilliam Square together before going their separate ways. Will's first house call was to an elderly female patient who lived on Mount Street Lower and as he strode along the east side of Merrion Square he heard a sharp intake of breath from a man who halted about ten yards ahead of him. It was David Powell and Will bit back a curse. He knew he would meet David at some point but after such a pleasant luncheon, he wasn't in the humour to deal with him now.

"David." Greeting him curtly, Will transferred his medical bag from his right hand to his left, went to go past him and sighed angrily as David blocked his way.

"Will, I'm sorry."

"No, you're not," he snapped. "You're not sorry at all."

He was gratified to see David flush and he went to walk on again but David stood in his way for a second time.

"I am sorry and I want to apologise to you, Will, for my sudden departure from both practices."

"You've been replaced in both practices."

"And Alfie?" David asked quietly. "How is he?"

Will saw red and he grabbed David by the throat. "How dare you ask about Alfie – how fucking dare you—"

"Will." He heard footsteps behind him on the pavement then felt someone tugging at his hand. "Will, let him go." The voice was female and calm and he tore his attention away from David's face. "Let him go, Will." Harriett Harvey was nodding at him, encouraging him to stop and he released David and pushed him away. "Good," she said. "You," she added to David. "Be on your way. Will, you come with me."

"I can't—" Will began as David turned and hurried back the way he had just come.

"You need to calm yourself so come with me." Taking his arm, she walked him to number 68 and Johnston, the butler, admitted them to the hall. "Some whiskey?" she offered and he took off his hat and shook his head, not wanting to present for house calls with alcohol on his breath. "Thank you, Johnston." Mrs Harvey dismissed the butler and he left the hall.

Dropping his hat and medical bag onto the tiled floor, Will went to the stairs and sat down, lowering his head into his hands.

"That was Dr David Powell, I take it?" Mrs Harvey asked and he raised his head. "I have been following the goings and comings at your medical practice," she explained. "And next door," she continued. "Your father has barely been at home. I had not heard of a courtship, so it didn't take me long to realise he was behind Dr Powell and Margaret Simpson's engagement. What I didn't realise was that Dr Powell had abandoned Isobel's brother in order to acquire a wife, a house and to be able to set himself up in his own medical practice. Poor Mr Stevens."

Will groaned and lowered his head into his hands again. He had allowed his temper to get the better of him and to reveal Alfie's secret. You bloody fool, he raged silently.

"I haven't told a soul about your father and Maria Simpson and I won't tell a soul about Mr Stevens and Dr Powell. I swear it, Will."

"Thank you, Mrs Harvey," he mumbled before heaving a sigh and getting to his feet. "And thank you for intervening."

"Dr Powell deserves a throttling," she said briskly. "But Merrion Square is rather too public a place in which to do it. Your father also deserves a severe talking-to. He is quite the matchmaker but what I cannot understand is what Margaret Simpson acquires from the arrangement – oh, I know you cannot tell me but please allow me to speculate – God knows my poor brain doesn't get much exercise."

"When will men cease to underestimate how clever women are?" Will asked and she gave him a wry smile.

"Have you attracted much ridicule for engaging Dr Barton at the practice?"

"Only from my father," Will replied. "But then he received a taste of his own medicine."

"From the *Freeman's Journal*." Mrs Harvey roared with laughter. "Have you lost many patients to Dr Powell's new practice?"

"Yes," he admitted. "But it was inevitable – those who disagreed with me for engaging Dr Barton – and those who simply wished to continue with David as their doctor."

"May I register with Dr Barton, then?" Mrs Harvey inquired. "And recommend her to some friends and acquaintances?"

"Of course you may," he replied. "And thank you."

"Jim is still registered with Dr Smythe," she said, shaking her head in clear incredulation. "It's just as well he has the constitution of an ox because, as a doctor, Jacob Smythe is neither use nor ornament."

"Give Jim my regards. Thank you again for intervening, Mrs Harvey."

"How are the children?"

"Eating and growing and growing and eating – John included," he said with a smile. "Call to number 30 and see them?" he suggested. "The past few months have been demanding on all of us but I think – I hope – that the future will be calmer."

"When do Dr Powell and Margaret Simpson marry?"

"The first Saturday in May. We will be with Alfie that day."

"How is your mother? I know today is her wedding anniversary."

"She is spending the day at number 30 and I will walk her home after dinner."

"Then, I shall call to her this evening," Mrs Harvey told him firmly and he gave her a grateful nod.

He confessed his blunder to Isobel in bed that night and she took him in her arms and kissed him.

"I would have done exactly the same," she said. "And Harriett is a clever woman, it won't take her long to work it all out."

"As long as she doesn't tell Jim."

"She doesn't tell Mr Harvey anything," Isobel replied and frowned. "How they came to marry is a puzzle in itself. But I'm too tired to ponder it now."

As the date of David and Margaret's wedding approached, Isobel racked her brains as to what they could all do to occupy Alfie on the day. Miles had never seen the sea and young John hadn't seen it since he had been brought to Dublin from London so a day out in Kingstown was arranged with luncheon in the Royal Marine Hotel.

To her frustration, the destination had to be changed a few days beforehand when it was announced that William Forster the chief secretary for Ireland had resigned in protest at Mr Parnell's release from Kilmainham Gaol. Mr Forster's successor Lord Frederick Cavendish and the newly-reappointed Lord Lieutenant of Ireland Earl Spencer were due to arrive in Kingstown on 6th May. To avoid the brouhaha – as Will put it – Bray in Co Wicklow was chosen instead and he sent a telegram to the International Hotel reserving a table for luncheon.

Westland Row Station was bedecked with Union Jack

flags and they boarded a train which trundled south along the coast from Dublin in bright sunshine. Young John and Miles' eyes were glued to the sea views, their jaws dropping as the train passed through Kingstown where buildings were decorated with bunting and crowds were taking up positions on the slopes overlooking the harbour and along the railway line.

"Two important gentlemen are arriving today," James explained as young John peered at them with a questioning expression. "They may even be on board that boat, there," he added, pointing to a steamship lying alongside the pier.

"It's like the boat I was on with Will and Isobel," the boy said, turning back to the pier. "Look." Nudging Miles, they gazed in awe at a military honour guard who were wilting in their heavy tunics and headgear beside a brigade of riflemen, a brass band comprised entirely of young boys and two lines of Dublin Metropolitan policemen who stood along the short distance between the landing stage and the railway station platform.

"Good God, what a fuss," she heard Will mutter under his breath and she squeezed his hand in agreement, glad they would be away from Dublin and streets which would be as crowded today as two days ago when Earl Cowper the previous Lord Lieutenant had departed from Ireland.

The imposing three-storey International Hotel was conveniently situated across the street from Bray's railway station and they enjoyed a pot of excellent coffee and young John a glass of milk before walking to the seafront. Many people were taking advantage of the glorious weather and were strolling the length of the mile-long promenade and children were paddling in the shallows. Will led John down onto the beach and they began to build a tower with pebbles. Miles was content to sit on a bench with Will's mother and the Ellisons and watch the waves so she took Alfie's arm and they went for a walk in the direction of Bray Head.

In the distance, a church bell rang out eleven times and he halted and shrugged helplessly.

"Thank you for today, Isobel, I would have just sat at home and moped."

"I didn't really know what to do today," she admitted. "But I thought it best for you to be out of the city altogether."

"I haven't seen the sea for a while," he replied, giving it an appreciative glance. "So this is very pleasant. I'm starting to feel hungry, too. I wasn't in the humour for breakfast."

"Will has reserved a table for us all for one o'clock so I'm afraid you'll have to postpone your hunger for a little while," she said and he smiled as they walked on.

"When Kenneth offered to go to the wedding and sit at the back of the church, I thanked him but I don't want to hear about it – there's no point – even though he wishes to view as many weddings as he can in preparation for his own eventual nuptials."

"His own?" She stopped abruptly. "But—"

"You thought he and I might eventually..?" Alfie asked before laughing kindly and shaking his head. "No. Kenneth and his cousin Imogen have been in love since they were both sixteen. They will marry as soon as he graduates from Trinity College."

"I'm sorry," she said, rolling her eyes, furious at herself for assuming.

"Kenneth is a good friend to me, that is all. He's asked

me to be his best man so that is something to look forward to a few years from now."

The photograph of Will, Fred and Jerry taken at the time of Margaret's first wedding sprang into her mind. Margaret's framed copy was now most likely at the back of a drawer somewhere.

"How is Will?" Alfie added. "Number 1 Ely Place Upper is no longer the Simpson house, it is now the Powell residence."

"He wrote a long letter to Jerry the other day to tell him. He said putting it all down on paper helped a little but he never ever expected David to step into Fred's shoes."

"Are you and Will completely estranged from Will's father now?"

"Yes, I think we are," she replied quietly. "Despite everything, Sarah isn't happy with how matters have turned out. She thinks we shouldn't be using the children to punish John but I simply can't trust him anymore."

"Trust once lost is all but impossible to regain."

"Sadly, that is very true. Shall we turn back?"

After a delicious luncheon of chicken consommé, poached trout and steamed vegetables followed by vanilla ice cream – which Alfie thoroughly enjoyed – they all took a stroll along the promenade before returning to the hotel for afternoon tea. They arrived back in Dublin in the early evening, Sarah was dropped off outside number 67 and their cabs proceeded on to Fitzwilliam Square. Mr and Mrs Ellison and Miles went straight into number 55 but Alfie accompanied Isobel, Will and young John into the gardens.

"Stay where we can see you," she called after the boy as he ran onto the lawn and he waved a reply.

"Can we sit down?" Alfie asked and they sat on the nearest bench. He gazed up at the sky and shaded his eyes against the setting sun. "It's so warm it feels like summer. If this weather continues, I may be able to do some studying out here."

"And watch your niece and nephew crawling across the lawn and attempting to stand up, too?" she asked and he nodded. "You watch all of Belle and Ben's attempts to stand up, don't you?" she continued as John returned to them and climbed onto her lap.

"Ben tries to pull himself up the table legs in the nursery and then he falls onto his bottom and Belle points at him and laughs," the boy declared.

"And do you laugh at him as well?" Alfie asked and John shook his head vehemently.

"Ben is trying very hard – I won't ever laugh at him."

"Good boy." Alfie gave him a grin. "It's been a long day, shall we bring you upstairs to the nursery now?"

"Yes, please."

"Would you like me to carry you?"

"I'd like to walk, thank you, Alfie," John replied, sliding off her lap.

"Of course." Alfie got to his feet, took the boy's hand and they set off towards the gate.

Isobel smiled and Will kissed her forehead before they got up and followed them into number 30.

They helped John to bed and kissed him and the twins goodnight then went downstairs to the morning room.

"Are either of you hungry?" she asked as she sat on the sofa and the two men in the armchairs. "I instructed Mrs Dillon not to cook dinner for us but I can ask for some sandwiches?"

"Nothing for me, thank you," Will replied.

"Nor for me," Alfie added, crossing his legs. "Well, David is lost to me now," he said matter-of-factly. "And it's time for me to stop wallowing in misery over him and move on with my life. It's also time for me to end my visits to Dr Harrison."

"Are you sure?" she asked and Alfie nodded.

"He's helped me immensely but I need to stand on my own two feet now. Mother, James and Miles need to look at me as Alfie their medical student son, step-son and nephew and not as Alfie – David's former lover – there is much more to me than that. I may find someone else to love eventually – I may not – but I have a few more years left at Trinity College and when I graduate, I'm going into general practice. Kenneth can carve out a path for himself in psychiatry – I just want to be a doctor – it's all I've ever wanted to be."

"Well, when you graduate, the third surgery in the practice house is waiting for you," Will told him and Alfie's eyes widened.

"You don't mean that?"

"I do." Will smiled. "Fitzgerald, Barton and Stevens – three doctors in the practice – just how it was in my father and grandfather's day."

"I can't thank you enough, Will."

"No thanks are needed. Just study hard, write your thesis and receive your M.D."

"I shall. From now on, my life will revolve around my family, my studies and Greene Hall. I have decided to spend one weekend per month there so I am not altogether an absentee landlord – I'll be careful," he assured them. "I want to get to know my estate, my new land agent and my new solicitor and try and do what is right for my tenants."

When the clock on the mantelpiece struck eleven, Alfie got to his feet.

"It's time to go home," he said. "I can't thank you enough for today. The weather was wonderful and so was the company and the luncheon."

"We all enjoyed the day," she replied, getting up and hugging and kissing him. "Will and I shall see you out."

In the hall, she passed Alfie's hat to him and Will opened the front door.

"It's still warm," Alfie informed them as he went out onto the steps. "Long may this good spell continue," he continued with a smile before glancing at two constables approaching from the direction of Fitzwilliam Square East. "Good evening," he said cheerfully as they stopped at the bottom of the steps and touched their helmets on seeing her beside Will at the door.

"Good evening, madam, sirs, have you been resident here all day?" the taller of the two constables inquired.

"We spent the day in Bray and returned to the square at approximately half past six this evening," Will replied. "And, apart from a few minutes in the garden, we have been in the house since then."

"You have noticed nothing unusual over the past few days or this morning? No uncommon comings or goings?"

"No, not a thing."

"May I ask why you are questioning us?" she asked and the constables peered briefly at each other. "Has something happened?" she persisted. "I can't remember when I last saw a constable on the square never mind two."

"Foot patrols have been stepped up because a most heinous crime was committed early this evening, madam," the second constable told her.

"A most heinous crime?" she repeated. "You may elaborate, I am not squeamish."

"A double murder – in the Phoenix Park – the deceased were stabbed to death and are believed to be Lord Frederick Cavendish and the permanent under secretary, Mr Burke," the constable explained and she gasped, clapping a hand to her mouth.

The new chief secretary had been murdered less than twelve hours after setting foot on Irish soil, she calculated quickly while she exchanged horrified glances with Will and Alfie.

"We passed through Kingstown this morning and saw army and police and hundreds of people waiting for Earl Spencer and Lord Cavendish to disembark their ship," Will said, slipping a hand around her waist. "Good God, this is…" Tailing off, he shook his head.

"Well, I…" Alfie struggled to pull himself together as he went down the steps to the pavement. "I had better be on my way home."

"Will and I shall accompany you to number 55," she said. "Thank you for informing us, constable. It is, indeed, a most heinous crime. Goodnight to you both."

The constables touched their helmets again before continuing on along Fitzwilliam Square South and she joined Alfie while Will closed the front door.

"I can't help but now think of David and Margaret," Alfie murmured. "Their wedding day will be forever marred by a political double murder."

Would the murders be a harbinger of doom for a marriage such as theirs, she pondered. They certainly would never be able to look back on 6th May 1882 with any fondness whatsoever. Never had the saying 'Marry in May, rue the day' been so apt.

And what about Will's father? Would John regret his machinations – the estrangement from his son and daughter-in-law – being barred from visiting his grandchildren? Only time would tell.

"But we shall remember this day as a happy one," she said firmly in an effort to not just convince Alfie and Will but herself as well. "Yes?"

"Yes," they replied together and she took their hands and walked in-between them around the gardens.

Approaching number 55, she saw that the gas lamps in the morning room had been extinguished. Good. Her mother, James and Miles had gone to bed and so would not hear of the murders until breakfast.

"Just a moment," Will called as Alfie went up the steps and opened the front door. "Remember what I said earlier – when you receive your M.D. the third surgery at the practice house is yours. I was the last to use the room and it will need a thorough dust and polish," Will added with a wink and she was relieved to see Alfie grin.

"When I receive my M.D. I shall acquire a duster and some furniture polish and give the surgery a jolly good clean," he replied. "Goodnight, and thank you again." He went inside and they waited until the door closed before turning away.

"We have cheered him a little but I cannot help but think of David and Margaret now, too," she confessed as Will linked his arm through hers and they crossed the street. "When we married, it was because we loved each other and nothing overshadowed our wedding day."

"And we're muddling along, aren't we, Mrs Fitzgerald?" he asked with humour in his voice and she spluttered a laugh and gave him a grateful kiss for raising her spirits.

"We're muddling along very well indeed, Dr Fitzgerald."

"Good. Let's go to bed and tomorrow we shall resume our usual routine and bring the children to feed the ducks in St Stephen's Green. Who knows what the future will hold but we shall continue to do as we always do."

THE END

Other Books by Lorna Peel

The Fitzgeralds of Dublin Series

A Scarlet Woman: The Fitzgeralds of Dublin Book 1 -
http://mybook.to/ascarletwoman
Dublin, Ireland, 1880. Tired of treating rich hypochondriacs, Dr Will Fitzgerald left his father's medical practice and his home on Merrion Square to live and practise medicine in the Liberties. His parents were appalled and his fiancée broke off their engagement. But when Will spends a night in a brothel on the eve of his best friend's wedding, little does he know that the scarred and disgraced young woman he meets there will alter the course of his life.

Isobel Stevens was schooled to be a lady, but a seduction put an end to all her father's hopes for her. Disowned, she left Co Galway for Dublin and fell into prostitution. On the advice of a handsome young doctor, she leaves the brothel and enters domestic service. But can Isobel escape her past and adapt to life and the chance of love on Merrion Square? Or will she always be seen as a scarlet woman?

A Suitable Wife: The Fitzgeralds of Dublin Book 2 -
http://mybook.to/asuitablewife
Dublin, Ireland, 1881. Will and Isobel Fitzgerald settle into number 30 Fitzwilliam Square, a home they could once only have dreamed of. A baby is on the way, Will takes over the Merrion Street Upper medical practice from his father and they are financially secure. But when Will is handed a letter from his elder brother, Edward, stationed with the army in India, the revelations it contains only serves to further alienate Will from his father.

Isobel is eager to adapt to married life on Fitzwilliam Square but soon realises her past can never be laid to rest. The night she met Will in a brothel on the eve of his best friend's wedding has devastating and far-reaching consequences which will change the lives of the Fitzgerald family forever.

Historical Romance

Brotherly Love: A 19th Century Irish Romance -
http://mybook.to/brotherly-love
Ireland, 1835. Faction fighting has left the parish of Doon divided between the followers of the Bradys and the Donnellans. Caitriona Brady is the widow of John, the Brady champion, killed two years ago. Matched with John aged eighteen, Caitriona didn't love him and can't mourn him. Now John's mother is dead, too, and Caitriona is free to marry again.

Michael Warner is handsome, loves her, and he hasn't allied himself with either faction. But what secret is he keeping from her? Is he too good to be true?

Mystery Romance

A Summer of Secrets - http://mybook.to/ASummerOfSecrets
Sophia Nelson returns to her hometown in Yorkshire, England to begin a new job as tour guide at Heaton Abbey House. There, she meets the reclusive Thomas, Baron Heaton, a lonely workaholic.

Despite having a rule never to become involved with her boss, Sophia can't deny how she finds him incredibly attractive.

When she overhears the secret surrounding his parentage, she is torn. But is it her attraction to him or the fear of opening a Pandora's box that makes her keep quiet about it?

How long can Sophia stay at Heaton Abbey knowing what she does?

Only You - http://myBook.to/onlyyou
Jane Hollinger is divorced and the wrong side of thirty – as she puts it. Her friends are pressuring her to dive back into London's dating pool, but she's content with her quiet life teaching family history evening classes.

Robert Armstrong is every woman's fantasy: handsome, charming, rich and famous. When he asks her to meet him, she convinces herself it's because he needs her help with a mystery in his family tree. Soon she realises he's interested in more than her genealogy expertise. Now the paparazzi want a piece of Jane too.

Can Jane handle living — and loving — in the spotlight?

About The Author

Lorna Peel is an author of historical fiction and mystery romance novels set in the UK and Ireland. Lorna was born in England and lived in North Wales until her family moved to Ireland to become farmers, which is a book in itself! She lives in rural Ireland, where she writes, researches her family history, and grows fruit and vegetables. She also keeps chickens and guinea hens.

Contact Information

Website - http://lornapeel.com
Blog - https://lornapeel.com/blog
Newsletter - http://eepurl.com/ciL8ab
MeWe - https://mewe.com/i/lornapeel
Twitter - https://twitter.com/PeelLorna
Pinterest - http://www.pinterest.com/lornapeel
Goodreads - http://www.goodreads.com/LornaPeel
Facebook - http://www.facebook.com/LornaPeelAuthor
Instagram - https://www.instagram.com/lornapeelauthor

CPSIA information can be obtained
at www.ICGtesting.com
Printed in the USA
LVHW030032030420
652092LV00005B/1402